WORDS THAT BURN LIKE ASH

KENDRA MASE

*To the literary heroines who made me feel powerful.
I'm happy to add Avril to your ranks.*

CHAPTER ONE

*A*vril managed to see a few of the great wonders and even greater parties in her life. Once, she might've expected more of herself. Attending a gathering of stuffy middle-aged people who drank cheap wine out of tiny plastic cups wouldn't have been high on her list of achievements.

It was a universal rule, however, that whenever Avril attended a gala in the city's finest institution, her life went to shit. So, perhaps tonight, she should've played along.

She should've twisted her vibrant ginger curls into a classic chignon rather than let dull red hang in a loose knot at the back of her neck. She should've worn a dress that made her look like a sculpture made of flesh rather than a simple black sleeveless number that caused her to blend in with the student gallery assistants. All of whom were trying not to look sly as they swiped another pour of pinot.

If only she cared.

Tonight, there were no photographers from *Page Six* to question her interpretation on the art.

What a waste.

Or call her *elegant* or even *tasteful* after running out of other adjectives, like *crude* and *indelicate*. They tended to reserve those for when they made visits to the more entertaining nightlife Ashton had to offer.

Her home, as the Queen of Burlesque. Just *Queen* when writers were trying to fit her latest bits of scandal onto a single page. They sold more magazines that way.

But no one knew Avril was here.

Or perhaps they did and just didn't care anymore after so long.

Stars, her head was spinning.

With little care, Avril twisted to the installation aside of her, nearly knocking an elderly couple into the artist's self-portrait. Short, wavy black hair cut sharp around her chin with compulsory narrowed eyes glared at the viewer. The painting was only half completed, the background made of ripped articles from *The Times* and *Leader*. The words *assault* and *rape* were exaggeratively boldened for a cliché effect.

Avril snorted.

She threw the last bit of watery grapes to the back of her throat, dropping the empty cup in the nearby vagina sculpture. Liquid red dripped down the inside. Call it art in motion.

A laugh stumbled out overtop the rumble of voices.

Avril searched across the room for whomever it was. Their laugh was deep and loose in all the right places to make a woman's toes curl. Letting her hair be a conspicuous barrier, Avril waited a beat even though her heart didn't before she turned toward it. Behind another group, shaking hands and offering subpar aperitif, a man she knew all too well was attached to that laugh, that smirk. Of all the people to show up.

Stepping back, hiding—no, not hiding because Avril did not hide—she positioned herself behind a partition and watched her friend. He was more at home with himself when surrounded by enamored crowds, wholly at ease as he glanced down at the girl tucked easily into his side. The striking pair fit together as if they had been made to mold into each other.

Jack and Kit smiled at everyone, his easier than hers—then again, it always had been. Jack's constant smirk was something that had made him rather the icon when he stood alongside Avril for years. Her friend showed up in those *Page Six* tabloids almost as much as she did. After a while, he had just as little care as Avril did. No matter what they slung his way, he remained unflappable. Except for when his ex-girlfriend had ratted him out to his small-town family.

Ever since Kit had come into the picture, his devilish smirk had turned as soft as her curves, and Jack's dreams had taken a turn back to what had brought him into the city to begin with.

Avril never got to tell him how stunning his photography was in *National Geographic* last winter.

She never got to congratulate Kit, her timid friend who had managed to take Jack as hers. Kit had taken everything Ashton offered her in the palm of her hand and decided to keep it. While Avril's career had burned down to the ground in spectacular fashion, Kit had rebuilt a life, starting with the lingerie shop downtown that Kit's aunt Emilie had left to her. They always made Avril the most beautiful pieces to wear onstage.

Avril could still imagine that red crystal set that had glimmered under the lights as she stomped her feet at Rosin. How the crowd had cheered for her.

Now she hid behind a wall, wearing a little black dress that wasn't even hers.

Avril blinked. She was staring.

Jack left his slightly crooked yet endearing grin on full display. Kit attempted to copy it, slowly arriving at an expression that appeared almost coy. Her dark hair looped up at the nape of her neck, which Jack tenderly held. The puffed crinoline sleeves of her vintage Dior gently crinkled under his arms.

His thumb stroked an easy rhythm before he leaned in. He whispered something. Kit's eyes narrowed. He turned—

Avril started walking.

She couldn't talk to them. Him. Not now.

Gaze straight forward, head held high, people moved out of her way, and she ignored the movement of feet behind her.

Personnel Only loomed in bright letters—a heaven. Avril didn't question the exit as she yanked on the handle. Sounds faded behind her. Jack's snarky, deep laugh disappeared as the door clicked shut. Leaning back against the flat surface, Avril shut her eyes to take a deep breath. However, she had little time to be thankful for her swift escape before a hand slipped around her waist.

"There you are."

Before Avril could utter an exclamation, she was lifted. A hand on her chin. The mouth on hers was like a shock of electricity. Her lips were so cold. They ached from the sugary dregs of wine she had gulped. But the warmth of his lips, this kiss, Avril couldn't help herself. She leaned into it.

That small movement seemed to be all the encouragement the stranger needed. His hands, heavy on her hips, began to roam the rest of her body. When he twisted her around, Avril hardly realized she was lifted off the floor until she looped a leg behind his back for stability. Fingers dug into his forearms, bare up to the elbows, where the cuffs were rolled.

Only for a second did Avril question what was happening; however, she couldn't bring herself to care enough to stop—or want to.

Everything but the sudden pleasure was thrown far out of her mind. From Jack and Kit to the question of how many tiny plastic cups were enough to get one drunk. The stranger tasted similarly of wine as he pushed her lips open with his own. The bitter taste mixed with the sensation of the kiss and slipped down her throat, swirling into something much sweeter in the pit of her stomach.

Situated back down on the edge of a hard table, she was finally the perfect height to grab his neck in the darkness.

Avril quickly tilted her head up in search of anything more he would give.

His teeth scraped her bottom lip. His hands, stars, they were wide as they skimmed above her knees. A tremor coiled around her spine so that when she curved to eliminate the sliver of space left between them, she gasped.

The sound was high and unusual, falling out the back of her throat, which she would be all too happy to bear and let him go to town on, if he wanted.

Only he didn't.

Long eyelashes fluttered open. When he broke the kiss, his eyes widened at what he saw—or who he saw positioned on either side of his legs.

Quickly, he stepped back, and a muffled curse left his lips as Avril's eyes began to adjust to the dark. "I am *so* sorry. Who are—"

Before he could go on, Avril jumped up off the counter in a graceful movement, given the circumstances. Her skin was still humming from his touch as she rushed toward him. As her eyes adjusted, she realized this was no ordinary supply closet, but a safe place for layers of paintings. French posters stuck in frames as well, seeming to stare down on them in judgment. Coming to her senses, Avril realized she heard sounds drifting through the thin walls.

There were voices outside the door.

On unsteady feet, the stranger caught her elbow as she put more than just her body weight against the door for leverage. Positioning the unusually tall stranger against it, she lifted a finger to cover his kiss-swollen lips.

"Shh-shh-shush."

"Who—"

"Do you not know the meaning of the word *shush?*" Avril snapped through gritted teeth.

Lips sealed, the man glared down at her with clear gray eyes and carefully shifted her finger away. He seemed disgruntled at the contact for someone with her saliva coating his tongue.

The sharp tones of murmurs radiated outside of the door. Then faded.

Whatever air still remained in Avril's lungs released along with her hands, drooping to either side.

"Someone you'd rather not see?"

"Who were you hoping for?" Avril asked, not answering his question. Shutting her eyes, Avril rubbed her temples and leaned against the metal filing cabinet she had likely been groped against moments ago. "Of course, I have been told I have the kind of face that inspires instant lust."

And him?

When Avril opened her eyes, her lips parted. No words came back out. In the dark, she had not noticed before. He certainly did not have one of those generic guises about him either, though his angled cheekbones weren't the reason for her stare. Tall and lanky, he towered over her with a graceful distaste shining in his light-gray eyes. They were framed with thick-rimmed glasses that had fallen from the top of his head during their impassioned interlude.

She couldn't believe she hadn't knocked them off.

Those eyes, though, those eyes swirled with flecks of stone and the darkest brown nestled above what Avril could only describe as one thing.

Shadows.

Shadows, like the ghosts she had seen all her life since she had been a child, stuck under his eyes, curling around his hairline. They moved like snakes, twisting around his neck and flickering like twilight stars before moving across his skin. She stared at them, wondering how they trailed under his button-down.

"Are you all right?"

Avril blinked, swallowing her shock at how many there were. They sought her out when she least expected, like sticky drips of soot, and coated her life in the same sheen. Her mother had always been convinced her daughter was more sensitive to the world than others.

Avril used to like the sound of that. She tried to think of the gray shadows like little ghosts that teased rather than warned. They could be figments rather than monsters under the bed. Apparitions that stuck to people or places like memories that faded over time or disappeared altogether without notice.

Either way, she never really questioned what she saw, only followed the rules her mother had given her. One, *don't talk of the shadows*. And two, *ignore them*.

Only when she had gotten older did she begin to question the specks after her best friend, Reed, made her go to therapy.

"Just to try it out," he'd insisted, more worried about her last year than even she was, unable—no, not wanting—to leave the house.

The therapist had sat on a crushed blue velvet chair across from Avril for less than an hour, exuding false calm, while Avril fidgeted on a flimsy folding chair. She probably pretended to listen to people's problems and problematic sex dreams all day long while sitting atop her velvet high horse.

So, Avril figured she should give her something to remember.

She seemed to like Avril's reasoning on shadows and memories at first. But as she began to read through the rest of Avril's file, she questioned the root of the issue.

Trauma left marks.

Some marks were more visible than others.

She'd never gone back for the second session.

Shaking off the memories, Avril focused back on the man as her mouth turned dry. She had never seen so many shadows on anyone else, excluding herself when she looked in the mirror for too long. If she blinked enough times though and ignored all the shadows, she could cut through them.

They'd be gone. It would only take a minute.

Smooth skin tinged with petals of purple replaced the shadows as he squinted at her.

"I don't know," Avril choked, quickly finding her words. "Like I said, it isn't often someone attacks me without my consent in …" She looked around them again.

"Archives."

"What?" Avril refocused on the man in front of her.

He rubbed his neck as he stood still—too still. "The art archives. Where they keep the artwork before and after shows. Some pieces are left behind, but others move on to grander pastures."

Right.

Avril glanced back at the door. At this rate, she should probably head back out. Or see if there was a side door to the archives and make a run for it, but for some reason, she seemed stuck in place, waiting. "You didn't answer my question."

"You didn't answer mine."

He'd asked one?

The stranger rolled his eyes, suddenly at ease, and gave a low laugh. He stepped toward her, cocking his head down to look her in the eyes. "Are you drunk?"

She glared. *Probably. Not enough.*

"If you were, it would make much more sense," he grumbled.

"Excuse me?"

Another huff of laughter, but it didn't sound amused. "Why would you just let me—"

"Now, you stop right there." Avril held up a finger. It was getting its workout today with this guy. "Because if this is going to turn into some slut-shaming spiel about letting you ravish me, I assure you, we'll be here all night."

She was the one still in front of the door, and for some reason, she was beginning to think that the man with grandpa loafers on wasn't going to be the type to physically move her.

"Ravish—what were you even doing back here then? Can't you read the sign?"

"I can read," Avril retorted.

He waited.

"Like you said, I was trying to get away from someone." Avril cleared her throat, trying to stand taller in heels that pinched her toes much more than she remembered. On reflex, she produced one of her old friend Jack's famous smirks he'd taught her long ago.

The mask easily slipped into place. That devilish smile had gotten both of them out of several sticky situations over the years.

This time, she folded her arms over one another, maintaining that inch of distance between them as he stalked closer to hear her well-prepared comeback. "You, on the other hand, are obviously blind unless—"

The door behind her creaked on rusted metal hinges.

When she swung around at the sound, the stranger reached out to grasp Avril's elbow again, keeping her from tilting to the right, effectively pulling her into him.

Avril had seen the woman before in the gallery. She had mingled between groups, flowing between them on simple black flats. She smiled and barely drank an ounce of the golden ginger ale that bubbled up from the bottom of her flimsy cup.

Her almond eyes had stared down at Avril from newspaper headlines with feigned disapproval.

The artist—what was her name?

Celia—or something—stood in the open doorway. Her short, dark bob filled with stripy red highlights did look similar to the loose hair falling around Avril's low bun. She faced Avril, eye to eye, obviously not expecting to see anyone back here. That would make three of them.

"Oh." Cynthia shook her head, rapidly attempting to form an explanation for the peep show she'd walked in on. "Excuse my intrusion."

Avril glanced back at the stranger behind her.

His eyes widened.

"No. Wait. Cyn!" His hand reached out, but the door closed.

He'd let it close.

Neither of them was able to hear her steps as she scurried away.

Avril waited for him to say something. She was about to herself before the insult died on her lips. Eyebrows scrunched tight together, he turned his stare from the door, and the glare he gave froze the room as well as her as she waited for him to say something. Anything.

She waited for him to yell at her.

To tell her that whatever was going on was her fault.

She'd heard such accolades before. She knew them well.

Thanks for the help with fucking up my life.

The stranger's lips remained closed for a long moment. Maybe he was waiting for her to say something too.

But Avril didn't say sorry. She would never say she was sorry, and now, out of all the things she felt, sorry wasn't one of them.

The stranger shook his fair head as he held the door open and looked back just in time for the bright light to slice through. He watched Avril wince.

"If you drove, ask someone to call you a cab."

She hadn't driven. Still, somehow, body turning back to numb and lifeless, she nodded.

With another short stare, the stranger ran his hand through the front notch of dark-blond hair that splayed upward.

The shadows were back from where he touched, nestled around his temples. Curled around his wrists. They swirled slower this time. Avril took a step, her foot slipping on something small and round.

When she glanced down, beneath her foot was a small ring. Reaching to pick it up, the band was thin and gold, yet somehow the metal warm between her thumb and forefinger. A tendril of shadow twirled around the one side, but before Avril could see any engravings or chips it was trying to conceal, the shadow jerked and faded so quickly that Avril wasn't sure if she'd merely imagined it.

Before she could find reason to stop herself, however, Avril was back up off the ground, reaching for the door, still partly open. Her mouth opened to yell something after him. Something like *wait* or *stop*, but he was already gone, leaving her to trail him on her toes. She ran through the office and gallery, gripping the ring that fit perfectly in the center of her palm.

She didn't care if Jack or Kit were out there anymore, showing off their love for each other while on some sort of socially acceptable date. She didn't care what the stranger must have thought of her either when he turned his back on her and her flushed cheeks.

Avril followed the dark gray button-down out of the corner of her eye. He turned out of the gallery and down the stairs. Her heels strummed with each step, echoing through the space as she made it to the door leading to the parking lot.

She flung it open, swallowing the cold, bitter air to find her voice loud and clear.

"Hey!"

But he was no longer there. Avril glanced back down at the ring in her hand and shook her head at the flimsy piece of metal.

As if he had not ever been there at all.

CHAPTER TWO

*T*he cold always found Avril an easy home, settling inside her bones. Whatever heat Avril felt inside or against the body of the stranger, warm and steady, was gone as she wandered the edge of the sidewalk. Taxis slowly went by, waiting for her hand to hail before speeding away.

Avril's feet hurt enough that she was about ready to brave the muck-infested pavement and sit down right there, pry her shoes off, and pop the blisters that were sure to greet her. At the same moment of painful desperation, however, she stopped in her tracks. Avril had two other options. One had never occurred to her in the past few months as she crashed on couches and in beds that didn't belong to her when she could no longer stay upright.

She could go home.

Her eyes were heavy.

Her back ached.

Phone palmed in her hand, she raised it into the air. A taxi slowed and then stopped. The rusted red door was a hundred pounds as she let it slam behind her.

Tapping through her Contacts, her thumb hovered over the Call button for a second too long as she found a different sort of solace in the too-squishy, ripped cab seat. If only it would swallow her.

"We just drivin' tonight?" the cabbie asked after they passed the next light.

Avril put up a single finger. Unlike the guy in the closet, that shut the driver right up as the tune of call waiting at once sang to her like a siren pulling her in. There was no turning back. She pressed the cold metal tight to her ear.

A voice cut the hum off after the second ring, somehow slow and even. Avril knew better than to think he hadn't already been asleep for at least an hour by now.

"Darling?"

"Reed?" Avril's throat cracked when she spoke his name, heard his honeyed voice. She had thought about him and doing this a few dozen times in the past few weeks; now, the whisper of a command was on her lips. "Will you unlock the door?"

She could hear him swallow.

"I'll wait by the stairs."

Nodding only to herself, Avril listened as he waited for her to hit the End Call button. The heel of her shoe knocked twice against the plastic divider. "Riverside and Malley."

"You got it." The eyes of the driver shifted in the rearview.

The mirror was covered in spots of soot, likely from someone else sitting just where Avril was, admiring themselves after an evening they were trying to leave behind.

"Hey, aren't you that dancer? The one from the burlesque lounge down the way? My wife—"

"No."

His eyes averted back to the road as he made a left. The tires bounced as they hit the bridge.

Lights streamed by the windows. If Avril closed her eyes, she could still feel the rush of water that constantly streamed beneath them, roaring as it hit the posts and continued on. The rapids did not let anything stay in its path for long. The first time she'd wandered over the bridge wasn't long after she started working in the city, repairing ripped seams in costumes, only to make bigger holes somewhere else in the fabric, however less noticeable, before sending each dancer, one after the other, out the famous Rosin stage.

Stars, from the moment Avril had entered that club, she'd wanted to be up there, on stage, right aside them, tights torn or not. For a while though, according to the burlesque lounge's owner, Cherry, Avril was too young and too sparkly to be shaking her hips to a crowd's unadulterated glee. People already pushed to get closer and see just another teasing inch of skin she happily kept exposed near the top of her garters the moment she revealed herself via the backstage doors. It was only right in her mind that she also took a bow.

And then they thought she was someone else than who she was back then. She could see it in their eyes. To Avril, that meant she was finally beginning to become the someone she always wanted to be as she made her mark in Ashton.

One of the girls had even gathered Reed up with her in her arms each week after a particularly good show. Avril was one of them, she'd insisted, along with the fact of how it was already after midnight anyway, and Saturdays meant they had to party.

The dancer—Avril couldn't remember her real name—hosted one of the first merry festivities herself that Reed and Avril both got the invite to. She opened the front doors wide of her boyfriend's house—a fifty-three-year-old stockbroker—and let anyone who cared to be anyone cross the threshold.

Avril raided the wine cellar in the basement, danced on a coffee table trimmed in art nouveau gold, and fell asleep on top of Reed, who, at some point, had lost his socks.

The two of them walked to the bus station in the morning together when the sun was too bright to ignore any longer. Reed was barefoot, complaining how there was sand or lint he never noticed before in his crimson high-tops. He closed his eyes halfway across and lifted his face, so his chestnut locks could fall away, exposing his cheeks to sunlight. Avril let him have the moment. Where else did they have to be?

She leaned over the railing of the bridge until he looked back at the rows of townhouses they had left, as if the whole night had been a dream.

But it wasn't.

Avril reached out the palm of her hand and swept it over the line of colorful residences, as if she could feel the crisp, saturated paint swirl beneath her fingertips. All of them were much more unique than any simple brown or greystone crushed between skyscrapers.

"I'm going to have one of those one day."

"What?" Reed's long lashes were stark against his cheeks. *"You plan to settle down and marry a rich old man?"*

"Nah, we both know that's your dream."

Reed grinned through his hangover. Cars honked. People cursed over apartment fire escapes as they attempted to toss down a bundle of keys to the person below.

"Nope. If that's what it takes, I'm going to pull a Cher. I'm going to be a rich man."

AVRIL BLINKED in the back of the darkened taxi as it slowed, curving toward the sidewalk. Somehow, it managed to find a rare gap between a dozen cars parked and never moved from the curb.

"This it?"

In answer, Avril swiped her card and hit the button for a good tip. She didn't look back when the door slammed in signal. He began to pull away and made a narrow turn back toward the city. Back to life.

Her heels moved, a painful soprano their only cries.

The door opened before Avril made it to the top step of the narrow Victorian townhouse, painted in a deep royal plum.

Leaning against the frame, Reed didn't look at her up and down. He knew what he'd find there, however hard she attempted to keep it hidden. The deep-set eyes. The slump of her shoulders as she stumbled her final pained steps.

He only quirked a gentle smile, as if it would conceal the worry flooding the rest of him.

"Hey, darling." Reed gathered her into his arms.

She let him. Avril collapsed deep into his oversize T-shirt that smelled like him—a strange combination of cherries and leather.

Her arms didn't hug him, however, and he didn't quite hug her. In that moment, he seemed to understand Avril better than she knew herself and perhaps ever would again. She just needed someone there—the closer, the better—and the heat of him through his terry-cloth robe had already begun to melt the frost on her elbows. He didn't comment that they were bare or how she wasn't wearing a coat.

Perhaps he also knew why she'd left those months ago.

For one, Avril couldn't stand Reed mothering her. He shelled out overbearing tendencies better than his mother had subjected on her own children back when they were in high school. Paula never let a night go by without saying good night or pressing them to finish their vegetables. Even Avril, when she sat around the dinner table with the family. Even though she'd hated warm carrots.

Reed tried to take care of her similarly. He had given her direction in the past year when she wouldn't beg for someone else to figure out her life for her. At least she wouldn't do it aloud. Reed just knew. The only thing he didn't seem to know was which direction was the right one.

For that while—still sometimes—she hated how well Reed knew her.

She squeezed his arms, still not quite believing she was back in them. "Hi, Reed."

He kicked the door shut and slid the lock before he let go.

The townhouse—her castle—looked as she'd left it, albeit a tad cleaner. Her things were no longer strewn over the back of the couch. The walkway was cleared of left-behind shoes she never took upstairs after kicking them and whatever filth from the streets she'd trailed in and onto the Oriental runner.

Home. As much as Avril made it be, anyway.

"Let's get you cleaned up."

Avril nodded but did not meet Reed's molten eyes as he followed her up the stairs, one careful step at a time. Her back, more than her feet, barked with irritation. The base of her spine burned low and steady. From the cold or exertion—probably both.

She could let him mother her for a few hours. Just a few. It was the longest they had been apart, the past eight months.

Her knees bent, wilting into her friend, who carefully wrapped his arm around her for support.

She was so tired.

"All right."

SHE WAS UNDERWATER, and she couldn't breathe.

Avril sat in the bath. Water tumbled from the faucet after the first layer turned cool. She loved to lie, soaking in the silence and light sound of music she'd put on in the other room for as long as she could. In the bath was no different. Avril floated with her ears submerged, and all she could hear was the hollow sounds the water droned as it made room for her wide hips.

In a proper soaking tub, like this, Avril often wondered if these moments were what people meant when they said they were at peace. That they'd found their *happy place*—at least for a little while.

Twisting the faucet to a light stream, Avril only then noticed the figure out of the corner of her eye. He stood, leaning against the wall of the doorway. Teeth punctured his bottom lip in boyish pleasure.

Caught ya.

"Care to join me?" Avril lifted a leg to show him where there was plenty of room.

He chuckled as he walked closer, hopefully to take her up on her gracious offer, kneeling down before the edge. His finger trailed along the surface of the water, turning iridescent bubbles to gray. To shadows.

Tilting her chin up, he traced Avril's lips before kissing them.

Avril lifted dripping skin into the chill of the air to get closer. Her lips. Her jaw.

Hands trailed along skin as he hummed against it, as if he was determined to touch each and every inch.

Then, he pushed her under.

She thrashed beneath the tight hold, kicked at it, only to slide farther against the slick slope of porcelain. She didn't understand, unsure of what to do before her body took over.

Air. She needed air.

Her foot connected with the faucet, scraped against the harsh old-fashioned metal no one ever replaced when they remodeled.

She couldn't die like this.

Avril did not die like this.

Choking on bubbles evacuated from her lungs, Avril held on until they burned. Then, she opened her mouth.

The hand yanked her back up by a clump of hair. Globs of water rushed down her face as she quavered, mouth wide. Even her lungs shook. Dark eyes so deep that Avril could see herself panting within them as they began to shift, turning to gray and then silver.

They stared at her with merciful sadness. *"You said you trusted me."*

AVRIL GASPED for air when she burst through the water's surface. The bath chilled in the darkness, and a dim shade of light flared through the lavender shades draped over diagonal witch windows.

She knew those windows. Those drapes.

Reed stumbled from where he had fallen asleep in his chair next to the bathtub. He caught himself on the lip before tilting all the way back, but Avril had already started to haul herself out. Droplets dripped onto the plush bathmat that molded to her toes.

She shoved air out of her lungs one breath at a time, her own version of screaming. One after another.

One more time.

"Hey, hey." Reed quickly adjusted himself to help, wrapping a towel over her shoulders and holding it tight. "I'm sorry. I'm so sorry. You dozed off, and I thought that it would be fine for just a few minutes, so you could sleep, and I—I'm sorry."

Shaking her head, Avril shrugged him off. She shut her eyes as shadows gripped the sides of the tub from where her fingers had been.

It was fine. She was fine.

Still, she shook from the cold. It had to be the cold, didn't it, that caused a whimper to escape her lips?

"I'm sorry, Aves."

She shook her head again, feeling for the tips of her fingers. One after another, she tapped them against her thumb.

One, two, three, four.

Five, six, seven, eight.

Slowly, the numb feeling that had invaded her began to reside. Reed watched her. "It's okay."

"I know." Her voice began to steady, pulsing as it snapped at him.

She swallowed, looking around again, just as she had when they first walked back in and Reed unzipped her dress before helping her swollen feet escape cheap patent leather.

Though the rest of the house had returned to its immaculate state. Her room and bathroom remained the same as she'd left it. Her curling iron cord trailed off the edge of the sink. Her toothbrush fell against the side of a mason jar, crust and mold accumulating at the bottom. Her trail of heels were bread crumbs back into her closet. And on her bed, blankets were tossed and jumbled. They never managed to stay tucked in at the sides.

"I'm so tired."

"Okay," Reed said, moving with her each way. Reaching to the bottom of the tub, he pulled the plug. Water gurgled down the drain. "You can sleep."

Without waiting for permission, Avril was across the room, letting her steps leave wet footprints. She crawled beneath the blankets, letting the towel drop, damp and cold, on the floor.

The sheets stuck to her, and she shivered beneath them.

She felt him watching her.

"Go to bed, Reed."

Opening his mouth, he hesitated. She listened as he walked to the door and shut it softly behind himself. It was already light out, but still, Avril closed her eyes. Then, she blinked them back open through the darkness that once again settled around her like a swath of silk.

She couldn't see any shadows now lingering after her. She'd learned that trick long ago.

But she couldn't close her eyes either.

When she did, she could see *his* face.

"You said you trusted me."

Avril rolled over to the other side, trying to muffle the sound of his voice against her pillow, which caused her body to quake—and not for the reason it once had.

He had been persistent. She found it attractive in a man, almost as much as his big vocabulary. He never ran out of ways to tell her how gorgeous she was. How fabulous they could be together, and she'd agreed like the good little lady he thought she was, especially when they ended up somewhere between slamming his apartment door or his bed frame into the wall.

He wrapped a hand around her throat in the darkness, now twisting around her ears to whisper, *"So, you love me?"*

Her mother would be turning over in her grave.

As she sat up, Avril was pretty sure she was rolling in hers.

Posters were rolled up and tucked behind her wardrobe of dance costumes she hadn't opened in over a year. Dust clung between crystals and sequins. Moths had probably gnawed holes through already-sheer fabric that she had worn while she posed for one of those posters. It might have been her favorite picture of herself, taken three years ago when she'd returned after touring in Europe.

Smooth velvet encased the throne. Her leg kicked over the one arm. Her body on the other side arched back, a thick crown of gold and stars tilted from where she held it on her head, hair perfectly coifed with fiery-red curls. Her eyes were closed, but her bloodred lips stretched into a wide, openmouthed smile.

She was Queen.

Was.

It didn't matter that the taxi driver had looked at Avril as if she was someone special when she climbed into the back seat. As if, with her smeared mascara and lipstick looking more like she was a clown than elegant royalty, she really was still somehow the same Queen as when she'd danced and strutted downtown without anyone daring to stop her.

Squeezing her eyes shut again, for a moment, she was sure the darkened features were still there, waiting for her the moment she let her guard down, but instead, Avril paused, confusion wrinkling her brow.

Those eyes she saw, they weren't dark at all. Not at all the ones she tried so desperately to get out of their line of vision. They were light and solid, like stone.

They were stranger's eyes, wide with shock as he realized who she was—or rather who she wasn't—in the Art Institute's gallery closet. Those eyes, rimmed in shadows, molded into the rest of him. The darkness peaked and turned around his neck and wrists, as if they were holding him together entirely.

When Avril had first started to see the shadows, it had been hard not to stare at the people or objects that seemed to bend with them. It was usually only little things. A man with a splotch of darkness smeared over his throat, as if he was trying so hard to keep something in. Her mother, who picked at shadows she didn't know were embedded in the crevices of her nails.

Avril herself would stare at her reflection in the mirror, and over the years, some of her shadows had grown, thickening, while other new ones formed.

Her mother would pinch her in warning.

"Ignore them," she'd tell her daughter. "Stay away from them. They can only bring bad things."

Of course, she had known that already.

The more Avril brought them to her mother's attention after all, the more the fear of them seemed to grow. That the shadows were coming to get her, her mother had insisted at one point, and eventually, they did.

She thought they had.

Heat bloomed, dull in her chest. Avril shoved the plush comforters off her shoulder as she stood up and made her way across the room to the mirror leaning up against the wall.

Twisting over her shoulder, she saw the way the shadows draped over her own pale skin like charcoal. They collided at the base of her back, where, before, they'd made a home, growing since they'd started over a year ago and taking the place of bruises saturated with yellow and shades of purple Avril had never seen before.

The pattern was similar—not exactly the same, but similar. The darkness seeped like blood through veins, as if alive, just like the stranger's in the closet as he'd stared down at her with stone eyes, empty of any emotion. Empty of any recognition.

"Stay away from the shadows," her mother had warned her.

"Stay off the stage," the lounge owner had insisted.

"Rest," Reed had pleaded.

Avril was never very good at following rules.

CHAPTER THREE

$\mathcal{A}$vril felt the pull the moment she stared back at herself in the mirror. She wouldn't be going back to bed.

Throwing one of the many robes draped over the back of the bathroom door over her shoulders, Avril dropped her knees on the floor, where her clothes lay in a pile. Rapidly, she searched each pocket and small compartment of her purse until her fingers found the cold piece of metal.

When she lifted it up to her eyeline, sunlight snuck through the shade reflected off the ring, spattering in color.

It was only gold. Avril narrowed her eyes, turning the tiny band over her hands before she saw it. Embedded into the band was a sparkling diamond. It was small but powerful as the stone twirled light around her as bright as any little star trying to fight to be seen through darkness.

Tucking the ring into her robe pocket, Avril maneuvered back through her room and to the door, grabbing her laptop as she went. Her hand was on the knob, about to swing it open, but halfway, sunlight coated her toes, and Reed's voice, now a clumsy mezzo, floated down the hall in hushed tones.

"No, it's fine," Reed murmured into the phone. "I don't know if she is staying, but I need to be here for her right now. Okay? Yes. Soon. I will."

"Who was that?" Avril let her head lean against the molding of his bedroom, so he could tell she'd been there for a while.

"I have research I've been putting off," Reed lied smoothly as he shoved his phone back into his pocket.

"Research?"

"Yeah. Everyone is racing to get things published before the end of the year. Fine-tuning, taking last-minute research trips for the hell of it."

"Are you going?"

"What? Where?"

"On another trip," Avril said slowly, raising her eyebrows.

She thought of the last one he had been on after putting together his PhD dissertation. Both of them had managed to somehow meet up together at the same time in Paris. Neither of them did their best work on stage or in old buildings, where Reed always put his hands against the walls, insisting how they seeped knowledge.

History pressed deep against his palm lines.

"No."

"Why not? You should. Didn't you bow out last year?" Avril asked before she realized what she meant.

Reed hadn't bowed out last year. He'd had to fly home.

For her.

Avril shifted in the doorway. His bed was made, comforter stretched to the top and pillows hanging off the sides.

His eyes narrowed down at the laptop in her hands. "What are you doing?"

"Recon," Avril answered simply, still taking in his jeans and sweater. His chestnut hair, which needed to be cut, was even brushed. "Not sleeping?"

"I got a few hours before. Like I said, I need to get some work done—unless you need me."

She nodded. "Have fun."

He nodded, slower than her. "What kind of recon did you say you were doing? I could stay here, help if you want."

"Not sure if you'd be much help," Avril said, taking a deep breath. "I'm looking for someone."

"Who?"

"Not sure."

"Maybe I wouldn't be much help then." Reed tried to laugh, but the noise came out stiff. "Where did you meet them?"

"When I was out last night. I was actually at the institute."

The unease turned a bit lighter, loosing Reed's shoulders as he began to walk around his room. He gathered notebooks and his planner, shoving them deep inside of his backpack. "Why were you there?"

"I don't know." She had seen a poster and decided, *Why not?* Her calendar wasn't very full these days. She'd needed something to do. "Cheap wine. To make fun of neo-modernist art. I saw Jack."

Reed raised his eyebrows. "That's good."

"I guess. He looked good. So did Kit. She was with him."

"They seem happy. Jack and she just got back from traveling with his job. She hired someone else to take care of the shop while they were gone, I heard. They're good for each other. You called it."

Yeah, she had.

Kit was all Avril had wished she might be once upon a time. A girl, new to the city, with confusion and hope, mixed into one fantastic potion. Avril had helped Kit drink in one swift gulp. Kit swallowed back shot after shot on her birthday that same first night they met properly last year. They played Passion and Prose when everyone was still together with the deck of tarot cards still stacked on the high bookshelf around the fireplace.

It had been a good night.

It had been the first night, too, that Avril noticed the way Kit looked at Jack.

The way Jack glanced back at her. It was a slightly different look than Avril had seen him give before. He didn't stare her down. No, she caught Jack as he pressed his lips together to hold back one of his stunning grins until she was watching.

Then, he couldn't help himself but let it escape. His eyes had crinkled with wrinkles in the corners.

Avril wondered how long it had taken them after she left to realize they had been made for each other, like in all the gooey love songs. Probably too long.

"You didn't talk to him?" Reed asked. "You realize he probably has connections back at the institute now. He'd likely know whoever was there that you're trying to find."

"I'm not asking him."

"Why not?"

"Because I didn't talk to him, okay? I can't talk to him."

How was he not getting that? She couldn't talk to anyone. She couldn't look at anyone, especially not Jack. Not yet. The thought that she'd even had an option last night to set her cup down to follow the sound of her friend's boisterous laugh instead of just staring at him had twisted her stomach and made it hard to breathe.

Made her run and hide.

She couldn't talk to anyone. Not at Rosin or the clubs or anyone in the city. That was why she'd left. It was why she had to keep leaving.

Reaching down to her pocket, she felt for the tiny sphere inside again. It was why she was trying to find whoever it was that this stupid ring belonged to. She needed to find the man whose shadows had clawed at him, trying to break through skin.

It was stupid, but the image of them, of him in her mind, tugged at her, trying to keep her moving. Whether finding him meant setting her life right or finally being at the end of it altogether, just like her mother, she had to figure it out even if it did make no sense… and she did still have this flimsy piece of jewelry.

Reed watched her. "Okay."

"I just need to find this guy, all right. I might've done something, and he left something, and I need to track him down, and that's it."

"What did you do, accidentally stab him with a plastic hors d'oeuvre utensil? I don't remember them being particularly sharp."

She glared at him.

"I didn't realize you were going through some sort of messed up twelve-step process then. Lots must've changed in the past eight months. Am I on the list of people you need to find and apologize to or whatever?"

Avril tilted her head up straighter and looked at Reed once more. He passed her going into the hallway, making way for the stairs with his heavy-looking go bag. His face had gotten thinner since she'd been gone.

"Would you like to be, darling?"

"No."

"Then, you're not."

He paused halfway down the steps before continuing. Avril lazily wandered behind him at his back, watching as he carefully shrugged on each arm of his coat before reaching for the buttons at the bottom.

"Great."

Avril sighed, fighting not to roll her eyes. It was just like Reed to be moody when he didn't get at least seven hours of sleep. Of course, that was partially her fault. "What?"

"Are you planning on being here when I get back?"

Avril shrugged. "I don't know."

"Well, if you could, let me know."

"It's my house, Reed."

Reed froze, turning back from the door to look at her. "I know."

"I can come and go as I please. The mortgage payments are coming out of my bank account. I can stay in my own house whenever I want to."

"I know."

"Good," Avril huffed. Her fingers gripped the railing.

Reed opened the door. "It would just be nice to know. I hate to see you this way."

Yeah, well, Avril wanted to say, *this is me. Take it or leave it.*

"Your phone is charging on the counter. Take it with you if you go or stay. Guess I shouldn't care what the fuck you do, huh?"

"Reed."

Before Reed said anything else, though, he turned out the door and let it shut behind him.

Reed didn't get mad. He got frustrated, but this?

Avril opened her mouth and screamed.

The sound filled the house until she heard the echo of crystal ringing through her ears.

Clearing her throat, she walked to the kitchen, unplugged her cell phone, and slammed it right back down on the counter. Let it die.

She didn't like keeping the damn thing anyway now that she didn't do anything on it besides call Reed. She answered nothing. She posted nothing on social media—Reed had already hired someone to do that for her alongside her agent, who directed all inquiries to him. The only reason she kept it was to appease her friend. But he wanted to be an ass today.

So be it.

Avril popped up the screen of the laptop and positioned herself in front of it. The blue light was her companion after an hour of scrolling for nothing. She stared and stared at the search engine.

Who was she even looking for?

A man with terrible fashion sense. A man with a reason to be hanging out at the institute gallery. A man who could ruin her once and for all.

She scrolled through five pages of new faculty, and not one looked as young or stuffy as the stranger in the closet had. Most appeared to be far past their tenure or coming in from PhD candidacy, a little too excited to teach the history of Shakespeare and scene painting.

Though their marble work was impressive.

Maybe her hunch that the shadowed stranger was a professor was wrong. He wasn't coming up when she searched for artists either, only college magazine articles with in-depth interviews that all asked the same three questions.

Maybe he wasn't there at all. Maybe Avril was just going crazy already, and she didn't need whoever he was to pull the final trigger on her sanity.

No man. No shadows.

Her mother's face flared in front of her once more. Green eyes, rimmed with red from not sleeping. Trailing through the apartment night after night, whether or not there was a special visitor there, she'd tell Avril not to interrupt her.

Avril shut the laptop.

Grabbing one of the fizzy probiotic drinks Reed stocked out of the fridge, Avril also reached back on a shelf, breaking a plastic container of chocolate pudding free. She didn't dare check the date. The only person who ate them still after a pudding shot gone wrong was her. The cup looked fresh enough. Even when she broke the seal, the all-natural scent of cocoa powder and gelatin was immediate, and she scooped a bite into her mouth.

When the fridge beeped at her, Avril used a foot to shove it closed, the movement exaggerating the twinge in her back. No matter how far she stretched to either side, her back stuck, as if a fist gripped her lower spine.

An array of paper coated the sealed fridge. Postcards from Avril or any of the others who often shared the Riverside castle whenever they needed a place to crash for a while. They'd remember to send at least one back as their compensation of sorts when they left. It was a vicarious way to induce wanderlust for whoever was still occupying the place.

The postcards littered the top in a sort of wallpaper, starting in Chicago and ending in Bilbo Baggins cottage in New Zealand.

Old Polaroid pictures were also pinned up, as well as a calendar that hadn't been changed since February. They had started so strong since Reed had put it up at the start of the year, though they hadn't beaten their record of remembering to tear off the front page till August.

Then, there were all the Post-its.

Avril didn't pay attention to most of the notes Reed had left. They were everywhere. They had been since the day she'd met him. It was obsessive, the way he labeled different books and information on different colors and then deciding to switch them halfway through whatever project he was working on since they had run out at the stationery shop.

On the fridge, however, the sticky notes were all the same light-green color.

Little reminders for appointments were quickly underlined. Last-second thoughts for a new thesis he didn't want to forget but rarely ever used, forgetting what his entire follow-up would be—besides *history*—were also there. Avril used to find those the most humorous. Next to one of those Post-its, commenting on medieval weaponry in the Arthurian era, the tickets from *Hamilton* with the original cast that he'd made them go to twice were also tacked.

Avril narrowed her eyes at another note her swaying gaze had caught on. It was similar to any long grocery list they hired out for delivery. Only this was pink and prefaced with a single bold **A**.

Avril yanked it down. Sticky glue remained behind, where it must have been for some time. The *flower power* magnet next to it stuttered before reattaching to its surface.

SIGNATURES NEEDED *for DuCain booking 1.18*
   Back rehab to be scheduled. Rescheduled.
   Kit called about order (invoice paid) set for pickup.
   Rosin called 4.21
   Dentist appointment rescheduled. To be rescheduled again.

THE LIST WENT ON.

Avril's fist flinched, wanting to crumble the entire note that Reed had kept for her in her hand. Instead, she read it line by line. There had to be dozens of calls she'd missed and quite a few he'd returned by forging her signature on appointments she never planned to keep.

Avril paused, however, on Kit's name. She remembered Reed making the order for her when she'd gotten home. She'd left a lot of her things behind in the apartment she moved into, farther into the bustle of the city for a while. All her lingerie, camisoles, and slips she mainly wore were still there.

No one had countered her when she insisted on not going back for them, questioned whatever had happened to them.

She was still down to mainly cotton underwear, some of which she had no qualms borrowing from Reed or whoever else she had spent the night with the past few months, wherever she was. Whoever she was.

Avril's thumb stuck on another appointment she'd missed in the past few months. Sighing, she looked around the place, walls inching closer in on her with each thought invading her mind.

She loved this house.

Right now, she just couldn't stand it.

CHAPTER FOUR

*A*vril looked up at the low first-floor window.

She used to scale these kinds of things in her sleep, in and out of houses. It was like a party trick. Reed had practically pretended he was Juliet in high school, sneaking her into his room at night, unbeknownst to his parents. The occasional party that ended too soon in a raid spruced up her skill. Everything had prepared her for this moment.

But Avril hesitated. It was similar to the hesitation she felt before she struggled into suitable clothing and left the house. She knew she had to do something or else she would scream again, but glancing back to the computer, she still tried one last time to think of anything else she could do in order to put a name to the shadowed stranger's face, if she could even still remember it correctly.

The lack of answers spun a hollowness in her chest.

One task off the list that Reed probably didn't even think she'd notice, and then she would be back. She'd figure it out.

No one was inside the room she stood outside of. It wasn't early or late enough for Kit to be moseying around on a random project she'd dreamed up in her head like a fairy princess. She was probably busy out front, where the store's lights shone over the satin delights Kit made and sold online and in store in record time, compared to their late Emilie, who had passed on the rent-controlled building.

Avril had been in the store enough to know where everything was and what she'd be looking for. *Set for pickup*, as the note Reed had compiled read.

Now or never.

Before she could psych herself out, Avril wiggled the cracked window frame and shoved it upward. There, step one done. Now, all Avril had to do was hoist herself up—

Her back shrieked as it reached toward the ground. A low grunt ripped from Avril as she suddenly realized how weak she had become, how much less graceful as she tumbled inside of the shop.

Her heel slipped off as she landed, clanging against the uneven hardwood.

Frozen, Avril waited.

Someone had to have heard her. The shop was too silent as Avril winced and slowly lifted herself back onto her feet.

In the far corner, *A. Queen* was written on the darkest maroon ribbon sitting atop her stack. Silk, lace, and all the fabric in between looped on top of one another. They were just where she'd expected, waiting to be picked up. There were angels singing as Avril transferred her new treasures into her arms.

Oh, how she'd missed pretty things. How had she not thought of them before? Notice that something was missing as she put on her simple black dresses with no frills when she went out? She thought it would be simple to disappear. She hoped that maybe, eventually, she wouldn't care for these sorts of finely extravagant items.

But her heart thrummed in her chest at the delicate stitching.

How ridiculous she'd been to ever think that.

"You should at least let me wrap those up for you."

Avril's breath caught before it reached her throat.

Kit stood by the doorway.

Her hands in her skirt pockets and hair twisted at the nape of her neck, she looked the picture of unsurprised. No, with thin cat-eye glasses perched on her nose, she looked a lot like her aunt Emilie, minus the wigs.

Avril almost had to do a double take.

"You should probably also use the front door next time." The corner of her pink lips turned up. "You know, for insurance purposes."

Avril swallowed. "Wouldn't want you to deal with that."

"He isn't here, by the way."

"What?"

"Jack," Kit explained. "He isn't here. I figured you didn't want to see him, and that's why you're testing your acrobatic skills."

"Oh, right."

"Because I sure hope you weren't trying to avoid me."

Avril said nothing. That was exactly what she had been trying to do.

"I saw you, you know."

"What?" Avril said, her voice skipping. She cleared her throat and started again. "Shimmying up the drainpipe into your sewing room?"

"At the gallery show opening last night?" Kit said, though it sounded more like a question.

If Avril said the word that it wasn't her that she had seen last night, Kit would believe it—or at least pretend to.

She looked different somehow from the last time Avril had seen her this close. Kit was no longer the little girl Avril had met when she first arrived in Ashton, lacing Avril up in a corset so Jack wouldn't ruin it after his own feeble attempts at figuring out what was right side up.

Jack only ever knew how best to take things off.

"I saw you when we walked in. You were near the corner.

Black dress. Heels. You looked gorgeous somehow, per usual. But not … yourself."

Avril couldn't help the pull at the side of her mouth as she looked down to the pile of garters and stockings. She hadn't had any of them last night. If she put them all on right now, would she look more like herself?

"Jack saw you just after I did, but I told him not to leave me. You looked like you were trying not to be found." Kit shrugged. "I told him that maybe you'd come back when you were ready."

"I'm not."

"What? Ready?" Kit supplied.

"Coming back." The words slipped from Avril's lips.

They felt surprisingly easy to say. When Avril had imagined herself having to say the words to someone else—like she'd insisted early on to Reed, who only looked at her with something between remorse and shame—Avril had seen herself choking on the words. She'd imagined they would burn like embers she was forcing to turn to ash deep in the back of her throat.

Yet somehow, Avril still stood tall in front of Kit.

Perhaps it was an act Avril had played the part of so well over the years that even she believed it.

Kit only blinked.

"I should be going."

Without pausing, Avril's heels resonated on the newly installed floors of the shop as she tried to make it to the front door. One of the only things that remained from the original decor Emilie had put together was the door. The wood had been slathered in layers of white and silver glitter that reflected off the corsets still displayed in the windows, like the most fabulous brothel.

Everyone couldn't help themselves but come inside.

"Wait." Kit stopped her.

Avril, despite herself, waited, staring at it all. She even took a moment to stare at the other girl in the building she hadn't noticed until then. On the other side of the counter, dark-polished fingernails were poised over the improved computer system. She didn't say a word.

"You have your employees well trained."

"Her name is Perse," Kit said quietly, catching up to where Avril had stopped. "Like the Greek goddess, though I'm almost positive she's actually a Victorian child. Not to be seen or heard. It's a bit unnerving some days, honestly. You wouldn't be able to stand it."

The wide-eyed girl still didn't make a sound.

"Do you want to come up for a while? Like I said, Jack won't be back until later. I know you hate tea, but I have chocolate biscuits as long as someone didn't eat them all."

Jack, like Avril, always had a strange addiction to sugary snack foods.

"Okay."

"Okay?" Kit's eyes lit with joy. Within them, though, there was also that something else Avril hadn't wanted to see. Another reason she hadn't wanted to see any of them or anyone who knew what had happened last year. Not even people who cared enough to give a wild guess.

Pity glimmered behind that expression, however deep and covered they attempted to conceal it.

Kit took Avril's things out of her hands.

Halfway up the staircase, she turned back. "Coming?"

For the first time in her life—or at least a long time—Avril followed.

———

ONE THING that hadn't changed since the last time Avril had been in the lingerie shop was the apartment above.

Emilie had not been one for minimalism, and not having much stuff of her own, Kit had seemed to grow into everything left behind. The '50s circle skirts she wore in her daily wardrobe. The mismatched appliances seemed to somehow work together as Kit opened the cabinet to pull out two differently shaped mugs. The only thing out of the ordinary from classic Hermès scarves tied round the coat rack was the gym gear hung by the door.

"You two are both living here?"

"We figured it was a good option for now. I'm right here with the shop and since we've been traveling …" Kit trailed off to the sound of the stove burner. Blue flame leaped under the kettle. "We went to Prague recently."

"Did you?"

"A few months ago. In the spring," Kit told her. "It was so cold for some reason, but we still ventured out one day after he was done shooting. He took me to a place that he said you and he had gone together. It was that cinnamon pastry stand. Trdelnik! They made it right in front of us before covering it in chocolate and whipped cream and everything."

When Avril had had a shoot in Europe, Jack had exclaimed how he had never been abroad. They sat in line for hours at the government offices until they issued him a passport before they had to leave. Somehow, his picture turned out good. Even the man at the airport looked a little curious about how perfect the dimple on the one side of his face was.

Then again, the man at the airport had also complimentary upgraded them after thinking the two of them were a newlywed couple. Thus, the beginning of their international country-hopping and first bottle of celebratory champagne.

"We were so hungover. I think it might have been our last day or the day before last." Avril's smile burned as she remembered the Nutella and marshmallow combination. "I ate at least four."

"He said seven."

It had definitely not been seven. However, Avril didn't counter. It sounded much more impressive.

"I never got to..." Avril paused as she looked down at Kit's hands.

A Band-Aid was wrapped around her one finger as she set down the package of cookies. Kit took one out for herself and immediately bit into it. She shoved the blue plastic toward Avril.

Sitting down, Avril immediately felt relief flood her lower back. She had known that she was pushing it, walking most of the way here. Through the window. Up the stairs.

She twisted the top of the sandwich cookie off to get to the cream center.

"I never got to properly congratulate you two," she tried again, tense. "Reed told me."

Kit smiled wide. When she reached up to her neck, it was only then that Avril noticed the chain. When she pulled on it from under her collar, there hung a small antique ring. The band lifted into the diamond bezel, delicate and dainty, as she held it out for Avril's inspection.

"Thank you. I had to put it on here after it got caught a few too many times while I worked. No one wants pulls in their lace."

Avril held it for just another moment before letting it drop back over Kit's heart.

"Another adventure. In Paris."

"I thought you two got engaged at DuCain, in front of everyone."

Avril tried to remember what Reed had let slip, however few details. He likely hadn't wanted her to upset herself. But she wasn't upset. She felt the one side of her mouth begin to curve, imagining the spectacle they'd caused.

"Oh"—Kit nodded—"we did. But we did it for just ourselves first. Jack knows better than to do something like that in front of a lot of people."

"He probably would have to assure everyone your overstimulated silence was code for yes."

Kit laughed. "Exactly."

"Will I be invited?"

Kit held her smile softly, something gleaming there. For a second, Avril could have sworn that devilish glint only belonged to Jack. "And here I thought we were friends."

Avril snorted.

"If you have to ask, you aren't coming." Kit shook her head. "I can't believe I let you up here to eat my cookies while my fiancé is out."

"Are you trying to tell a dirty joke, Kit?"

"Is it working?"

Avril pressed her lips together so that the laugh she had wouldn't break through. Apparently, it was.

"If you aren't at our wedding, Avril … well, you'd better be there."

"I await the invitation."

"Good," Kit said finally. "I missed you."

Avril rolled her eyes.

"I did."

Still, Avril wasn't sure how or why. The statement stirred something inside of her nonetheless. The image of silver eyes and pitch-black shadows curled around her line of vision.

"Last night."

Kit perked up. "Yes?"

Yes. So prim.

"I—I met someone, sort of," Avril said.

"Oh?"

"Yes, oh," Avril muttered. "But I didn't get his name."

Kit's intrigue turned more tickled.

Avril stopped her before she could even attempt another dirty joke. It was painful to watch. "Don't even. If I wanted to, I could say that this was all your fault. I was hiding from you and your atrociously nosy husband."

"Fiancé."

"For all I know, you two already got married and plan on just having another show for the hell of it. Anyway …" Avril, for a moment, felt something stir inside of her. It felt light. She ignored it and kept on. "I need to find him."

"Why? Was he a good kisser or something?"

He was actually.

But that wasn't the point.

"Wow," Kit said by the lack of answer.

Avril reached into her jean pocket. She dug until her fingers clasped around the object. Pulling it back out, similar to how Kit had with her own from beneath her blouse, Avril extended the ring.

"Oh," Kit exclaimed. Waiting for permission, she extracted the gold from Avril's fingertips. "Very pretty. Simple. Looks really tiny."

Before Avril could snatch her hand back, Kit slipped it on Avril's finger.

"Fits perfectly on you though."

Immediately, Avril reached to yank the ring back off her hand, but before she did, she stared down at it. The diamond flickered again. More carefully, Avril slid it off, putting it back in her pocket.

"You want to find this random guy you ran into last night to return the ring?" Kit asked, raising her eyebrows. "That's all?"

"That's all," Avril insisted.

It even sounded like a terrible lie to her own ears.

"He obviously didn't drop it on purpose, Kit. He needs to get his ring back. Or whoever's ring it is he was holding on to."

"Maybe it is meant to be your ring."

"Did something go to your brain?"

"Just love."

"Even worse," Avril countered. "At this rate, it doesn't matter. I tried searching for anything I could think of. He might as well be a ghost."

"Maybe I know him."

Avril forced herself not to look unconvinced. Kit, social-anxiety debutante, who'd just recently scored the most scandalous man in Ashton.

"Try me. Describe him."

"Fine. He was …"

"I'm going to need a little more than that."

"Tan-ish. Tall."

"Ish?"

"Tall," Avril confirmed. Taller than average. "Glasses, I think—they were on his head for a while."

Another short laugh.

"He wore appallingly worn loafers." And he had gray eyes and sharp features and had looked at her in only a moment as if she were the only one he cared about, no matter who it was that had caught her basically in his lap last night.

"Dark brows, lighter hair?" Kit reached up, as if to mimic how it stuck up before falling.

"You know who he is?"

Kit raised her eyebrows. "You wanna know?"

CHAPTER FIVE

*A*vril had loved the library when she was small. It'd be a lie, however, to say she did much reading. It was the one place left, her mother used to say, where you could go during the day and not have to buy anything. So, they went often.

Some evenings, Avril's mother even dropped Avril off in a corner for a few hours, warning her not to draw attention to herself while she ran errands or went out with a new boyfriend.

Avril twirled through the back reference aisles. She read about theater and famous people who had more than one volume dedicated to their lives. She watched old black-and-white movies on VHS tapes in the kids' area when no one else was there.

The librarian who saw her often didn't seem to mind after she asked Avril where her mommy was.

Avril would only glance over her shoulder and point to another section. "Looking at the grown-up books," she'd say. Just like she'd practiced.

Hours passed differently when Avril was in the library. Hours felt like minutes, easily spent by flipping through the pages of Venetian art and Greek goddesses. Avril had traced their curves and squinted her eyes so that when the figures looked at her from the page in vibrant color, she'd stare right back with emerald-gilded irises.

Avril couldn't find the art history section in this library. She never set foot in it before. Never thought to, like the art students positioning themselves around low tables, running their fingers over the pages like Avril strummed hers over the end of each row of shelves she wandered through.

A throat cleared across the corridor.

As if the image in her head had come to life, at the end of the row was the stranger. For a moment, Avril closed her eyes before opening them again, making sure she was actually seeing him right there in front of her. There he was.

Ian Whitlock. Temporary librarian at the Ashton East Public Library.

He appeared much more well kempt this time, though the drab outfit seemed to be a personal uniform.

As were the shadows. They looped around his wrists like cuffs. Fingerprints stained the covers of the thickly bound books he carried to reshelve. He noticed her a moment after she saw him. His fingers relaxed for only a second before gripping the sides, as if he controlled the darkness pooling himself—inviting her in.

"Why, hello there, stranger." Avril attempted the practiced words, though for some reason, they sounded strained.

Jury, meet executioner.

She swallowed and forced herself to look somewhere else as she calmed her heart, that had taken up a hasty strum. The building was a recent affiliation, to be kept alive by The Ashton Art Institute. The students needed somewhere to print out their references, after all.

Avril forced herself to turn her attention back at the man Kit had carefully described as if she herself knew of him intimately and not just when she had come in to get a library card. Still, Avril hadn't asked her for more information. She had taken what she had been given and left soon after. Her fingers had started to fidget against her friend's table as they were now, thumb strumming against fingertips.

Five, six, seven, eight.

She shook the hand out to the side. "Why, if it isn't just the man I was looking for."

Her mystery man didn't move. Not that she'd expected him to run away.

Not exactly.

He only narrowed his piercing stare, more of a scowl than anything else. "What are you doing?"

"Looking for a book, of course. What else would I be doing in this fine establishment?"

"I thought you just said you were looking for me," he said blandly.

Then, why had he asked?

Avril leaned against the shelves. "I can have more than a few things to be looking for, can't I?"

He raised an eyebrow, but his face remained impassive. "Which?"

"Which what?"

"Which book were you looking for?" His voice was deep and steady as he continued his glower at her empty hands.

"Titian."

"The artist." It wasn't a question.

Avril could have sworn there was a twinge of pleasant surprise that crossed his face.

It disappeared just as quickly.

"I've always been fascinated by the *Venus of Urbino*. The rich color of virginal red. The way she looks into your sinful eyes."

It was only then that she noticed him more fully. His lanky body filled out those carefully pleated dress pants. Tortoise-shell glasses drew attention to his scrutinizing gaze, as stiff as stone. Setting the stack of books down on the edge of the shelf, he pushed the spectacles back up onto his head, dirty blond and ruffled.

She couldn't believe she'd pegged him for a professor.

Without a word, he turned and led her down a few more aisles. Turning another corner, he stopped so suddenly that the movement almost caused Avril to run into him. With a swipe of his finger across the shelf, following decimals, he slipped out a heavy book of Venetian art.

It was the same edition she remembered as a child.

Avril's hand slowly slid across the embossed lettering on the cover.

"Is he your favorite?"

"No."

She could tell that the librarian was trying to stop himself from asking the next logical question: *Who is?* She bit her lip, waiting for it.

"Anything else I can do for you?"

Avril raised her eyebrows. She didn't open the tome. "I wasn't looking for a book."

"You don't say?" Ian took it back for her and put it properly on the shelves. After that, he began to turn around at her apparent dismissal, leaving her to trail after him.

"Could you not?"

"In case you haven't noticed, ma'am—"

"I prefer madam, if we are being formal."

"I'm currently at work. I have a job. So, if I can no longer be of service to you…"

The words rang a bell somewhere deep inside of Avril. Perhaps the librarian wasn't all gentle breeding and manners. Avril quirked a smirk.

"Are you offering your services to me, Ian? Because if so, I would love to inquire about the ones you serviced me with last night."

He stopped walking, but not before leading her directly to his office. "Who told you who I was?"

"A little bird this morning while I was getting dressed." Avril swayed back and forth in her leather pants before moving past him.

His office was rather orderly to the naked eye. Mostly sparse, but upon closer inspection, she noticed the librarian was a bit of a mess. Papers stuck out of stacked books that were never put on the shelf. None of them appeared to have a real subject connection.

Avril perched comfortably on the edge of his desk. "I'm the crudest Disney princess you've ever met."

She also was quite sure that in most fairy-tale storylines, it wasn't the princess who saw the darkness and shadows looping around her like the foreshadowing of an impending death. Queens did though. So did monsters. Maybe that was what the man was in front of her, watching her.

But the shadows still circled his wrists like binds—or not—no longer there.

He lifted his sleek wrist and took a look at whatever it was that caught Avril's attention. "Dust?"

Ignoring him, Avril blinked, as if it had been dust that got in her eyes.

Ian dropped his newest stack of books by the small table in the doorway and stuffed his hands into his pockets as he strode farther inside the small office.

"Are you done wasting more of my time now?" He practically shooed her off his desk.

"Because," Ian intoned, fixing something she hadn't even touched over his calendar, which was as wide as his whole freaking desk. He barely looked up when he spoke. "Like I said before, which you ignored, I'm busy."

Slipping off the wood surface, Avril made herself even more comfortable in the round-backed chair in front of him.

She waved a hand out to the side. Even his walls were bare. "Not even a thank-you?"

"What on earth would I have to thank you for?"

Without circumstance, Avril shoved her hand into her pocket. Ian glanced away at the movement, but his eyes froze as she carefully dropped the ring down onto his desk with a resonate clang. The circle strummed before settling.

Ian stared at it for a long moment.

"Don't tell me you were going to propose."

Ian said nothing as he reached out and took the ring in his hand, looking at the band and the tiny diamond on the other side. Tension seemed to seep from his shoulders.

"Where did you find this?"

"It was on the floor in the closet."

He cringed at the reminder.

"Archives. Whatever. It's yours?"

"Yes. It's mine."

Avril narrowed her eyes. "Look, if I made trouble for you and your girlfriend the other night, honestly, she should be flattered."

"Flattered."

"That you had to tell your girlfriend about how you had such apparent and unbridled passion that you were about to fuck her in the archives closet, absolutely. Ladies these days eat that shit up. Blame it on all the erotica."

The side of his jaw ticced. "She wasn't my girlfriend."

Of course she wasn't.

About to snap out something else to attribute to her bland disbelief, Avril paused. She had come. She had seen. She could get up and leave right now, now that her act of goodwill was completed. She was almost certain that was what Ian was waiting for her to do. But Avril sat and stared at Ian.

The man of shadows.

He'll cause your ruin. Avril heard a familiar voice again in the back of her head, settling into her as she sat, waiting for it. Once and for all.

"Hey." A guy with hair tied back into a small bun smiled from where he looped around the office doorway. Immediately, his eyes caught on Avril. A tawny eyebrow slanted. "I'm Noah. Are you—"

"No."

"All right then. Ian."

Ian did not look up. Apparently, much to Avril's prediction, he was rude to everyone.

Noah continued without pause, "I'm just about to head out for the day and thought I would say *see ya*. I need to run home and change into more company-official clothes before the meeting-party thing tonight at Wexler. You're bringing Cyn, right?"

Ian's bright eyes flickered up from his desk toward the intruder.

The man stepped back to leave.

"All right then. Let me know if you need help finding the place," Noah said. He glanced once more at Avril. "Nice to meet you."

When he rounded the corner outside the glass windows, Ian's head turned back down to his hands. He held the ring with sharp reverence before stashing it away.

Avril made herself all the more comfortable, kicking her feet up to the edge of the desk. "You intimidate them."

He looked at her eight-hundred-dollar scuffed heels with disgust.

"And you know it."

At that, his gaze turned up again, giving Avril a similar stare, but then again, he must have been giving her that stare all along. Or maybe he was like a turtle. A rage-filled turtle who let his glares keep him company when he was nervous. But he didn't retreat into his shell. At least, not completely. Maybe that was the point.

Avril had no shell. Dropping her feet back down to the floor, she leaned forward until there were only a few inches between their faces on the desk, balancing her head in her hands.

"Take me."

For the dimmest moment, Avril was positive Ian was thinking the exact same thing she was. The images flowed freely of him sweeping aside his desk planner and cup of dried-up pens and laying her down on it. Save him the effort having to pick her back up again on a table, just so he could accurately reach her mouth and, well, the rest of her.

There were enough curtains behind her on the windows that no one would notice. And if they did, she was certain whatever glare Ian produced then would be enough that no one would utter a word about the temp's kinky work behaviors.

"What?"

"Don't pretend that scared guy with the freckles and Harry Potter glasses was an illusion. You need a date. I scared yours off, didn't I?"

"You did not scare her off."

"I appreciate a man who stands up for women, but yeah, I'm pretty sure I did." Looking around the room, Avril mimicked looking for the long-lost girlfriend before putting her hands to either side.

Ian didn't appear to appreciate her acting skills.

"Come on. Let me be your office party date so you don't look like a lonely, coldhearted loser. I've never been to an office party before. It's the least I can do."

"You ask so nicely," Ian gritted out.

"I try."

"I was being facetious."

"And?"

"A *please* would be warranted."

"What? Did you go to finishing school?"

He only waited, looking down at her across the space between them.

"I don't say *please*."

"And let me guess, you don't say *thank you* either."

Like he did?

"You're catching on," Avril purred. "And aren't I the one offering to take you on a free night out with me? I have a feeling that if you are as prim and proper as you think, you should be thanking me."

He said nothing.

Avril couldn't help herself. She knew why she was here, somehow even if she wasn't positive. She was here for him, Ian Whitlock. The man of shadows she had been warned about since days before her mother's death. There was a pull to him and the shadows circling around the two of them, like they liked whatever game it was they debated on playing.

Avril took a deep breath and leaned into them. Let them take her.

Whether or not she could feel the edge of her mask she knew was so well slipping into place, she grinned at his displeasure. "Last call."

CHAPTER SIX

"You clean up nice."

Ian twisted from where he stood at the base of the marble steps that led up to Wexler. Once the original all-male college, it was still a formidable-looking building. All angles and no shutters over brick. Ian looked even more so. He was dressed in dark slacks, a thick camel-colored wool trench, flipped up around the collar, where the shadows liked to twist light tattoos around his throat, begging him to speak their darkness.

Their darkest fears and trauma.

The closer she got, the more noise seemed to radiate into static in her ears.

She focused on Ian's eyes, widened at the sight of her. Opening her deep red coat, Avril exposed the loose sheath of her tank top and high-waisted black pants. She'd figured it was an office party though and added some sparkle dangling from her ears. As they swayed, she could see them out of the corner of her winged eyes, which had taken a few times more to perfect from lack of practice.

He cleared his throat before extracting his hands from his

pockets. They were similarly gloved to hers in short black leather.

"I guess I should say the same then."

How chivalrous. "I'm waiting."

"You look nice," he said stiffly.

"I should consider that compliment one of the most detailed I've ever received."

He huffed. "Your outfit. It's mostly appropriate."

"You're getting there." She closed her coat back up, as if they were going to keep standing outside. Her breath escaped with a ghost. "Now, is that a hand you were about to offer so that you could enter your party with your scandalous guest? Or will I have to traverse the marble steps in these heels with only my talent?"

Ian blinked and shook his head without humor. He extended his arm.

Avril hesitated at what she knew lied beneath wool before accepting. "Why, thank you."

He was even taller than she cared to remember. Even on her heels, she arched her neck to meet his face.

"I thought you mentioned not saying *thank you*?"

"And *sorry*," Avril reminded him. "Only when I mean it."

He made a strange sort of sound. "And so, when will I begin to know when the department holiday party is thoroughly scandalized, as promised? The library has been associated with the English and art history departments. I can't imagine they are easily put off."

Wait a second.

Avril stopped walking.

When she peered up at him, his face scrunched as he looked back at her, as if he'd just noticed a bit of dirt caked on his shoe. "What?"

"You honestly looked into nothing about me since the last time we spoke. Not even after your library boy looked at me like I was all he wished for in his dreams?"

"It has only been a few hours. Like I said before, I had work to do."

Like she could believe that. There were only so many books to shelve. What was he doing, reading them one by one to become the goddamn library?

She would have at least suspected after the way Noah looked at her that he would have done a quick Google search on Ashton and his date's name. If he were a woman, Avril would have scolded him about participating in such risky behavior.

Then again, he had already had his tongue down her throat.

The memory spread a different heat from the back of her neck.

"Are you kidding?" Avril couldn't help herself but ask again, searching his blank face, curling with shadows, the more he scowled, declaring him above everyone else. Literally and figuratively.

"Excuse me?"

"You don't know who I am?"

He stared at her.

"Not a fucking clue who I am?" she asked, as if that would clear things up further.

"Should I?"

"I'm just making sure I have this right." She couldn't believe this. "You think I am, what? Just some woman you accidentally and thoroughly, I might say, ravished in an office last night?"

A flash of disgust crossed his face.

"Honestly. You're serious?"

"Honestly?" he mocked.

"Honestly." It was likely the thing she valued the most at this point.

"Sweetheart, I'm not even sure if I remember you telling me your name."

All the breath seemed to be swirling around Avril. He had no idea who she was. Not a clue, and he didn't care.

The shadows roared in her ears. A voice warning her to stay away, run far away, trilled, not far behind.

"Let's make a deal."

"Are we on a game show?" Ian asked, looking around.

A cloud of his own breath formed a ghost. The wisp traveled upward, toward barren tree branches. A couple passed them on their own way inside, chatting about something that didn't matter.

But what Ian said did. It mattered so suddenly that Avril was full of the idea that swam through her vision like a dark cloud as she reached her own hand out and caught Ian's arm before he thought to join them without her.

Her heart raced. The wind pounded into her ears. She felt it all for the first time in, well, maybe longer than even the year.

"Listen to me."

"I think I have been."

"No, I want to make a deal." She had to think fast. "I fucked things up for you and your girlfriend."

"Not—"

Avril swatted away whatever ridiculous argument he was about to make. "Whatever. Look. You have what? A few of these events you've been invited to already over the holidays?"

Ian didn't reply. He must've been smart enough to know that she'd already seen the unanswered invitations scattered across his desk. He was an RSVP's nightmare.

"I'll be your date."

He looked up once more at Wexler. "And this is?"

"Not only tonight. I'm talking for the rest of the holiday season. You are new here, obviously."

"I don't need a date."

"You did last night."

"Excuse me?"

"Your artist chick. You wanted her for a reason, and I can't imagine that it was to go to a boring office party, correct?"

Ian said nothing.

It was all falling into place.

"You need a companion of sorts. I can be that person. No one will try to set you up or bother you. I am very good at parties. No one will question it, and I do owe you after all."

"I don't want whatever you owe."

"I'm offering," Avril said, taking a step back so he could take in exactly what she was offering if he really wanted to look again. To be honest, she wasn't even sure.

"I have work to do."

"So?" Her grin widened. "There is one condition, of course."

He rolled his eyes and laughed. It was a dry, deep laugh that held little humor. "Of course there is."

"You can't know who I am."

"Well, I think that will be relatively easy."

"No," Avril maintained. "You can't know who I am. When I am with you, you cannot look me up. You cannot conveniently overhear any whispers that happen in there tonight or at any other point. You cannot ask anyone who I am specifically from this moment forward."

"More than one rule."

"I'm not a fan of most rules if it makes you feel any better."

"You just like to make them," said Ian.

For a second, Avril was about to give him another reason, feeling the strange tang of rejection starting to permeate on her own tongue.

"I don't know you."

"Exactly. What better for basically your holiday rebound?"

Ian chewed on the inside of his cheek for a long moment before he threw a hand to the side.

With a breeze of wind, Avril wondered if her heart had stopped. "Fabulous."

She had no idea what she'd just done or started.

All she knew was that she was standing next to him, watching the shadows dance over his skin and slip back down under his tailored coat, and for some reason, it set the whole idea at ease. As well as her name in stone.

The deal was made. She took another step up toward the doors.

"But," Ian began, unmoved.

Avril stopped, turning around. She was almost as tall as he was now. Almost.

She set her hands on her hips. "But?"

"I get to make my own rules."

"You have rules?"

"The rest of them. They're mine for the rest of this ... experiment. It's only fair, as I see it, if you are going to play pretend at someone you're not. That is your goal here, right?"

Only Avril didn't want to play pretend. Not exactly.

"And as of now, it's on a trial period."

"A trial period?"

"Tonight," Ian explained. "If tonight in there doesn't go well, this whole thing is off."

"And if it does?"

"Then, we'll make a deal. Until I leave."

"You plan on leaving the party so soon? I think we have to make it inside first." Avril made it up another step before turning around.

He still wasn't following her.

He looked around himself. The buildings. The trees.

"Ashton?" The thought made something in her chest clench. "You're going to leave the city?"

"I'm only here on a sort of periodic help basis at the library after I was told there was a job opening. The only reason I'm in Ashton is because I'm finishing up some work on a property that was given to me."

"Impressive gift."

"It'll be sold by the end of the month, and our deal will also be off. So, if I follow your rules, you at least pay attention to mine. Is it a deal?"

She'd started this mess, but still, Avril paused. He hadn't said that she had to follow his rules, whatever they were. Not exactly.

Did it matter?

Swallowing, Avril nodded. "Fine."

"Deal?" Ian asked again. He peeled off his glove and put it in his pocket.

A pattern of swirls decorated his wrist, all the way into his palm, just as she'd imagined they would.

She tried to swallow the hesitant shake in her voice as she yanked off her own glove and sealed her hand in his. She felt the shadows pulse against calluses.

Mine. Mine. Mine.

"Deal."

CHAPTER SEVEN

*A*s she'd suspected, office parties were boring. Somehow even more boring than Avril imagined. She'd had a slight hope after Ian admitted the art history crowd was also invited along with the English department. Only a few guests tottered, dry elbows shaking above canes as they sat down in flimsy folding chairs and ate tiny cubes of cheese off toothpicks.

"Well, this is invigorating," Avril murmured, trying to be on her best behavior. Reaching out, she stole a second glass of champagne off a tray. The bubbles were dim, but not uninviting.

"Hey, guys."

Ian stared at the man approaching. His hair was more delicately swept away from his face than it had been earlier today. Less curls, more gel, but not yet transitioning to crunchy.

Avril stepped forward, shoving her almost-empty glass into Ian's chest. He caught it in his hands and brought it directly to his mouth, swallowing the rest.

"Noah, right?"

"You remembered." He smiled. "This is my friend Wanda."

Wanda flashed a hesitant smile. Only it slowly turned into confusion and then, "Oh my God, are you—Noah said, but—"

Avril smiled politely as she shook her head. "No one of interest currently, sorry to say."

"Oh, I, uh," Wanda stammered.

Noah only hugged onto the sides of her shoulders.

Avril attempted not to notice the suddenly rapt attention on the back of her own from Ian.

"Don't mind her," Noah said. "I thought that Cynthia was in town, Ian. Figured she'd be here with you after you finally said that you were going to meet up with her at the show. It's awesome that the university liked her work so much. I still need to go and check it out sometime. Been wondering if I could catch Cyn before she leaves the city to get the inside artist's scoop on what all the squiggly lines and naked women meant as a whole."

Ian's eyes finally caught Noah in a similar glare to the one he had given him for interrupting them earlier today. "I didn't realize Cynthia's art was still of that much interest to you, Noah."

"I just wanted to say hello. Haven't seen her since that show back in—oh. I thought—you and she didn't—right." His eyes shifted between Ian and Avril.

Both of them were unsmiling. Though Avril wouldn't bend her neck to look up at him, whatever look he was giving seemed to wither Noah in his dress pants.

"Well, now that both Wanda and I have put a foot in our own mouths yet again, we were just looking for the champagne or whatever is being served before it runs out," Noah said with a smile.

It appeared he was used to the unusual contortion.

"A great idea." Avril lifted her own flute back out of Ian's hand. Their skin brushed together again, sending a tingle toward her fingertips. Carefully, she brought it to her lips as Wanda continued to closely watch her down the single drip Ian had left, obviously unperturbed.

"But I—"

"I told you not to say anything," Noah mumbled to her as they walked away.

Wanda scuttled along with him, still glancing back. "I'm sorry, I couldn't help myself. She was right there. In front of me. Here of all places."

Ian reached for another glass of champagne for himself off the table beside them. It was the last of few. Still, he downed half of it in another easy gulp.

It tasted like Welch's grape juice.

"So, I can't ask?"

"Not the slightest bit."

He stood up to straight while the room wandered around them.

"So, conversation?"

He raised an eyebrow. "What conversation?"

"Not a conversationalist then, I see," Avril said. When he didn't respond, she shifted her weight onto her other foot to take it out of her back. "Fine, I'll start. So, your girlfriend was the artist?"

Ian's jaw clenched.

"What a way to ruin a show opening in Ashton. Damn."

"Again, she wasn't my girlfriend."

"Uh-huh. She just had the whole shocked facial expression down."

Was this hell? If this was going to continue, no emotion in his voice or care in the world, Avril was going to need another drink soon.

She saw a few over there, still sitting on a covered table, where Noah and his pearly-cheeked friend had gone. When she took a step in that direction, a hand caught her elbow. Avril almost gasped before catching the sound back in her chest.

Ian gently pulled her a step back in line with him. "She wasn't my girlfriend. We were friends in college. I wanted it to be something more, but I never stepped up. She gave me my chance a while ago. The only reason I was in that closet with you was because ..."

Because he'd planned to make a move.

Avril's eyes widened. In the dim lighting, she imagined their similar black dresses. Her height in stilettos. "You were really going to propose."

"I was not going to propose."

And she thought he was dull. "Ian."

He closed his eyes when she said his name.

So, he might have been a tad constrained, but last night—to the artist, to her even though he didn't know it was her—for a moment, Ian wasn't. Not at all.

Avril could work with that. If she was going to be stuck with another angry pile of regret, she'd have to. She hated feeling the emotion herself enough that she felt it emanating off of him.

He twisted his hands that held themselves, if only for something to keep them occupied while he returned to intimidating silence. He stood as if he presided whatever dominance he had oozing out of him and into the room.

"Do you want to get out of here?"

Ian glanced down at her. It was only then did she realize that he didn't have his glasses that had been previously atop his head earlier today or last night.

"I'm serious. After all, I did say that I was going to accompany you to a party."

"Are you drunk?"

"Stars, I only had two. Most of one drank," Avril muttered.

"Where do you think we are?"

She popped a laugh. She understood. "We came. We saw. This is not a party."

"What is it then?"

"Terrible."

She saw a twitch at the corner of his mouth. It smoothed too quickly.

"We don't need to talk about your—"

He gave her a look.

"Artist. Awful art. Hate to even think of it."

He cocked his head to the side, an invitation.

It felt as if he had taken the time to engrave it, and Avril accepted swiftly. "For some reason, I have a feeling you've never been to a real party."

"A real party? Is it different from a fake one?"

She ignored that. She already had a feeling she was right. She didn't need more ammunition. "A fun party. A party that you look back on and cringe and smile about at the same time, feeling the grit of whatever the hell someone had just poured into a cup for you out of their bathtub, just from remembering it?"

He narrowed his eyes again, studying. "Has anyone ever told you that you should be a writer?"

"No, mainly because I'd only write the terribly scandalous scenes."

"The next Anaïs Nin then."

Avril raised her eyebrows. "Very well read, Mr. Whitlock."

"Doctor actually."

A well-educated man, of course. Where else would he have learned to do all that brooding?

"Doctor. I'm shocked."

Shaking his head at the name, Ian finally turned his gaze down to her. His eyes smoldered as they met. "I've done plenty more things that would shock you."

"Doubtful."

Ian rolled his eyes.

"A remedy," Avril suggested, reaching up to take Ian's cup from him. She tossed it into one of the potted plants. They deserved some fun too. "Ready?"

"Ready for what?"

"A little trust. Do you think I would lead you astray?"

"I think I'd count on it."

At least he was finally catching up. Perfect.

She was willing for the first time in a long time to play.

They didn't say goodbye as they slipped their coats over their shoulders and slipped out of Wexler. Her hand didn't shake when she grasped him on the sidewalk, looking both ways. Uptown, downtown, to the villages.

"What are you doing?"

"Deciding."

"Deciding?" Ian looked around, as if it was incredulous that they were already out on the street and she hadn't decided to button up her jacket yet.

"Now, shut up," Avril rebuked. "You said I was the one to show you, out-of-towner, around Ashton before you care to disappear from its wonders and usually much better holiday parties." At least when she threw them. "Will you let me, or would you rather head back inside to that misogynistic Wexler building, where the most interesting thing was Wanda and counting how many different shades of periwinkle she has hidden underneath that pixie cut?"

Ian sealed his lips.

Avril pursed hers at the pleasure of silencing him of her own accord. DuCain and Rosin flared to her mind first as the perfect places to take him. Drinking sparkling cider out of coupes or crisp liquor over spheres of ice in art deco golden-rimmed glasses. She imagined him rolling his eyes at the casual sadomasochism and amount of latex people wore this time of year. She'd be laughing as she made a strange joke about the ambiance.

Avril shook the thought that felt like the most vivid memory out of her head.

Avril raised her hand, and a taxi stopped immediately. She swung inside, leaving the door open for Ian.

He slowly maneuvered under the low ceiling after her.

"Sixty-Third and Calico."

"Sean's?"

Avril clicked her tongue and pointed at the gruff driver. "You know the place, darlin'."

"Your accent," Ian said suddenly. The driver nearly took off with Ian's leg hanging out. "What is it? Welsh?"

Avril cleared her throat to mask it once again. "Nope."

"It's gone again."

"I learned how to cover it." Most of the time. The only time she let it slip out often was when she was home with Reed. Or drunk.

"Why?"

Avril turned to face him as a flash of car lights blew past them. "Aren't you full of questions?"

The driver laughed—at his radio talk show or at them, it really didn't matter. After a few more moments, he pulled over behind a row of cars. Avril swiped her card and nearly pushed Ian out onto the sidewalk before he realized they were at their destination.

"Calico. Who named these streets in Ashton?" Ian stared up at the crooked green sign.

"Whoever wanted to."

He smirked back up at it again, noting the numbers that appeared to have been hand drawn on in thick white script. "I'm serious."

"So am I. You know, Ashton was an artist commune once. For a short period, near East Bay Park. When they disbanded, the city was basically up for grabs. That's why there are so many streets with people's names." She glanced upward, toward the extra loop on the C of Calico. She'd never noticed that before. "People's cats."

"I'm still not sure if you are trying to pull something on me."

"Believe what you want. It makes no difference to me." Avril shrugged and walked her way down the pavement toward the sounds of rowdy banter.

"Are you sure we are going the right way?"

"Yes."

"Where are you taking me?"

"My, oh my, I didn't take you as such a curious person," Avril said. "My mistake, obviously."

"I prefer to know what I'm getting into."

"You didn't seem to be concerned with that a few hours ago. For all you know, you made a deal with the devil."

"I'm more likely to believe that at the current moment." Ian fought to meet her pace as she wrapped around the corner.

A small cluster of people passed a joint back and forth under the lamppost outside the staircase. It led down.

Reaching out, Ian's hand caught Avril.

He didn't touch her, however, not exactly. His index finger and thumb hitched on to the edge of her coat sleeve.

She paused and looked down at it. Immediately, she wanted to shrug him off.

But she didn't. She only looked upward, and for the first time, whenever she turned around to meet Ian, she didn't see the shadows. Not at first. There were none there. Only the ones jumping onto them both from the gentle flicker of the post in need of a bulb change.

It hesitated before growing brighter, as if debating something.

Ian had a similar expression, glancing up from where his fingers gripped gently on to a wine-red trench. "Are you the devil, Avril?"

She certainly wasn't a khaki-colored private investigator, trying to blend in.

Avril pulled her hand back and placed it naturally on her hip. Ian had let go with little resistance. The city pulsed around them when she shrugged.

"Just one of his happy little helpers."

He huffed out something Avril could almost interpret it as a laugh.

"Any other questions?"

"You're taking me to a pub. So, you don't plan to scandalize me? I thought that was part of the deal you promised."

"Would you like it to be? It can be arranged," she said, but before he dared to answer, she forced a laugh. Or maybe it couldn't be arranged—at least, not now. "The terms of agreement to our deal are still up for debate."

She looked down at her shoes and shuffled the nonexistent dirt off them. They were still scuffed, just around the toe, like those of a hooker skittering up and down the pavement all night long. These had become one of Avril's favorite pairs when she came home a year ago. She trusted them to get her from point A to B, with only a little cringing from her feet or vertebrae. She hadn't trusted herself to try anything taller, more elaborate, more expensive.

She wouldn't dare victimize them with the possibility of needing to put slips of blue memory foam in the soles, like she imagined grandmothers did to their penny loafers.

Like the ones Ian wore.

He really needed better shoes if she was going to take him anywhere worthwhile.

"Not tonight. Like I said before, I am taking you out for a drink, and we're going to party."

"And the pub is a party?" Ian looked skeptical.

"Anywhere can be a party if you want it to be. Or is your imagination not broad enough?"

"It is plenty developed, thank you."

Avril only hummed at his displeasure with her. "Open mind."

"Another rule."

"A human rule. You act like you've never had any fun."

Ian didn't reply. She could see the trill of something, however, dance behind his eyes. Was it possible that she had a secret party boy on her hands? Or not. Then again, little Kit with her doe eyes had surprised them all after meeting her as well.

Ian looked like he would rather be anywhere but there.

Avril huffed. The door opened and closed below, loud guffaws echoing toward the surface out of the bar. The sound of so many people made her fingers twitch. She took a deep breath though.

She wasn't going to drag him in.

"Fine. Whatever."

"What?"

She was already turning around. This was a bad idea. A terrible one, though she couldn't say it was her worst.

Ian trailed. "Where are you going?"

"Getting a cab."

"Why?"

"Because. I am trying to be *nice*." Avril seethed calmly through her teeth. The tone came out in a little spirited haze in front of her in the cold. She shoved her hands back in her pockets. The fabric hugged close to her. "In case you haven't noticed, it isn't a mannerism that comes to me often."

"I apologize if I offended you."

"You—" She snapped her mouth closed before finishing that sentence. The shadows were back, as if they knew that she needed a reminder of whatever they were trying to do to her. They were why she was out here with all these people. Why she was with him. "You didn't offend me."

"I see." Ian adapted a similar stance in front of her, tucking his hands into his coat pockets.

She couldn't imagine how they looked, both of them standing there in the middle of the sidewalk. One tall, one...Avril.

"You could at least try to be...I don't know. Pleasant?"

"Pleasant."

"Or nice. I usually don't care for niceties."

"So I've noticed."

"But I don't know ... maybe you'll convert me," Avril went on.

Ian shook his head, confused. A hand flew out to the side, as if he were trying to catch the next few words he was searching for as they actively swirled around that big brain of his. "You want me to be nice to you."

"No."

"No?" At this point, he looked like he was about ready to leap into traffic.

Avril wasn't even sure where she was going with this. She took a deep breath. "I want you to take whatever giant prick is up your ass and find it a new home because, darling, I'm exhausted with playing nice, and I'm getting real tired of looking at it."

Ian stared at her for a long moment. Amazement crossed his face, as if he couldn't believe what she'd just said to him. Pressing his lips together, he looked like he was holding something back as well.

"Go on. You can say it. Get whatever it is out into the open. Ashton doesn't give a flying fuck what you say out here."

A mother—child grasped tightly in her hand, also laden with groceries—shoved past them with a glare at her. The child, on the other hand, nope, she definitely didn't care.

"Go on," Avril encouraged.

Lips curling back, sharp canines protruding forward, Ian laughed.

The unnatural sound caused Avril to tilt back on her heels.

Ian lifted his hands to his chest, as if it might cause him physical pain to continue on, but he did for a long minute.

"You just—not even a stick. My God." He cringed. "You want me to be nice to you."

Avril still stood in slight astonishment. "Or at least pretend to like me. No one will believe I'm your willing date if you can't even look at me. Stars, they'll think you have me chained in your basement—which, I mean, if you're into that."

Ian shook his head as the final chuckles were released from somewhere deep in his stomach. He coughed once to clear his throat, blinking to right himself again to his uncompromising self, less flexible than most city-funded statues. His shoulders remained loose as he stood, once more no longer held back by any shadows.

His sharp chin turned back over his shoulder before he met Avril's eyes again. His own, the color of steel, seemed to melt around the edges. "You want me to pretend to like you."

"It would certainly be a suggestion."

"Do you do that often? Pretend to like people?"

What an odd question.

Avril lifted a shoulder in contemplation. "If it suits me."

"Much like if it suits you to stop being yourself for a while? Cover an accent. Put on a mask for the day."

"Sounds like playing dress-up."

"Isn't it to you right now?" Ian asked, his voice more sincere than harsh.

"No," Avril said immediately, letting her answer rush out between them. "And if it were, my mask would fit like a glove."

"Come along then, my rose."

"Rose," Avril repeated the soft, delicate calling card of a name.

"Well, as we went over, I can't trust you."

"Perhaps the first smart thing you've said tonight," Avril conceded.

"How am I even supposed to think Avril is your real name?" Ian asked as they walked back toward where they'd left minutes ago.

The cold had begun to settle into Avril's bones like icicles. A tingle shot through her toes with each step.

"I follow the rules and won't magically find out if you lie about your entire self, but if you want me to play nice, well…"

"Pet names?" Avril wrinkled her nose.

"One of my rules."

"Does it go both ways?"

"Absolutely not." Ian looked repulsed by the thought.

"Yet now, you're suddenly much more on board with this arrangement of ours? I didn't expect cheery names to seal the deal of tying us together for the next month."

"Which I still don't understand, but you forget."

"What, that you have all the rules?" That, she remembered quite clearly.

"Roses have thorns."

Avril paused as they made their way back to the bar.

"My, my." Avril licked her lips as she looked him up and down. "Aren't we the poet?"

Ian stepped aside. He extended an arm to let her traverse the steps downward in front of him.

"And in case you forgot, you are still on a probationary period."

CHAPTER EIGHT

*A*vril shoved a glass into Ian's hands while he eyed the walls, covered in road signs and chipped paint so you could see the wallpaper underneath.

She clinked her own drink against his and tilted it back.

The strong burn of bottom-shelf alcohol slid all the way down into her chest. From there, it spread into the rest of her body.

Breath exhaled through pursed lips.

"I still don't think this can be considered a party."

"I never said it could be," Avril said. "If you wanted beer on the floor, you should have said so. I thought you were more sophisticated."

"So, you brought me to a dive bar."

"A more sophisticated dive bar." She hadn't been to Sean's in ages. The signs were the same. The mirror behind the bar, reflecting a minimal bottle collection, was still growing a speckling of what could only be described, but never convicted by the board of health, as mildew.

She was overdressed, but no one but the owner knew her. He shifted a free first round to her before yelling at a customer for rushing them in an accent she knew well.

All good things.

She tapped Ian's hazy glass. He was still scowling at the well-worn single booths, where customers chugged their pints and had to raise their voices above the noise of the competitive dartboard players.

Near the back, another group gathered around the green-lined pool table. The starter broke the set with a crack.

Ian considered the drink in his hand, as if just realizing it was there. "What's this?"

"Drink up."

When she turned back to the bar, her glass had been refilled, and she took it down fast and straight with him. He didn't flinch.

The alcohol stung the crack in the center of Avril's lip, hidden in matte color. It didn't matter. Whiskey set a small fire in her throat and over her taste buds in a sort of concerto. Tiny embers flared into the memories of her first sip off a man's lips, who'd tasted like fresh oak bourbon.

A couple extracted themselves from their seats at the bar, and Avril quickly climbed onto the vacated stool. Before she could motion for another round, Sean murmured something to the bartender before disappearing to the back. Two more drinks, these on the rocks, replaced the last.

Ian sat beside her. "Do you come here often?"

"Is that a pickup line? I thought I was your beautiful, blooming thorn of a rose a few minutes ago."

His jaw clenched. A slight flush from the whiskey heated below his ears. "You know what I mean."

"I used to. Once in a while. Moons ago."

She'd found the place with Jack on St. Patrick's Day. She still remembered standing on the other side of the bar with her boobs popping out of a *Kiss Me, I'm Irish* shirt cut above her navel.

Ian raised an eyebrow.

"It isn't one of my main haunts."

"So, no one will recognize you."

He was catching on.

Avril took a sip of her refreshed drink with a wince this time before glancing back at Ian. His thumb mindlessly rubbed over the inside of his pinkie finger. One of the shadows twisted there, a timid vine.

He paused, noticing Avril's fixed stare. Clearing his throat, he took a small swallow of his drink. There was a slight cringe this time.

"Not a fan of whiskey?"

"Have never been much of a drinker," Ian said. He looked down at the dark-brown liquor. His thumb slid back across his palm.

"The ring."

His gaze shifted toward her from the corner of his eye. "What about it?"

"Whose was it? It's fine if you don't want to tell me. Just figured since I'd found it—"

"It was my mother's."

For some reason, the possibility had never occurred to Avril before. His mother's. "You just carry it around with you?"

"Most of the time," Ian admitted. "I used to wear it right here on my finger, but after a while, it didn't fit anymore. I didn't want to risk cutting it off."

Avril imagined gold where the shadow indented skin.

"She passed away almost sixteen years ago."

Studying him, Avril tilted her head to the side. "I have something like that. Kind of anyway."

Ian said nothing. Avril couldn't even tell if he was listening anymore.

"My mother, she died when I was young. But she had these beautiful pins—antique brooches really. They were filled with twisted metal and gemstones. So, when she wasn't there anymore to yell at me not to touch, I took them." Avril glanced down to her legs. When she was onstage, she almost always wore one, if not all four of her mother's brooches at once, stuck through her garter belt. "I used to wear them all the time."

When she lifted her gaze again, imagining the jewels catching the Rosin stage lights, Ian stared at her. His eyes had softened at some point.

For a moment, Avril held her breath, as if he could see right through her.

"How long ago did she die?"

"I was nine."

Avril blinked away the memory of it all. She didn't like to think of it when she could or else it would stick in her mind for days. Her mother screaming at her in the bathroom, tears running down her face as her body seemed to melt onto the avocado-green tiles.

"I'm sorry for your loss."

She shook her head. "Don't be."

Ian nodded after a moment, as if knowing not to push. "The property I'm fixing up, like I told you, it's actually a house. I only found out about it recently, but it turns out, I've been a home-owner for quite some time since my mom left it to me."

"Sixteen years, and you just found out?"

"My father isn't the most giving of important information."

Mr. Marcus Whitlock, investment banker of Ashton. It hadn't taken as long for Avril to find information on him, compared to his son. Whitlock was practically an industry filled with interns and cold, hard cash.

When Avril remembered the fact, it was hard for her not to narrow her eyes at Ian, wondering where the resemblance was. The connection at all really. The only family photo found online was over a decade old, including Mr. Marcus Whitlock, his other son of the same name, and Mr. Whitlock's wife, who looked like she had somewhere much more interesting to be. They were all pressed and posed, unsmiling at the photographer.

There was likely a good reason Ian wanted out of that house, this place.

"At least I'm glad I didn't screw up you and your not-girl-friend's proposal." Avril stuck her hand in the bowl of mini pretzels across from them. They were nearly tasteless and made her teeth ache, but she bit down on another anyway. "I know I said we didn't have to speak a word of her. But I feel like I must know if our scheme is going to work properly."

"Is this going to be your excuse for the ever-intrusive question you ask?"

Probably.

"You two were lovers?"

Ian relished the tingling burn this time as his drink passed his lips.

"More than a lover then," Avril concluded.

"We were not lovers."

"Not a label guy?"

His eyes narrowed over the edge of his glass.

"What? I appreciate that," Avril said. "Labels …"

"Complicate."

Avril raised her glass to that. "Cheers."

"Cheers!" two guys a few seats down from them hollered, raising their own glasses.

"See? Even they get it."

Ian shook his head, but there was amusement toying in his expression. Look at that—the man of steel was opening up.

He touched the rim of his tumbler to hers. A satisfying clank sounded.

"I met Cynthia when I studied abroad," Ian began, a husk restraining his voice, tucked in the back of his throat. "I went along with Noah. You've met."

Of course she'd met his quirky coworker. Probably the person he mentioned who had also gotten him the job in Ashton.

"How cute. Where did you go to school?"

"Princeton."

Avril raised her glass once more, impressed.

Ian stopped her before her lips could open and encourage their watching friends. "Don't."

"I'm not. Go on."

"We met in Florence. She studied art, obviously. The three of us became a group. We traveled together and visited museums. Cyn always had something to do. We were never bored. We went to the gardens, cathedrals, the Uffizi—your *Venus* was there," Ian said, remembering their earlier conversation of Titian's master-piece only hours ago. It could've been days.

"I know." Avril balanced on the edge of her seat as she listened, not daring to interrupt him now. "I was there once."

"You were there?" Ian asked.

She tried not to be offended at his disbelief. "Yeah. I flashed her."

Ian's eyes widened. He obviously hadn't expected that response. "You did not."

"It felt appropriate. I also was really hoping I made some security camera man's day."

"My God. Anyway, the things Cynthia could do with a paint-brush—stop smirking. Not like that. Even then, she was talented. She was the first person who got me to admit what I thought maybe I could be in my life."

"A librarian."

"A writer," said Ian.

For some reason, Avril blinked with shock at the admission. When she looked at Ian—when she looked at anyone, she could usually tell who they were or desperately wanted to be in the blink of an eye. With Ian though, in his crisp white suit shirts, she still couldn't get it out of her mind that when he'd first grabbed her with such conviction in that archives closet that she believed him more of a stuffy physics professor than a writer.

Even without the tie that loosely hung around his throat, like it did now.

"I didn't know that it was what I wanted until I said it that night to Cyn. And when I said it, she looked at me differently, like I was worth something. I wasn't all an Ivy League brooder—whatever she'd meant by that."

Avril held back a smirk behind her glass. Oh, she had an idea.

His eyebrows scrunched at her similarly drained glass when he went for another sip. "I was going to write articles, short stories, or even a novel. I went on and on to her like I knew what I was talking about."

"Like a dream."

His eyes lifted to meet Avril again, pulled out of exactly that. A dream.

Avril always had an appreciation for them. Even when they stopped.

"Exactly. She kissed me at the airport before we got on separate flights, as if nothing had really happened and it was over," said Ian.

"So, why didn't you?"

"Why didn't I what?"

"Become a writer."

"You can't just become a writer."

"Why not?"

"Why not?" Ian asked right back. "I needed a job. I was an English major who realized that no matter how many half-assed articles or short stories I was sending out, basically copies of the ones I'd read, I wasn't getting published, certainly not in *The New Yorker*. I needed a job or a place to hide out."

"So, you tagged along with Noah."

Ian nodded. "I figured, why not?"

"Never pegged you as a bottom."

His eyes narrowed with surprise; a distasteful, deep look appeared to prove her wrong. A shiver traveled up her spine, but she began to shrug out of her trench anyway. She let the arms hang over the back of the stool.

"He always talked about becoming a librarian. He wanted the small town. *Two-point-five kids* deal. I figured, why not hide out in school for a little while longer? Then, after that, I decided to stay again and get my doctoral in literature. I was certainly good enough at it."

"So humble."

"Noah and I met up with Cynthia over the years. Whenever she had a new show, we'd try to see it. For years, this went on, and we played around one another, Cyn and I. We would have a … flirtation."

"More than that, obviously."

"I don't know," Ian said. "I was thoughtless. She wanted to run back off to Europe once, and I wanted to. I did. When I was around Cynthia, I felt like that guy on the rooftops of Florence, who had declared he wanted to be a writer even though he hadn't managed to write more than a few pages. Yet I turned her down. There was just something about her, the way she carried herself."

"I think it's called confidence," Avril supplied. "Something I am sure you have plenty of somewhere in there."

"You think you know me?"

"I know I do," Avril said before she could stop herself. She sighed. "At least, more than you'd probably like."

"This have to do with your secret past?"

"No. But it's either confidence or arrogance, whether or not you have the fucking courage when it comes down to telling a girl you think you maybe, possibly love her."

Ian cringed at the easiness of Avril's speech. The word.

Not so much love then.

Ian managed to surprise her.

"Ian, Ian, Ian."

"Don't say my name like that."

"Like what?"

"Like you're cursing me."

Avril chuckled. She had curses covered for the both of them.

"What are you thinking?"

"You didn't love her."

Ian flinched as if she'd hit him. He'd all but admitted it a second ago. "How do you know?"

"First of all, it took you some time to realize that I wasn't her in the gallery closet," Avril offered.

Sighing, he turned his head back away from her, but a hand shot out for her to continue.

"You liked who she was. You liked what she did for you. You might say that I have a mask sitting in front of you, darling. But you'd be lying if you said you didn't have one or two of your own, pretending to be someone you have no right being."

He blinked.

Avril shook her head. "You didn't like her. You just wanted her."

Not saying anything at all, at least he was smart enough to know the difference.

"Now that we've gotten that sorted, come on." Hopping down from the stool, she left her coat to hang across it.

"What are we doing?"

Avril extended her hand to the heavy beat that vibrated through the crowded space. "Enough drab, sorrowful life talk. Dance with me, Ian."

CHAPTER NINE

*T*he night moved around her. She could smile and laugh without a care, and in front of her, much to her disbelief, the stubborn librarian slowly pulled himself off his seat to stand. He followed her toward the small space in the floor before the dartboard and pool table, where couples leaned into each other to the beat of whatever pounded through the speakers.

"You said you wanted to have a night on the town—or whatever it is you old people say."

Avril lifted her hands up to shake and twist on her toes. It had been so long since she'd felt free. Even this little bit.

Her one hand caught Ian.

He only looked at her with raised eyebrows. Amusement covered anything they'd spoken of moments ago, and he only watched her.

"It only encourages me," she warned him.

"I had a feeling."

"You're still thinking. Too much. Clear your head." Avril demonstrated, swirling her own hands around her ears. Tiny puffs of hair curled with unmanageable frizz, but she didn't care.

She was dancing.

The movements were easy and didn't hold any pressure. It had been so long since she'd last danced, last wanted to. She closed her eyes when the beat fell and let her hips sway. She laughed at Ian's blatant awkwardness, keeping closer to her as the song turned into the next and into the next.

She missed dancing so much. It was just like how she missed bars and good lingerie and her mother's pins that had winked at her each night she put them on. She didn't understand for the slightest second why she would stop until the twinge yanked in her spine, right between her hips.

She slowed, swallowing, as if saliva could coat the pain.

A strident beat changed to a slow melody.

Maybe it was the liquor and how she hadn't eaten for most of the day, but Avril's breath caught when Ian's hands grasped hers, them both moving, dancing.

Relax. She needed to remind herself.

Relax. Her hands softened, focusing on the soft calluses below Ian's fingers.

Carefully, Ian pulled her a step closer to him, both of them still dancing in their own way, only he led her this time without a question. Her leg brushed against his, but he must've not noticed, moving as his face softened out of ease or concentration—Avril couldn't tell.

"This is a bit better," Ian murmured.

She danced slowly without having to think what to do next. Her mind emptied, and she felt only the steady pulse of air still between them.

She'd only ever been able to dance with this sort of ease with Jack before. Even Reed got a little stiff, thinking too much, questioning which foot after already completing the task just fine. It was as if he couldn't help himself, face screwed in frustrated focus by the second half of the song.

Ian, however, he knew exactly what to do.

"What?" He noticed her stare.

"You learn how to dance at a debutante ball?" she teased.

He opened his mouth, as if he couldn't stop himself, and he let loose a single laugh. "Something like that."

Avril smiled as well, eyes wide at her own deductive skills. "Why am I not surprised? What comes next? Prep school? Private tutors?"

"Have to leave something to keep you amused."

Raising his dark brows at her pleased expression, he lifted her arm and gave her a twirl. As she twisted all the way around on her toes with simple grace and elegance, Avril paused at the sharp pain again when she came to face him. It felt like someone might as well have stabbed her. She recoiled aloud, stumbling over her one foot.

Anger bubbled where there had only been mystic easiness seconds ago.

She had been fine. Fine for all of those seconds.

She tried to go back to them, ignoring the pain when she looked at Ian. He slowed his movements with her already.

"Tell me," Avril insisted.

Intrigue coated something else that Avril noticed often in men's eyes.

"Would you like me to beg?" Avril tried to piece herself as well as the conversation back together. She still held on to one of his hands. The other dropped down at her side in the music that seemed too loud once again.

She lifted her voice. "I don't do it often, but all of a sudden, I'm in a rather good mood."

"Is that right?"

Her eyes trailed back down his body, as if that was what she'd stumbled at. It certainly wasn't a body of a god, but ... the movement of her own making sent a short wave of heat into her stomach. Or maybe it was still the whiskey, not yet danced away.

A sharp grin, which had only been a smirk moments ago, grew. "No."

"I didn't say a thing."

He looked down at their locked hands. "Of course not. You say far too much with your face. No one has said that to you before, have they?"

She knew exactly what he saw there. "Am I supposed to deny the fact that I find you attractive, Ian?"

She could see the gears turning in his head.

"Because, right now, Ian, I do. Blame it on your dancing skills."

He gave her another twirl.

This time, Avril couldn't ignore the strike of pain. The sensation grew and burned and struck, as if the shadows were using her spine as a ladder, trying to get to the top, where only they could addle her mind. Already, they were back, turning, swirling.

Bitterness coated her tongue as she yanked her hand away from Ian.

When she took a step back, she almost collided into another group. Ian's hand caught her elbow, yanking her away from the guy before he could put his arm around her to steady her feet. Quickly, she righted herself.

"Are you all right?" Ian asked, concern wedging into his words.

Avril nodded. Blinking. She had been a little blurry there for a second. But the noises, the people, the shadows—they had all pressed in on her until her bones ached.

She was moving before she realized where she was going. Ian followed after her until they got to the glass front door. Panes were hazed from the change of temperature outside clinging to get in.

The air was just as frosted when she stepped out onto the somewhat-empty sidewalk. People still walked along, running up the sidewalks on the other side of the street in some sort of game Avril believed she had played in this city before.

Come and catch me.

"Just some air."

"Are you sure you're all right?" Ian came up behind her, laying her coat over her shoulders.

She'd forgotten about it inside.

Avril shuddered as she stepped out of reach this time, still feeling the warmth of his fingertips on her skin, which was now covered with thick cotton. She could keep herself standing just fine.

She was, "Fine."

His hand dropped through the thick air.

Her own turned to brace herself for a second while she still stood, unwilling to lower herself into a crouch, even for a second, while her back pulsed, tensed, and loosened. It was still deciding whether or not it wanted to cramp.

She shook her head as Ian watched her closely, sighing in frustration.

He wouldn't stop looking at her.

"It's not you," Avril professed. She needed to say something before his face turned any flatter and more dour. She had seen that smile of his, that glimpse of teeth. She didn't want it to disappear. "It's my back."

Opening her eyes now, she only expected to see the expression she might've hated more than someone forcing themselves to be a wet blanket. Concern mixed with all the other deplorable stares.

But Ian only looked at her hand, bracing her lower back with interest. "Does it hurt you often?"

"It happens sometimes. It's fine," Avril tried to explain. Her head was already becoming clearer in the cold again. Her back fizzled to only a slight ache.

"An injury."

Sucking in a breath, Avril shook her head. Yes, an injury, reminding her exactly where she stood.

Clearing her throat, she nodded. "Let's forget that happened. Okay?"

Ian looked confused, conflicted, but after a moment, he nodded with her. "All right."

"There is still one thing I want to show you." Even though it wasn't the most opportune time, they weren't far away from where she was taking Ian next. The image flashed into her mind just as swiftly as any discomfort.

"Where are we going?"

"Now, where would the fun be in telling you?" There wouldn't be any, surely. "It's not far. Promise. Don't you trust me?"

A deep rumble of laughter sounded behind her. Ian's two steps caught back up with her half dozen.

"Not in the slightest."

"Wow," Ian breathed.

Avril agreed as she stared. The light shone just enough for them to see the tiny waves as they crested, like at a beach. They beat down the ground a few feet in front of them.

They passed the metro, where the last train of the night rolled beneath them in a tunnel of saturated graffiti. They also passed the alleyway, where she'd once found a roller rink in the basement. Seventies music played until at least three a.m. before switching to the eighties to encourage the techno-averse to get out.

She could hear the disco through street grates.

They continued to walk down the block and down the small hill of a gated cemetery, where she'd once hooked up with a guy in bell-bottoms she'd met at that roller rink. She wondered if after three years, the man they'd lain on top of had forgiven them for christening his resting spot.

Avril only stopped them when there was no more sidewalk to walk on, a few blocks down from Sean's Pub. She heard where they were before they were close enough to see, but it led her all the same in companionable silence.

You hadn't been to Ashton until you appreciated it at night. You needed to stand on the edge of the river that washed up with abandon toward its city. The Ash River, after all, was a deep, solid black, no matter the time of day. Like the most beautiful of smoke-filled powder, constantly trying to be washed away.

Like shadows finding their resting place, they never wanted to go easily to.

Side by side, they breathed in the tang of air.

"This is your ideal night out on the town? Drinking, dancing, a midnight view of the river?"

"Honestly?"

Ian shrugged a single shoulder. "Why not?"

"If I were taking you out ... this isn't my home I showed you. It's the city though. A start." She imagined how else this night could have gone, especially now that she stood right there in front of the river that people floated down on particularly sunny days to see the entire city in a short amount of time.

If this were her city still, tonight, she would have taken Ian to the bar she loved and often had late drinks after a show with the girls. Or she would have taken him straight to DuCain, the local BDSM club she'd once basically lived at, just to see the look on his face. Maybe she would have even let Jack, if he were there, still dolled up in his dark eyeliner and gear, help her horrify him a little more.

If she were still able to talk to him.

She'd see if Ian was the kind of person she was beginning to think he was. All hard exterior with something she recognized deep inside.

The cold, hollow feeling of shadows was called at the thoughts.

Tonight, though, Avril was as much an outsider as Ian was.

The last time she had been at the river, the water had roared beneath her. Now, there was only a small hum. The last time, she'd stood on the bridge. She wasn't coming home from work that evening. Instead, she clutched her waist as she looked out over the edge. Her eyes had burned from the cold spring air.

"What are you doing?"

Avril reached down, using Ian's arm for support as she pried her heels off her feet. The edges stuck to her slightly swollen skin from dancing on them so long. She let them drop on the ground next to her, not bothering to roll up her tight pants.

She closed her eyes as she stepped into the dark water.

"That water has to be freezing."

It was the same thought that had run through Avril's head the days before her birthday when she stood up on that bridge, wondering how it would feel if she tripped on pointed toes.

Not yet, the water had seemed to reach up to say to her though.

Not yet. The fire in her soul ached for her to hear it among the loud shadows twisting up her legs and banisters.

Avril had dropped that day to her heels. She'd looked up when she couldn't look down.

And those damn stars.

Not yet, they gloated until she could feel them on her skin.

Somehow, she'd managed to lower herself back down to the pavement. But she didn't want to go home back then, not yet. So, she hadn't.

Now, she was back.

Here I am, she offered herself up.

The only sound that replied was the sound of her own hum that matched the water. Turning around, Ian watched her.

He'd picked up her shoes, and he held them carefully in his

hands. She glanced between them and his face. The water was freezing, and so was the previous glacial appearance of Ian's disposition, now sturdy, unmovable.

Avril blinked and felt a cold track run down her face. She reached up, playing it off as just a splash that had gotten her.

Ian said nothing as she dragged her feet from the river, pleasantly numb against the sharp rocks. Without question, she looked up at his face as she brought her hands to where her heels were positioned in front of his shirt.

She placed her hands over his.

He didn't move an inch. "What are you doing?"

Bewitching you, she used to tease men who asked her such ridiculously beautiful questions.

Those were men who hadn't been marred by shadows. When her hands touched Ian, the shadows only spread like a smear of charcoal crayon rolling away from Avril.

The space between the two of them was a lot shorter, she thought, when he met her halfway and his mouth pressed hard against hers.

They were back in the closet at the gallery. They were standing in the cold right now, and neither of them moved for more as they gripped on to hands and lips, trying to find purchase.

Ian was kissing her like she had never been kissed before in her life.

Avril let out a soft breath before coming back for more. Shadows turned soft as they lifted up the side of his throat, and she couldn't help herself but trace them with her gaze. But that wasn't what she was focused on.

Instead, she pressed herself farther into his body, slanting her lips over his. It was as if they were just talking, breathing, aching for something neither could describe to one another. Only they wanted and burned until they turned to ash and soot, and Avril could barely breathe. More and more. More.

Maybe this was how she would die in the shadows, just like her mother.

Maybe it wouldn't be such an awful way to go.

Ian broke away, breath harsh and eyes wild. He slipped his hands out from under hers, leaving her with only her heels. "I apologize."

"Don't." She felt the comfortable weight and underside of the stiletto against her hand's lifeline.

"Can I see it?"

"See what?" Ian looked around, as if something tangible were there.

"Your house. The one your mother left to you when she died and you're fixing up so you never have to come to the city again."

"Why do you want to see that?"

"Can't I have an interest in architecture?"

"Why do I have a feeling this deal is more than you're letting on?"

Because they were both lonely, standing there on the edge of darkness—the edge of Ashton—and they were terrible at making it less obvious.

"Can I see it?" Avril repeated the question.

He nodded before he seemed to make up his mind. "Tomorrow. You can see the place then if you want."

Tomorrow.

"You passed." His eyes swirled in the darkness as he took a step back and turned around. He shoved a shaky hand through his flop of hair on the top of his head, all the way to his neck. "It's a deal. We should get back."

Yeah, maybe they should.

The breeze swept under her hair and against the back of her own neck, warm as Ian's hand was against her skin.

Her heart hammered in her chest as she looked back and forth for the cause in the swath of darkness where she was no longer able to see any shadows. Not of his. Not of hers.

None.

"It's a deal?"

"One word, one problem, and you're gone."

It usually didn't take much more than that.

"I have enough issues in this city as it is."

And she was going to be another, he was sure.

Ian bowed his head. "It's a deal."

CHAPTER TEN

*K*eys was the coziest coffee shop in Ashton. With low lighting and just enough bookshelves that didn't know the meaning of alphabetized, it was also an ideal hiding place when you didn't want to run into a one-night stand from the night before while nursing a hangover with caffeine.

The hot spot had great cappuccinos and open mic nights that somehow never managed to disappoint. Even when slam poetry and folk singing night got their scheduling confused.

"Thanks, Marley."

"You just make sure to come in here more often, all right? If I don't see a regular face, after a while, I start to worry. Don't I, Kit?" The gruff café owner tilted his head up toward Avril's friend behind her.

Kit gathered her wide mug in two hands. She nodded over her steeping tea.

Avril only played, leaning over the counter. "Did you really miss my wonderful presence that much?"

"You want me to say no?" Marley asked, but a smile quickly broke through. "You all always bring some much-needed color to this place."

"And make your life so much more interesting?"

With a grunt, that was a yes.

Lifting her giant hand-spun mug—one of the dozens that lined the walls of Keys and you could pick one to be yours from the moment you walked in to the morning, afternoon, or even all day—Avril stuffed a few dollar bills into the tip jar. She winked at the employee cleaning off the espresso nozzle behind the counter.

Marley laughed and waved her off.

"You seem to be in a good mood," said Kit.

She sat in their usual space. The cushy love seat had seen more stains over the years but never stopped being the perfect place for Avril to throw her feet up on the coffee table, covered with textbooks. She collected the glares of students being interrupted in their studies.

Avril only raised her eyebrows to each. *Say something*, she dared them.

But they never did.

She rolled her eyes and turned back to Kit, who was still watching her.

"Was that a question?" Avril asked.

"Sort of," Kit clarified. Her chin tilted downward toward Avril's pants. "And what are you wearing, or do I not want to be an accessory to whatever you plan on doing today?"

She didn't think they were so bad. She wasn't someone who wore ripped jeans, but this seemed like the day. Avril had still also yet to open the good side of her closet. She'd thought about it, reaching for her other heels and sheer blouses that hopefully still fit, but just couldn't.

After she had gotten home last night, she'd watched the clock tick by until she finally walked next door, climbing into Reed's bed. He didn't say anything to her. He barely opened his eyes before letting Avril up on him like a cat.

When she'd woken up, Reed had already left.

Kit barely shook her head. "Seriously, what are you doing today. Manual labor?"

"Maybe."

She raised an eyebrow.

"I'm headed uptown and to the right. I think I might become an interior decorator."

"Who's the client?"

"Ian Whitlock."

Kit paused, leaning back to the table beside her. She set down her mug with a light cling against the glass. "Avril."

"Don't *Avril*. At least wait until I am dead to use my name as a swear word." Gods, she sounded like Ian. "Or don't. I kind of like it."

"Avril."

"There you go again. Did you miss me that much too? Should you and Marley start a support group?"

"What are you doing? I know I told you who your mystery man was, but Ian … he's not exactly—I don't know if you've realized this, but Ian Whitlock is not rebound material."

Rebound?

"If that is what you are looking for."

"Kit," Avril cut in. "If I am looking for a rebound, it has come, gone, and I think, by now, come a few more times by the amount of people I have rebounded right on and off of since last year. Very happy customers, coming and going."

A boy across the table glanced back up from his books.

"Would you like to be a part of this conversation?"

His head turned back down.

Kit pressed her lips together, not to laugh, but her eyes still held that look in them. Since when had Kit suddenly come to the realization that she could judge Avril? Hadn't she just said that she looked happy?

"I'm just seizing an opportunity."

"What does Reed think about it?"

Avril reached for her drink and swallowed a large gulp. She let the milky caffeine settle into her nervous system. "He's on protest currently."

"Protest?"

"From speaking to me."

"I see," Kit said. "Wow."

She and Avril both. Reed and Avril had had their fights before, but not the kind that Reed didn't talk to her after a twenty-four-hour period.

"It doesn't matter. He's likely going to go off on another research trip or something anyway by the end of the week." Avril waved her off. "Also, if you think just because Reed isn't talking to me that he isn't already up in my business and knows exactly what I have been doing and whom with in the past few months, you're the crazy one."

Kit's face blanched. "I didn't say anything about you being crazy."

Avril only let her eyebrows flare. "You don't need to worry about me. No one needs to worry about me, all right? I thought we were past this. You and me."

"I'm not worrying. Or I am, but you know that's all I do. I worry. I stress. It's what is basically holding my life together at this point. If Jack wasn't the one who wanted to plan the wedding, I'm sure I would be in front of you in a heap of mess right now. But, Avril, I love you."

The words yanked something inside of Avril. Still, she looked away from Kit.

"Psh."

"Psh." Kit made the noise right back. "So, tell me more."

"More about what? My fabulous life?"

Avril motioned her to pick up her tea again while she stared at her. Kit held the cup in her hands as she fixed the crinoline under her skirt to sit flat.

"He doesn't know who I am."

Kit squinted. "What do you mean?"

"He doesn't know who I am," Avril replied curtly. "To him, I am just some random woman he mistook for another chick he wanted to confess his love to in a closet."

"Wait, what?"

Avril waved that off. "Beside the point."

"Is it?"

"Completely. I showed up at the library—"

"You ambushed the man?"

"Do you want to hear this story, darling, or not?" Avril asked.

Kit said nothing.

"Lovely. So, I went to the library to see if your information was correct. It was. Of course, he wasn't all that pleased to see me. It turns out though that he needed a date or something to an office party, and, well, I was there, so I went with him. A sort of *sorry the artist of the exhibition thought we were fucking when you planned to express your unrequited love.*"

Kit's eyes stared wide. "And?"

"And he took me up on the offer, sort of. It only dawned on me that Ian, however smart you might peg him, isn't less smart than most girls. When I showed up, he still had no clue who I was. I was surprised his little library friend hadn't let him in on it. He totally knew who I was, and it was easy to see why after I met his periwinkle-haired girlfriend. Anyway, Ian and I made a deal."

"A deal."

"He doesn't know who I am. I will be his replacement for the holidays. He is also helping fix up his mom's old house or something like that." Avril was still fuzzy on the whole family-dynamic issue, but still, she itched to see Ian's house for some reason. To see him.

She looked down at her hands, as if one of his shadows had tangled around her last night, but nothing.

Kit cleared her throat, obviously waiting for something more.

"So, I plan to seduce him, and both of us will have a very happy holiday."

"You have too many stories that end up like this."

"It is all on my terms. I call the shots, and he'll never know. Probably the safest business deal I have ever been in." Avril took another sip of her drink, finally cool enough for her to gulp half of it down in one go. She was going to be late at the rate of all this sisterly bickering.

"I don't know, Avril."

"Well, that's good. Because I do. How about you? How is your life going?"

"It's busy. I have a few packages to deliver and alter at Rosin today, if you want to tag along." At Avril's expression, Kit didn't try to convince her. "Seriously, it doesn't seem like something Ian would do, jumping into whatever this is blindly."

Avril didn't add in their extra time about the town last night. "You know him that well?"

"No. I just … from what I heard, he isn't someone who takes things lightly. I couldn't imagine that he would take you lying as something casual."

"I don't think it's lying. He knows I am lying, and it isn't like I am lying, *lying.*"

Kit only stared at her again, holding back whatever she wanted to say.

She was glad her friend was beginning to understand. "It's omission. Lawful, understood omission."

Even if he didn't believe Avril was really her name. She never realized; it did sort of have that showgirl vibe about it.

"Just be careful," Kit said. "He's not like us."

"What's that supposed to mean?"

"It means, Jack told me that you've always had a tendency to adopt people."

"So?" She really didn't want to think about Jack right now.

"Ian is not one of those people, Avril. He isn't a lost thing for you to collect. He has an intimidating reputation for a reason."

Avril paused as she considered this. She was right, after all. Avril had called Ian out on his cruel disposition the moment Noah leaned in the office door. From Ian's sharp, pinpointed eyes to the way he remained quiet and as unmoved as Avril did when they each silently debated on who would break that kind of noise first. Kit knew these kinds of traits, being around Jack, but Avril knew them better.

But Ian, she wasn't so sure he did, and that, to her, made all the difference.

And reputation? "Don't we all?"

CHAPTER ELEVEN

*A*vril leaned against the short library shelves. A few parents noticed her presence before glancing over the children. They were probably wondering if they'd spot a fiery-headed toddler among the mix. Avril, however, was only there to watch Ian as he playfully bared his sharp canines at the bunch as he spoke of the Wild Things.

"He's good with them." Noah appeared next to her. He leaned against the top of the bookshelf, arms crossed, like hers. His hair seemed to stand up in the front by some unforeseen force today. "You wouldn't think it by meeting him, but over the past few months, he's settled in."

"He's great with them," Avril commented. "I would've pegged you for the tiny-tot storyteller."

"Had an appointment. I got out early enough to catch this, though," Noah said. "And for your information, I'm usually first on call when it comes to sensory play day in the back room, not story time. I get nervous in front of crowds."

They watched as the one child on the left of Ian attempted to blow his arm like an elephant.

Avril turned back to Noah. "Terrifying."

"I prefer the pumpkin spice Play-Doh."

"Who knew you sort of library men were such balls of fluff? I expected spectacles and increasingly angry stares about the art students who use the back corner to make out between Shakespeare and Cyrano."

"I leave that part to Ian."

"Probably for the best."

"You know, the other day, when you were in here, in his office."

Now, Avril had her own pointed stare to give.

"My lips are sealed, Queen."

She was about to open her mouth and tell him just where he could shove his title. Before she could, Avril felt a tall and looming presence overhead.

"What was that?" Ian asked.

Noah's beaming smile turned wide as he looked up.

If Avril could have taken him back to DuCain and dragged him down to the dungeons right now, she would've. The thought stirred excitement in the pit of her stomach as she remembered the last time she had been in DuCain, Jack at her side.

Noah would probably like that too much.

She turned on her heel to face Ian with a similarly goading grin. "We were just talking about how in your element you appeared with the Wild Things."

"Well, as we all know, I'm very … wild," Ian said flatly.

"First word that comes to mind exactly."

Noah remained silent, but Avril noticed he was struggling.

"Weren't you going to get some of that fancy homemade Play-Doh you were talking about, Noah?" she asked.

"Right." He shook his head and made his way in the opposite direction. "Gotta go before we have a revolt. See ya on Monday, Ian."

"What was that?"

"What?"

"What did you do to Noah?"

"Have you not noticed I am very intimidating and inappropriate? My presence must've been too much for the kid."

"Noah is thirty-one years old."

"Age means nothing to me." As if to prove it, she glanced at him up and down.

His interest plummeted. "Let's go."

"Wild? More like increasingly bossy. Don't be upset, Dr. Ian. I have lots of older man friends. I even shipped one of them off to marry one of my favorite eligible, kinky, young friends recently."

"Your only one?"

Awe. He was trying to make a joke.

"It took them a while, but I have a feeling they were meant to be. You should keep in my good graces."

"I'm thirty-one."

"I'm twenty-four. On death's door."

He huffed as she trailed him across the library, away from any impressionable individuals. "I'm surprised to see you up and moving so early."

"I can handle myself." And her liquor. Avril now only had to keep up with his ginormous legs. "You were good with the kids."

"They're more well behaved than others I know."

"You are starting to think you know me already," Avril said. "You are starting to like me."

"I don't go back on my promises."

Good to know.

"I need to pick up a few things from my office."

A few tables sat outside of his office. Students sprawled out with books spread open and headphones in. Another was an older gentleman with a magazine in front of him that he didn't look to be reading. His feet were propped up on the seat beside him, eyes closed.

Avril leaned in the doorway of the office, taking in the space once more. For some reason, it still didn't quite scream Ian to her. Whatever that meant.

He itched his neck, opening drawers before closing them again, not grabbing anything out of them.

"You read all those?"

He glanced at Avril before up at the floating shelves. "Some of them. Most were left by whoever else had this office before me."

"Can't be very good then, huh?"

Ian didn't answer that. He shoved more things, however random to Avril, into his very businesslike briefcase.

After seeing Ian with the kids and Noah, however, her perception of librarians needed an update. Business on the outside, the shirt Ian wore still looked oddly similar to the one he'd had on last night. Creases bent around his elbows from where he'd rolled up his sleeves.

"What about you? Should I be asking if I should be impressed by your morning punctuality?"

On his way back to the door, Ian stood, unmoving, in front of her. Avril comprehended once more how small she was in comparison to the tree of a man. Instead of moving out of the way, however, as was likely his intent, Avril made herself more at home, settling there.

She smirked at the spaces between his shirt buttons.

With a wave of his hand, he shooed her out the door. He hit the lights and twisted the lock as he went.

"What? Early day?" Avril inquired.

Ian cleared his throat as he tapped the laminate table of the sleeping man. He snored sharply before popping upright. "We're closed to nonacademic visitors by three today, so you're aware."

"Ah." The man began to collect himself. "Right."

Avril raised her eyebrow at Ian's now blatant disregard of her. At least he was creative about it. The rest of his route was straightforward, waving to one of the student staff at the front desk, checking books in.

They glanced up and continued their work hastily.

Avril continued to follow him in a similar silence, she realized, until they came up to the curb.

She looked back and forth. "No car?"

"Haven't been in a place long enough to need one."

A taxi stopped, and Ian held the car door open for her.

Tapping her foot as she looked at him again, she ducked inside.

"You should put on your seat belt."

"Concerned for my well-being. I'm touched."

When he reached over her, Avril shrank beneath his frame. Pausing as he yanked on the belt, he stopped halfway, pulling himself away at the involuntary reaction.

Retreating, he offered the stretched polyester. "Well, you are mine for the holidays, right?"

Avril blinked. His.

Right.

"I'd rather you not crush your skull against the partition if we're in an accident."

Avril pursed her lips as she adjusted herself to sit up. She was now properly strapped in for whatever ride she was going on. Kit had warned her about him, yet still, when she looked at him and the sharp contours of his cheekbones, sharp and foreboding, she still couldn't see it. The story behind the man.

Not like hers. She could see it just as well as most of the taxi drivers through the rearview mirror. Her makeup was smudged from what she hadn't managed to get off last night.

"Glad we are still on the same page."

Ian said nothing else as he looked forward. His Adam's apple bobbed when he swallowed.

All so serious again. Where was that wild thing?

Wanting to tease, Avril held back and merely snorted.

The city was busy in the early afternoons of the weekend. Tourists came in to visit and see the holiday decor strewn about in haphazard formations across park benches and solitary Christmas trees left to rot on street corners. They bought tickets to see the latest off-Broadway musicals in Midtown that always seemed a little tone-deaf.

In opposition, the financial sector lost life, trying to escape out of the city by bus, train, or rideshare. Whichever would get them home the fastest after telling their significant others that they'd had a late dinner meeting the night before. Double points if the method of transportation to the suburbs had a mirror. That way, they could see themselves from the back seat. Their reflection was optimal for scraping the lipstick from their stubbled jawlines and the scent of floral delights off crisp cotton.

Avril wasn't sure what she expected as they headed farther from the center of the city. When Ian had said house, she'd thought of her own. A tall brownstone built before it wasn't the status quo to not have the bathroom positioned in the kitchen came to mind. Avril was in love with the idea of those kinds of baths. She admired them whenever she was invited inside an apartment with such a one during a party.

She could hold court from those tubs.

City homes were a different breed of home sweet home. They were sharp edges and cramped when people wanted sunlight and open concept. Only as the cab pulled up to the nearly empty curb, private lots likely nearby for residents, Avril couldn't help but think *home* the moment she laid eyes on the place from the smudged window.

Ian held the cab door open as she stared in awe at the Queen Anne estate.

"What?" Avril gaped. "Was your mother a witch or something?"

Ian's eyebrow crinkled as he walked up the front porch steps of stone that looked shone and newly leveled. "Not that I'm aware. Though she did have a proclivity for fortune-telling."

Even the lights framing the front door looked new and fresh. A lantern hung on either side.

"She used to have some kind of fancy cards with her."

"Tarot cards," Avril mused to herself. She turned around as she took in the view, tall trees and space all around the courtly park. She could walk straight into the city from here with enough time and decent weather. "She had taste."

He waited for her to pass him before shutting the door behind the two of them, leaving them in the empty square entry. "Yeah, my mom and I didn't live here for very long. A lot has already been done recently to get it back up to how it should've been updated."

Stained glass ran from the bump out upward, like she was in the narthex of a church. Faded greens and warm roses reflected across the deep hardwood flooring. Many of the more auspicious Ashton residences, including her own, boasted original vertical planks in various finishes.

The kitchen had to have been gutted, leaving clean cabinets missing their tops. White walls were nearly in every room—a base layer of paint likely covering left-behind glue from peeled wallpaper.

Ian was living in what was basically a historic home show model, updated from the early 1900s. At least.

"On the right is the kitchen. Across the wide opening, here is the living space that leads into a study or office, the realtor told me. All the bookcases in there were emptied by the time I came in. All that was left when I arrived were random pieces of furniture and trash lying around. It's coming along," Ian explained.

He dropped his coat on one of the pegs beside the front door. He extended a hand to take hers as she dumbly looked up toward the smoothed ceiling.

"I had a friend helping me work on the place, but after demolition, he had some other things to attend to, so it has just been me and the crew I've hired to get in the granite, electrical. Things he couldn't explain to me how to do before he headed out."

"A bit of a money pit, huh?" A beautiful, stunning money pit.

Ian's hand shot out as he walked in front of her, making her flinch. It only found its place when he grabbed the roots of his hair.

"Yeah. Guess so," he said lowly.

She put her hands on her hips as she looked around the place with a smirk. She watched the flecks of light catch on dust falling around them.

"Where do we get started?"

"You seriously want to help?"

"What else do I have on my social calendar, except you?" Avril joked, taking a step toward him.

AVRIL HAULED the heavy can of paint closer to her feet. When she tilted it over, the color washed into the tray Ian had set in front of her when he came back downstairs after changing into a similar outfit to her own. His jeans, on the other hand, already had bits of paint on them.

The color was basically as beige as the fresh, dry wall.

"You couldn't have picked a more interesting color?"

"What would you suggest?"

"I don't know." She lifted her gaze from where she squatted down with her tiny paintbrush.

Directly across the room, Ian was already getting to work, covering the wall in a bland tint.

Why hadn't she gotten a roller?

"Something that didn't remind you of your time in a psychiatric ward. Something with actually a little color."

"That is a color," Ian informed her, but he was definitely

smirking already. "There are flecks of blue in it. Apparently, a very popular color."

"According to whom?"

"*Home* magazine."

She really thought for someone who wanted to be a writer, he would have a bit more creativity to his wit.

"The realtor said to stick to neutrals."

"Neutrally boring. Whoever stays in this place long enough is going to stare into the void and have an existential crisis of whether their living room is gray, blue, or beige."

"Whatever gets you painting, Rose."

Avril glared at him.

"I'd rather get at least a section of the room done before the new year."

She hoped he could feel the hole she was burning between his shoulder blades. She kneeled down to stir the pan, lifting the brush he had given her for emphasis. "And what the hell is this?"

Glancing over his shoulder, Ian glanced at the toothpick of a painting utensil. "I believe it is called a paintbrush."

"It's a baby paintbrush. This thing is tiny. You expect me to paint this whole wall with this?"

"Would you rather have the roller?" He held up his own, which was swiftly being shimmied into a vat of depressing paint.

"Yes."

"Paint."

"But—"

"Paint, Rose," Ian said. "Start with going around the taped-off molding with that one, all right? Then, if I trust you enough, I'll give you a bigger brush."

Avril made a noise that sounded more like a growl than a rebuff.

"I never asked." Avril ground her teeth together. Fine, she'd use this paintbrush. She would be the best goddamn tiny-paintbrush painter there ever was. A smear went over the very helpful tape as she began. "How did your mom leave you this place?"

"She didn't. Not exactly. Before I went to college, my father did mention that my mother had a lockbox, but I didn't know that inside it was a set of keys. That man barely spoke to me, and now—"

"You got a shiny, old house with mold running up the banister."

Avril waited for any sound of delight made at her apt description.

Per usual, she was met with disappointment.

"At that point, I got in contact with a friend I knew from the area, who found out about the position where Noah works, and here I am."

"How convenient for you."

Ian's rolling paused before starting again.

"I've always had a strange fondness for houses." Avril swooped her brush into the deep pool of paint she dragged alongside her, hunched over at an angle to smooth it along the wall. She let the excess drip back in thick blobs. "Growing up, I didn't really have a house. I looked at these places like they were mansions, compared to our apartments. We usually lived in studios or one bedroom stuck between two others, where the landlord didn't care that we had been kicked out of our last one for being late on the rent a few too many times or for making too much noise, but we never had a real house. With all the rugs and trimmings."

"We," Ian repeated. "You and your mom?"

"Just us."

"Why aren't you spending your holidays there, then? I didn't ask. Family? Friends?"

"Isn't it best to have your holiday lover at your side in all moments?" Avril filled the blank quickly.

"No." Ian stopped his work. The syllable came out similarly as it had last night, only she could tell there was less tipsy of a smile to go with it. Turning over her shoulder, she met his eyes, already waiting for her. "Lovers weren't in the deal, if I remember correctly."

"And if you didn't?"

"I did."

"What, nervous?"

Ian's eyes burned with something that certainly didn't look like nerves. He blinked, turning away, back to work.

"You are, aren't you?" Avril pursed her lips. "Is that why you are being all dull and dour this afternoon? Is this about our little kiss last night?"

She sighed when he didn't continue their game.

Her eyes blurred as she went on section by section, cracks of shadows sneaking out behind corners as the day turned to evening, as if they wanted to play instead, teasing Avril of her own submission.

"Well, this is an exhilarating task."

"Do you ever stop talking?"

"Only if you put something in my mouth," Avril said flatly, turning to see a twinge of response.

Ian didn't answer her as he continued to work, not even a grunt.

Avril began to hum a tune that she couldn't quite place. The melody echoed in the empty space.

"Must you?"

"I thought you weren't talking to me again."

Again, Ian went back to silence. His unamused stare was enough for an answer.

At least to him. To Avril, she raised her eyebrows.

"I could stop, you know. Leave you to your painting. Your brooding, as Cynthia called it. I could be drawing a cute little stick figure family above the fireplace."

"In case you haven't noticed, I care very little of what you do."

He didn't care. Then, why did it look like something had been eating him up from the inside out from the moment he walked in the door of this place?

He was always so serious. So high strung that even the shadows plucked and pulled against all his sharp edges. It was like he wouldn't even allow himself a single moment of enjoyment or fun. The shadows even agreed at her assertion, peeking out of his shirt collar as he squatted closer to the ground. The dark tendrils wrapped up toward his temple the longer he ground his teeth.

One step at a time, she crossed the floor, drawn to them.

"Is that so?" Avril murmured. "Because I could do all sorts of things. Many of them I am most certain you'd like."

Ian continued to ignore her, eyes not even flicking toward her over his shoulder.

"I could take off my clothes right now. Truthfully, I'm not wearing very weather-appropriate clothes. There are not many layers between me and the world. Or I could sneak up behind you and kiss you like last night."

Still no response.

"You can't deny that you liked that unless something else in your pocket was very excited to see me."

A shocked grunt sounded as Ian cleared his throat.

She grinned, coming up beside him, and he finally had to turn, eyes closed, as if giving a prayer to whatever god he believed in before he could face her. "I've been told that I am very good at kissing in a manner of ways. Care to take a few guesses?"

No? Well, this was going to be a very boring month together.

"Or I could do this."

As if she had no control of her hand, before Ian could realize what she was doing, she followed that shadow and swiped her brush all the way down the side of his face.

He stared at her for a long moment.

"You're right. You really can't trust me with this thing."

CHAPTER TWELVE

*B*efore she could move out of the way, a flash of paint swiped down the side of Avril's face. The next, she saw coming, and yet she did nothing. She only waited as the warm and slightly callous fingertips of a librarian, carrying books up and down stairs to the collections, gently scraped in one smooth swish across her cheek. A caress.

Speckles jumped, mimicking her freckles.

"Don't start something you don't want to finish."

At the demand, something stirred. Avril's fingers pulsed before she could restrain. A shadow followed her own thought, and the darkness climbed up his spinal column to the nape of his neck.

With her tiny paintbrush, she coated it all the way down.

Ian's eyes turned around at the crime she'd committed. Was it possible that she'd shocked him? Before Avril could contemplate how to do it again, his hand dipped into the vat. Gray paint splattered against her once-pristine jeans.

She gaped. "Are you serious?"

"You wanted a war on your hands." Ian cocked his head to the side in bravado, but he couldn't help it. All she saw was pure delight.

Flecks of paint flew. Avril couldn't help herself as a shout of laughter pealed out from the back of her throat. It was rough, as if she hadn't used the sound in a long time. Really, she hadn't. Not like this, when she couldn't stop.

Ian paused at the sound, setting his hands down from where they'd reached out, covered in another healthy coating of gray, set to make its mark. Only it didn't. Paint dripped from the tips of his fingers, as if he were turning into a marble statue, molding every detail.

He made a sort of sound, like, "Huh."

Avril swallowed as she looked down at herself. She was much less Greek statue and more *Carrie*, if blood wasn't red.

"You're lucky I put down drop cloths for this floor. My shirt, on the other hand …"

If only there were an easy remedy to that.

When she moved forward again with her hands covered in paint, Ian took a step back until he realized what she was doing, her palms skimming underneath the hem of his shirt.

His stomach was surprisingly toned beneath her hands, and he just stared down at her, waiting for her to do whatever it was she planned to do next. Lifting his shirt up, he tugged it over his shoulders.

That was one way to fix the problem. Below him, she continued her exploration. She heard him inhale as her fingertips trickled around his waist before she slowly kneeled down in front of him.

Brazen, her lips skimmed over his hip. His skin tasted like salt and citrus. She looked up at him.

His light eyes turned molten.

Gripping on to the top of his pants, Avril never had trouble with getting a single button undone. Fire breathed into the back of her neck before, suddenly, it was pulled away. Ian took a step back, nearly pulling her forward with him.

Avril tumbled forward from her knees.

"Come on."

Brushing off her hands, Avril narrowed her eyes at him. She hadn't realized how loudly her heart was pounding in her chest; she didn't hear the cars going by or the heat start to flow through the air vents under the window. "What are you talking about?"

"I'm putting something in your mouth," Ian supplied. A scowl tainted his lips as he reached back for his shirt, tugging it back on overhead, as if he now, all of a sudden, didn't care that it was covered in paint along with the rest of him.

All the shadows were gone. All that was left were thick lines of gray-blue paint.

The gray matted against his skin in mismatched swirls and strikes. It looked almost like a tattoo. If tattoos were as silver as his eyes, drying darker. Avril stared at the stagnant pattern. The shadows' pattern.

Only now, Ian could see them. She waited to see if there was any sort of recognition, but he didn't say anything at first.

Neither did Avril.

He tossed her coat at her. "Let's go."

Clutching her jacket to her chest, Avril watched him as he made his way back to the front door, holding it open and not saying a word. He wouldn't even look at her, control thinning. Standing, she slowly slipped one arm through the sleeve and then the other.

There was no denying it. Avril smirked, watching him. Ian Whitlock wanted her.

———

AVRIL REACHED for another bag off the shelf, shoving the cheese puffs into their shopping basket.

Ian promptly took them and placed them back on the other side of the aisle.

"Excuse me?"

If he kept doing that, the two of them were going to have some problems. He'd already scared her off pop-toasties and their likely carcinogenic yet colorful qualities. Not to mention the fact that she'd be living without peanut butter for the next who knew how long after he informed her of his allergy.

"Forgive me for being concerned for your immediate health," Ian rebuked. He reached for another odd bag of puffs. "Compromise."

Avril peered at the logo. "Those look like they were made for children."

"Healthy, likely gluten-free children, yes."

Rolling her eyes, Avril followed Ian into the produce section, opening the crinkly bag and stuffing her hand inside.

Ian looked at her like she'd robbed the place. "When was the last time you ate?"

Thinking for a minute, Avril shrugged as she leaned against the shelf. "I had coffee this morning with a friend."

"You have friends?"

"Ha ha. You do have a sense of humor," Avril muttered. "How come you don't have food at home? It's a good thing we are fixing this if I am going to be over."

"Who said I invited you back?"

Avril stuffed another cheese puff in her mouth. They tasted like cardboard. Slightly sweet, bearable cardboard, but cardboard nonetheless.

"I eat out most days or pick up meals by work—" started Ian.

"Are you always at work?"

He was a skinny guy, but Avril never thought it was by choice.

"Noah and I stick around sometimes late and order in."

"You two dating?"

"What?" Ian was obviously still getting the hang of her humor. "We go over things."

"Things. Like what?"

"Programs and professor schedules for the weeks leading up to the winter break. There was a lot that went into the merger of the public library. It's adjusting to being partially academic since the institute took over, which isn't a common scenario."

Avril still couldn't get out of her head an image of the two of them sitting late in Ian's office while he likely ran overdue book numbers. "He's probably afraid to leave."

"What do you mean?"

"Noah had a job as the children's librarian before you came around, right?"

Ian gave her a single look in agreement, still not sure what she was getting at.

"He is probably afraid to be the guy leaving earlier."

"I never asked him to."

"No offense there, Ian, but you are not exactly the most laid-back, non-intimidating person. But you already know that, right?"

"I believe we went over it."

He cupped at least a half dozen green apples for firmness. He did the same with the avocados. He even looked at the date of the lettuce.

Avril leaned on a display for support as she rolled her eyes once more at his meticulousness.

"Should I call for medical assistance?"

"My God, what are you even going to do with all this?"

"Well," Ian said, as if he was really thinking it over, "that is the thing about vegetables. You're supposed to eat them."

At this rate, Avril wasn't going to have any eyes. They were going to roll out of her head.

"I eat vegetables," Avril said. "I'd just prefer not to."

"When is that?"

When she actively needed to keep in shape for work, it felt easier. Though burlesque dancers like herself were encouraged to look womanly, she still needed to be fit enough to get through more than a few shows and practices each week. At least one day a week, she would attempt to cook something healthy in a pot.

Reed always gave her the extra onions she snuck in.

"The occasional belly dancing. Bodybuilding competitions. To ease the scurvy."

She got the slightest twitch out of that. His cheek flinched.

Pointing to it, she chuckled.

He swatted her hand away. Only a few shoppers glanced over to watch their discussion as they continued past a colorfully assorted stand of potatoes.

"What's your favorite fruit then?" Ian asked.

"My favorite fruit?"

A terse nod.

"I don't know." She never really thought about it before. "Strawberries."

"Strawberries," Ian repeated, neither pleased nor displeased by the discovery. Reaching down the line of plums, he grabbed a pint, carefully settling the small, plucked berries into their basket.

Avril stared down at them. Ian didn't even look at them or the price. "Thanks."

Ian peeked at her. "They're out of season."

Giving a shake of her head, Avril huffed as they eventually reached the front of the store to check out. Before they turned the corner, she stretched onto her toes.

Avril's heart stopped in her chest. Across the aisle, the back of a dark head was there, wide shoulders and arm reaching up toward the one shelf with a flex of a hand.

"You coming?"

How could he be here? There was no way he could be here in the city, let alone at this store, standing there—

"Avril." A hand was on her shoulder.

Swinging around, she met Ian. His eyes narrowed, studying her expression. She swung back to the man pushing his cart down the aisle. Walking around the front, he lifted a small boy up into the cart with ease.

It wasn't him. She blinked.

"Are you all right?"

She stepped out of Ian's hold. How ridiculous she was being. Of course it wasn't him. "I'm fine."

In her hands, she brought down a bottle of wine and then another.

"What are you doing?"

"What does it look like?" Avril raised her finds up for his appraisal. "Red or white?"

He continued his drab stare.

"Red or white? You said you weren't a hard drinker, and you definitely don't casually reach for a beer on your days off. Not with those hands."

She watched the internal struggle as Ian forced himself not to glance down at the back of his soft palms.

Avril raised the bottles of cabernet once more.

"Red."

"A red it is." Handing him the other bottle for safekeeping, she swiped a third much lighter shade off the shelf in case they felt adventurous. "I think we're set."

Without any small talk from the cashier, Avril and Ian made it back to the metro and home in record time.

"Look at us, all domestic," Avril continued to tease as they hugged their bags of groceries.

Ian grabbed one and then another out from Avril's laden arms.

Ian kicked the door closed with the back of his foot. One item at a time, they unloaded until the kitchen actually looked mostly usable.

Folding up the paper bags, Ian reached for that lonesome pot

Avril had found earlier. Water bubbling on the stove, Ian shook a box of bow tie noodles he'd left out, balancing precariously on the edge of an uncovered cabinet. "Pasta?"

"Only if it's instant," Avril moaned.

"You can wait. It's cooking. It won't take that long."

Avril grumbled, "I can't. I can't do it."

"You ate half the bag of chips at the store."

"All this waiting is making me get hangry. Just because you are unprepared for a dinner party—"

"You have random dinner parties often?"

He was trying to distract her, trying to make her think of all the times a group of people would just show up to the townhouse on Riverside and scatter themselves around the table, squished on the sofa, where the cushions had been turned a few too many times from stains, eating, and laughing. Most often, everyone migrated there after a dress rehearsal of a new show. The girls would still have glitter up to their brows.

Jack would let them practice their newly acquired looks on him.

No, Ian's tactic was not going to work.

"You'd be surprised. But right now, if I have to wait any longer, I might do something I could regret. Likely not, but I've surprised myself before. Or maybe I'll just pass out. Will you be there to swoop in and catch me?" Avril feigned a swoon.

Ian gave the pot a single stir. "No."

With another high-pitched moan, Avril slumped out of the kitchen, leaving him to do whatever it was to make buttered noodles for dinner. She couldn't remember them buying any sauce.

Her heels clicked as she crossed the hall back into the living room, piling up the mess they'd left for themselves in the corner before turning around to the door on the back wall. Walking toward it, Avril always knew she could never survive Bluebeard's castle as she turned the knob.

She was far too nosy.

The study, as Ian had referenced it when she walked in, was empty. The moonlight was bright as it streamed through the old French door panes leading out to a wide, fenced-in backyard.

Avril skimmed her fingers over the empty shelves. She maneuvered around the boxes, flaps open to reveal stacks of books and what appeared to be old paperwork held together with thick bands. Only one, stuck into the corner, wasn't made of rubber.

Picking the object up, at first, Avril thought it was a jewelry box of sorts for how long they were, but no. They were a deck of cards.

The shadows holding them close together pulsed before vanishing.

"Weird fuckers," Avril muttered to herself.

She almost put the cards back down. Tarot cards, after all, were deeply personal objects, meant for one handler at a time. Not feeling the same deep foreboding in her chest, however, she spread them.

The symbols were traditional illustrations, sturdy and opaque. The coating of the card brushed her palm, edges well worn and soft.

They were beautiful.

Flipping the top card, Avril paused, staring at the dark, swirling shadows imprinted into the paper, a knight breaking through.

"What are you doing?" Ian stood in the doorway, a wide bowl in each hand.

Avril's heart hammered in her chest. She cleared her throat before she could take a full breath as she lifted the deck up. "These were your mother's?"

Ian stared at the cards as if he hadn't seen them before. "You plan on replying to my questions with another all the time?"

"What do you think?" Avril grinned. "Maybe."

"Yes, they were."

Avril walked toward him. She still held the cards in one hand as she reached to take a bowl with the other.

He shifted his shoulder farther back, taking the food with it.

Avril muttered, "Must I say please?"

Ian handed her the bowl into her awaiting hand. A slice of bread balanced on top.

It was all Avril could do to make it to the center of the living room before she collapsed on the covered floor. She stabbed her fork into the pile of noodles. Before peering back up.

Ian stood above her. "Sitting on the floor?"

"Picnics are quaint. Especially when you don't have a table."

Taking a bite of her food, she looked back up at him, still standing there, as if debating something. Likely wondering who the hell he'd let in his house.

Excuse her. *The* house.

Avril set aside her bowl on the sheet while she went to get the wine and cups she'd left in the kitchen. When she returned, Ian settled himself on the floor, waiting for her before he took a bite from his own bowl.

Avril took her spot back up and began to shuffle the cards once more. They felt comfortable in her hands, bending similarly to her own set, though different in design. While Avril's were covered in stars and pops of color, these were mainly black and white.

She narrowed her eyes down at the face card that had fallen out. She flipped it over along with a few others, unsurprised by the order they had fallen in. She'd seen this spread before.

The cards easily slipped back in as Avril continued to remix. "Did she draw these by hand?"

"Yes."

"They're gorgeous. You want to know your future? Let me guess. You're a Libra?"

Ian didn't dare reply to that. He was still looking at her hands. "You know how to read them?"

"Intrigued?" She raised her eyebrows.

"Where did you learn?"

Avril paused at the question. The spread she'd pulled a moment ago flared to mind again when she blinked and took another bite of her dinner. There was something about plain noodles that was the most satisfying. "A friend of my mother's taught me."

She remembered her time at that friend's house in another time and another city.

Suzanne had a deep laugh, and her fingers had been stacked with rings. Avril had always noticed them as Suzanne shuffled her own large deck of cards.

A FLURRY of color flew between palms.

The apartment itself echoed those cards, perfectly in place within the deep pink and almost-red tiles that ran up the walls. Multicolored rugs sprawled underfoot. Suzanne made them herself during one of her "hobby phases."

Sweat, however, in the apartment was constant. Beads dripped down the back of Avril's neck, even after they took their coats off at the kitchen table. Heat seeped up through the floorboards from the Laundromat below.

Avril always liked Suzanne's, filled with stuff and warmth. There were hardly ever any shadows sticking in the corners either. The only whispers of smoke sat under Suzanne's deep-set eyes.

The only thing she didn't like of Suzanne's were the cookies that tasted stale as sawdust and the tea she encouraged Avril to drink, a remedy for her ongoing nightmares.

At first, she drank the murky cure only so Suzanne would read her leaves left at the bottom, like she did for her mother. When that proved inconclusive, Avril just choked the concoction down bit by bit whenever someone tapped the rim of her cup in reminder. It was awful hot but even worse when cold.

Then, Suzanne read her cards from that ornate, colorful deck she held close to her heart. She had Avril pick them out from her hands. Avril created decks and chose from whichever one tingled beneath her palm.

Striking figures tinted with gold foil filled the table.

They illuminated shadows that seemed to move just below the surface in little bursts of light. Avril itched to reach out and sweep her fingers across them to see if they stuck like the other shadows did, but she knew better, even then, as a child.

Suzanne narrowed her eyes until a light expression of shock swept up from her cheekbones.

"You will meet a man."

"My stars, Suz, she's a child." Avril's mother, Isobel, spoke up from the other side of the small lime-green table she leaned over, resting her head in her hands.

"Your child." Suzanne tucked a strand of tight black curls behind her ear as she waggled her eyebrows.

Avril grinned.

"Suz."

"I didn't do anything!"

"Of course not."

Avril's mother rolled her dull green eyes, reflected in Avril's, much like the rest of her was. She went back to picking at the skin around her nail beds.

Suzanne waved Avril back in. Her chair squeaked as she leaned closer.

"Your life, like last time, still doesn't have much course yet." She pointed to one of the cards and then another. "But see these cards here, the ones with the swords?"

Avril intently looked at each pointed tip.

"Those generally mean action. Something happening. Choice. And

these"—*Suzanne sliced her finger across, toward another section of the layout*—"are face cards, or the major arcana."

"Kings and queens."

"Yes, like that. Only each card means something different. They reflect things or people that can affect you. Like here is The Magician, The Lovers, and The High Priestess. Very mystical cards, filled with passion to manifest."

"Manifest?"

"Bring to life." *Suzanne sprinkled her fingers over the cards like fairy dust.* "Like a wish."

Avril always loved wishes. She'd try to pick out what star she saw first when she looked out the window at night and not to lose it as she said the rhyme, in case it would suddenly disappear before she could finish.

Not that any of her wishes had come true.

"Hmm, but like your tea leaves last time, all I saw was shadows and indecision. A man of shadows is what this means here. Darkness. Tall, dark, and handsome perhaps?"

Suzanne chuckled, but it sounded less amused this time, smoothing out the card to get a better look at the man illustrated on the front, sword raised high as others came for him, twisted in dark, swirling dust.

No, shadows.

"That could be your Knight of Swords right here, next to the King. A ruthless card, based on ambition. He could either cause rise or ruin."

"He looks like a nightmare."

"From where he is placed, it will be very important."

Avril forced herself not to mimic her mother and roll her eyes. It was better than the shiver that ran up her spine.

Suzanne must have noticed, trailing backward before she lost Avril's attention. "Six of Wands here. Eight of Pentacles. Queen of Wands—"

"Why don't I have any of those?" *Avril pointed back to the few cards caught under her mother's arm from the remaining deck.*

"You didn't draw any. They're like the swords, but in general, cups are a little different when it comes to the suits. They are filled with emotions or feelings. Many reference the hearth or home and family."

"I won't have a home?"

"Perhaps you will be a world traveler or a roadie for a punk rock band," Suzanne suggested. "Maybe all those face cards, like the Father of Swords and Son of Wands and the rest of what is basically most of the major arcana you pulled, will be your family."

"But I don't have a family."

"Never said you couldn't adopt one, in a sense. That's what me and your mama did."

Avril's mother peeked back up again, circles lining her eyes.

"And that card?" Suzanne had skipped over it before, but Avril put her finger right at the top, where lightning struck stone.

"That's The Tower card."

"Major arcana."

Suzanne grinned as she brushed her tight, dark curls behind her ears, pleased. "Exactly. A big player."

"But what does it mean?"

"What does it look like it means?"

Immediately, Avril traced her finger through the clouds. "A storm. Like the man of shadows?"

Her mother's friend nodded sagely as the realization appeared to her as well. "The man of shadows."

Avril's mother quickly cut them off after that, something fearful and wild in her eyes despite Suzanne's insistence of how Avril was attuned—or however she'd put it. It didn't matter to Isobel. As Avril was pulled out of the apartment, it didn't matter how much she wanted to reach back to Suzanne to finally ask her, did Suzanne see them? Did she see the shadows too?

But she didn't get to.

Only once they were outside the building and Laundromat did Avril's mother stop. It no longer smelled like rosemary bread and lavender candles, but bleach and dryer sheets. Her mother's huffs of air were hot against Avril's skin as she bent down.

"Your name is Avril Isobel Maison, yes?" Her mother straightened the edges of her puffy coat. No longer her size, it strained around the zipper. "Yes?"

Avril tilted her chin down once.

"Say it for me."

"My name is Avril Isobel Maison."

"And no one else's."

Nothing else's. The words remained unspoken.

"And no one else's," she repeated.

"Don't you forget it."

AVRIL HADN'T FORGOTTEN IT, not until she had for a short time. She was reminded again as she shuffled the cards, giving Ian the shortened version of her strange friend and the kitchen table the color of limes. She shrugged, as if the meaning of tarot was the kind of thing any child learned before they knew how to count to a hundred.

She took a sip of the dark-red wine, curling her lip to the side. "Nowadays, I've transferred my knowledge of prophecy into house parties and drinking games."

"Must be quite the party trick."

"Want to play?"

"With you?" That seemed to snap him out of whatever funk he'd slipped into.

"I appreciate the momentary self-preservation. Come on though. Have a little fun. Or are you allergic to good times like you are to peanut butter cups? You'd be terrible in an '80s rom-com."

"What kind of game do you play with tarot cards?"

"Nothing that will make you think something terrible will happen to you. Usually anyway," Avril assured. "Not building a card house, either. The cards will simply be a guide to follow.

Think of Passion and Prose as a *choose your own adventure* of sorts."

"Passion and Prose?"

Avril had adorned it such, or maybe someone else had. All that mattered was that after the first time they'd played in the townhouse, the rules never written down yet the stakes high, it'd stuck.

"People tend to get a little passionate when they play."

"Passionate." Ian swallowed.

"The drinking. The voices rising over one another. The secrets spilled that no one remembers anyway the next day. Reincarnations of Lord Byron reveal themselves to get out of thick situations, so they don't have to take the risk. Tricksters too. The game has led to more than a few torrid affairs in my family."

Laughter bubbled up from inside of Ian's chest. "Your family continues to sound more and more interesting."

It was good he thought the game was ridiculous. She did, too, sometimes. Those sorts of games, after all, were the best kind.

"See? Breathless? A little nervous. Shaky hands. This is how it all starts. A lot can happen, among other things, before the sun comes up."

He glanced away, though there was no denying that Ian Whitlock wanted to smile. "You revolt me."

"Forgive me if I never believe you from this point forward. Need I remind you of our closet rendezvous? We would at the very least be fabulous in bed. Don't you agree? No matter how dreadful your imagination must be."

"See, I worried that it was me who had done the awful thing at first that night, seducing you."

"Please," Avril groaned. "Seducing me?"

Avril wasn't sure she had ever been seduced before in her life, let alone by him. She swallowed, getting back to carefully shuffling. Another card almost fell from her hands.

"I'm beginning to understand who I am dealing with."

"Is that right, darling?"

"Already look at those manners, though," Ian commented. "Slipping out in my good-natured presence."

Avril slapped the deck of cards down on the floor. She held back a grin as she narrowed her eyes at him. Her verbal sparring needed a bit of practice to be up to what it once had been, but his quick wit almost reminded her of her and Reed's conversations. They would fight for the last word when, in all actuality, they never minded which one of them got it.

Her palm vibrated over the top of the sparkling deck, as if she were nervous what it would be when she turned it over.

He wanted to play?

"Let's play."

CHAPTER THIRTEEN

*I*n true Passion and Prose form, the rules became a little fuzzy by the time the first bottle hit the dregs. Avril tilted it over to watch the final drop of warm red slip down the side of the tinted bottle before plopping into her overfilled glass.

"I still don't understand the game." Ian took another sip of his own glass. At some point, he'd mistakenly poured the red in his white, turning his drink into a pink-hued elixir.

"That's the point. Stars, I made the whole fucking thing up, but damn, it's fun, isn't it? Plus, I've never tried to play with only two people, so..."

"You're kidding."

"Turn a card and see if you get to ask me how it all started. I might tell you anyway."

Ian reached for a card. He turned it over.

"Lovely. The spirits have spoken. Well, you see, I love parties. When I came to Ashton and my life was something of a..." She drifted off.

"A secret when it comes to me knowing?"

Avril tapped her nose. "Exactly. But I had a place and a fantastic roommate and was making real money with real badass people. So, I decided to throw a party. Finally, one of my own, where I could afford the booze—good booze, mind you, none of the *mystery juice that stains the bathtub* shit. Of course, it came to my attention very quickly that though parties usually run themselves, I wasn't much of a host. It was a flop. The whole thing. People were sitting around, talking about their week. I could've puked."

Ian smirked.

"It wasn't funny. But then my friend—my roommate," Avril clarified, "he was imbibing after a strenuous exam week. He suggested a game. Of course, I nearly shot him straight down. What were we going to play, Monopoly? But then, smart guy, he said, 'Make something up.' So, I did. I grabbed the most expensive beautiful bottle of vodka and slammed the thing down in the middle of the living room, and we played. It was a much better game than whatever you just got. Everyone remembered that night. My parties from then on reigned supreme. As they should, thank the gods."

"But why Passion and Prose?"

"Ah." Avril took another sip of wine to coat her throat. "Because in the beginning, when I first came up with the game off the top of my head, that's how we'd see who'd be sacrificed to the lions—or forgive me, tarot—first. Everyone had to go around the circle. Each gave a passion and put it into prose."

"Prose."

"Yeah, like life. You make it sound prettier than it actually is." Avril tried to further explain. "Whoever couldn't think of something good enough, fast enough, was already one shot behind—or rather, ahead of everyone else. It certainly got the game rolling, no matter what. Intentionally or not, the game has changed a lot since then."

"Why is that?"

"Because Reed continued to be a dirty cheater. He always won."

Until Kit had come along and blown them away. She was such a hustler that night. It was one of the last nights that they were all together, laughing and screaming at each other through the veil of liquor of glee, as if nothing was wrong in the world. For a few hours, there hadn't been.

"I don't know really though. Time changes a lot, changed the game. And the world goes around and round. Plus, Reed always picked the same passion."

Ian's smile reappeared. His lips were pulled up at the one side, more casual than his usual dapper smirk he forced at people, like the cashier at the store. It was a smile of someone like the children at the library this morning—completely content while listening to a well-told story.

"And what was that?"

"Sex. What a terrible question, Ian," Avril said. "Though I will admit, he got very creative. What he could do with three letters might as well have been passion, though he would never change it, and he says that I'm the stubborn one."

He let his head drip toward his shoulder. He stared at her.

"Stop that."

"Why?"

"Because I shouldn't like you."

Ian snorted an obvious tune. "Shouldn't doesn't mean doesn't. And to be frank, I don't really think I should like you either."

Avril blinked at the sudden absurdity of their statements. Reaching for the other bottle, she topped off his cup.

Ian didn't notice until he brought the wine to his lips. "Are you drunk?"

"Stars, no. How could I be with the pound of noodles you gave me? Hats off to the chef."

He was still staring at her.

"What now?"

"It's your accent." Ian smiled as he caught the twang. "You've been talking with it for a while now. You never answered me last night about it. What is it again?"

"Irish." And a mix of American hillbilly likely.

"It makes you sound like a goddess."

Avril raised an eyebrow as she leaned farther onto her elbows and then her back against the hard floor. "And you're asking if I'm the tipsy one."

"What are you doing?"

"Stretching," Avril whined as she reached her arms above her head on the floor.

"Is your back bothering you?"

She shook her head, feeling down for it but only feeling the numb ache she always felt when she focused on it. "Not really. The wine helps."

Ian barked something that had to be a laugh—unless he planned to take over the world.

Avril only shrugged. "Don't worry; I'm positively A-OK. I watch myself not to overindulge. I learned my lesson this past year, if I hadn't already. Bathroom floors and I don't have positive memories."

"So, you *really* like parties."

"You couldn't tell?" Avril asked rhetorically. "I've loved them since forever. I've always imagined them in my head. The loud music and the people pressed up close to one another. Parties, no matter what or who they are thrown by, are filled with life and sorrow, desperately trying to capture the best bits in only a few hours. Parties like that hold the most truth in the world —let alone in whatever person I end up with after midnight— lost and fully at ease with themselves, if not a little terrified about how much they don't want to go home. At least, not alone."

"You've spent a lot of time with other men?" Ian asked before it seemed like he realized what it was he was saying. He shook his head, but Avril only smiled. His tone had held no verdict on whatever that meant.

At some point, they had moved closer to one another.

"Yes," Avril said. "Mostly men."

"Why?"

"Why?" She'd never been asked that before. She focused her gaze on him with a simple shrug. "Because I can."

When she had run away from Reed and Ashton at the beginning of the year, she couldn't tell herself how many parties she'd managed to make her way into. How many beds she'd woken up in after usually whatever guy she passed the time with passed out. She lost count of the number of arms she'd carefully maneuvered around to leave come morning. She'd slept with them because at the time, in the darkness and heady rooms she found herself in, it felt right. She could feel right and empty for a while, where the shadows and voices inside of herself normally screamed in frustration.

She'd kept safe. She'd watched for herself when she edged too far over the cliff of no return. No one could tell her not to do whatever the hell she wanted.

She was no one else's. Not anymore.

"Does that bother you?" Avril asked.

"No."

Avril searched his face for any untruth there. None showed. "Care to rethink your previous decision? Don't act like you haven't thought about it since last night. It wouldn't be so bad."

"What exactly?"

"Company."

He hummed low in the back of his throat.

"Why not?" Avril was a breath from his lips. "You said the terms weren't fully set yet. A date."

"That was the deal."

"So was not being lonely."

"Who said I was lonely? I like to be alone."

"Being lonely and being alone are two very different things."

Ian stared at her for a long moment, something flickering in his gaze. A muscle twitched in his neck. She wondered what he held inside there, bursting to get out.

"So, why not?" Avril leaned forward on her knees as she crawled under his gaze. Only, there was no submission in Avril as she did so. There rarely ever was. There was only power she felt as the man in front of her watched.

Ian's eyes drifted from the tips of her feet against the floor to how she cocked her head to the right. His pulse jumped once more.

"Why not more than that? I can tell you want to, Ian. Holidays might be a sad time of year for many, but they are also for lovers, aren't they—"

Before she could finish convincing, it appeared she didn't need to.

Ian cupped the back of her head and shoved her mouth open with his. The sudden ferocity turned Avril breathless as she stared up at him. She tilted her chin down and watched his dark eyes swirl.

The same sort of power she'd felt moments ago was in his tongue as it swept over his one grinning canine. "You sure you're up for some revisions?"

CHAPTER FOURTEEN

*I*t was a fight for power when their lips met, and for some reason, for the first time, Avril wasn't sure she'd mind losing.

Just not today.

His hands surrounded her as they kissed, never fading as they slid up her ribs, as if it were the most casual thing in the world to find them placed on either side of her face. She arched her neck to expose her throat, and Ian greedily took her up on the offer.

As she took a deep breath, her own hands skimmed down, feeling the way his body was formed, starting with his shoulders. Though he was tall and lanky in vision with his oversize button-downs and glasses, Avril now took the chance to sit to the side. Ian still felt strong and at ease with himself as he moved, as if they had all the time in the world and he'd take it so long as no one had issue with it.

Maybe even then.

As she slid down his chest, Avril's tongue created a trail while she pushed him back to the floor. He let her. This time, there was nowhere for him to go when her fingers sought his tricky pants button. He strained against the fabric as she tugged at the waistband, and he finally slid free into her hand. He was long and thick as she curved her fingers around his length.

Avril gave him a single stroke and reveled in the sound that ground between Ian's teeth. He stared down at her, watching her every move. With another stroke, Avril leaned down close to stare at the wetness forming at the tip.

Ian shivered when she used her thumb, rolling it into the sensitive head. Her lips hovered right above him.

"Not so serious now, are we?"

Before he could argue, her lips closed over him. Taking him into her mouth, she felt his heat against her tongue, pulsing. She stroked and teased. She knew if she was good at anything in the world, this was it. She reveled in the sounds and shuddering shakes men made underneath her as she slowed and quickened, their pleasure all in her hands.

When he reached for her, she paid him no heed, continuing her work until he thickened in her mouth, hips lifting as he came. She sucked and dipped her head once more before coming away from him with a satisfying pop.

"Company," he murmured her earlier words.

"You sound a little breathless there, Ian," Avril commented. "Perhaps we have different definitions."

"A clarification we'll have to make."

She was sure now; they would be going with her suggestion.

Reaching out, his hand easily tangled through her hair as he pulled her back against him, lips pressing against hers and requesting entrance, which she gave without question. His tongue tangled with hers, as if they had done this dozens of times before, knowing how she twisted to get the advantage he no longer appeared to want to share.

Light, spattering kisses were placed along her jawline. Avril licked her lips, and a yelp popped out in sudden surprise at the gentle bite beneath her ear.

A low, rumbling laugh sounded.

"Don't be so proud of yourself," she huffed, letting him continue his sharp onslaught, slipping her out of her shirt, still coated with dry paint, and tossing it across the floor.

A clatter of where it hit against their dishes didn't deter him.

He kneaded her breasts in his hands, pinching her nipples as his teeth grazed the sensitive skin. As he was poised between her legs, Avril felt him harden against her thigh once more, and her head fell back to the chilled floor. Or maybe that was her as a shiver spiraled up her spine.

Her chest pushed farther into his mouth, seeking more attention, sensation, as she shut her eyes.

"Uh-uh." Ian nipped at her ribs, his hands almost casually slipping between her skin and jeans.

She helped, kicking to get them down her legs, and he did the same. His cool gaze locked on hers as his fingers traced lower. He tapped at her inner thighs—an order that she spread without question—seeking pressure as he toyed with her.

"Eyes open. I want you to look at me when I take you."

Slithering farther up her thighs, his fingers found her slick with wetness. He parted her folds, sliding his fingers back and forth but not entering her. Tilting her hips toward him, she hoped that he got that order while the rest of her body shivered.

She was acting like a wanton virgin.

"What was that about how I shouldn't be proud of myself?" he asked.

Avril didn't answer as one of those fingers finally—*finally*—slipped into her, joined with a second not long after. He explored her with his hands, watching as he slowly fingered her, in and out. He took his time, much like the rest of her, watching how she flinched or shuddered as he pressed up inside of her with a curl of his knuckles.

Eyelashes fluttering, Avril gritted out, "Are you just going to play all night, or are you going to fuck me?"

Those fingers disappeared, leaving her empty and lips parting in revolt.

"You really need to work on those manners."

He slipped inside her with a jolt. A sound lodged in the back of her throat sprang free as he pushed himself with a thrust and then another before he was able to fully find himself settled between her legs. Swallowing, Avril took a deep breath, her heart strumming in her chest. She felt full, so full and warm—hot even, compared to the cold frost of the shadows swimming all around her again.

He pulled out and thrust back into her once, hard enough that they both grunted from luxurious impact. A warning. A beautiful warning as she arched her hips to meet it.

Fingers brushed her cheek. "Eyes on me."

Eyes on him.

She leaned up, keeping control as they shifted and ground against each other. Her nails dug into his one shoulder as she held on to him, baring her teeth as if they were animals, primal and taking as he pumped into her, thrusts hard and swift.

He was no longer taking his time. He wanted to see her break.

He saw it happening a moment before she did. Avril tipped over the precipice and continued to fall as he kept the pace, thrusting into her with a similar abandon to the cry slipping past her lips. She clenched, muscles in her thighs straining to pull him closer as she came.

Blinking back up toward the sky, Ian pulled himself out of her before he spilled upward against her stomach, swallowing his own sounds of pleasure that she wanted to lap up as they still echoed through the empty space.

Rolling off of him, Avril waited for something to happen, but nothing did. All that did was the stagnant, chilled air of the house settling over her as her breaths slowed, no longer hammering against the cage keeping them contained. Curling over to one side, Ian watched her.

What was he thinking? Did he know that he'd just managed to give her the best sex she'd had in—not ever. It couldn't have been the best sex she'd ever had. She'd been to orgies in luxurious palaces, where she was fucked up against walls with gold foil trapped in the wallpaper while wearing ridiculous yet very sexy period-appropriate clothing.

And yet...

"YOU SAID you never played P and P before?"

Ian glanced at her. He was still catching his breath as he tugged his jeans over his hips, prudently tucking himself back inside. He didn't answer.

"Because, like I said, if you ever caught a real game of P&P, it can get pretty raunchy," Avril went on, the world starting to trickle back in around her voice. "So, you won, we'll call it. Congratulations."

Still nothing.

"I think that's why Reed insists we can only play it on special occasions now. He doesn't like the cleanup. The last time we really played was a little over a year ago."

"You mentioned him before."

Avril inhaled. At least she hadn't screwed him into a mute. "He's my best friend."

"Does he live in Ashton?"

Avril glanced back to where their cards were now sprawled across the floor. A few had managed to stay in a deck, and she gestured to them. "Care to take another card?"

They both knew how their last game had ended.

She looked him up and down.

He only waited for her to answer.

With a sigh, she sat up, but made no effort to reach for her discarded clothing. "Most of the time. We still share a place. Reed and I met when I was fifteen, I think. We've been together ever since. He saved me from a fistfight. Which, of course, I had totally been winning."

"I wouldn't doubt it."

Avril rolled her eyes as Ian stopped his pacing to stand in front of her, but said nothing about her continued nudity.

She thought about Reed and her then, the day they'd met, sitting on the grimy linoleum floor together until the next bell so that her head could stop spinning. Her lipstick, which she'd stolen from another girl at the group home she lived in at the time, had been smeared across her face. She'd left it like that for most of the day.

She touched her fingers to her bottom lip. "I thought Reed was the most gorgeous boy I had ever seen at the time. We were always a compact deal after that. He thought I was bizarre, I'm sure. Still, he snuck me into his family's house for at least three months while we were in high school once he found out I was basically wandering Ashton suburbia late at night. I didn't want to go back to the home I was living in."

"What happened?" Ian asked. He moved forward now, extending a hand to her to stand up.

"What are you doing?"

"You can stay. It's too late for you to go home."

Avril didn't know what to say. Though she wasn't against staying the night, her lips parted to nothing.

"Just for tonight though." He gestured her to follow him toward the stairs, not concerned by leaving the mess on the floor.

And oddly, Avril stood.

She followed.

"So, what happened?"

"Reed's mother found out I was staying there. I'm pretty sure his younger sister had tipped her off after I ate her leftover birthday cake in the fridge. She wasn't much of a fan of me. But Paula, his mother, kept our secret for a while after Reed talked to her. After that, she was seemingly unconcerned about the wicked girl who hogged the shower. That was, until Reed's father came to wonder why they were spending so much on groceries." Avril remembered the red in that man's face, putting up with her. "I had to get a job after that to appease dear old father Mike."

"But he didn't kick you out either?"

"No, but don't think it was because he liked me," Avril said. She took one step at a time upstairs.

She couldn't believe the whole thing now that she thought back on it, either. She was most certainly not Mike's cup of tea. Still, he put up with her to this day, likely for Reed whenever they visited together over holidays. She wondered if Reed was going home soon to celebrate Christmas with them this year.

"I'm sure his wife pulled a few favors. I'm also pretty positive he was near overjoyed to believe his son was fucking me."

She could see the question in Ian's eyes. Her amusement should've been answer enough.

"He was only partly right. Reed and I, we've been a fantastic duo in crime together. For a long time anyway." Avril dropped her chin into her hands as she told the story. "Recently…"

"Another reason you've involved yourself in a deal with a stranger?"

"You were just inside me and are asking me life questions. Not so sure I'd call you a stranger. Not even sure if we could call this a cheap date."

When he didn't respond, she rolled her eyes, with a hint of a smile pulling at her lips before she noticed.

"We all have our reasons."

The only reason she knew the room they had come to was Ian's bedroom was due to the fact that it was also the only room that was sans dust. Utilitarian was the only way to describe the space. Sparse and lacking even a simple rug under the box-spring mattress combo.

Ian didn't call this place his home, and it showed. Mostly

anyway. A lamp was on the ground next to the mattress, where there should have been a bed. An alarm clock was plugged in with bright red numbers, balanced atop a stack of paperbacks with worn spines.

"So, what happened?"

Her eyes continued to trail around the space, looking for—well, she wasn't quite sure what she was looking for now that she stood in the center of the floor. "He cares about me."

"How dare he."

"I know, right?" Avril shook her head. Her lips were loose and moved easily. "Something happened last year, and he—we've been on edge ever since. But there's a fine line between caring and caring too much."

Ian tilted his chin in a single nod, as if he understood.

"It's not that I don't appreciate Reed. He's done a lot for me and everything after it all happened."

"It?"

"Yes, *it*." Avril pointedly repeated. The tight feeling around her heart began to ease when Ian did not pry further. "Without him, I'm not sure exactly what I would've done at the last year. I wasn't … good. Sometimes, I'm still not sure if I am or not. It doesn't matter though. Because now, he just keeps staring at me. He can't quite separate what happened. He doesn't *see me* like he used to."

Of course, then again, neither did she.

"So, you're giving him space too?"

That was one way of putting it.

"He was always on top of things. The one thing he couldn't keep in his tidy box was me. We evened each other out in that way. But now, when he looks at me, it's more than that. And I can't breathe."

"Not so laissez-faire?"

"Hey, I am very type A in the right situations. A fantastic delegator."

Ian raised his eyebrows.

Avril laughed. "You don't know me."

"I think I'm beginning to."

Avril held her gaze down to her bare feet, one toe slightly crooked. She wondered what Reed would think at this time of night. If he would worry about where she could possibly be.

Maybe he'd be relieved.

Ian gestured to the other door. "The only finished bathroom is through there. Do whatever you need to. I'm going downstairs to clean up, and then we can figure out—"

"New negotiations to our deal?"

He shook his head, lifting this chin back to the en suite while his eyes glanced at her frame again, up and down. Turning around, he headed back out the door again. "Clean off the paint. It's late."

Avril didn't move until she heard him hit the steps, a light creak still lingering in them. Looking around the room one more time and still not finding whatever she was searching for, Avril trailed through the door.

The bathroom was gorgeous. Modern tile with a hint of what must have been left behind in the old, bygone Victorian dream house, including a wide soaking tub sitting in the corner with brass clawed feet.

Such a beautiful tub.

Trailing her hand over the cool porcelain, Avril patted it once, promising it another time as she stepped into the shower. The water was warm as it cascaded down her. Tilting her head back, she let even her curls get wet, sticking to the sides of her face as she lathered the rest of her body with Ian's black block of soap.

Whatever swirls of gray paint were left on her were swept to nothing.

Standing under the rain for another minute, Avril blindly reached and swiped the handle until the stream stopped flowing. Drips trickled down to her ankles as she stepped out, reaching for the nearest towel, soft and fluffy enough that it was obvious how new it was—probably picked up at the department store not long after Ian had arrived.

When she wrapped it around her chest, Ian was already back inside his room, running his hands through his hair.

"You all right there, tall, light, and scary?"

Twisting toward her, Ian widened his eyes at the sight of her. "Going to rinse off."

She stepped aside gesturing toward the shower. She was about to say another wit-filled remark, but whatever those words were, they died on her lips. She shut them as he shuffled by her without a glance.

He let the door swing mostly shut behind him.

The water ran.

A sour pain entered Avril's gut as she stepped back into his dimly lit room. She'd exposed too much of herself.

But when did she ever care about that?

Breathe, Avril.

Goddamn it, she needed to calm down and get it together.

Just breathe.

Somewhere, a piece of air got caught in her stomach, escaping from her lungs and making a home of its own, swirling around in there.

Avril leaned around where the door was partly open again, catching Ian. He ran his hands through his hair as the paint swirled down over his body and down the drain.

The shadows were gone.

It was only then she realized that the shadows were gone.

She blinked once. Before she could contemplate what that meant, however, Ian reappeared. Sweatpants hung long on his hips.

"Like I said," he started, still drying his hair with a towel, "this is the only room I have set up yet."

Avril glanced behind, at the bed beneath her, immediately catching what he meant. "I think we've moved a bit past that."

He gave a single nod.

Instead, he focused on the towel still wrapped around her.

"I didn't think to bring pajamas." Unlike him.

She glanced at him again, up and down, at how the cotton hugged his legs. Ian Whitlock was hiding a lot more than he let on under those awful academia clothes.

Without saying a word, Ian walked over to his one set of drawers in the closet. Coming back to her, he extended a plain white T-shirt.

Avril slipped it overhead. It clung to her warmth, and an unease settled into place with it.

And there they were again.

Even his shirts had shadows threaded into the hem.

Maybe if she just lay down for a little while, then she wouldn't feel so lightheaded.

Avril shuffled over to the mattress. Perhaps Ian was right. She had drunk quite a bit of wine compared to usual.

Usual. That sounded bad, didn't it?

She needed to sit, was all.

Perched on the edge, she rolled onto her back. When she lifted her chin back up, Ian was still staring at her.

"So, ground rules?"

"What?"

"You look like someone who likes rules," Avril explained, trying to focus her mind anywhere else from where it wanted to go. "Structure, organization. I'm very used to them in my day-to-day life dealings—or was—whether you'd think so or not. I figure you want to put those corrections to our deal?"

"Ground rules," Ian agreed, walking around the other side of his wide mattress before he sat down with a sigh.

Her head fell back down, so she no longer had to crane her neck to look at him.

Ian raised his eyebrows as she stretched herself out. "This remains professional."

"It didn't feel that way when you turned into a wild beast and mounted me on the living room floor. Ah, don't look like that. How will I ever tell you to do it again?"

He gave her a pointed look. Case and point.

She batted her eyelashes.

"One month," added Ian. "Then, I am gone. I am leaving this place once and for all. You understand that."

She shrugged. "Maybe I'll be leaving too."

He nodded, as if he couldn't care less what she did. "Sex."

She grinned.

"Is on the table."

"I'm a bit comfortable here right now, but I like where this is going."

"Rose, serious."

Of course. She put on her severe face.

Unfortunately, he didn't look very convinced. "You're my date for the merrymakings. We aren't alone for whatever the hell this month turns into—"

"Merrymakings."

"And then that's it. Understand?"

Simple enough. Poor guy looked like he could sure use some of that … merrymaking.

"If either of us does anything or says a single word—"

"Are you suggesting a safe word, Ian?"

Another look. If he kept it up, they wouldn't be able to finish this conversation.

"I knew you had a little kink in you."

He only shook his head.

"A lot? You're only turning me on by not denying it." Avril looked him up and down. "So, that's it? What you really want to say here is that our month company has turned into a companionable thirty-day sexcapade? Our relationship of convenience has taken a turn. You sure know how to draw a girl in."

"Rose."

"As for birth control."

Ian's eyes widened as he just thought of it.

Grinning, she basked in the horror for a short moment. "It's all taken care of. I've had an IUD since last year."

"Good." He hummed as he stared into her. "Also, one more thing."

"Yes?"

"You take off the mask when you're with me."

Whatever Avril was about to say dissipated from her tongue. "Mask?"

"Whatever that smirk is on your face right now. Yes, that mask. Persona. Whatever you'd like to call it."

Immediately, it fell to a scowl.

"The act and pretending—for whatever reason, I know I am not to know about—you take it off when I'm inside you. Deal?"

Startled at the idea, Avril quickly took a breath. Fine then. She rolled her eyes. "Safe, sane, consensual. That cover it?"

"Don't make this a kink thing."

"Why not? You'd fit right in, and life is so much more fun this way," Avril said, though she trailed off toward the end.

"One more thing. You can stay. If you want to."

What had happened to this being a one-night-only event? Avril looked down at how she pressed into his comforter.

"You said you didn't want to go home for the holidays," Ian said softly. "So, fine. Stay here. Paint—preferably on the walls. It would all be convenient."

Convenient.

I want you here, with me. How else would I keep an eye on you? Another voice seemed to add in the back of her mind.

Ignoring the thought, Avril let her mind's eye drift back again to the more exciting moments of her time here so far, not long past … and down Ian's body. She could deal with quite a bit of that sort of convenience.

"Impressive when you do that."

"What?"

"The eyebrow thing."

"You can't?" Avril seamlessly shifted to her other eyebrow.

Ian gave it a shot, both going up before he could help it.

Avril laughed louder than he did. The sound was almost a rasp, as if she hadn't laughed so easily in a long time. She listened as it bounced, echoing off the undecorated walls. Maybe she did look a little ridiculous—however impressive, apparently.

"Fine then, seriously, come here. Lesson one. If you are going to be an intelligent yet ultimately domineering fool, you at least have to master the eyebrows."

Avril kneeled in front of him, both of them nearly at the same height this way. When she lifted her hands toward his face, his eyes caught hers, holding for a long second.

They were beautiful then, gray and swirling, as if the shadows had calmed but were still alive somehow, still inside him. Captivated, she fell into the hourglass and felt quite at ease, wading through the seconds.

She cleared her throat, the sound also seeming to startle Ian, who suddenly looked from her to her hands.

"Are you going to tell me what you plan on doing with those things?"

"Oh, nothing you wouldn't like. Relax. I'm teaching you the art of lifting your eyebrow. No one will dare question it. Now, lift —no, gently," Avril scolded.

Carefully, her fingers resting on his temples, she smoothed one, holding the other. Glancing back down at his eyes. They were staring at her again.

She shifted back. Something odd disconcerted her all of a sudden, but that couldn't be right. Avril was never weird after sex or talking about sex and the many positions it took place. She just wasn't.

She cleared her throat again.

"There, you have it."

"I fear I might need more practice." Ian relaxed down on the bed next to her.

"Just stare at yourself in the mirror for a while. You can't find that hard."

"Is that how you mastered such a variable expression?"

Avril immediately saw her mother when she blinked. Avril saw herself staring at her when she put on a new dress one day, in the doorway of their bedroom of their tiny studio apartment somewhere—she couldn't remember where.

"How do I look?" her mother asked coyly. She raised her eyebrow and pursed her lips, to her daughter's delight.

After, Avril stood in front of the mirror for hours, trying to do the same.

"Plenty to look at," Avril answered, looking down to her bare legs.

Ian seemed to follow her eyes, snapping back up when she narrowed hers. "Can I have one more question?"

Avril leaned back onto the bed, cradling her head into her hands. "Why not?"

"You have a back injury that causes you pain, yet you still wear heels," commented Ian.

"Is that a question?"

"I guess not." Ian settled. "But they're important to you?"

"Why would you say that?"

"Because you step over puddles. For some reason, I figured you were someone who didn't care about stepping right on through city puddles or dirt, but you didn't last night or on our excursion to the store, either. And so far, I've never seen you not wear them. There must be a reason."

"I just like them," Avril said lamely.

She looked down to the raised edges on the back of her feet from when she'd had to rebreak in pair after pair when she got her collection of shoes back and not taken them off since. At least, not after Reed had told her she was given the doctor's approval to take her usual routine easy.

At those words, Avril had expected to only feel relief. She did, but not completely. Instead, she felt her schedule filling back up as if nothing had ever happened. But it had.

She knew it had.

So, there would no longer be lunch dates with gossip columnists to keep them on her good side. There would no longer be Pilates on Thursdays and choreography practice on Tuesdays before the run-through for the weekend, starting at one in the afternoon on Fridays at Rosin. There would be no fittings and no dance lessons every day of the week or at parties she deemed absolutely mandatory since she arrived in the city on Saturdays.

Heels had become the only part of the routine she went back to wholeheartedly. A good thing too. Her legs looked like a pudgy toddler in ballet flats.

"So, that's why you came here to the grand city of Ash?" Ian asked. Only an ounce of mockery hid in that statement somewhere. "To wear heels."

Her eyes flared.

"Not just any heels, darling Ian. Expensive heels." Unable to hold her straight face, she forced herself to laugh again before she caught it. His expression did too. But he wasn't inside her, was he? "When I came to Ash, I wanted the whole world."

"Did you get it?"

Avril's heart stopped at the question as she stared at Ian. A hand cushioned his chin as he listened to her. Every word.

"For a while, I thought so."

Tiny wrinkles around Ian's eyes squinted as he seemed to search for the next words to say, something that was—

Blinking a few times, her eyes were so heavy. She let them close.

———

"WHO SAID YOU COULD HAVE THAT?" A voice as smooth as silk swept over her. The tips of his fingers traced up her arm from wrist to elbow.

Avril hummed at the pleasant touch. "I missed you."

"That's mine, you know."

She thought she was his.

Still, she blinked her eyes open to stare with unabashed longing. She tugged on the hem of his shirt that she had taken from his closet, still smelling of his brisk cologne. She unbuttoned the top loop to expose a little more skin as she attempted a smile. "I missed you. You didn't miss me?"

"I could've had anyone I wanted while I was gone."

She sat back on her heels. "Yes, but—"

"But what?"

"That's," Avril stammered. A creased threaded into her brow. "That's not what I meant. I was just…"

"Just?"

She didn't know what she was doing.

"You don't even get dressed up for me when I show up anymore. No wonder no one wants to be around you. Why no one calls."

Avril shook her head. This wasn't right.

"I was waiting for you."

Fingers clawed at her throat as she was suddenly dragged away from where she had been sitting. Her feet fought for purchase as they went wherever he was taking her, holding her until she couldn't breathe, until all she could do was choke.

Her head lolled against the tiles of the bathroom floor as she heaved.

"You are disgusting. Where is she? Where is the oh-so-special Queen now?"

Nowhere. She was nowhere.

Avril spat down onto the floor. Her mouth tasted like bile and iron.

When she turned over, her eyes connected with someone else standing not in the hall, but far away. She wasn't in his bathroom —the one with the cold gray stone shower that scraped her feet. No.

Emerald octagon tiles stared at her until she lifted her head.

"Mum?" Avril croaked at the redheaded woman.

Her mother only shook her head down at the sight of her bleeding on the floor. She blinked twice before meeting her daughter's eyes, identical to her own.

"Mum?"

"Close your eyes."

CHAPTER FIFTEEN

"*A*vril? Avril, please. Rose." A hand gently turned her chin back to face the voice calling out to her from somewhere far away. Down the hallway. Another world so dark that she couldn't break through.

Blinking. She blinked.

Immediately tilting her eyes down, Avril noticed his hand—not *his* hand, but Ian's hand—was covered in charcoal or soot, smudging her skin. The shadows coaxed softly from his fingertips, bleeding like a dull pulse. His other carefully held her up from where she must've been thrashing, even as she startled away.

Her mouth opened in horror. "I'm sorry."

"It's okay."

She shook her head. "Don't."

He put up his hands, and she scrambled toward the other side of the bed. His eyes flashed. The yellow light on the nightstand was on as she looked around the space. It was all just as she had fallen asleep in, only a soft blanket draped across her feet.

Closing her eyes, Avril swallowed the bile caught in her throat.

Her mother had been right there in front of her. She was sure of it.

"You're all right."

As she swallowed, it felt raw.

She was fine. Perfectly. She released a slow breath, and only then could she compose herself. She was on a bed. Ian Whitlock's bed in his house. They were in Ashton. There was a blanket over her to keep her warm.

"Rose."

Opening her eyes, she focused on Ian.

"You woke me up," she said.

"You were screaming. Trying to …" He shook his head. "Should I not have?"

Avril swallowed. Room. Ian's room, where he sat with his well-defined thighs clad in soft pajama bottoms. Her name was Avril Isobel Maison McClair Queen. No one ever woke her up until she woke up herself, afraid her eyes wouldn't refocus like the first time when Reed wasn't Reed and Avril couldn't stop the low pained sound that had cried out of the back of her throat.

Now, the room was quiet. The only sound was their breathing.

Ian tilted his head low, catching her line of sight. "Are you awake? You're here with me."

Avril nodded, staring at him. The shadows that were normally there, surrounding him, were gone suddenly. It was just him. His soft fingers also were no longer covered in the thick smudges of paint she'd flicked at him.

"A dream," she said. Mostly a dream.

"Do you want to talk about it?"

Turning her head away, Avril remembered the dream in splashes of dark vignettes. Her jaw clenched, forcing her to catch each breath and slow them all down. "No."

No, she most certainly did not want to do that. But as she looked up at Ian, his one hand outstretched from where he was on the other side of the bed, she had a much better idea as the images, the words still flew around inside of her head, loud and mocking. She couldn't get them to stop, filling her ears—all of her.

In two shuffles, she was back toward him, her hand reaching around to the back of his neck.

The fear. The anger. It burned low in her stomach.

"What are you doing?"

Avril swallowed, blinking at the confusion on his face. "Kiss me."

"What happened?"

"Nothing. Please, just kiss me. Please." For a moment, Avril inched herself closer to him. She placed her hands on his shoulders, surprised to feel how sturdy, how strong they were as they rotated to hold her, as if he were holding her up completely.

"Please, I need to make it go away," she pleaded. Just cover it over, as if it'd never happened at all.

Because she could. She could do whatever she wanted.

She was no one else's.

And right now, she needed something or someone to make her forget even if it was only for a little while. Now, as much of her shook with hesitation, with bitter hope, Avril also ached. "Please."

She drew his mouth down to meet hers. They were warm and heavy, just like they had been in the closet the other day. She imagined again how he'd wrapped his arms around her, his hands skimming up toward her hips. But this time, Ian hissed.

"Avril."

The sound of her name. Avril. Not Rose, as he called out to her, pulling her out of that dream. That darkness.

The name made her pause as it came out smooth and empty on Ian's careful lips.

She pulled back.

"No." Ian shook his head as he began to stand.

"It's no different than before. Our deal." At this point, Avril couldn't stop herself, reaching out like a child. She snatched her hand back into her chest. "Wait."

"I can make up a bed on the couch or another room."

Avril closed her eyes. "Stay."

His mouth opened in thought, or maybe shock, and seconds passed before he swallowed.

"I won't. I'm sorry," Avril croaked, hating the way she sounded, flushed with anger and loathing. "Stay."

Ian looked at the expanse of the bed. There was plenty of room as she shifted back over to her side, where she must have lain down at some point and fallen asleep and dreamed. "Fine. I'll stay, but that's it."

Avril nodded. "Fine."

"Avril."

Rolling over, she pretended not to listen, as if Ian had said nothing. He shifted to adjust the sheets and turn out the light, truly swathing them in darkness. She almost thought of turning back over again to him, whispering something to him, asking him again with a calmer voice, without the painful rasp of the scream still lodged in her throat, gasping awake at her dreams she did not want to return to.

But Avril did not beg.

She would not allow herself to reach out a hand again, not even across the sheets, to feel him breathing like all of her other lovers she had taken, so she knew where she was. Her heart continued to pound in her chest while her eyes shifted back and forth between nightmare and reality when all she could see was a stagnant precipice.

They felt the same.

Turning around, Avril looked to see if Ian would say anything at all at her tossing, but his breath had already begun to turn long and full. She tiptoed to the door and down the steps, careful to hold on to the railing, and brushed the dust off her hands when she reached the bottom.

She wanted to run out the front door and not look back. If she did, it would put an end to everything. It wouldn't be the first time she had taken that avenue—wandered until she found a cab and paid the driver when she reached Riverside. Tonight, under the lamplight that came through the window, she paused. Her hand hovered above the knob.

Run, her instincts called. *Run far away and don't look back.*

From the nightmares. From him.

The man of shadows, the name called out just as Suzanne had told her all those years ago.

Avril wandered toward the living room as she decided, staring down at her bare feet as she walked farther inward, back toward the study. Classics and textbooks sat on top, but near the bottom, book club top picks and best sellers also were stacked with bent edges.

Avril let the pages of books run through her fingers, walking back out with the less common romance novel, fitted with a swooning woman on the cover in a regency gown and all.

Throwing away the sheet over the divan in the corner, Avril carefully sat on the edge. The crushed fabric bent underneath her, cradling her body and spine as she leaned back. If she shut her eyes and curled up, maybe she could fall asleep.

But of course, that wasn't what she wanted. Or perhaps she wasn't even sure what that was after so long.

She turned to the first page and blinked until her eyes cleared enough to see the first words on the page. She traced her fingers over the crisp piece of paper, worn from others turning it.

Or one person many times.

Though it didn't start with *once upon a time*, Avril could almost imagine her mother telling her the story like she always used to after she'd woken up from her nightmares as a child, though they had taken different forms. Monsters were in the closet back then. Nights would envelop her whole.

Once upon a time, her mother would always begin, like a fairy tale, though neither of them knew any.

———

AVRIL WAS STILL READING by the time the stairs groaned under steady weight.

"I never took you for a bodice-ripper fan."

Ian quickly glanced between her and the book. "I'm not."

Good. At least he wasn't a terrible liar.

"About last night," Avril peeked over the top of her page, noting the slow gait in his step as he headed toward the kitchen.

His bed head carefully sculpted to the side.

"We don't speak of it. Ever."

He nodded again, as simply as he had when he came downstairs, seeing her still there, as if he hadn't been sure if she would be.

She hadn't been either.

Returning from the kitchen moments later, Ian held a second ceramic mug, along with his own. He set it with a clink on the wood table next to her. "Already forgotten."

CHAPTER SIXTEEN

*R*eed must've forgotten to turn out the lights before he left. Maybe he'd thought that she would have been back here at some point in the past few days to turn them off. Instead, of course, she'd been living in Ian's oversize clothing to paint in while he was at work.

Still, the house was left clean yet. Shoes seamlessly lined up by the door. Coffee table was, well, mostly clear. The Christmas tree, however, was up. She didn't remember it being put together in the corner before she left.

Branches were spun in the gaudiest tinsel and antique ornaments she and Reed had found one of their first Christmases in the city. They'd had a cactus for a while, which they'd draped in fairy lights, but that had quickly died that year after Reed overwatered it. The next, they bought a real tree off the side of the road. It, too, withered, scattering needles, which they tracked all over the place because Avril never realized they were supposed to be watering it at all.

The artificial silver tree was the only compromise they could make after their many holiday disasters. Reed decorated it with increased care while aggressively spirited music blared throughout the townhouse at the same time Avril sang along off-key in the kitchen, where she attempted whatever new sweet recipe she'd found online.

No matter if it was cookies or babka, it usually came out underdone and in the form of a delicious, chocolaty goo. She and Jack devoured it anyway.

Jack was almost always in the house around the holidays. He lived in the guest room whenever his yearly lease, shared by three other roommates, was up by December. He was still too afraid to go home to his family once they figured out what he did for a living, even after his sister-in-law sent him a Christmas card. He coped by waving Reed off as a fun sucker as he ate the dough off the beater, ignoring the warnings of salmonella.

Reed had rolled his eyes at the both of them as he decorated the tree though. He'd never let anyone else do it, barely conceding to letting Avril put on the star that had already been placed proudly on top.

Avril dropped her purse and leaned farther into the living room, listening. "Reed?"

The house remained silent, a stagnate buzzing noise she had only just gotten used to over the past few days, working alone in Ian's house. When it started to unnerve her, Avril ended up finding some speakers in another box Ian had left in the study and let whatever was on shuffle stream through the house.

Ian was not a fan of Avril's choice of full and heavy rock music that it usually got around to by the time he came back through the front door. She couldn't help but notice, however, that he knew all the words.

He'd also gotten really tired of Avril borrowing most of his clothes and toiletry items, even though he wouldn't say so.

As she made her way upstairs, it sounded just as quiet, even as she waded through her room, still in disarray toward her wardrobe. Yanking the doors open, she reached below for her deflated duffel bags.

She dragged things off hangers and out of drawers, one by one. Underwear, deodorant, and the rest of her skin care were stuffed to the bottom. She also had to make sure that she had something suitable—as Ian would put it—even holiday-worthy, if Ian still planned to go to whatever party Mr. Sourpuss had been invited to tonight.

She fished out a few other dresses and stockings to carefully lay on top.

Walking over to the other side of the room, she yanked the window shade up to shed some light onto the lid of her jewelry box. She needed earrings or something, though she doubted Ian would appreciate her jingling with her red and green bell drops she had been gifted from...stars, she didn't even know anymore. Someone who hadn't understood her taste or the likelihood of daily annoyance.

She remembered wearing them until after January on principle.

Avril paused. Three jewel-encrusted brooches sparkled up at her.

There had been four antique pins before. Kit probably still had the other Avril had thrown at her at the beginning of last year, white gold spun around amethyst. Beating hearts.

"For protection and inner strength," Avril's mother instructed her when she found the brooches the first time, hidden in the far back of her drawer.

"Emerald is for balance and emotional stability. Ruby, passion and power. And diamonds are filled with the potential of inspiration and love ... and they're pretty." Her mother had giggled, covering her mouth with the side of her hand.

They were the only things her mother had ever taken from her own past life when she ran away from home, Avril eventually found out. Avril had been letting the dainty trinkets tag along with her in much the same way, though she had never seen her mother wear them.

That was part of the reason Avril had done so often when she first made it to Ashton, much like Ian and his golden ring.

Maybe that was her first mistake.

Scooping them up, sharp edges digging into her palms, she wrapped them in one of her T-shirts. They bounced to the bottom of her bag.

Before she could change her mind, Avril zipped up the overflowing overnight bags up and stepped into the hallway to head back down the steps.

Someone stood in front of her.

"Fuck, Dixon! You scared the shit out of me!" Avril slammed her hand onto her chest. Her heart was still there, still beating.

"I'm sorry. I should have said something before."

"You think?" Closing her eyes, she took another deep breath.

When she opened them again though, there, Reed's mousy-haired pet was still standing with a slightly nervous look on his face. He looked like he was debating whether or not to bolt.

"Is there a reason you almost gave me a heart attack?"

"I didn't mean to."

"I hope not. Reed isn't here."

"I know. He said I could stay here for a while. If that isn't okay—"

Avril waved him off. There went the mystery of the lights. "It's fine."

"He said that you probably wouldn't be around, but…" Dixon paused, trying to find something else to say. It was only then that Avril realized that he was standing out of Reed's bedroom door.

Avril wet her lips with her tongue, trying not to display the shock on her face but it cracked through her voice instead. "Are you two…"

He pushed up his round wire frames. "I'm not supposed to—"

"Are you two fucking again?"

He froze before he at last nodded.

"Since when?"

"He told me not to say anything."

"What?" Avril couldn't believe this. "Why not?"

To that, Dixon said nothing, but this was no time to start following the rules Reed had laid out all of a sudden.

"Dix, has he been here, with you, in the past week?"

The tree was put up. House had been kept clean. The phone call Reed had had the other morning that he quickly hit the End button to when he noticed Avril standing in the doorway...

It was all coming together.

How could he have kept something like this from her?

She asked Dixon as much by the time they made their way downstairs. She shut the door to her bedroom behind them both.

Dixon looped her second bag over his shoulder and carried it down like the gentleman he was. He set it on the floor next to the table. Even the kitchen was suddenly very well stocked now that he was here. It was one thing for Reed to insinuate that he'd figured Avril was going to have another existential crisis and run off the moment he wasn't in town, but—but...

Avril looked up from her hands pressed against the cool granite countertop. "How long have you two been together?"

Dixon scraped his bottom lip with his teeth. "We started to see each other again, um, back in April."

"April," she breathed.

Avril had been gone by April, not long after her birthday, when Reed tried to hold her back from running away the first time. When she wandered off with no intention of setting a date to be back to the city, if ever, Avril didn't expect Reed to wait by the door. She didn't even expect him to look for her. He had known better than to after the years of spontaneous adventures and stories that made it back to him before she did. Yet for some reason, a weight settled in Avril's stomach at the fact that Reed hadn't.

It'd crossed her mind, after all, by the time she hit the bus station, that she could have asked him to tag along. But she knew that no matter what, at that time, he wouldn't have. He would have tried to take her home, wrapped up in one of his warmer, more seasonally appropriate coats, and tuck her into bed to rest, so he wouldn't have to worry about her and her back and what she planned to do next.

He'd made it about him. Avril sneered in her own mind at the fact. She gritted her teeth and thought, but never said it most of the time, that he had taken care of her. When she let him take care of her, not seeing any other option. Not seeing anything really at that point.

Not until she decided to do what she and her mother and what everyone around her, growing up in a dozen different homes, had said she was best at. She ran away.

So, Reed had run to Dixon.

For years, Reed and Dix had been an on-again, off-again thing, but the sadness in Dixon's eyes now held something else other than unrequited love. The moment his eyes collided with Avril in the hallway—

Avril groaned. "Stars, you guys are finally giving this an actual chance, aren't you?"

When he opened his mouth, all that escaped was a heavy sigh. Dixon nodded.

"But he didn't want you to tell me."

"It wasn't like that," said Dixon.

"Oh yeah, then what was it?" Avril asked. "Tell me, Dixon."

"He didn't want you to think that he wasn't focused on you."

"He was always focused on me."

That was the problem.

Dixon said nothing against the statement. They both leaned over the island, mainly so he didn't have to shout.

Dixon's soft-spoken tendencies were low and soothing. "You're not mad."

"No. Of course not." She was glad in a way, though her face certainly didn't say so right now. She had seen Reed so easily relax into Dixon's shoulder during game nights and summer holidays. "I wish he had said something. I would've…"

Dixon waited.

"I don't know."

"That's okay."

"It's not."

He really hadn't wanted her to know. Or had she just not noticed?

She lifted her head. "When he left for California, for all those trips last fall?"

Dixon's head dipped as she stared at those piano fingers that had entertained Orange County for the past three years after Reed broke up with him the first time.

"He was with you." Avril had to laugh at it, but it came out curdled. "Wow. I really am fucking blind, aren't I?"

"You've had other things to worry about."

Slowly, she turned her gaze back up to meet Dixon's. Those eyes that stuck to her like the sourest of honey. "He told you."

"He…" Dixon looked away as he thought about the right way to phrase whatever it was. "He needed to tell someone."

"Fuck." Avril curled her hand into a fist. She wanted to bring it back down, but she didn't. It was still sore from the past few days from holding a damn paint roller. Her thumb was still covered in a speckling of gray and dark forest green from the office that just wouldn't fade.

She ran a finger over it.

How could Reed?

She didn't care about Dixon, not really. But how could Reed have betrayed her trust?

He was the one who told her to be careful about things she shared with others, and now here he was, blurting out her secrets —her life—to whoever he cared to. At the very least, he could at least make it glow in thick printed letters on the headlines of every gossip blog.

Let her agent suck in the publicity she was probably dying for.

Then again, she had been stupid enough to believe Reed trusted her enough to keep house for a few weeks. To think that they were still close enough for him to tell her when he was finally going to give a chance to the love of his fucking life he'd kept throwing out the window every other year.

"I can't tell what you're thinking."

"That makes two of us."

"You seem better."

"I am." Avril's voice turned tense. "I actually have to go. I'll probably see you around. If you need anything, I'm sure Reed gave you my new number."

Debating, he nodded after a moment.

Always nodding. Always so soft and agreeable, Dixon. No wonder Reed had finally realized he needed to fall for him.

"Good."

Dixon reached out for her bag as Avril leaned to haul the light weight off the ground. "Let me help—"

"No, don't." Avril put up a hand as she swung her bag firmly over her shoulder. She took a step back toward the hall. "Don't tell him about this, all right? Just don't bring it up. It will be something of this past year to go how he wants it to. I'll wait for him to tell me."

Dixon cringed, unsure.

"Let him tell me."

If he ever did.

"Okay."

"I'm really happy for you two."

"Really?" A small smile puckered Dixon's lip.

Avril bit the inside of her cheek. "Really."

"Didn't anyone ever tell you that it's unbecoming to be a snoop?"

"Yes," Avril answered, looking back into the room where Ian stood for a moment.

She'd left open his top dresser drawer after she came back. She'd shoved over the shirts of his she'd been wearing of his all week, the room becoming communal with little conversation about it, considering he'd noticed Avril rarely stayed in bed long enough for him to get awkward at night. She wandered the halls instead in his oversize sweats.

Now, her own clothes were also available to her in that top drawer instead of just Ian's socks. Nothing beneath the socks.

"You might've said something about the sort many times recently since I've been here, enjoying your flair for cotton."

"So, really not only a snoop, but a thief as well."

Now he was getting it.

"I thought about finishing the one wall in the study," Avril said. Her hand flopped over the edge of the bathtub. She wore her own ripped, paint-covered jeans and another one of his white tees, also worse for wear than it had been when she arrived. With a deep breath, she sighed, sinking lower into the empty basin. "I didn't get that far. Good intentions and all."

"Did you get back from picking up your things?" Ian asked. He obviously was looking for a sign of how long she'd been in there.

Avril focused on her feet on the other end. "Sort of. I got distracted."

"What? Was someone there you hadn't expected to be?"

Avril twisted around with narrowed eyes. "Did you follow me?"

"Why would I …" Ian shook his head before his eyes could flare with confusion. "No. What are you doing in there though?"

"It's a nice tub."

Ian slowly walked into the bathroom. He kneeled down at the

side of the basin. "You know, when you get in a bathtub properly, there is usually water in it. Sometimes bubbles."

Avril glanced at him. Both of their faces seemed to be drawn at this point. She hadn't noticed that before. Still, Avril plastered on a winning smirk just for him. "See? I knew you could talk dirty."

"You look tired."

So did he. Neither of them had been getting much sleep the past few days, though not often for reasons worth Avril's favorite pastime of kissing and shouting it to the world. Ian had been slowly coming to terms with Avril's late-night jaunts up and down the staircase when she couldn't—wouldn't—sleep.

"Like I said, it was a rather busy morning."

He just stared at her, neither of them speaking.

The stretch of emptiness ran on for so long, shuttering between them in dark specks.

Avril shut her eyes so she wouldn't have to look at it. Anything.

"New rule."

"I thought the rest were mine," said Ian.

"New rule," she repeated without a single care. She'd make all the rules up as long as her head stopped doing whatever it was that it did when he stared at her. "Don't look at me like that."

"Look at you—"

"Concern. Pity. Worry for my perfectly A-OK peachy-keen well-being. All right? Wipe it off that serious face of yours and leave it at the recently reinstalled door. Which, if you are really trying to sell, you should probably paint it a different, ugly Pantone color and get some sort of quirky welcome mat while you're at it. Rich arm holders love that kind of charm when they have to be this close to their husband's battle ground uptown instead of an hour away in a nice suburb with Froyo instead of Starbucks on every street corner."

"A good tip," Ian said. "You said you designed a house like this before."

Her castle. She made no intonation for yes.

Her house with Reed was nothing like this place.

"Is something wrong?"

Such care. Such concern in his voice. She'd heard better from Dixon from walking into her own house.

"Nothing."

"You are a terrible liar."

"You're wrong."

"Where am I wrong?"

"I am an excellent liar."

"Really?"

"Exceptional," Avril snapped. "I've been lying to you all this time, haven't I?"

By the end of their time together, if things went as she'd planned according to their deal, he'd find out just how exceptional at it she was. He would eventually find out he was pretend dating or almost fucking a washed-up stripper who was going to disintegrate into nothing, just like her mother had. Just like everyone had looked at her and thought she would since she had been in school.

She wasn't anyone's cup of tea anymore. Not even her own.

Ian obviously wasn't ready to figure it all out now, clearly.

Clenching his jaw, he stood up from where he'd squatted in front of her. With slow steps, as if he was deciding whether to turn back, to say something, he made his way back to the door leading through to his bedroom.

All work and no play made Ian a very dull boy.

He cleared his throat. "I have to go."

"You have to go? Now?"

"Yes."

"Why?"

"Why?" Ian asked as if it was the most ridiculous question asked all day.

She was pretty sure he'd won that contest if he thought she would've answered where she had been, who she had been with, why her fucking life was just getting better and better. She was already letting him know too much. Even her clothes that she'd packed, she realized, if he had any care in the world, they would've been a dead giveaway that she wasn't likely some laid-off sales associate at a local boutique downtown or whoever he thought she was. Might've been.

"I have to go see someone. Do things. I can't just sit in a bathtub all day."

Avril huffed yet made no effort to move. "Oh, yes, go to see your mysterious friends that you don't talk about in the city you despise, I'm sure."

He gripped the doorway and stayed silent.

"You have something you want to say?" Avril asked.

With a dark smile, he shook his head. "No. I don't."

"No. Please, go on. Tell me why you are in such a fucking pleasant mood too. What, is it *shit on me* day?"

Without a pause, Ian pushed back through into the bathroom. Only a step, but the solid vigor made any other sharp words die on her lips as Ian looked at her. A hand went out to his side, grasping for something. Words likely. The other went to that hair of his. That fucking gorgeous hair that Avril still wouldn't—couldn't—touch.

"Look."

What else was she doing? She let her hands fly out to either side of her, too, mimicking him. She was looking.

"I'm sure it comes as a shock to you, but the entire fucking world does not revolve around you."

She had never heard him swear before, and for some reason, Avril wasn't sure she liked it. It caught her attention, and her mouth turned dry as he stared at her with cloudy, dark eyes.

He looked like he was about to say something else, take it back, but instead, all Ian did was turn around and stalk out of the bathroom without a single syllable. His footsteps pounded quickly down the stairs of the house, echoing in the empty spaces. The front door slammed behind him.

Turning her head down into fisted hands, Avril screamed.

The sound in the claw-foot tub resounded.

CHAPTER SEVENTEEN

*A*vril waited for him to come back.

He had to show back up at some point, even though she wasn't sure what she planned to say when he did. Nothing? Tease him for probably having no actual life? Right now, he was probably wandering around the city, like a well-dressed hobo with no place to go, just as nervous as she was about what they would do when they faced each other.

She was nervous.

No, that wasn't right.

If anything, she was mildly distressed as she paced. Her pair of thick socks slipped back and forth over the freshly waxed floor. She slid from the entry to the kitchen, now inset with countertops, before turning back around to the fireplace. There was no point in actually getting dressed in the outfit she'd brought from the townhouse yet if Ian was going to be dramatic and pull an all-evening disappearing act.

They were already late for whatever holiday get-together Ian had mentioned the other day.

He couldn't have just left her alone in the empty bathtub for fifteen minutes, could he? If he had, well, she would still probably be in a piss-ass mood, but she might not have directed it at him.

Not right away anyway.

To occupy herself, Avril sorted the few pieces of mail Dixon had made sure she took with her before she left. Shoved along the inside of her now-emptied duffel bag was a fan letter, dated about a month ago; a credit card application; and a blank letter of somewhat. It was addressed only to the current owner.

Avril ditched all the flimsy correspondence in the kitchen bin along with coupons to the makeup counter. There was only one envelope she paused over.

The card stock was thick and lined with black-and-white roses.

She'd jokingly asked Kit if she was going to be invited to the wedding, and now, here was the proof of it. In her hands was Avril's very own wedding invitation, printed on sleek card stock, asking her to come celebrate the small affair of Kit and Jack's big day on the first day of spring.

The people she'd decided somehow were her best friends were getting married.

Guessed she didn't have all that many to pick through these days.

So she wouldn't forget to fill out the RSVP, knowing that she would be there somehow even if the cursive note filled her with nothing but a new layer of sickness coating her stomach, Avril stuck it to the fridge. On Ian's new fridge calendar, she counted how many days she had to put it off until it was due. He'd posted the printout a few days ago to mark his hours he'd be at work, so she would know when he'd be back.

Twisting out of the kitchen once more, Avril truly started to pace.

When Ian sold this place, it was unlikely that the study would stay as its intended purpose. It was a sort of medieval man cave, and she found herself drawn to the room when she wasn't sure what else to do, like now. The space would likely be rearranged into a children's playroom or a sitting area, where a family would pull away the curtains and let the sun stream in from the backyard. A plot beside the fence, dripping with wild vines, would be perfect for a garden if anyone had a green thumb.

The desk was still covered with paperwork and folders though. Ian's degrees, with line after line of concentrations and honors, were still stuck in their fancy padded folders. Avril always thought those things were only decoration. Now, she could only imagine Ian in some ridiculous, poofy hat, like a court fool at graduation. A dozen multicolored tassels would weigh his shoulders for good measure and academic morality.

"Nerd."

A nerd with a penchant for dirty novels, which she had been excited for each time she found over the past week of procrastinating any task he'd left her with. She nearly always managed to trick him into telling her the endings because she knew that he knew exactly what they were.

Nonetheless, she still read them each night. Her latest floppy paperback sitting on the built-in bookshelf was left upside down, so she wouldn't lose her place. Other pages were dog-eared as well, the perfect parts to read aloud to Ian's deaf ears until they turned a shade of crimson.

It was a surprisingly becoming color on him.

The last book she'd finished was good, though it'd had a sad ending. A happily ever after, sure, but Avril couldn't help but think there was also something else behind the conclusion. A *for now*.

Avril stared back down at the diplomas.

She hoped when she peeked underneath the three of them, she would also find a photograph. Instead, a blue folder was bent at the corner.

Lifting her head, Avril glanced toward the front door, but no sounds came from anywhere in the house to interrupt her continued snooping. No doorknob creaked or front porch ached under the pressure of impending company.

The sharp edge sliced through her finger as she opened it with a hiss. She stuck the paper cut in her mouth, but it didn't deter her as she read the heading of the document through her glare.

The last will and testament of Vivian Louise.

Avril paused, looking up again as if she would be caught, but still, no one was there.

She read on. It was a short note, single-spaced, that barely took up a page and a half. She'd left whatever she had in her life to Ian, which wasn't much, but each word laid out the terms clearly. Whatever money. Whatever items of worth.

It all went to one person. Ian Whitlock.

He had no middle name. Only one.

There was an amended section—added by Ian's father, Avril assumed—near the bottom. It was an insubstantial footnote she'd almost skipped over. But there it was in print, leaving him the house in Ashton. Behind the will was the death certificate, notarized on the border of California and Arizona.

Avril traced over the flat printed date, copied in a lawyer's slanted hand, before closing the folder back up. She moved everything right back to its proper place and grabbed her jacket as she headed out the door, where the cold air seeped into her bones and whisked the air in her lungs.

It could be as if she had never been there at all.

THE BUSES WEREN'T RUNNING, especially not on the residential side of town. The snow came down thick and wet. Flakes melted against Avril's jacket. She buttoned it up as far as it would go to her neck, and she made it down the street and through the park, where the bustle of decorating one of the large trees still rooted in the ground took place. People giggled, tugging knitted caps over the ears of children, who threw snowballs at one another. They disintegrated into cold air before making contact.

Avril tucked her nose farther down into the thick wool fabric of her scarf—Ian's scarf that she'd grabbed off the hook without thinking. She couldn't remember a December as cold as this year, but the red and green lights made her keep walking even if it wasn't to the kids singing "Jingle Bells" in a loop.

Avril knew Ashton better than she knew most things or people in her life. She knew where the best coffee was and the best place to scour for designer vintage. She knew where the best views were and where the bartenders didn't measure out their shots when they poured a drink.

And once she had seen the address lying on the desk, the date, she knew exactly where Ian was.

She twisted her arms over one another, close to her body, to keep the heat that seemed to have already left her completely as her boots crunched over the thin layer of snow while she passed through the open gate and around the twisted white trunk of a tree. Its roots lifted the stones around it, trying to find room to grow, to stretch.

Avril stood next to the tree as she looked over the embankment toward the edge of the cemetery near the stone mausoleum.

There was a man of shadows there.

He knelt at a grave.

CHAPTER EIGHTEEN

*J*an kneeled in the grass, knees broken from frost. His long legs seemed to indent the ground before becoming part of the earth. He must've been there for a while, just staring, unsure exactly what to do.

So, he did nothing.

He sat. He stared. At some point, his fingers traced the pressed letters of his mother's name against the headstone, no longer sheen like the rest around them in a hazy, snow-covered fog.

The metal fence whined shut, rocking on its hinge.

A ghost of a breath escaped him, hollowing his body, as if he knew exactly who was behind him without even having to turn. Avril never thought of herself as having heavy footsteps, but she could hear each one as she trudged through the light layer of snow.

"I never understood why she was buried here," his voice croaked.

Avril took another step forward toward his back, only slightly hunched, unwilling to give in to less than mostly perfectionism.

She, on the other hand, still stayed a few inches away on his right, staring at the date he'd left covered in flakes.

Vivian Louise.

She didn't have a last name. She was thirty-five.

"She grew up west of here. Her parents emigrated from somewhere in the Middle East. She didn't even remember. I never knew what had happened to them, but I always thought, growing up, that eventually, she would go back home even if it was to be buried there. But there wasn't one for my mother. Home," Ian repeated the word.

"Sometimes," Avril whispered, thinking about the similar words she'd spoken when she first entered Ian's house, looking at the beams and arches in awe, "some people never have a home. Not exactly."

"Her parents were gone, I found out eventually, or I was told. They died or dropped her off somewhere when they could no longer care for her, thinking someone else would. She'd been making her way on her own for most of her life."

The cold seeped through Avril's jeans that she'd slipped on before walking out in sweatpants. Cold melted right behind where her joints bent. Unable to keep herself above snow level, Avril let herself soften into it. When she sat like this, her back didn't protest any louder than the sturdy cadence of Ian's voice.

"Until, of course, she met my father. Me. I guess he still loved her on some sort of level." Ian glanced up at Avril, as if still somehow surprised that she was sitting in the snow next to him. "To bring her all the way back here."

Avril ran her tongue over her lips, though she knew that they'd crack. "I didn't know."

Ian shook his head. "It's the first time I've actually been here to visit the grave on the day she died. I never could bring myself for some reason. Ashton, whenever I even thought about it, gave me this feeling."

That Ashton was the place where everything would change.

When he closed his eyes, Avril couldn't mistake the saltwater tracks that had begun to dry down his face. A fresh tear only made it down from the corner of his eye before Avril couldn't help herself. Leaning forward, she was done waiting for a sign or letting another stupid question pass in front of her.

Another regret when she used to say she regretted nothing.

She caught the tear with her lips, swiping it away in perhaps the first movement Avril had ever made that could be described as soft.

He didn't jerk away from her. Slowly, he only turned to stare at her with wide, unreadable eyes. He stared at her as if he had no idea who was sitting next to him.

And he didn't.

That was what Avril had told him earlier, after all, wasn't it?

His chest heaved with another harsh breath, filling before letting it come back out. His hand reached out for her own, still digging itself its own igloo trench in the snow.

Forcing herself not to flinch back, she let him take it.

"It's cold."

Avril sniffed, trying to smile even though she knew it wouldn't help as the snow continued to fall. And she didn't feel like smiling anyway. It had been a long time since she was at all in the snow like this. Letting it burn and not care. Her first years in Ashton, the first years she'd met Jack, he'd make everyone who was in the house at that point run out to the backyard one morning, still in pajamas, to make snow angels.

When she looked around, it was only then that Avril realized that they weren't the only ones in the cemetery. Another shadow out of the corner of her eye bent down to place a poinsettia atop a flat stone.

"I know how we can fix that," Avril offered. "Are you ready?"

Clenching his mouth shut, he nodded and stood, brushing himself off before helping her to do the same. His hand slid over her hip. A chunk of slush fell to the ground. "I'm ready."

CHAPTER NINETEEN

*S*he didn't lead him back the same way they had come. He was still holding her hand, however, as she led him farther into Ashton. Lights glowed brighter as exposed balconies competed in a contest of glimmering lights.

He didn't try to correct her if they were going in the right direction. He only followed. This sort of silence was different from the others that they'd shared, usually out of frustration or anger or a test to see who couldn't help themselves but talk to the other first.

It was the only game Avril could admit to herself that he won.

This time, Ian's eyes trailed along the sights until she stopped before the wide door's alcove.

Looking down at their hands, carefully, she slid hers away.

"Stay here or come in. Warm up. I'll be right back."

The warmth of Keys dripped into her muscles from the moment the bell above the door chimed. The place hummed with voices of students still awake, laced with exhausted laughter. Syllabi had been ripped and tossed into the recycling bin next to the door until it overflowed.

Finals week was her only guess, and from the lack of coffee

mugs on the wall and live entertainment up on the stage, she'd be right.

"A special. Two big-ass cups of hot chocolate, too, to go," Avril ordered at the counter, disrupting a rather tired-looking employee from her copy of *Anna Karenina*.

Bending over the page, she stood up with the speed of a snail. "You mean a large?"

With her plastic tongs, she placed two bite-sized biscuits inside a white paper bag.

Avril gave the girl a look that would cause mountains to fall. "I mean, *big ass*. Load that bag up, sweetheart."

When she turned around, Ian stood near the doorway, stepping out of the direction of bug-eyed students packing up their backpacks decorated with enamel pins. His hands delved into his pockets as he looked around. His attention focused on her.

"Give her a few extra too."

The robust, slightly lumberjack figure of Marley pushed past the curtain leading to the mysterious back room of Keys. "Emergency?"

"Something like that."

He chortled down to himself and grabbed the large cups, the ones with the extra-wide rims, off the top of the espresso machine. "Good to see you again. See, you didn't lie about coming back to see me this time. I'm glad. Just earlier, your other two were in here."

Avril quickly glanced around the space, air caught on something in her chest.

"You probably just missed them."

"Well …" Avril forced herself not to sigh in relief. She reached to grab the generic white paper bag away from the cashier, who stared at her sugar-filled order with questioning eyes. Had she never seen an art student in need of a sugar high before? "Maybe next time."

"He seemed a tad shocked when he heard that I had seen you."

Avril's eyes locked on Marley. "He did?"

"Looked kind of broken up about it actually."

Avril slid tall cups he'd topped with whipped cream and lids across the counter. The heat seeped through the cardboard. "Thanks, Marley."

He stopped, holding on to the top of one of the cups before she could flee. "You should call him, you know."

Biting the side of her tongue, she knew. Avril was about to tell Marley just how much she knew, emotion rising in her throat. Yes, she should probably call Jack or go see him, but the temper in her system was still lingering from earlier, sharpening her forgiving edges back to points.

Again, she gave the slightest tip of her chin. "Thanks."

"Have a good night."

Clutching her to-go order, Avril maneuvered around a couple waiting in line against the couch and extended her left hand to Ian. He took the cup from her, holding open the door leading back to the cold. She barely had to duck, going under his arm.

She looked back and forth from the honking horns up the road as the light turned from yellow to red before twisting back to Ian.

He continued to stand, watching her. "Now, what are you planning?"

"We are going home for you to wallow."

He didn't comment.

She shook the bag as she took a step back toward the street. "I have cookies."

A sprinkle slowly fell from the bottom.

Ian looked up at the sign that swayed above the large bay window. "That place."

"Keys," Avril informed him. "It's a student hot spot. They have great drinks though. Marley doesn't kick you out if you fall asleep on the couch during *Jeopardy* night either."

"I like *Jeopardy*," Ian said.

He ceased to surprise her.

"Of course you do."

"What did that man inside mean by your other two? Were you supposed to meet someone this evening?"

"Besides you? Absolutely not."

Ian didn't quite look convinced by her bravado.

"Unlike you, darling, I do have friends." Or had them. If she had found Ian much earlier, she knew that there would have been almost no helping that she would come face-to-face with Jack. And with Jack, everything else. There would have been no going back. She swallowed. "But like I said, I'm trying to separate myself this month. Holiday stress and all that."

When she threw up a hand, a cab immediately flipped its light in front of them. The bite in the air was already beginning to dig through her coat and skin. Screw the affordable metro.

She opened the door and slid across the seat.

"I got it," Avril said as Ian ducked under the ceiling with her.

She swiped her card with little care on the machine so that they wouldn't have to worry about it when they got back to the house. She was hoping to be heavy and warm with at least three cookies in her by then.

"It must be exhausting," Ian murmured.

"What?"

"Putting on that mask all the time."

Avril's eyes shifted. "There is no mask."

"If you say so."

"I am very honest with how I present myself. Pure of heart." She dropped the white bag into his lap, and she reached to slam the door he hadn't yet closed, cold air rushing in.

"This stuff is—"

"Exactly what you need in your life right now?" Avril held up an oatmeal chip cookie from the bag as the driver pulled back out onto the road, the steady sound of music and scraping windshield wipers floating around him.

Ian looked like an oatmeal guy, and when he plucked it from her fingers, she smiled in triumph. "Exactly. Drink from the cup."

Pausing, if only to retaliate for a second, Ian lifted the to-go cup to his lips. Pulling it back down, he looked at the lid for a long second.

"What did you expect, a shot of rum?"

Ian smirked. Her plan was already working.

Gorge him with comfort until he smiled at her again, even if it was sardonic enough to make her question her intelligence on a universal level. Until he never looked at her with that distaste he'd had in the bathroom earlier, leaving her to stew in an empty tub for too long before she realized he wasn't going to return to apologize or pull her from over the edge to sit on the more comfortable bathmat that had cushioned her feet.

"I expect nothing but the unexpected. Hot chocolate."

"Best in town."

She took a sip of her own, recoiling when it burned her tongue. "I just hope you don't have an aversion to marshmallows. Marley always adds a few extra when I order it."

"Why's that?"

"Hot chocolate usually means emotional crisis. And what is hot chocolate if not consolation? Plus, he likes me, so …"

"He likes you?" Ian asked, as if there had to be something else going on.

But Avril only shrugged and reached her hand in the bag, feeling around for something sweet and frosted. "Who doesn't?"

"I think there must be a line started somewhere."

"Look at you, trying to be funny," said Avril. "In case you haven't noticed just yet, I am full of never-ending talent that people like to have around."

"Is that right?"

"I'm very charming for one thing."

Ian narrowed his eyes.

"I'm an amazing dance partner. Always know where the good parties are. Also, one of the best travel buddies you can have."

"What? You don't get jet lag?" Ian asked, already slightly impressed.

"Oh, no," Avril corrected. "I get that terribly. But I can get you to the hotel and call up room service to order you a gin and tonic in at least eight different languages. See? I impress you."

"What languages?"

"We're back at the house," Avril said, reaching over his lap to the door. She pushed Ian onto the sidewalk.

He was obviously still waiting for his answer as he stumbled all the way up the steps and inside, where they both began to shuck off their damp coats.

Avril started yanking down her pants to throw them straight into the dryer.

"What are you doing?" Ian put a hand up, as if that would stop her.

If anything, it would only impede his view.

"I sleep without pants almost every night, and now, you have a prude problem?" Avril shook her head as she yanked her pants the rest of the way off. Maybe Kit was right about not wearing them often. They *were* like boa constrictors for your legs. "I'm wet and freezing. I think this is actually the moment where you cloak my body in yours and offer to warm me like an innocent deb on her wedding night, Ian."

"Go get changed."

"I'm taking the cookies with me."

"If you get crumbs on my bed," Ian warned, already following.

She dropped the paper bag on the duvet.

There was a grumble behind her, but she didn't look back as she tugged out the drawer of her clothing, pulling on layer after layer over chilled skin.

"So, tell me."

"What?" Avril teased, knowing exactly what he was talking about. Very one-track mind.

He leaned against the wall at the head of the bed. He changed into comfortable clothes as well. They hung off him when he stretched. How long must he have stared at her, waiting for her to turn around as she brushed through her thick hair with only her fingers? Must've been a while.

She pretended not to notice as she took inventory of the bag still sitting where she'd left it. She ripped the paper flat for a makeshift plate.

"The languages you know."

"Plan on taking me to Brazil and challenging me to order you a whiskey ginger?"

Swallowing, Avril debated lying to him. Crawling across the bed—if there was ever a time where she could divert him, tonight would be it—she wasn't sure that he would stop her from her slow seduction.

They both had things they wanted to forget.

Masks that took time and care to plaster on after they'd been so quickly stripped.

Avril was still sure she had enough of hers still on as she slid the paper-bag plate between the them. She lifted a non-fun plain cookie up like a sacrifice, offering it to him. He could at least pretend to enjoy her picnic of sugar and—nope, mostly sugar.

He accepted, extending his long legs out with a sigh. His thick wool sock hung off the side.

"The first language I ever learned, only in pieces, was a cheap form of Gaelic. My mother, as we've previously discussed, was Irish. Thus, the hair."

"The accent."

Avril hummed in assent. "When she died, I ended up living with a distant relative of sorts with the same heritage, same brogue. Honestly, he was probably the only reason I hung on to the twang."

"Was he kind?"

A low, humorless laugh rumbled through her. Or maybe it was sort of comical. "He yelled so often that I started to pick up the swear words I'd heard my mother use as well and then came the rest. He seemed to like me better some days when he was home. I understood him when he was drunk.

"Of course, without as much practice over the years, it turned pretty much into only comprehension. After that, in school, I took French and continued with it. I thought it was pretty. Someone once told me that French was the language of sex, and I liked that. It also helped soften out my accent that I was already getting skilled at covering," Avril explained rather quickly. "People have a tendency to look down on people they can't understand as easily as themselves. So then, I decided to try my hand at a little Italian. A bit of Spanish and German. Though in Amsterdam, they spoke English mainly anyway. Also, Czech."

"Czech?" Ian raised his eyebrows at the statement.

"I'm not fluent," Avril said. She wouldn't classify herself as such for any of them.

As she talked, she finally decided on which cookie she wanted next—a lopsided reindeer that looked more like an alpaca if any four-legged creature.

Ian handed her cup over from where it sat on the floor next to him. She took a large gulp to wash her large bite of baked good down.

"I had a lot of free time in Prague once and took a library workbook from the shelves. I never did return it. My mother would have been furious about that. She was always, if nothing else, diligent about library due dates."

"I know you mentioned that you and your mother didn't have the ideal relationship most do," said Ian.

"My mother."

"You don't have to talk about her yet, if you prefer."

Yet.

She shook her head. A veneer began to slip over her expression she tried to hide by focusing on her cookie. She dipped it into her hot chocolate. "My mother ... she killed herself."

Ian blinked. "I'm sorry."

"Don't be." Avril sighed, pulling her cookie back out. A crumb fell, plopping into the abyss. "It was sort of like she was dying all my life, and it wasn't her first attempt. She usually freaked out a little before the end, pulled back in time. Until, well, she couldn't. It was too late." Some pills just got a little too cozy after a bottle of tequila helped them go down.

"You were there?"

Avril chewed. "Sometimes, I don't know. I feel like she's haunting me, or whatever had haunted her, transferred to me when I was there that day. I think of it randomly sometimes." *See it.*

"You think you're cursed?" Ian smiled, as if that were the funniest thing he'd heard from her yet.

When he said it like that, it almost did seem ridiculous. Still, Avril blinked and could see the scene unfold behind her eyes, as if she'd never left that single moment fifteen years ago.

"Please." Light-green eyes stared into Avril's dark, glimmering emeralds.

Her mother clutched her throat, shoved her hand through her thin ginger hair.

Bile stuck to the corners of her mouth as she gasped and retched. No matter what she did or how far she slid her fingers down her throat, she couldn't bring back all the little green-blue pills she'd shoved down.

"I don't know what to do. Do something. Call someone. I don't know what to do!"

· · ·

AVRIL COULDN'T REMEMBER if she was the one who had made the call or if someone had simply heard her mother's screams. She simply sat there in the bathroom, counting tiles.

Her mother's body always covered half of one.

"You'd be surprised. I'm not sure if that helps you feel better or anything. To know that you aren't the only one who has lost a mother, I guess. No matter how long ago it was."

He nodded, though it was less assured than hers. "How old were you again?"

"Nine."

Ian stared at her for a long moment.

She shook her head, pulling away for the hot chocolate. Beside her cup on the floor were the tarot cards they'd played with the last time they sat across from each other so casually. She took a sip of her drink, and the sweetness coated her throat. Then, she started to shuffle.

Ian looked down at the cards but didn't stop her fidgeting.

"Go on now," said Avril. "I bared my soul. Your turn."

"My turn?"

"Yes, your turn. It's only fair. You are the unexpected man who nearly froze to death in a cemetery and all."

Ian shook his head with her, as if debating, and then stopped. "Okay."

A stillness settled over Avril. "I'm all ears."

"I was fifteen," Ian said. "We lived in California for a while, where it was warm. She said it helped her condition."

"What did she have?"

Ian's expression contorted. "I don't know. A kind of cancer, I imagine. There was never an autopsy done. Never anything done. It's the only thing that'd make sense unless it was something more involved with what she did while I was growing up to put food on the table and all. But like I said, I don't know. She never got it checked out."

"Why not?"

"For the longest time, she insisted on my father never helping us financially after we left. She got sicker, even as she tried to work. We went to the beach every day to watch the sun go down, and one day, she just couldn't get up."

Avril's eyebrow furrowed. "What did she do?"

"What do you mean?"

"To put food on the table. You said her illness could be related," Avril said.

"Right." Ian took a deep breath. His silver eyes catching on hers as some sort of connection. They reminded Avril of something. Someplace. "She was a prostitute. A companion of sorts."

The words settled into Avril. She waited for more.

"That's how she met my father. She told me that he picked her up one day, and they fell in love. She said it was meant to be. Of course, my father already had a wife at the time and kept my mother for a while. He was always kind to her, but eventually, I guess neither of them could handle each other or what they were. My mother left, and he didn't stop her. Or maybe he didn't know."

She ran, Avril heard herself think. The words rose from the shadows pooled between them.

"We lived here for a while." Ian looked up toward the ceiling. "He was the one who bought this house for us, just far enough away from his other family."

"And when she died? How did your father hear what happened?"

"It didn't take long for social services to find out who the guy on my birth certificate was. They said I was lucky to be going back to him. He even put me on a plane to get there and then another when he sent me off to boarding school. New girlfriends don't really appreciate a long-lost child of a dead lover showing up."

Avril tried to smile at his attempt at humor. "I always wanted to go to boarding school."

"Yeah?" The thought seemed to amuse him.

"Yeah," Avril said. "I always thought about the clean uniforms and how there must have been such interesting people there who could take care of themselves. I always wanted to meet the people who threw those big parties you always imagined, like in the movies. You'd dress up, and the next day, you'd barely remember what happened. All you'd know was that it was one of the best nights of your life."

Whimsy overtook their faces at the image.

"I always knew I could take care of myself by then, though I also probably would've been accused of violating that dress code once or twice. Starting a secret society. You know, just putting down my territory."

"I don't know what fifteen-year-old Ian would have done if he'd met fifteen-year-old you."

Avril at fifteen. She had basically already been living with a bushy-haired Reed and his family not long after that birthday rolled around. She had worn scuffed combat boots and ripped jeans. She'd hated school.

Still, somehow, she couldn't help herself but smile at Ian. "I'd have advised him to run."

He laughed, a deep hitch in a low rumble.

"I don't know though," Avril added without a thought. She let the image of a gawky, likely less assured Ian running amok through her head. He was all perfectly pressed in his button-down and school-issued tie.

She tapped the full deck of cards she was still moving through her fingers against her palm. "You probably would've turned into my Reed."

Ian noticed the sour taint that suddenly coated her friend's name. "Doesn't sound like such an honor anymore."

Avril huffed a single laugh. "When I ran home today, Reed was supposed to be in and out of town until Christmas. The house though, it wasn't empty."

"Someone was at your place?" Concern edged sharply into Ian's voice.

She waved him off, setting the cards beside her knee as she thought about the day's events. "Someone is almost always there. We've always had an open-door policy on our guest room, but it wasn't just anyone, and they weren't using the guest room."

Sorting through the cookies again, Ian handed Avril the last of the snickerdoodles.

Taking it, she smiled at the cinnamon sugar she licked off her thumb.

Ian watched the movement intently.

"Reed has a boyfriend," Avril explained. "Not just any boyfriend, but Dixon. This guy—they've been skittering around each other for years, as if it wasn't obvious that they were fucking. Anyway, they've been together since April."

"This is a bad thing?"

"I didn't even notice it. He didn't tell me. Maybe he just didn't want to. Or likely, he thought I wouldn't even care about whatever he did back then, which I wouldn't have. I wasn't here anyway at the time, which Dix so plainly laid out for me."

Snickerdoodle lodged in her throat.

"And he was," Avril finished. "It's stupid."

"If it matters to you, it's not stupid," Ian murmured.

"It is though. I've told Reed enough times to grow some fucking balls and do what he needs to do in his life, and now, he has. Like I said, it doesn't even matter. Maybe he's finally starting to see what I've seen this past year all along."

"What are you talking about?"

"I had a birthday this year," Avril said quickly, so her voice wouldn't crack. Too much sweet. Too much comfort. She would not cry. She did not cry. She swallowed as a compromise. "Obviously."

"Happy birthday."

Avril forced a smile before shaking her head.

"Not a birthday person? Consider me surprised."

Avril always loved birthdays, though he was right. Ever since she could celebrate them on her own, they'd become things she planned for. The more extravagant and gaudier, the better.

"My birthday was back in May. I left the city not long before. I needed some space…or something." It all didn't matter. She glanced up and saw exactly what she had known she would see in front of her.

Her eyes met those inky, dark shadows swirling everywhere on the only person she had left in front of her—from his loose shirt neck all the way to his hands. They looked like someone had drawn them. As if she had. They were exactly like the edges of the card in Suzanne's kitchen.

Avril glanced back at the foreboding tarot cards at her side. It was all just another sign of what she knew awaited her. At first, she denied what was coming for her as she fell deeper into her own personal well of shadows last year. Now, well, Avril still never did anything in peace.

"My mother died when she was twenty-four."

"And you're…" Understanding dawned on him.

"Set to go crazy just like her?" Avril gathered up the cards. What else was supposed to happen to an indelicate daughter who happily became a stripper as her calling? Her parents were an unknown and a fifteen-year-old runaway who somehow made it alive as long as she did. "The thought has crossed my mind."

"You know that doesn't mean anything."

"Doesn't it?" she asked.

Ian shook his head, a serious look on his face. "No."

"I have gray hairs at twenty-four." Avril tucked a few strands behind her ears. "What's the difference?"

"You dye it. You are not going to die."

"You sound so sure."

Severity coated him. "You should be."

That was the thing all along, and now, for some reason, she

wanted to prove it. She wanted to stare Ian in the eye and tell him that the shadows twisted like the most intricate of swirls, locking him inside. Yet he couldn't see them. No one but she could. At least here.

She was just like her mother.

For the first time, though, the statement sounded more like a question.

"No."

Avril blinked, focusing on him once more. "What?"

"That's it," Ian said. "No. You aren't going to die."

"You have some magical immortal power you haven't revealed until now?"

"No, I'm making it one of my rules. Avril, Rose"—Ian's tired gaze locked on hers—"you are not allowed to die. That's an order."

An order.

Not to die.

Someone had stolen a breath of air from her lungs. Saying nothing, Avril looked down and began to shuffle the cards in her hands again. She split the deck into three.

On impulse, Ian pointed to one and then the other.

She stacked them back together as such before pulling out the cards for him. They collided. They pulsed with prosperity and then confusion and hard work, but no reason to get there.

Avril's forehead wrinkled as she looked down at them.

Ian only stared, as if he wasn't surprised by whatever he saw.

"These make no sense together, really," Avril mumbled quickly. She pulled the cards back into her hands to shuffle again.

"My mom always said that when I wanted her to show me my cards."

"You could never get a clear guidance?"

Ian reached for another sugar cookie. "She would sometimes try and give me a reading anyway, but they always showed me what I knew instead of what I wanted to know. It never bothered me much. I've never been one for predestination or anything like that anyway."

That's not what the cards showed, Avril wanted to say. The words, though, felt like a lie to her now after this past year. She'd invested so much into them, needing to put faith into something.

Pausing her hands, she shoved the deck to Ian. "You do it. Just shuffle and pull a card."

He raised his eyebrows, but did as Avril instructed. Splitting it into three, he mixed the cards and then pulled a single one from the top.

Queen of Wands.

Avril pulled the next.

Avril peered at the King of Swords looking up at her. A strong card of decision. A card of clarity and compassion, but reversed, it was a card indicating a misuse of power and manipulation. So close to the Knight that slipped out of the deck.

Her hand shook. How had she not noticed before?

"Is this you?"

"Oh, I don't know." Ian stared down at the card. "Maybe. My mother told me she drew each card with a person or subject matter specifically in mind. She was working on this section when I was young. Probably why the edges are drawn in so dark."

"What do you mean?"

"I had a lot of nightmares as a kid."

Avril's mouth turned dry. "Nightmares. What about?"

"I can't remember them all. Most of them made no sense. I dreamed about the sky a lot, I remember. Drifting away upward until I couldn't see down. Probably why there are so many clouds." Ian flipped over the card for Avril to see again, but they weren't clouds swirling around the figure to Avril.

They were shadows.

"This card kind of looks like you too, doesn't it?" Ian chuckled, pointing to the Queen of Wands before leaning back against the headboard. "We really need sleep."

Avril's attention snapped to the card. A figure oozing confidence and determination sat upon a throne, head tilted up and a crown not quite centered on her head.

"Are you well?"

She couldn't take her eyes away from the card, even when he set it down among the others. She knew what she was seeing. Shadows, or maybe it was something else that swirled in her stomach, pulsing high and low in her chest until she tore her eyes away. "Course. Ian?"

"Yes—"

Before the word was fully out of his mouth, the cups and cookies between them were hastily set aside. On her knees, Avril leaned over him. She fisted his shirt and leaned close to his ear, so she was the only thing he could hear.

"Use me."

CHAPTER TWENTY

*S*he pressed herself farther into his body, slanting her lips over his. Without question, he reciprocated, tilting himself to gain leverage as his lips parted.

He breathed into her.

They were all hands as they roamed over each other, swiftly discarding their loose clothing they'd changed into from the snow. The tingling coldness in her fingers and knees disappeared completely. She was all fire.

Ian lit a match and watched her rage higher.

Tilting her head back, she gasped as his mouth trailed, biting her throat and letting his tongue create a line down the center of her chest, holding her so closely to him that she was no longer sure where she was touching and where he met her, overpowering her as he ravaged her body.

His mouth hovered low, heading to dip down before she tugged on his arms, bringing him back up to her mouth. Her teeth caught his lip as she grinned.

"Please." She was willing to beg at this point. She needed him. "Now."

He made a low sound into her ear as he twisted her around,

scraping down her spine before layering it with featherlight kisses.

Avril shook and was met with chuckles as a hand slipped between her legs, feeling her heat.

Maybe he wasn't just the casual librarian kinky. He was a sadist.

She was already ready for him as he poised himself behind her, over top of her.

"Wait."

Ian stopped. Not only did he stop, but he also started to push away.

She took a deep breath, reaching for his wrist. "Just not like that," Avril tried to explain.

But that was all she needed to say. Readjusting again, Ian gave a single nod as she rolled over, and as he leaned back in, he pulled her back on top of him.

"Better?"

Avril poised herself against him, pressing her hands against his chest. She grazed her thumbs over his nipples. Much better.

Thank you, she wanted to say.

She didn't, curving herself over him instead. She rolled her hips, sliding her wetness over him. She chuckled when his eyes rolled back. She brought her mouth back down to his skin, flushed with heat. He was so warm. Hot.

Her tongue ran up his chest and throat until that groan became a hiss.

Ian's hands gripped hard into her thighs as his cock jolted against her. "God."

"And the rest of them," she purred.

She wanted him, wanted him so hard that her bones shook as she took him back in her hand and positioned the tip of him against her. Heat slunk through her as she slowly lowered herself onto him, one inch at a time.

Ian's hand reached up to one side of her face. "Eyes on me."

Eyes on him. Eyes on his gray eyes that swirled like a trickster and lips lightly parted as they turned up to her with a sort of reverence. Eyes on him as she held him in her hand and slowly dipped, feeling the way he stretched her before she rose back up, only to lower again, taking him deeper.

Avril bit her lip as he slid farther into her. She watched as he trembled with need, trying not to grab her hips and bring her all the way down onto him in a single stroke.

He didn't move, eyes connected to hers as she gently shifted down on him. Her heart hammering in her chest. Eyes on him.

Him.

"Eyes on me."

Ian.

Avril blinked quickly as she focused on Ian, so big and lanky compared to her, now fully inside of her, so full that she couldn't breathe, so instead, she laughed. The two of them somehow fit together nearly perfectly. At the sound, Ian unleashed himself, swiping his hands up around her breasts, gripping her as she began to ride him.

A wide grin came with a sigh that hitched when she rolled her hips.

"That's my Rose."

She leaned down, and a pleasure-filled moan escaped her as she continued to move, getting a rhythm in her seat. Filled and stretched open in a way she hadn't been in so long, Avril held on to his shoulders, digging into the soft, malleable muscle across his stomach. She felt them ripple when he grunted, covering a gasp.

She ground down into him, thighs straining as she lifted and pressed deep onto Ian. She could feel him up to her stomach, pressure building as much as the heat swam through her veins, her bones, all while keeping her eyes on him.

"All eyes on you," Avril huffed. "I never pegged you as the vain one."

When he flipped her around, another cry of enjoyment burst from Avril's chest. Ian chuckled, baring his teeth as he grinned at her before capturing the sound with his mouth.

He gripped her hips, lifting up into her faster. The way Ian fucked her, he must've been waiting to, wanting to, as long as she had since the moment they'd gotten back to the house. From the second they'd noticed each other in the cemetery, he could have shoved her down into the patch of snow and gotten to work. Or it sure felt like it.

From the first time she'd laid eyes on him.

Or rather, his lips.

Unable to take it any longer, with a swift and unforgiving thrust, he pushed inside her.

Avril was nudged back into the bed from the pressure, but he was there still to meet her, driving into her again and again with a groan, harder each time.

Mouth open, Avril swore she saw stars.

He bit her neck and the space right below her breasts he'd moments ago treated so tenderly. Noises climbed up her throat, thick and low, that collided with heavy pants. Hips met each of his thrusts as they came down on her over and over again while his thumb found the place above, where she watched him before meeting his eyes once more.

No, they were never gray. Silver. The most stunning metallic, purer than gold. More heart-stopping than strips of shadow.

Avril felt the pressure burning in her hips as she curled up to his chest, twisting as she cried out.

He kept thrusting as he bit into her one last time, and their heartbeats synced for one moment, as if he were sucking out her soul.

Perhaps he was.

Maybe she'd let him as long as he shared whatever he found in the space it held.

"Dear Lord," Ian gasped, similar to her own sentiments that

she managed to keep in her head as she gulped down a fresh breath of air into her lungs, her brain.

When he pulled out of her, Avril immediately felt empty and damp from the sweat that coated her.

"Sex fixes everything," Avril said with a deep breath. Almost everything, at least. "It's basically magic."

"Magic?" Jaw set, Ian reached out to push a curl away from her eyes.

She shrugged. "There is so little in the world. A good orgasm has to be some kind."

"Be quiet."

Avril barked a laugh. "Only for you, darling."

She stared up at the ceiling.

"Ian?"

His mumble turned into a deep breath low in his chest.

Turning, she stared at how his lashes settled over his cheeks. She was a little tired herself for once. Instead of rolling over toward the edge of the bed, Avril curled in, wrapping her arm around her pillow.

She shut her eyes. "Night, Ian."

CHAPTER TWENTY-ONE

*A*vril never thought she would ever get to wear the dress.

She had seen it the moment she opened her package from Kit's shop. Along with her usual essentials, her friend had layered her up with extra pieces of lingerie, and at the bottom was a single dress. When she opened the smooth fabric in her hands, the dress unfurled off the hanger, and a slip of paper lightly danced its way to the ground.

Swiping the slip up, Avril narrowed her eyes at the final piece of her package.

I still have your corset ready.

Staring at the notecard, Avril blinked before tossing it aside. She hadn't needed to wear a corset in a long time, at least not the exquisite detail-filled ones Kit and her aunt used to make for her.

Funny to think of Kit dressing her now. When she'd met the timid seamstress, she had been too nervous to put together an outfit that fit, for fear someone would dare give her a second look, even if her style was more pinup than femme fatale.

The dress was neither sexy enough for her to wear to event nor sweet enough for any other day when, most recently, she had been in jeans and one of Ian's old shirts before both articles were suddenly discarded to the floor of the kitchen after insisting the new granite countertop was in need of christening. It certainly wasn't the most expensive dress she'd ever put on, but now, as she stared at the hanger hanging on the back of Ian's bathroom, Avril touched the sleek hem with reverence. She hadn't worn something so extravagant in a long time.

After getting dressed one layer at a time for the night out, Avril started with makeup. She drew each line and splash of color across her skin like painting, smooth and precise. Freckles popped through on her cheeks.

She slipped into each separate piece of lingerie Kit had added into her simple undergarment purchase, thinking she was sneaky. Each segment of lace fit her perfectly as the deep color—not quite black, but also not bright enough to be a royal purple—curved over all the edges she once remembered.

The more she added, the more herself she felt. Avril twisted in the mirror to see herself better and snap garter to stocking. Once upon a time, when she had taken her time to get dressed like this, Avril would be preparing for something grander—like when a layer or two came off and all that was left was the moment where all eyes would be on her.

Tonight, no one's eyes would be on her.

They would be on the stage.

It was apt, all the better. Avril finished up her final touches. She flipped her hair upside down. Untamable curls bounced before she clipped and twisted them up into a coiffure at the back of her head. She looped a string of pearls around her neck, and as she reached for a bracelet out of her bag, she hesitated.

A jewel glimmered there.

Reaching for it, Avril held one of her mother's brooches in her hand. At first, she'd thought it was the ruby, bound in pewter. She always seemed to draw it when she wasn't looking while getting dressed.

But Avril stared at diamonds. Each was clear and cut to catch candlelight rather than fluorescents.

Piling up the long skirt in her hands that fluttered below her knees, Avril hitched the fabric up until it was near her hips. Carefully, Avril clipped the diamond pin into her garter belt just so.

So it wouldn't pull. So it would be there, just for her to know it was.

The soft fabric fell back down where it was supposed to be, and Avril looked up again into the mirror above the sink. She used the counter to balance as she slipped on her heels. For a second, she hardly recognized herself.

Swallowing, Avril looked at that person in the mirror.

She hadn't seen her in a long time.

A thin line of a shadow curled up the back of her neck.

When she shook her head, a curl escaped from her chignon, covering the darkness as easily as she'd noticed it.

She turned the lights off as she made her way down the steps.

Ian stared at her from the bottom of the staircase for such a long moment that Avril paused halfway to look down at herself.

Had she forgotten to snap a button?

The dress shimmered under the chandelier above the two of them in the warmest shade of a young lover's rose. In a structured frill, the fabric twisted over her breasts.

A perfectly wrapped gift.

She smirked when she found nothing amiss, stepping down the final steps. "Are you gawking, Ian?"

He licked his lips but didn't take his eyes away. "You look beautiful."

The words seemed to escape him before he even realized what he was saying. That must've been it, though he was in no hurry to redeem them.

Avril had been called many things in her life. Stunning, gorgeous, even striking in a Bettie Page sort of way, but rarely beautiful. A simple, easy word that could be expressed without thought, only a breath.

She glanced around at the bare walls, as if something far more interesting were there, but she couldn't help her bloodred smile.

"Thank you." Avril shrugged a shoulder toward him. "You don't look too shabby yourself."

He looked better than that even. Pressed black pants perfectly shaped around his hips and behind as he turned around to reach for their coats. He held open her opera coat, warm and lined on the inside, and Avril slipped one arm through each hole at a time until she was directly in front of Ian.

With nimble fingers, before she even had the chance to do it herself, he fastened the top button.

"Are you ready?" Extending an arm, he bent it at the elbow.

How chivalrous.

Avril looped her own around his. "Onward, my lovely escort."

The moment they hit the taxi already waiting for them at the bottom of the steps leading out of the house, Avril probed him all the way into Midtown.

"Where are we going? Where are you taking me? Somewhere fun? A gala? A saucy show to get us in the mood? That's it, isn't it? Finally going to admit that you want to get in my pants? Or panties. If I'm wearing any."

He glared at her.

The driver glanced back in the rearview to see her wagging eyebrows.

"I hear there's a pretty popular cancan spectacle in town these days."

Ian still said nothing until they pulled up to the Shabelle Theater.

He swiftly paid and pushed the door open into the small crowd of people gathering in front of the theater. "You're in a mood."

"An entertaining one, I hope," Avril said as they walked through the circle door and into the lobby.

Ian did not respond. He seemed much more content to hold on to her arm. He hadn't stopped touching her since they left the house.

"*The Nutcracker*?" Avril looked up from the poster stretched on the easel. She smiled as she pointed at the little girl on her toes, grinning up at her fancy new culinary toy.

"What did you think I was taking you to see at the theater in the middle of December? A rock concert?"

"I do see you as someone with a secret love for Metallica."

Ian only stared, but a feeling of pleasure strummed through her at his lack of denial.

She shrugged. "I'm always prepared for surprises."

"Have you seen the show before?"

"I think so. Or at least, the Barbie princess version."

"I'm unaware of the child doll version."

"The colors were out of an acid-trip nightmare. The true definition of sugarplums dancing in your head."

Avril remembered more of the film as they walked. She remembered the lights almost all turned off when her and her mom watched the tape that eventually got stuck in the player. She'd stand up and spin around on the shag carpet as her mother clapped, reminding her to bow when she finished with a flare of her hands to either side.

Thick lashes fluttered against her cheeks. Avril swallowed down the memory, glancing down at her hands to shadows flickering on her fingertips. She tried to shake them off like any other grime as Ian let her arm go, extending tickets to the man near the door.

"Well, let's hope you find this one as entertaining."

"Up the steps and to the right," the man informed before handing them back. "Enjoy."

"And such fine seats," Avril commented.

"If you are a fan of the balcony."

"Oh, I am. Seeing little girls break their toes in pointe shoes from above is all I need for a good time, as long as there's no one like you in front of me, blocking the view. And all sorts of other things happen in the balcony." She trailed an agile finger up the back of Ian's neck.

He flinched before grabbing it, holding it in his hand. "None of that."

"Not into exhibitionism? I'm learning so much."

She smiled and dutifully nodded in order to be released.

"Were you even invited to this?"

"Not exactly," Ian admitted.

"You didn't have to come to this holiday tradition?"

"The school offered free and discounted tickets. I thought you'd enjoy it."

Avril leaned her head around his shoulder to beam up at him. "That might be the sweetest thing anyone has ever said to me."

Ian turned away, so he didn't have to look with that practiced scowl of his to hide whatever pleased smirk he wanted to display. He'd likely steal the show if he did—the utmost plot twist.

He pointed her to sit.

Scooping her skirt underneath her, she sat down and batted the folded cushion beside her.

Ian sat down as he'd planned to, however begrudgingly.

"Great view."

"You're one of those people who talks through the credits, aren't you?"

"How'd you guess?" Avril grinned.

The crowd trickled in around the theater, chatting and squeezing by on the way to their seats and to other friends with a better view who'd bought tickets ahead of time. The lamps flickered above them like a calling before they turned out all at once.

The thick curtains rose. Clara danced and bounced among the other children surrounding the tree, coated in oversized ornaments, holding her shiny red nutcracker up to the light. Its golden crown glowed.

It felt like only minutes went by as Avril sat in the silence, transfixed by the stage, letting the soft maroon threaded cushion hold her up until a hand gently touched her hand, gripping the armrest.

"Intermission," Ian said softly.

Blinking, Avril pulled her eyes away from the stage. Others around them stood up and stretched.

"You should stand up. Let's take a walk. We have thirteen minutes."

"Ideas?"

"Unless you count using the restroom." With a hand, he motioned her to rise.

She rose.

Filing out with at least two dozen others making their way down the narrow staircase back to the first floor, Avril let her hand slide over the ornate patterns in the banister. Ian held his position close behind. At Rosin, the colors were similar, a deep red and gold that made the speakeasy lounge feel like you were stepping into a sexy, secret alcove from the '20s.

Avril turned from the bottom of the steps as she looked at others milling around. Parents bought carnations to present to their exhausted dancers at the end of the performance. Others purchased chocolate mints.

The rest of the theater appeared to have the increased urge to use the restroom all at once. The line looped out the door.

Stopping on her toes, Avril turned back to Ian, who'd already come in and out of the men's restroom, leaning against the wall to wait for her.

"Not going?" Ian asked.

She stepped back beside him, smoothing the fabric down where the diamond seams angled at her hips. "Waiting till the line goes down."

"How do you like the show so far?"

"I haven't just watched a show in a long time," Avril admitted.

She remembered her first show she'd ever seen in Ashton, in this theater. It was nothing special exactly, though it was to her. She had never been in the city just because, let alone to attend something that cost half a paycheck.

A contemporary troupe had come from Canada. They were tall and sleek. All of them were beautiful as they swayed into each other to the beat of the piano. They caught themselves like a breath each time a partner lifted them. They were just as graceful as anyone would assume a ballerina.

After the show, Avril had made sure to catch them as they left the dressing rooms. She invited a few of them who had been willing to chat for more than a moment to a get-together that Saturday night with the girls of Rosin, who always admired other dancers, no matter the type.

Avril had been invited to their rehearsals to dance with them every time they were in town since. Except for last summer, when they usually came around. Avril wasn't in the city to notice.

It didn't matter that she was short or had curves where they were toned in a different sort of way. They all danced, and somehow, in the end, that was all that mattered.

"You were a dancer," Ian said more than asked, noting her pause.

Whether she was or wasn't anything, Avril was always a dancer.

"A long time ago?"

A long time ago was practically asking her if she used to take toddler tap or point her toes in her mother's bedroom slippers. The scene of her dancing in front of the fuzzy television set flashed back through her mind again. Her mother smiling. The gentle claps.

She rubbed her fingers together again, as if she could feel the dark gunk staining them once more. "Sure feels that way."

When she glanced over her shoulder, the line to the ladies' room had already gone down.

"I'll be right back."

"I'll wait here."

Coming out of the stall, Avril paused in the mirror. Other women also stood, glancing in her direction. They all fixed their red and green blouses, giving them a quick shake to release the wrinkles from sitting for so long. They probably wondered if she was someone special or thought she was, wearing what she did, standing how she was, taking up space as she blinked at herself with a small smile.

For the first time in a long time, as she reached into her clutch and pulled out her lipstick to reapply a fresh coat, she did think she was someone special.

And she didn't give a damn what anyone else thought.

Giving them all a grin, Avril turned to see a more familiar face staring her up and down.

"Kit?"

Her friend grinned, clutching her tiny beaded bag. She was dressed more similarly to Avril than the rest of the line—1940s crepe silk cinched a fitted bodice with rosettes around her shoulders and waist. Her hair was styled in a similar fashion.

Her flushed lips parted. "I knew that dress would make you look like a sexy Mary Pickford."

"Should I say thank you?" Avril asked.

"Only if you mean it." Kit looked proud enough of herself for the both of them.

"How didn't I notice you? Are you here for the show?"

Of course she was. Kit. Here. With her, in the restroom of one of many Ashton theaters, likely giving their own version of *The Nutcracker*.

Somehow, over the past few days, Avril had managed to think that she lived in her own little world, away from her other life and all that had gone with it. Seeing Kit was a bucket of ice water, be it in the summer on a boiling day, pleasant.

She shook her head, and as she did, another thought popped into mind. "Is Jack with you?"

"He is. Probably backstage though. His brother helped design the sets."

"That's—" Avril had never met any of Jack's brothers. Heard of them, of course, but last she'd heard, Jack was still content, being estranged from them all. "That's fantastic."

"He ended up taking some words I'd had with him when we visited his family to heart and showed up on Jack's—or rather my —doorstep not long after. The poor Carvers have four sons, and hopefully, the first two stick to being farmers because at this rate, who knows what they'll do?"

"Must've been some words," Avril said.

"I'm very forceful when I need to be."

Avril knew.

"Are you here with…" Kit let the question hang with wide eyes.

"I am."

"My, oh my."

"Surprised?"

The last time they'd spoken, Kit had thought Avril's plan wasn't going to work after all, but her friend only smiled.

"Not in the slightest."

Something in her words caused Avril to sway.

"Are you all right?"

"Perfect," Avril breathed.

"I'm glad. Do you have a lipstick you wouldn't mind if I borrowed? You'd think the whole magnetic cap thing on most of them would mean less accidental smooshing, but—"

"You'd think." Popping her clutch open, Avril immediately handed her a tube. "Keep it."

"Till I see you next." Kit smiled. "If you can, remember to send the RSVP soon for the wedding. I sent one to Reed as well but haven't heard if he plans on coming. I didn't think it was a big deal if people just showed up since there won't be too many, but according to Jack…"

Say no more.

"Mark Reed down for two."

"Two?"

Avril nodded. "I'll send mine in soon."

"Perfect. See you after the show maybe."

Maybe.

Her heart started to beat in her chest. If they met up after the show, there was a likelihood that Avril would also run into Jack. There was a chance that the moment she stepped outside the restroom, Jack would be standing there, waiting for Kit, like the perfect gentleman he wasn't.

Avril only kept smiling as she exited.

Jack wasn't there. Neither was Ian.

He wasn't in the atrium, where she'd left him. Turning herself around to make sure that she was in the right wing, she noticed only the back of a dark-haired head, which she paused at but did nothing to move toward.

She walked along the velvet carpet to make sure he wasn't stretching his legs as well. It was only when she climbed the steps back up to the balcony in the theater, above where the string section was warming up for the second act, she spotted him.

He sat back down in their seats; his eyes latched on to his hands.

From what Avril could see, there was nothing wrong with them or the watch he fidgeted with. He unclasped and clasped the metal loops again onto his right wrist.

Smoothing out her skirt as she sat down, Avril hesitantly smiled at him. "Thought you were going to wait for me."

He glanced up at her and then back down. "Right. Sorry. I got distracted."

Something was different. The way he sat was stiffer, jaw clenched.

"Are you all right?"

"Perfect."

Lights fluttered one last time before settling into darkness. Still, Avril could see the familiar tinge of shadows and not from flashlights leading people back to their chairs, but in Ian's eyes as he glanced away from her. The curtain was beginning to pull back.

"Are you sure—"

"It's starting."

Eyebrows scrunched together when she stared at him for a moment longer. She didn't care about the music or anything. Neither did Ian until she finally looked away. She didn't understand. They had been having a good time. It didn't matter though whether he was in a mood or not; she was going to watch the show.

And she let it take her back away once again. She let it sweep her away from the scowling man next to her. The other man likely down in the audience somewhere, holding Kit's delicate hand, giving her a peck on the lips as she sat down, transferring Avril's lipstick onto his smile.

Avril pressed her lips together and calmed her heart, which had begun to race at some point.

Her eyes remained glued to the stage as she watched the tiny ballerina dance on her toes before being upgraded to toe shoes. She watched tutus drip with glitter. She remembered when she had taken a stage, like she and Ian had talked of before, and smiled wide down toward the dancer she didn't want to take her gaze from now.

Luckily, she never had to close her eyes, except to breathe in the space around her. She felt the pressure behind her eyes building, the same way the people's eyes and voices had called out to her in their own time. She'd never had so much fun. She never felt so perfect as when she danced like the girl onstage.

She bowed and grinned brighter than the light that shone down.

A finger reached out to brush away the stripe of wet tears.

Avril flinched away for a moment as the music continued below. Ian must've taken his turn to watch her at some point, eyes hard and steady. But his hand was still there, unmoving, as he stared into Avril's eyes, perhaps as awed as she was.

Both of them seemed to be thinking the same thing, remembering her tongue against his cheek as she swiped away his tears in the cemetery. They'd tasted like salt and frost.

The music swelled and pulsed for one last note before the audience applauded.

Avril wet her lips and tasted the cake of lipstick before she joined them.

CHAPTER TWENTY-TWO

*A*vril skipped down the sidewalk from where dozens of people were grouped together, talking about the show and hailing down cabs that pulled in with little notice.

Ian raised his eyebrow. He put his hands in his pockets and followed her lead, clearing his throat from whatever it was he wanted to say, but stuck inside.

"Where to, queen of the night?"

Avril smirked, happily continuing to enjoy herself as she rubbed her lips together at the calling card of a name. He had no idea. For some reason, she loved the sound of it all the more that way. "What? In a better mood all of a sudden?"

Bringing a hand up to his hair, he let it fall wide out to the side, like some sort of shrug she hadn't seen before.

Fine. If he was seriously asking. "I want to walk."

"Aren't you cold?" The question came out in frosted smoke.

Though the air caught beneath her swept hair and she could feel the redness reaching her nose, she shook her head at the sky and the rest of the people around them happily herding themselves home, wherever that might be. "Not yet."

Ian nodded, looping his arm into the crook of hers. "At least put your gloves on."

Plucking them out from her pocket, Avril extended her hand out in front of her. Before she could slip it on, however, Ian's hand caught it.

His thumb stroked the few lines marring the back of her hand and fingers. "How didn't I notice these?"

"Have you been studying my hands that closely this evening? I think there must be a fetish for that," Avril speculated.

She continued to slip her gloves on the rest of the way, buttoning them around her forearm. Ian helped her with the second one.

"Thanks. The scars are left over from when I was young, is all. I played rough."

"Why am I not surprised?"

"And why am I not surprised that you are going to go on, continuing like you weren't mad at me or something in there?"

Ian seemed shocked that she'd called him back out again on it. "No, I'm not. I'm not mad at you."

"I mean, I've been told I take far too long, primping myself in the bathroom, but never to such a stagnant arrival. Usually, my refreshed appearance wins them all back over."

"I wasn't mad at you."

Avril opened her mouth to disagree, but instead, she paused. She thought of all the things she hadn't said to Ian, even when he asked the past few weeks. The questions she'd averted and comments even more easily diverted with the threat of another paint argument.

"Okay."

He seemed shocked at her sudden turn.

Avril didn't leave him that way for long, arching her neck to look up at him. "Pick up the pace."

"Are you going to tell me where we're going then?"

To be honest, Avril didn't know. She found her reason only as quickly as she found her steps, maneuvering past anyone in their way. With him holding tightly on to her, she was at ease.

Her feet slipped from underneath her as they turned the corner to the main square, which was actually more of a hexagon, covered in little stands selling handmade gifts and *bouquinistes*, like the ones Avril had browsed along the Seine in Paris. In Ashton, they sold holiday titles from closely related indie publishers. Someone read into a microphone alongside one of them. Children gathered around as a reindeer found its way to the North Pole.

Before she could stumble back from colliding with another person, Ian already held under her arm, righting her.

"Careful."

Avril sighed at the sight of it all. She watched friends and couples wait in line at a fortune-teller's booth and stand in front of the twisting strands of lights that created a sculpture out of nothing. Most of the city patrons and tourists alike were bundled in scarves and hats. They held out their phones in front of them for a photo. They smiled and kissed and brought their tiny paper cups of authentic Belgian hot chocolate to their lips.

Avril remembered the stuff, thick as sauce and twice as good.

Ian scanned the place. "This is amazing."

"Every year at Ashton, the artists come out to play, and the city center has always been a place for them to show off their work. One thing left behind, I guess, from all those years ago, where they ruled the place before structural evolution and all," Avril said, taking in the wares of the glassblowing stand.

On shelves, tiny puckered pedants were strewn on ribbon. Animal paperweights were twisted as easily as intricately braided vases holding holly berries where people stood in line to turn their own ornament in any color already crushed into dust. The heat from the stove exuded out the sides, people crowding to watch as well as get warm.

"The city loves to celebrate."

"I had no idea all this was here."

"I haven't seen the lights since I first came to Ashton. The holiday market was on the way home from my first job I ever took here. One day, I made Reed come with me even though he knew we would miss our bus back home to his parents' house."

"You were in school still?"

Avril nodded. For some reason, when she thought of that, she felt older. "Remember my stint living with my friend?"

"The sister ratting you out to the family." He pieced it together for himself.

"Exactly. After Reed's dad basically challenged me to get a job while living under his roof, I decided to come into the city, though I had to take the bus every day. It was snowing, but for the first time in my life, I could buy gifts for people. I wrapped Reed in all the layers I had on me. He wasn't very happy and looked ridiculous but definitely pulled off a chic beret."

Ian let loose a deep laugh, pulling her tighter against his chest in the crowd, as if afraid she would get lost. "I hadn't thought of you as someone so strongly interested in celebrating the holidays."

"I loved anything that had a party involved," Avril conceded.

Love, she had to correct herself even if she wasn't positive that was true anymore. She wasn't positive it wasn't.

"What was it?" Ian asked as they continued to walk, not getting very far. "Your first job?"

Avril smiled again at that memory. "I was a fitter at a lingerie shop downtown. I applied to restaurants and clothing stores, but they looked at me like I was an alien. Then, I was wandering around downtown, and I saw the most beautiful mannequin in a window. The corset was unlike anything I'd ever seen before. It was filled with crystals and lace, and somehow, it was all so perfect. I never wanted to wear anything more. So, I went inside."

"And the owner was there?"

"That's right."

"She hired you on the spot?" Ian asked in disbelief.

She thought about Emilie and the shop Kit had taken over not long ago. Back then, she hadn't worn her wigs often, instead leaving her hair long and filled with silver grays.

Avril never had made it to the funeral.

"I was very knowledgeable when it came to the other wares also sold in the shop," she granted. "The owner was rather impressed, and I took to holding women's boobs up while they were being fitted for a bra, so, well …"

Ian laughed again.

She loved the sound of it even more than her first job with Emilie. From the daily tasks to delivering to the girls at Rosin she'd supplied, Avril could remember each day, especially the ones where she'd watched Emilie sew up something new a client had asked for but wasn't on the rack yet. Those bespoke pieces, like her corsets, fit like the most ornate second skin.

Avril smiled as she stared into the lights and how they changed from blue to red to green before lighting up in a single strand of gold. Looking down at herself, she was surprised to only see the colorful reflections rather than loose shadows from talking.

"Are you two in line?"

At some point while they'd stood there, the two of them had made their way to the front of the glass stand.

Ian put up his hand, looking around to decline.

Avril reached to pull it back down in front of her. She glanced up at him and smiled. "Why not?"

"Just one?" the guy in a singed apron asked, pulling a new, long iron rod out from the side before walking up toward them. His one hand was covered in a heavy-duty glove, the other bare with signs that he and the furnace had had a few too many close encounters. The rest of him, however, appeared as if he could've been working in one of the warmest climates—no coat, only a thin shirt to save him from any wayward sparks.

"Just one will do."

"Color?"

Avril glanced up at Ian. "Go on, choose."

"You want me to pick?" He seemed surprised, considering she had decided to make them both walk into the small hut.

"Pick something nice."

He narrowed his eyes at the wooden bowls. They all looked similar in the dim light. He pointed decidedly to one bowl and then another.

The glassblower nodded, prepping without another question. It was likely his hundredth ornament of the day. Gathering glass powder on the hot pipe, the guy waved them to walk over with him a few more steps, where duct tape lined the floor.

He stuck the pipe into the fire and spun, tilting it back and forth every few seconds before bringing out the molten glass from the stove. He never stopped his easy turn of the wrist as he dipped it into the scattered color Ian had picked.

The glass was as soft as gum as the glassblower laid it and rolled it into a bubble.

"You want to give it a blow?"

Avril grinned at the offer. Ian only extended a hand for her to go for it.

"Not the first time I've heard that question before."

The glassblower only looked down and smiled with light amusement. "Not the first time I've heard that joke before either."

"Here I thought I was special."

Both of them snickered, and he dipped the end of the glass in water. Keeping the process moving, he presented the rod to her.

"Go for it. I'll fix it if you mess it up."

"Always the magic words to a girl's ears."

Leaning down, Avril held in before blowing back out through the pipe. She was only slightly displeased when nothing but a small bubble appeared.

"Not horrible."

Avril shook her head as she found her place back with Ian, and a hand touched the side of her hip.

The glassblower brought the pipe to his own lips. He placed his thumb over the edge and blew slowly, and the glass took form before he rolled and shaped it on the edge of his workstation again. Without further ado, he turned the rod fast, clipping the ornament off and adding the top before it fully cooled, taking shape and color she hadn't seen in the shards he'd previously rolled it in.

When he slipped it off, Avril's lips couldn't help as they parted at the stream of colors captured in the rounded glass.

The sphere. It looked like her shadows.

Grays and white and silvers turned fast enough until they swirled. Speckles of red, however, darted between them, like burning pieces of ash.

Somehow, Avril was unable to say anything, though she must've planned to. Her mouth opened, but no words came out as Ian glanced between the final product and her.

"I haven't seen one turn out like that yet." The glassblower gave the piece a final twist on his fingers before slipping it into a padded gift box.

Avril couldn't help herself, still staring at the shadows captured in the glass.

Ian took it from the man with a gentle smile.

"Happy holidays."

"You too," Ian said.

Moments later they were back out, heat swept out from underneath the two of them as they moved out from the stand into the cold air. His arm had come around her shoulders at some point, rubbing feeling that had already been there back into them.

"Are you feeling all right?"

Avril crossed her arms over one another. She swallowed as she glanced around to all the people still stumbling in groups.

Smells of cinnamon and spice wafted through the air with an extra potency as she stared up at Ian, still unsure of what to say that had brought out silence.

"Let's get home?" Ian asked.

She nodded.

CHAPTER TWENTY-THREE

The world flew by above their heads. For someone who still didn't know the city all that well, Ian directed her to the nearest station fast enough, his body close to hers, as if she were a fall risk, as they walked down the concrete stairs and waited on the platform for a train to pull up. Only a few were left before they shut down for the night. Still, Ian chose the car with the least amount of people inside. He directed Avril to sit on the end, himself on the inside in case anyone else got on, which wasn't likely in the direction they were heading.

Avril turned and let her legs across Ian's lap. His hands went over them, as if a safety harness, as she sat sideways on the train bench. His thumbs began to massage, exploring.

Avril hummed in simple pleasure.

"You were the one who wanted to walk," Ian reminded her.

One eye open, she stared at Ian. "You act like you didn't have a good time."

"I had an amazing time."

"Queen of the night. Queen of the good times," Avril began to list with an appeased smile. "I should get a plaque."

"I think you are a little late on writing your Christmas list."

"I'm not sure I ever wrote one," Avril said, after thinking for a second. She was still too focused on the easy squeezes Ian distributed up her calves. She wondered how high he would go if she scooted down more, but knew better. Instead, she sighed and rested her cheek against a fist. "Explains a lot."

"You never wrote to the mysterious Santa Claus?" Ian asked. His eyes flickered to the end of the car with a young boy sitting next to his mother. Though he seemed a little preoccupied in his handheld game to notice if Avril suddenly got the urge to ruin childhood dreams.

She shook her head. "Nope. Never really celebrated Christmas."

"What did you celebrate then?"

"My mother turned us into something that occasionally made us sort of pagans. Neo-Wiccans? Not positive. A combination of everything and nothing I have ever seemed to be able to find in Ashton. I tried one year, which seemed impossible. But around Yule, the winter solstice, when the stars seemed brightest, we strung up paper ornaments on a tree, just like everyone else. Oranges were sliced and strung up over the fireplace mantel, if there was one," Avril went on. "There were also rituals."

"Consider me intrigued."

"Trade secrets, I'm afraid." Avril shook her head, thinking of Suzanne again and how she'd taught her the correct way to stir her tea in order to bring good luck.

Every year since she'd first come to Ashton and gotten in the holiday spirit, like she felt now, stirring like a heated wick of a candle ready to spark, Avril always had a solstice party. Summer or winter, she didn't pass it up, especially when her friends loved the strange tradition so much. They incorporated their own gift exchanges and games until the townhouse felt warm and inviting and filled with the best food all year, so Avril didn't have to celebrate all by herself.

"The solstice is the twenty-first, isn't it?"

"The twenty-second this year."

Ian nodded down to himself, as if committing the new random fact to memory. "You should celebrate."

Avril only shrugged. It'd been years. What was another one at this point? "Maybe."

His eyebrow scrunched when he was trying hard to concentrate. To remember something he didn't want to forget.

Avril followed the insanity from his temple down his sharp cheekbones and face. His neck tilted to the side against the train wall as it slowed down, stopped to let people off, and took off again.

The ever-present shadows she had seen earlier were still there, but already they began to fade, just a bit. They were only whispers.

She wanted to reach up and trace them. Preferably with her tongue.

"I don't like that look."

"What look?" Avril looked to either side of herself in innocence. All she saw was some man in a ski jacket and a few high school–aged girls looped in handmade scarves, whispering back and forth.

Avril hoped they were talking about her and Ian.

"You, smiling like that," Ian informed. "Stop it."

"I'm not smiling."

Ian narrowed his eyes.

"Just like you aren't glaring."

"I'm not glaring."

"Exactly." Avril smiled wider.

Ian playfully slapped her leg, but he still didn't push it away. "You wicked creature."

"It is like you already know what I'm thinking."

"You should stop."

Yeah, perhaps she should. But right now, in the cold air, heat pumped through the loose air vents above them and settled in deep in Avril's stomach.

Ian's gray eyes gleamed, as if something were alive inside, swirling.

She looked directly into them. "Why?"

As if the words had undone a piece of ribbon that also held his lungs so tightly against his heart, Ian leaned closer. For a moment, Avril was sure that he was going to say something against her lips. Tease her that it was her all along that wanted him and the deal more than the other way around. She'd just proven it.

Cupping her chin between his thumb and forefinger, he stared at her face and let his lips lock with hers.

CHAPTER TWENTY-FOUR

hrough the few kisses she'd had with Ian, the many
kisses she'd had in her life, this one pulled the breath
out of her before she breathed it right back in, filling up her lungs
with a hush from the rumble of the train and people sitting at the
other end, chatting to one another with headphones too loud.

Avril was here, grasping at the collar of Ian's shirt as he kissed
her to keep her hands from shaking with sudden need. His warm
mouth enveloped hers as he parted his lips.

A chuckle rose with Avril's eagerness.

He was the one pulling her to him by her pearls.

"I think we have a few voyeurs," he rumbled into her ear.

She didn't turn away from him to see who he meant. The
pressure of eyes meant nothing. She didn't let him go.

"Let them watch."

They could put on a show.

Ian's warm, dark laugh only erupted louder. Whether they
turned eyes back down to themselves or not, Avril didn't care.

The ride couldn't end fast enough.

By the time their stop came up, Ian picked Avril up with him
before the doors opened. A noise that could only be described as

a squeal passed her lips. He carried her past the open doors and across the metro until she jerked to be let down to the dimly lit sidewalk.

Kicking off her heels, she gathered them up by the straps to walk faster, nearly sprinting on her toes.

Ian looked down at her strappy heels and put a hand to his chest, keeping pace. "I'm honored."

She shoved him away with a hand on his stomach, if only to get up the steps and to the door first. Without a key, however, Avril was swung around, back against the solid wood door.

Ian's bottom lip trailed up the side of her throat.

The heat from his body and the cold outside sent shivers across her skin. A shock up from her stomach turned into a gasp she couldn't hold back.

From the way Ian's eyes met hers at the sound, she wouldn't dare.

"What was that about wanting to keep things in the house and professional?" Avril tried to tease. Each word was a huff of breath.

Her hands weren't the only ones shaking. Keys shuffled before turning the lock. The door fell from behind her as Ian walked them in, arm wrapped around her waist for support.

Starting with his own, Ian shoved his coat away and set the small ornament box beside the shoe bench before he kicked the door closed. Everything fell onto the floor, keys into the jar.

They knew where everything was, even when through hooded eyes. They'd placed them themselves.

When she pulled away, her opera coat slipped out of her fingers, and with one hand gloveless, Avril was turned back around by suddenly very assured hands as they bent her over the hall table.

"New rule." Ian let his weight gently press into her from behind. His hardness nudged against her, straining against his pants separating them.

"What is it?"

"It doesn't matter, does it? I'm just debating how many more times I'll have to remind you that the rest of them are all mine." Ian's hands searched for a zipper, running over her body.

"Between the straps," Avril nearly pleaded, reaching for it herself.

Along with a stream of release, she also heard the light rip and pop from the top button.

"Whoops," Ian muttered, already turning her back around to face him. His mouth found itself against her chilled skin. Her chest. Her jaw. Her lips as Avril's head slung backward, giving him plenty of space to roam.

"I don't care." Avril inhaled, still arched for support over the table while the length of fabric, tight and structured to her body, slid to the historical floorboards. She was easily lifted out of them and settled on top of the table, mail neither of them paid attention to and the extra keys. All of it fell, crashing to the ground.

She needed to catch up. It was only fair.

Quickly Avril undid his shirt, one slip of a cream button at a time until all there was left to do was place her hands on his shoulders and push it behind him the rest of the way down in the pool of fabric.

She ran her hands down his chest and lean stomach. Ian's forehead pressed against hers and watched as her fingers quivered. His hand twisted around the pearls looped around her neck with a grin, and with a gentle tug, he pulled her mouth closer to his but didn't kiss. He only listened to the sharp crescendo of breaths that escaped as Avril strained, trying to meet his lips while he pulled away.

He hummed with dark pleasure as he looked down at the perfect swaths of sheer black cuts of lace—the only things left still on her body.

Locking eyes with her one last time, both of them breathing

heavy, Ian ducked down and pulled one of her nipples into his mouth through the thin layer of fabric.

The warmth from his mouth felt as if it has set a fire in her, burning deep and low. When he sucked harder, Avril couldn't help herself but flinch. Nipping at her breast, Ian did the same to the other, taking his time as she melted.

A finger played at the edge of her panties. Something between a growl and whisper rumbled from Ian. "You're soaked, Rose."

Avril felt herself blush. Proving it, Ian turned his hand, slipping a finger inside her.

Another breathless sound came from somewhere deep inside of Avril when he added another. It was a sound she hadn't heard in a long time. Ever.

Ian paused, dipping his fingers farther in and out as he explored her. "I like that sound."

"Stars." She did too.

Ian was touching her. She was touching Ian, and everything else around them seemed to be far away. Everything she needed was right here, balanced on the edge of the hall table with Ian's fingers deep inside of her.

His free hand gripped where her stocking met flesh. Thumb still wandering, he grazed metal he hadn't noticed until then, staring down at the diamond brooch. The antique jewel winked under a car light passing through the window.

When he looked at her, she could tell he remembered exactly what it was, what it meant to her, like the ring that he could no longer fit around his pinkie finger.

He bent low, and Avril watched as Ian placed a single kiss on the bezel of tiny diamonds set in the center of her brooch.

A breath caught in the back of her throat at the sight, let alone Ian, so at ease, kneeling before her. He slipped his hands under her panties and garter belt, tugging them down her legs. Hot breath ached against her skin. Every inch set her on fire as he kissed and licked all the way downward—from the apex of her thighs, every spot where stockings slid up, to the arch of her foot.

He scraped his teeth against her inner thigh before he was no longer playing, listening to the hazy sounds of her reactions. In a swift movement, Ian licked her.

Avril leaned farther back, head hitting the wall as she gripped on to his shoulders, hips rising to the sensation of his tongue. He held her open as he sucked the bundle of nerves into his mouth, holding her there until she couldn't endure it any longer, grasping a hand into his tidy hair, so orderly, his head now at home between her legs.

Exactly where he was meant to be, or so she thought before he stood back up again, face flushed as she pulled him back down, tasting herself on his lips.

"You don't know how long I've been waiting to do just this," Ian murmured.

Not waiting for her response, Ian slid an arm back around her, picking her up for her legs to easily wrap around his waist. They didn't get far, melting back down into the hardwood. Drop cloth had been replaced with a carpet runner, soft and new against her back.

Avril wasn't sure she had ever desired someone before now, not like this, as she kissed the hollow of Ian's throat and heard him hiss. She involuntarily arched up to keep his hips, still covered, pressed into her aching center.

Staring down at her, his eyes caught near her shoulders, and before Avril noticed what it was, he flashed the glimmer of the diamond brooch in his hand.

He leaned back on his knees to study it.

"Are you going to wear that?" Avril asked, her voice hoarse as she took him in—all of him, including the painfully tight space of his dress pants.

Surprisingly, Ian chuckled at her tame joke, kissing her once so his voice hummed against her skin. "I have much better ideas."

The metal of the brooch was cold against her skin as it trailed down her stomach.

Holding herself up with one hand, she watched as he pushed a single finger back inside of her as he continued to trail the brooch across her skin. Cold as ice. Avril didn't know where to look as sensation took her over when another finger separated her folds. She panted at the extraordinary sight and feeling. Of him. When she glanced up at Ian, his eyes were only on hers.

There was something like reverence that pulsed through his cold stone eyes, mimicking the different shades of pearls she had left on. When she had them strung, she never cared how they didn't quite match. They were a gift.

They were suddenly one of her most favorite gifts.

He almost looked like a god, poised above her, and she was a ruler that would take and take and take whatever he gave.

Her eyelashes fluttered as she was stretched, and his fingers hit places she wasn't sure she'd yet discovered. Trying to stay up on her elbows, she could no longer help it, falling onto her back as he picked up the torturously slow pace, curving inside as he hit an angle that caused her fingers to flare for purchase against the floor, but they only found his knee as she squeezed.

Legs spread wide, Avril bowed off the ground with a gasp as he brought his mouth back down her, her brooch slipping with him until the cold metal and jewels caught at the apex of her pleasure. Her moans increased as he devoured her, licking and teasing turning into strangled cries. It never ended as he continued, even after her hips clenched in abandon, unable to contain the desire coursing through her, choking her like the most beautiful poison.

Catching her breath, she was unable to tell him how much she wanted to swipe that self-satisfied smirk off his face.

But it was actually quite a good look on him.

Hand still looped now up toward her neck, where her pearls lay between her breasts, Ian gave them a tug to lift her mouth up to his. An expensive leash. When he looped his arms around her, she was pulled once again off the floor. The brooch clanged to the ground, left behind with the rest of their clothes as they headed toward the stairs.

"Tired, Whitlock?" Avril provoked as she regained speech.

"Here I thought I'd rendered you speechless." Ian's eyes gleamed. "Don't worry. I'm not close to being done with you yet."

And he wasn't. He tossed her onto the bed, and his body coated hers, still limp from before, opening her legs back up to him. She didn't even bother leaning up to gain leverage before he entered her, already open and waiting for him. He rode her into the bed, pulling one of her legs up over his shoulder as he positioned himself, hitting a space inside of her that made her open her mouth wide, noises similar to his mixing between the two of them.

She spasmed, reaching for his arm as she came on him. She rode her climax as he continued to find his own pleasure, feeling every inch of him as he thrust hard and fast in her. The two of them kept going, on and on and on.

CHAPTER TWENTY-FIVE

*I*an held her against his chest. His finger traced along each freckle dotting her cheeks, as if they had all the time in the world.

Avril was rather in the admiring mood herself. Her body hummed pleasantly. Her eyes raked over him, peeking down between to where their bodies still met. "You're beautiful."

"Not handsome?"

Of course handsome. Hundreds of men were handsome. Quite a few women too.

She brushed a piece of hair back high on his head from where it had flattened. "Dashing really. Utterly fascinating in your good looks. Would you like me to come up with more compliments, or would you rather go fishing?"

"You realize I'm still inside you."

Avril squirmed a little more to watch his eye twitch and narrow. "I know. I rather like it. I might keep it."

"I'm not positive how that would work."

"I'm pretty sure it is like a time-share. Hard to get rid of once you put up."

Avril winced as he finally slipped out and rolled onto his back next to her.

"From this angle, you can really appreciate the coffered ceiling," Avril mused, stretching her arms.

"We just had sex, and you are talking about the architecture of my ceiling?"

"Would you rather talk about how many times you had your fingers inside me?" Avril caught him grin.

Dare she say it, with the way her heart stopped in her chest, that look nearly rivaled the dirty smirk of Jack the Ripper, who had torn through all the hearts downtown. Quickly, Avril brushed Jack out of her mind. She had a much prettier, accommodating man currently in front of her.

He traced his long canines with the tip of his tongue. "We can never prove that."

Narrowing her eyes, Avril reached for his hand, gently holding it under her small palm. She brought his fingers to her mouth and sucked the faint taste of him and her and sex still there. "I think otherwise. Don't worry; your expertise was noted."

"Do I see a blush, Rose?"

She looked away. "Absolutely not."

"Then, I think we will have to change that."

"Darling," Avril said simply, "I want you to lick, kiss, and fuck every part of me. No need to be coy."

He groaned as he ground his hips against her again, teasing and still hard, setting any embers left inside of both of them aflame.

"Now, who's blushing?" Avril asked, but she sounded breathless. She wanted to touch him. She had to feel more of him, as if she hadn't already once tonight. Her fingers twitched at all the new possibilities. It would take days for them to get through them all.

"Darling," Ian whispered against her skin.

"Oh, so you are stealing my endearments now?"

"Rose."

Avril raised her eyebrow the way he couldn't as he leaned down, his lips careful and soft and easy compared to their earlier rushed and vicious kisses. It was like this was just how it was. How they were meant to be. Lips touching, grazing, pulsing to pull one's soul out through their mouth. This one lingered, gently pulling on her bottom lip with a sigh caught between the two of them.

Before Avril could find it in herself to catch his hands, they slithered down to her waist and flipped her onto her stomach.

Her heart picked up a lost beat.

His warm hands started at the tips of her collarbone and traced back before his eyes, massaging the stiff muscles in her back carefully. His hand brushed the bottom of her spine as her legs slid against the sheets.

"I never noticed this one either."

"Do you have a scar fetish or something?" Avril asked, knowing exactly the space he was staring at. "It's small. I don't exactly put that one on display."

"It was from your accident? Last year?"

The edges, she knew, were still lightly puckered.

Avril swallowed. The images flooded to her mind as well as the minor operation when the bruising had turned infected. She'd screamed, holding on to Reed's hand until they had to put her out. Not from the pain, but all the doctors in their gloves, standing around her, touching her.

"There was a lot of external damage to my back. For a while, we didn't realize that fluid was retained. They didn't have to take out any discs or anything. They needed to release the pressure."

"Will you tell me more? About what happened?"

Pausing, Avril realized that she wanted to.

She stopped picking at the edges of the sheets as the words rushed to mind. But how could she ever explain? How could she tell a piece and not all? He was going to be leaving in less than a few weeks anyway.

What point was there to piece her life together, so he'd somehow understand her past year, where she'd self-medicated herself with liquor and men just to prove that she could after running away, hoping to at some point stumble upon herself again.

Wherever she had gone.

Been hidden.

At the moment, Avril realized, feeling her muscles tense, she must've found pieces of her, most of her right where she lay. Beneath who she lay.

Avril glanced up at him.

He waited with nothing but patience.

"Not yet. I'm not—not yet."

She could feel the shadows, his shadows and hers, and all the lies pooling like ichor down each vertebrae Ian so easily began to soothe. The shadows were what had brought her here. To him. They were what she deserved.

He kissed the scar, and Avril straightened from the avoidance of distress. "Okay."

"Just okay?"

"Okay," Ian said softly.

And then he kissed more than just her scars.

IAN KISSED her like she had never been kissed before in her life.

The man was insatiable. Almost as much as she was. Avril let out a soft breath before coming back for more. Shadows turned soft as they lifted up the side of his throat, and she couldn't help herself but trace them. But that wasn't what she was focused on.

It was as if they still continued to talk against one another. Only they ached and burned out words until they turned to ash and soot. More and more. More.

She needed to make the aching hollow feeling vanish—at least for a little while. And, stars, when he kissed her, something warm flared inside of her. A fire catching flame.

With a hand at her back, he angled his head to taste her, running his lips over the delicate skin of her throat.

Avril moaned, unable to help herself at the sensation.

It only made Ian become more ravenous, groaning into her mouth as he hauled her against him.

Only him. Him.

Him.

WHEN SHE'D FIRST MET him, she couldn't help but think how strong he was when he kissed her, forcing her mouth open with passion and heat. He never backed down when she demanded more.

And she always wanted more.

It was a challenge. He did it with his eyes open. He held her hands from where they desperately wanted to delve deep inside of his dark head of hair. His teeth tilted and bit down hard instead of nipped.

Blood rushed up against her lips, dripping from the corners of her mouth, hot and unblotted. Pushing him away from her, Avril stumbled backward. Her elbow hit the floor, sturdy and strong, to hold her up before the rest of her did. But he kept coming toward her with a chuckle.

She brought a shaking hand up to her mouth, but in the darkness, when she pulled it away, she couldn't see anything. She couldn't see anything at all but the dark shadows.

They were teasing her.

Testing her.

What was she doing?

. . .

WHEN AVRIL GASPED AWAKE, a hand was already on her back. Long strokes soothed rather than scored down her spine and then went up again. A light hum permeated the air instead of silence.

"Are you awake?" Ian whispered.

The humming stopped.

She wondered how many times he'd had to ask.

"Shh, shh, shh." Ian wrapped his arms around her as her hands came to her mouth again, her fingers solid and shaking.

She was sure if the light were on, shadows would be bleeding through her fingertips. Her eyes teemed with tears.

"Is it your back?"

Just a dream.

"A dream?"

Unable to trust her voice, Avril nodded. Her head burrowed itself farther into where he held her. She thought about pushing away and scooting back to her side of the bed. She must have been thrashing or rolling around to move this far into him unless he'd pulled her carefully through it all to his chest.

His heart rolled like the steady beat of a drum.

"Rough night."

Rough life.

"Have you always had them a lot?"

Since she had been here at the house, Avril had to admit that she hadn't had as many as she usually did when she let herself sleep.

While working in the house though, at night, when she wasn't reading or wandering the empty rooms after Ian fell asleep, she herself was too tired to escape the pleasant exhaustion that crept through her muscles like when she used to dance and learn a new routine in a single week, determined to get it just right before she debuted it to praise.

"I've always had them," Avril said quickly instead. "Sort of."

And sometimes, they just sort of flare, she wanted to finish with.

But she had a feeling the two of them would both know that was a lie. A piece of one at the very least.

"The only time I didn't have any nightmares was when I think I was about seven."

"I'm not even sure I remember anything about when I was seven."

Oh, Avril did. She remembered almost all those days. The ones that mattered.

"My mom once took us away from the cities we bounced from when I was seven. My head, I guess, was always blocking out sirens and yells. I think they were her comfort in a way though. The noise." Avril couldn't help but relate to her mother just then. Thinking how quiet it somehow had been, even on the outskirts of Midtown or downtown, where the nightlife was an entirely different species she had always been sure to count herself among. "But sometimes, when things got bad, she always talked about a place for women like me and her that would take care of us when we needed it. That was when she wasn't...good."

Ian ducked his head, as if he understood.

"So, she took us to the house that she always talked about in my bedtime stories."

"It was real?"

"Very real. I was so excited to see it right there in front of me. It was beautiful. A tall, rickety Victorian farmhouse in the middle of nowhere. This house reminds me a little of it."

She heard Ian swallow, focusing on her voice in the darkness.

It was easier for Avril to talk this way. She couldn't see the shadows even if she knew that they creeped around her, little reminders of her dreams. Her memories, like her mother's, she never talked of them often.

"We had been led to it by the stars. My mother pointed them out as we went, and to this day, I can still find each constellation. Back then, though, to me, they were just the few that shone the brightest that night after we got off the bus. We were outside of a tiny town that still had a clock in the center of it, painted an ugly teal color and rusted. The women at the house adored the stars. They worshiped them like goddesses."

"*Oh stars,*" Ian repeated her own words she said so often with a sort of reverence. His hand trailed down her back again, producing a line of shivers.

"Sometimes, I think that place was only a dream."

"Was it?"

"No. Maybe. I was told I was born there, in the house of stars. Young and pregnant, my mother hid it the whole time until suddenly, she couldn't anymore. I was born on the house's bathroom floor," Avril murmured.

Her mother had had a predisposition for them, it seemed. Giving life and taking it on unsterile tiles. Neither alone.

"She caught me in her own hands. That's why my mother always said after a nightmare, they'd protect me as long as they were out there, somewhere."

So, was it just a dream?

Avril shook her head again, the movement curling her farther into Ian's side, though she couldn't bring herself to stop. She was so cold, and Ian radiated something that seeped past her pores and into her bones.

He didn't tell her to stop either.

"You should write them down," he whispered after a moment.

Avril cleared her throat, not raising her voice any higher than his. "What?"

"Your stories. Your dreams or whatever you would like to call them when you remember them. You should write them down when you can't sleep."

"I told you, I'm not a writer."

"I didn't say you had to be."

CHAPTER TWENTY-SIX

*I*t was getting bad again.

Usually, it was Reed who was the one to tell her this, but he didn't have to this time. She knew. It was getting bad again.

The thick coating of shadow was still slick around items and her ankles as she walked. Just like every night, Avril got out of bed as Ian drifted deeper into sleep, and she walked.

She'd thought she was getting better. She'd tricked herself by saying the shadows and the bad dreams were gone. That something must've happened to change the course of the cards Suzanne had drawn for her long ago when her mother didn't believe in prophecy. That everything for once, was okay.

Then, they came back, as they always did.

The shades. The dreams. And she couldn't sleep again, knowing what lay for her, even in the darkness. Lurking inside of her own head, ready to pounce. Ready to drown her once and for all.

Avril held a blanket around her shoulders or wore Ian's robe, which was at least four sizes too large, as she walked down the hall, back and forth. Some nights, Avril continued down the stairs, one step at a time, and around the office until she looped back once again.

She had found a small cupboard under the stairs that blended in with the trim, and near the basement was a piece of molding that looked as if it had never been painted over, nicked with small pencil marks at varying heights for a small child. Avril squinted at the fading initials, unwilling to touch them too much. *IW.*

The memories, the shadows, snuck up on her. They were quiet like the thick shades of disappointment, and they weighed down her shoulders as they stalked her, pulling her mind down too.

Cheater. Whore. Disgusting.

Liar.

Avril flinched at the shadows' reminders, burrowing deep in the silence when they bared their teeth.

Eventually no longer able to make it back down the steps, let alone up from fatigue, Avril made her way back down the hall. Ian was covered in a blanket of swift shadows of his own, somehow softer as they curled around his shoulders.

Then, they all faded for some reason. As if it didn't matter whether they were there or not. Whether or not Avril still knew what they meant to him or her at all at this point. She'd thought she knew for the short amount of time between when she met Ian—the man of shadows—and made her deal. She liked to know.

Now, without realizing when it'd happened, she smiled at his sleeping form in the bed she had already grown comfortable sharing. More than comfortable when he cooed to her and read her classics alongside her more preferred bodice rippers, loosely bound in cheap, ugly covers. He'd hidden them in his closet and brought them out, stacked against the wall in easy reach to soothe her with Darcy and Franny and Mrs. Dalloway and her flowers.

All of them and him sputtered softly on as she slipped back to sleep after startling awake in the middle of the night when she could no longer keep her eyes open. No matter how hard she yelled.

Avril brought her hand up to her puckered lips that shivered as well from the cold while something else stirred in her chest.

Stars.

Gods.

Fuck.

CHAPTER TWENTY-SEVEN

*T*he knot of Avril's tied T-shirt dipped into her stomach as she bent over the floor. They'd managed to paint and christen nearly every room in the house. As of yesterday, they were onto the second bathroom upstairs. Each set of tiles was placed against smeared grout.

Avril glanced up at Ian as he put another heap on the flat metal tool, smoothing it beneath the light switch. His shirt hung off his chest when he leaned forward.

He smiled at his work. "Staring, Rose?"

She shut her eyes altogether to stop herself, turning her head downward so he wouldn't notice. "Not in the slightest. I'm a very diligent worker."

Ian made a noise that Avril might've mistaken as joy.

How unusual.

His shadows had come back again this morning, quiet, as if something was on his mind. Even though he smirked and played now though with dirt wiped across his jaw, the shadows flickered and twisted like a piece of jewelry over his collarbone and around his neck.

He grunted to clear his throat.

Avril reached for the next piece of tile. As she set the next tile down, not paying attention, she snatched away her hand.

The tile clanged against the floor.

Instead of the deep turquoise blue was a black so dark that it was as if all color had been sucked into the pads of her thumb and forefinger.

Avril shut her eyes again, but not for the same reason as before. A bitter taste coated her tongue, like soot. But when she did that as well, trying to clear the taste, the image, all she saw was her mother. Stark red hair glued across her forehead.

Avril sat still on the bathroom floor. Counting as she tapped her fingers.

Five, six, seven, eight.

Her body had always covered half a tile.

She must've gasped because Ian shifted over toward her.

"What is it?"

Opening her eyes, Avril looked down at the tile again. More green than blue but certainly not the darkest of grays. "Nothing. I thought I'd dropped it."

"Be careful of the edges. I don't want you to cut yourself." Ian had incurred quite a few scratches of his own. The back of his hand was taped over from where he'd tried to catch a few that slipped as he brought them up the stairs.

"Are you sure you're all right? Let me—"

Avril put up a hand to stop him. "It's fine."

"Would you tell me if it wasn't?" Ian asked. "You should go and rest. I know you haven't been sleeping well."

"I'm fine. I just thought ..." Avril wanted to stop herself. Instead, she ground her teeth down as a sort of punishment as she spoke the words. For some reason, a pressure dug deep behind her eyes. "A thought snuck up on me, is all."

Ian handed her another tile of the next color she needed, watching as she took it. He watched her fingers overtake their tremor. His hand, too, however, was also covered in shadows.

Avril shut her eyes tightly.

She was fine. Completely fine, though the shadows had become all she saw the past few days as she traversed the house. Even at night, she could no longer put off the dark spots as movement from outside snuck in through the window. The shadows surrounded her, thicker and thicker. It was like a warning whenever she picked snacks out of the cabinets or lay in Ian's arms to feel the warmth he gave off when he overslept, just to keep him as a barrier from the day. She needed that for another few moments.

Just don't get too comfortable.

The reminder broke her focus.

Always. Always those filthy words spoken to her with pure revulsion were ready to bite.

Worthless. Whore.

Liar.

"Rose?"

"I actually"—Avril hastily stood—"have an appointment to get to—a thing with a friend I forgot about."

Ian narrowed his eyes.

Shadows swept under them like paint before fading to lilac.

"All right."

"I'll be back later, okay?" Shuffling past the unfinished piece of flooring, Avril pounded the dust off her jeans with the backs of her hands. About to make her way down the stairs, she paused.

She looked down at her feet, poised on the edge of the top step as she held on to the railing. She never put her heels on today. She hadn't even noticed.

"They're downstairs."

Avril swung around to see Ian. He'd paused his work, watching her stare toward her feet with something she was sure could only look like horror as her arches comfortably flattened into the grooves.

Ian lifted his chin toward the stairs. "You left them by the couch last night when you fell asleep."

Avril nodded, trying to think of the moment they'd slipped off while they ate their late dinner. She didn't remember.

Not letting herself look back, Avril quickly walked down the stairs, seeing her day heels exactly where Ian had said they would be. She shoved one over the back of her foot before doing the same with the other. The heel was slightly lower than her other pairs scattered around Ian's bedroom. Right now, she was only glad of the sound they made as she walked across the hardwood.

Tugging on her coat, Avril paused as she looked at the table beside the door. Ian's keys sat in a small ceramic bowl he'd picked up from the school flea market set up outside of the library block. Her hand hesitated at her phone. Ian always set it there after finding it in random places Avril had left it.

Over the past week, she had been taking it with her whenever she went out, per Ian's request, and she hadn't balked at the request once.

Opening the door, she let it slam behind her.

THE COLD CHAPPED HER LIPS. Avril swept her tongue across them for the second of relief before her skin dried out once again, but she didn't care. She needed to keep walking, breathing. She shoved her hands further into her pockets as she went, not finding her gloves she normally kept inside. They were probably lying on the side table, where Ian's keys sat. All of her things were scattered around the house. Ian had constantly had to remind her where everything was recently, her mind elsewhere.

He saw more somehow than she did.

If she looked back, she was sure she could have seen the shadows like a cloak billowing behind her as she turned down Shiloh to Illyria.

The other day, she had shown Ian her favorite ice cream shop just around the corner, near another park. They went after the library had its own little party with the community, a holiday film streaming in the main room. Noah smiled with pleasant surprise, spotting Avril as he did a pom-pom craft, glitter glue sticking to his fingers.

Afterward, the two of them sat on a bench as the afternoon waned, where the snow had begun to mold together in dirty lumps. They watched others stare at them, likely wondering if they had anywhere else to be, sharing nondairy cream off tiny plastic spoons in paper cups. Ian had gotten something that tasted sweet, like honey. He flinched the moment the tart raspberry Avril had picked mixed on his taste buds.

Avril laughed as he forced himself to swallow after expecting bubble gum.

He'd started to laugh with her over his thick tartan scarf she'd pulled around him before they left the house.

She could hear him as if he were beside her now, walking a little slower to keep Avril's pace. The sound pulsed like the crowds of other people who actually had places to be all around her.

She swallowed as she paused on the sidewalk. Putting a hand on her stomach, she felt a string of darkness clench. She was drowning.

The shadows might as well encapsulate her right then and there, strike her dead while the sun shone, if that was what the world wanted. From a child to now, she couldn't even remember all the cards, but she'd made it to this point. The shadow man in her never-ending fortune.

She'd never expected to linger for so long after meeting him.

They were supposed to change her life. Wreck it with a sort of finality.

For some reason, when she'd started the deal with Ian, she expected that it would be all it took to set such things in motion.

She'd expected this to all be over by now, far before the holidays could drift into full swing. For better or for worse, she kept waiting, kept ignoring the warnings that had shouted in her head from the start.

Nothing good would ever come of the shadows. That was what she'd been hoping for the whole time.

She liked Ian. More than liked him.

And he was going to ruin her. Or at least, he was supposed to.

She was supposed to die, just like her mother.

Stars. Wasn't that what she wanted? Wasn't that basically the reason she'd sought him and his tortured, demeaning soul out from the start?

Also, she'd had to return his ring.

His simple, little ring he carried around for his mother, who she couldn't help but imagine wouldn't be very pleased if she found out who her son—her perfectly good son—was spending his time with.

Opening her eyes, Avril thought about continuing down the street and just heading back to his house—the house—as long as he hadn't already locked her out for how she'd been ignoring him all morning. But she couldn't do that.

So, she didn't do anything.

Beside her, someone with headphones on knocked into her shoulder and kept walking.

Avril almost yelled at him, but her voice was pushed too far down. Shaking her head instead, she glanced up at the street, about to turn around when her eyes caught on the low-level door of a greystone.

She'd been here before. She was sure of it but then not at all. It was the sign her eyes caught on that made her take another step back. Painted on the door was a traditional tarot hand, sheltered in an image of stars.

Eyes widening at them, Avril knew exactly which stars they were.

Her mother had made her point them out in the sky dozens of times. She'd made her promise not to forget.

The door opened as she continued to stare. A woman with a loose Afro looped her tote bags around her arms as if she was heading to the market.

But Avril couldn't stop herself, even though the words were a whisper. The woman saw her at the same moment, stopping in her tracks.

"Suzanne?"

CHAPTER TWENTY-EIGHT

*T*here was no doubt in Avril's mind of who the woman was in front of her. She had haunted her dreams, both good and bad, with her smile and smell of fresh bread, garnished with rosemary.

"My stars." Suzanne swallowed with a hand to her chest. "I thought I just saw a ghost."

Avril tilted her chin down. To think, she had been about to turn around, never noticing the door or the stars before heading back.

A crackling laugh creeped out from her cold, swollen lungs. She tried to smile at the woman who was basically her aunt, her godmother, and also no one at all. She was another person, another place.

But here she was, right in front of her.

They were both different from what they once had been.

"Maybe," Avril said.

Suzanne reached back to the door she hadn't fully closed yet. "Come in. It's too cold out here."

Avril followed Suzanne into her small apartment that smelled less of dryer sheets and more like cardamom and scented candles. Towers of twisted colors were scattered like a path on the tiled floor. White grout had long since turned gray. It was one of the reasons she'd managed to convince Ian to go with a darker contrast tile altogether in the bathroom, which he was probably still laboring over to make sure every corner was aligned.

Avril caught sight of herself in the round mirror Suzanne hung her coat beside. Plants grabbed on to the edges of the glass for support, and Avril's hair was loose as it fell around her shoulders in puffed coils. Her eyes looked dark and deep.

With an intake of air, for a moment, she understood. How could Ian look at her and see her as someone to smile with rather than worry over, like Reed did?

Not that Reed had called recently to see where she had gone.

She was nearly positive that Kit kept Reed up to date, at the very least, about how Avril was alive if she ever ran into him. She'd be unable not to; she was maybe one of the only people appropriately nervous around Reed's dry demeanor.

Apparently, hearing whatever she'd told him was enough now. Now that it wasn't just the two of them anymore, like it always had been.

She didn't go home first anymore.

He didn't need her to hold him up.

Shaking away the thoughts—the loose yet sticky tendrils of shadows following her, poking at memories like pressure points —Avril continued to trail Suzanne and her welcoming voice farther inside.

Art littered the walls along with posters and prints that it looked like Suzanne had painted herself. Beads hung over the doorways, and the lime-green table from the '50s was still situated in the center of the tiny kitchen.

Avril settled her fingers on the cool surface.

"Strange, huh?"

Avril looked up at Suzanne, who watched her closely.

"I feel it," Suzanne said. "The déjà vu almost. You look so much like her."

Avril tried to remember her mother sometimes, more than just her memory, trying to see where her mother's face seemed to mold into hers, like she always imagined it did. Like Suzanne had proclaimed, a doppelgänger. Still, somehow in her mind, her mother was different, sharper, and less full around the edges.

Avril was only a hollow for an odd yet hopeful projection.

"Over the years, I have made a bit of a business for myself. Small but growing." Suzanne caught up with a light smile. "I'm certainly no psychic to the stars, but it keeps the other three floors over my head. I have been keeping up on you too, you know."

Her godmother glanced toward the small stack of newspapers piled in the corner, where a plush chair was angled, likely for her more tender clients looking for foresight as well as a fluffy pillow.

Avril saw the magazines sticking out of one corner. She also saw her own face staring back at her.

It took all Avril had left of her self-control not to pick the old magazine up. She didn't know what she would do if she did. Rip the thing in half perhaps. Instead, she just stared at the image of herself in a red crystal-covered corset, hips back, tits out. Her hands perfectly poised on her overly cinched waist.

Suzanne continued to let the water run from the tap, filling up the glass electric kettle.

Avril didn't bother to tell her she didn't drink tea anymore.

"I wasn't looking for you."

Suzanne's eyebrows creased as she looked up again. She flicked the button, and the machine hummed before it bubbled. "Oh."

"I was just walking."

"Just walking?"

"Trying to figure a few things out," Avril clarified, as if that could explain all this to the both of them. "Sorry for the lack of grand entrance."

Suzanne sighed. "I didn't expect you'd be glad to see me."

Perhaps she was psychic. None of this made sense.

Gripping the chair in front of her, Avril carefully eased into it.

She was a child once more, watching Suzanne's each movement carefully, as if she would need one day to remember how to make herbal teas and shuffle the cards correctly on her own. She'd always thought of herself more like Suzanne than her mother when they visited over the years. She truly imagined one day, she herself would be a fortune-teller or a witch, getting to play with the magic Suzanne practiced, tattooed and in a tiny flat all her own.

"Your mother did leave me a note, you know, when everything happened," Suzanne admitted. "She left it with the rest of my mail by the slot. But by then ..."

Avril had already been gone.

She'd been loaded up in the ambulance with her mother, who had stopped breathing long before the paramedics arrived, yet for some reason, they drove them to the hospital anyway with no lights on. A social worker was called, and distant family was contacted with a possible uncle, who had a family of his own he spat Gaelic and cheap beer at. All when who should've been notified was Suzanne.

For years, Avril had had a feeling that was the case all along, but hearing it—well, it dug whatever it was already slowly eating away at Avril deeper into her chest.

She focused on the dozens of tea rings left behind on Formica.

Suzanne studied her movement. "I remember most of what was in it. Could probably find it if you want me to."

Avril didn't answer. She sucked on her cheek as she tried to figure out what to say to the woman who couldn't yet be fifty, older than her mother would have been, in a kitchen where she could far easier listen to the conversations of passersby above them.

"She made it clear that she didn't want you to be like her, so frightened of the world."

"I really don't want to talk about my mother."

"She wanted you so much to control your own life, your own destiny."

Avril gave Suzanne a single look. She didn't have to repeat herself.

Nodding, she gestured for her long-lost goddaughter to take the floor. "Go on then."

"Go on, what?"

"Ask what you want to ask me. Say what you want to say."

"Do you remember when I came here?" Taking a deep breath, Avril shook her head at her choice of words; she hadn't realized she did have something to say before it was there in front of her. Suzanne in front of her. "To your apartment, the one above the Laundromat, with my mother right before?"

"I think about it all the time."

"Do you remember when you pulled my cards?"

She blinked, perplexed, as she stood up. Going to her little shelf in the corner, she came back with her tarot deck. It was the same set Avril always remembered.

Suzanne sat it between them in offering. "I do."

Glancing between her and the deck, Avril reached out and grabbed them, shuffling like she always did before she was tempted to yank the first card off the top, just how she had for Ian the other night on his bed when he somehow was able to admire their own fates.

If only for a moment before they caught back up to her.

Avril slowly plucked each card she wanted out from the deck, settling them in front of herself on the table until they were all there, just as they had been when she was nine years old. All the cards began to make sense in a way they hadn't before.

The Magician.

The Lovers.

No pentacles, as if she was tainted.

The same steady gaze, but much less humorous carefully surveyed her work.

Avril started talking, forcing her voice not to shake as she tried to explain the cards, her life, everything. "It's all there. You remember that day, when you mentioned the shadow man for the first time and my mum made us leave?"

Suzanne nodded, still studying the spread.

"Do you see them?"

Pausing, Suzanne peeled her gaze from the table. "See what? The cards?"

"The shadows."

She remembered how close she had been to asking her that day as a child.

"Physically? No," Suzanne answered carefully. "I don't."

She must've seen the hesitation flicker over Avril's expression, hastily connecting the dots.

"You have, though, since that day. I saw you staring at the illustration here in the card, but I couldn't put my finger on it. That's why your mum tore you out of here. We both knew that you had some sensitivity, but she never said."

Why hadn't she ever said? The question hung for only a second.

"That's why Isobel felt like she needed to leave. She was trying to protect you because of what I'd said. You already had nightmares…" Suzanne trailed off, thinking as she put a hand over her mouth.

Avril swallowed before she nodded.

"You still see these shadows?"

Avril cringed at the casual reference, but she remained seated while the kettle beeped. Bubbles reached their peak behind glass before settling. The darkness appeared, too, like the word as well, licking up the sides of Suzanne's chair but did not touch.

"Let me guess, they are going to devour me whole?" Avril asked.

"Gosh, you remind me of her."

"Forgive me if I don't find that comforting."

Suzanne's smile faltered.

Avril cut to the chase. "Is that what you are trying to tell me then still? There's no way to escape the darkness? The shadows?"

"Do you want to?" Suzanne asked.

Did she want to? Avril almost rolled her eyes. Somehow, she managed to hold back.

Suzanne continued to look her over. "Darling, you're the one who made a home in the night."

"You know what I mean."

"I do."

"Then, tell me."

"Clairvoyance and being attuned to the world are very personal experiences for each individual. I mean, I've met more than a few over the years, but I don't have all the answers."

"Then, tell the ones you do," Avril snapped. Anger bubbled just as steadily as the unanswered pot.

"From what I understand, what I have pieced together from the cards and from others…"

Avril waved her on. Suzanne was hesitating for some reason.

"Heavy emotions linger on a person years after they happen. You know that," Suzanne explained, as if she knew exactly what continued to linger on Avril, creeping around her back like a vise, reminding her just where the pain had come from and how terrible it had been. "Your shadows could simply be similar to an aura."

"I'm not having headaches." Not often anyway.

"Not that kind of aura. More spiritually. Sensation. What makes a person who they are."

Avril shook her head, trying to grasp what seemed to keep going around what she needed to hear here. She wanted Suzanne just to come out and tell her once and for all.

"You're telling me that I see the worst in people."

"Yes. And no." Suzanne tried again. "Your shadows are triggered by what?"

Avril thought for a long moment. "Memories, I guess."

"Memories, so strong emotions are attached then. Think of it almost like a haunting, when people see ghosts. Shadows. Memories. It's all the same, isn't it?"

She waited for more.

"When people think pleasant things and remember beautiful emotions, they feel light and full of life. But, Avril, I've known you since you were a little girl. We've been over this. Like your mother—and, yes, I have to talk about her—I've seen you be left behind and ripped away from good things. Emotion to you has never been simple, has it?"

No, Avril thought before she could stop herself.

She thought of all those moments when she had been a child. She had never been unhappy with Suzanne and her mom. Not really. She just was.

"With your emotions, there comes fear and force of power over it." Suzanne sighed. "The shadows are a manifestation of deep and perhaps dark emotion on you and on others. Emotions and memories that can't be controlled or erased."

"So, I'm stuck."

"Avril."

"Don't. Just—" She tapped the Knight of Swords and then the King that seemed to stick to the back of the card like glue. She needed to know. She needed to get back on track about what she had been talking about. "My mysterious man of shadows— or whatever the fuck you called them. Right here. You said this man would end me, correct? Ruin me. My life. You said that about him and the shadows around him, reaching out for me years ago, and the cards don't just suddenly change meaning, do they?"

"Since when was your life currently so ideal, Avril?" Suzanne asked.

Avril said nothing. She was certain if she looked down at herself, she'd have a piece of the answer.

"The Knight of Swords is a card of action, of a decision that could be brought on by a person to stimulate a wild change."

"Like what?"

Immediately, she couldn't stop herself. The shadows rose and faded, as if they were short-circuiting around her. She swallowed them back down and shut her eyes, but when she did, she saw her mother—no, herself—on the bathroom floor. Worse, standing on the edge of the bridge and not stepping back down until they were coated completely in ash.

"I can't say. I'm not that person."

"But that is just it, Suz. There is nothing left for me then, don't you see? Shadows and sensitivity be damned. Maybe my mother was right then. That's what you are telling me. That's it. Those are all the cards—the same cards of my entire life that we thought made no fucking sense until right now, when you have a wreck sitting in front of you that might as well be the ghost of your dead friend. You pulled them. You showed them to me."

"Avril, you are seeing meaning here where there isn't."

Oh, so now she had *all* the answers.

"Your cards don't spell out your life. Your death. Whether or not for some reason you so desperately want them to. When the cards run out, there is only one place left to go. You will not die. Not unless you want to," Suzanne said with ferocity. She flipped another card over. The World shone back. "You'll have to rise. You don't like this spread? This story?"

Avril was struck silent.

"Start a new one. How wonderful. How remarkable. Like a constellation you notice for the first time." Her eyes sparkled.

With delight? Dismay? Avril could not tell. She knew which she preferred. "There is only one way out of the shadows, and that is all on your own."

On her own. Wasn't that always what she was? What she had been for the past year? Longer?

Avril at the current moment wanted to scream. She had no one. She had been parading as no one since the moment she had walked into a closet and been captured in the first goddamn shadows she let herself fall face-first into and never expected them to feel so smooth.

Suzanne sighed. "One thing that isn't your mother? You're stubborn, and it looks like you've gotten very good at masking yourself as someone who is so far above yourself that rarely anyone questions it. Don't let that be the thing that ruins you, Avril. If only for yourself."

Avril stared at her, remembering Ian's similar words. Her mask. She felt her eyes begin to water before she stood suddenly. The chair tilted as she shoved it back.

"I assume you won't be staying for tea?"

She needed air. She needed something as the tiny apartment slowly pressed in around her. Turning away from Suzanne, she wasn't sure if she walked or ran to the door. She flung it open, grateful she never took off her coat.

The frost broke through her skin and into her lungs as she gasped for a single breath of air on the sidewalk—and immediately ran into someone's chest.

CHAPTER TWENTY-NINE

*T*aking a step back, Avril caught herself before she fell. She stared, wide eyed, at the person in front of her, adjusting a wide tote bag over her shoulder, filled with fabric. Tiny scissors hung off the strap on a key chain.

"Kit."

She put a hand up to steady herself. Or Avril. Both of them teetered on heels, though Kit's were still significantly shorter. "Are you all right?"

Kit glanced over Avril's shoulder to the building Avril had practically run out of.

"Getting your fortune read?" Kit chuckled.

"Something like that," Avril said slowly. She stared at the sign again, the perfectly placed stars of something that was supposed to mean safety and solace. Now, they sent a shiver up the back of her neck.

Avril put a hand to her head.

"You look like you could use a coffee," Kit suggested before taking another look at Avril. She was still wearing her house clothes, covered in dust and now a layer of sweat. "Or something stronger?"

It didn't take much for Avril to be led back to Kit's apartment. She let herself be guided up the stairs, where Kit waved to Perse, the intern still at the front desk, staring at Avril with wide eyes. Avril even relented to Kit yanking off her coat when she stood in front of the door too long and hanging it on the rack over her own.

Kit draped a soft blanket around Avril's shoulders as they settled on the couch.

Avril adjusted herself, so she didn't sit on a lump of spring cushion.

"How long were you outside? You look freezing—in a completely ice queen sort of way, of course." Kit stared at her. "Will you tell me what happened that caused you to become silent? Because unlike Perse downstairs, it is actually starting to freak me out, and everything my mind comes up with is always a million times worse than whatever it likely is, but I'll still believe it all anyway."

Avril couldn't help herself. A painful laugh escaped her chapped lips.

"That's not at all concerning."

"I ran into someone before I ran into you," Avril whispered, regaining her voice.

Kit's eyes widened. "It wasn't—"

"No," Avril replied quickly, not wanting her to even suggest the name that flooded images inside of her head—and apparently not only hers. Shadows fed on it like dry paper to an already overpowered flame. She shook her head. "We don't have to worry about that."

Even if she did anyway each time she left the house.

Avril hadn't even realized that until now, the shadows calmer, her heart slowly returning to an average pace now that she was inside, wrapped in perhaps the world's thickest afghan.

"Oh good."

"I was taking a walk to clear my head. The door I came out of when you showed up, it was my sort of godmother's house."

Kit smiled with dull surprise, glad this hadn't gone in a different direction than she was likely thinking, obvious by her last inference. "Is that not good?"

"I don't know," Avril admitted. "I hadn't seen her in a long time. Not since before my mother died."

"Your mother?" Kit asked slowly, dragging each syllable out, as if it were a question.

Avril was almost impressed.

"Don't act like you don't know," she scolded. "I'm the one who told you Jack was god-awful at keeping secrets. I'm not stupid enough to think he didn't spill my life story out to you like a pleasant bedtime story."

Without holding back, Kit cracked a smile. So did Avril. She didn't realize she was baring her teeth in something that wasn't a sneer until then. It flinched before disintegrating as she remembered the way Suzanne had looked at her with this strange mixture of familiarity, sadness, and maybe even fear.

"I take it, it didn't go all that well?" Kit asked while Avril thought about the entire exchange.

It couldn't have taken more than a few minutes in her mind, but looking at the antique clock hanging above the door, Avril saw that it had been a few hours since she'd left the house.

"Did she tell you about your mother or anything?"

Avril shook her head. "It wasn't like that."

Maybe it could've been. If Avril were normal, seeing Suzanne likely would have made her gasp with joy, like seeing an old friend. Instead, Avril's heart felt like it was made of stone, still trying to beat when she'd sat in front of the woman—her executioner.

"I practically attacked the woman, if I'm being honest," Avril said.

Kit didn't seem shocked. "Well."

"Yeah, well."

"You know that you can tell me anything you want. Unlike Jack, I'm slightly better at keeping secrets. Or omissions. Or whatever you're calling them these days. I'm just a little shy seamstress."

Snorting, Avril raised her eyebrows. "You really must be throwing them for a loop at DuCain."

She shrugged, propping her head on the back of the couch. "I'm just saying, you don't always need a game or deal to come clean with me, Avril. You should know that."

Avril blinked at the words, taking a deep breath. In the back of her mind, she knew exactly what Kit was trying to get at. Perhaps out of all of them last year, Kit had managed to sneak into Avril's life and seen her at her lowest. Even when Kit had also been at hers.

"When I was little, before my mother left," Avril began, "she used to have a friend we would visit whenever we were in the same place."

"Your godmother."

"Yes. She and my mother considered themselves witches of a sort. Pagans by belief. I loved that. I still do, and I think about it all the time. I never got the full details besides the occasional holiday I soon realized no one else celebrated but us. But Suzanne, my godmother, she always had a remedy for me whenever I needed it. She also read tea leaves and palm lines, but what I always loved most were the tarot cards she had."

Kit sat, saying nothing as she listened, though Avril was sure she knew exactly what kind of cards she meant, whether from Passion and Prose or the fact that she wouldn't doubt if Emilie, too, had a few sets left around.

"Whenever she pulled my cards or tried to read my future in whatever capacity, it never made much sense. I was only a child. But then it did make sense somehow. Now, she can't even tell me what to do next. She can't tell me what the fuck I should do with them."

"You've been living your life like this? Through cards?"

Avril shook her head, letting the weight collapse in her hands. "No. Not always. Not until…"

Recently, she wanted to say. When she wanted nothing more than to disappear and the shadows thickened like vines, ready to strangle her.

She didn't know what to do. Avril always knew what to do. She was the decision maker. The doer. Reed was the voice of reason, even when she didn't like it or didn't follow it anyway.

But now, when her eyes were closed, she stared back at the cards that had been haunting her dreams until, suddenly, the past year whipped like a raging storm and she locked in on The Tower. Until she decided to escape that tower and run straight into the arms of the man Suzanne had said could tear her life down entirely. Brick by brick.

The man of shadows, the knight's sword raised and ready to swoop down through the darkness. She didn't understand why he hadn't already ended it all in one action.

One decision.

There was no pretending anymore that Avril thought it was him, like she had for a short while after she first left.

"Go on."

Kit narrowed her soft eyes. "What?"

"Say it. Say *I told you so*." Avril needed to hear it. "I should've stayed away from him or whatever."

"Ian?" Kit's nervous eyes turned lighter at the words, as if she might laugh. Luckily, she knew better with Avril's sour mood still permeating the space. "I'm not going to say that."

"Why not?"

"You really want me to?"

At least it would be one sure thing. Another mistake.

"Because I don't. Maybe in the beginning, but now? I'm not

sure if I should." Kit pressed her lips together. "I really never thought of you as being so morbid about all this. So unoptimistic. How did you ever become Queen?"

Avril rolled her eyes. "Exceptional timing."

That first night, she had been back at Rosin, grumbling about loose sequins she was horrible at fixing or the amount of foundation stuck to the toilet seats. She barely could think of those moments when their guest star didn't show up and there was no one else to go on and take her place. It all happened so fast—from the girls lacing her up in a pearl-encrusted corset she'd admired for weeks to painting her face in a dark, bleeding lipstick and shoving her out onto the stage. She was breathless as the light shone on her. For a moment, all she could do was gasp for air while the corset restricted her lungs.

But then she danced.

She'd never felt more alive, and from that moment onward, she had been allowed to dance, no matter the day of the week or who she was. She was just her.

Queen.

Kit hummed, as if she could guess what Avril was thinking about. "You're afraid."

Avril glared at her. "I am not afraid."

She only shrugged.

"You know what Jack told me when I first met you guys? He told me that you had a habit of collecting lost things," Kit said. "Lost people."

"Is that so?"

"I can't help but think that he was right even if you won't agree."

"If he was right, would I have abandoned you so quickly after?"

Kit shook her head seriously. "You didn't abandon me."

As she looked around the small apartment littered with her

and Jack's mementos, maybe Kit was right. Avril didn't abandon her. Not alone anyway.

Lost things.

It made them all sound like toys she played with. Reed, Jack, and Kit. A sinking feeling settled into her stomach at how well the title fit.

"Avril's miraculous talents continue." Kit shrugged a single shoulder. "I don't think they go away either."

"What are you trying to say?"

"That maybe you saw something—someone—that was lost. Maybe you didn't even notice it at first."

"Ian?" Was that who they were talking about here?

"Maybe yourself too," Kit replied quietly.

Avril shook her head, the words coming out before she realized how weak they sounded, even to herself. "I'm not lost."

"Maybe not as lost as before."

When the cards ran out, there was only one place left to go, Suzanne had said. For the first time in a long time, Avril saw a path. A different decision that she hadn't considered before. It made no sense. It made her stutter and freeze.

"I'm not a good person."

"So?" Kit asked as if it were the last thing anyone wanted to be in the world.

"He deserves—" Avril cut herself off.

Kit raised her eyebrows, unwilling to say the words again.

She was afraid.

Maybe not even afraid. Avril was horrified. She didn't deserve Ian, not from the start when he'd teased her. Not now especially. She didn't deserve a single ounce of him or his kindness or the way he looked at her with consideration, like he knew exactly what was spinning around inside of her head most of the time before she even did.

She was Avril. A stripper who never had a very good time at staying with one person. With being a person anyone wanted to stay with. Who would want her? The dirty, loveless whore who made her home in the gutters of the night and grinned, rather pleased with the hole she'd dug—raised—herself in.

How could that ever be worthy of Ian? A man so clean, yet willing to trample the whole world if it meant getting what was needed.

Kit looked at her friend with keen understanding. "You really messed yourself up good, didn't you?"

"Ready to congratulate yourself yet?"

Kit only sighed in good humor. "I'm just shocked you about admitted it. This is about him."

"No." Not completely anyway. "This is about me."

"Of course it is," Kit agreed.

"He's still leaving. He still doesn't even know who I am. I barely even know who he is really. Some trust fund baby who thought he was too smart to live it up like the rest of his family when he could. Real daddy issues."

"Uh-huh."

"He hated it in Ashton."

"Does he still?"

Avril paused. She thought about the smile on Ian's face as they'd traversed the holiday market. When he'd helped her slip on her gloves outside the theater that night, somehow even after he was frustrated with her for some reason only moments ago, wiping it all away along with her tears.

"Just the engaged woman here who fucked up her relationship royally once before due to terrible communication, but maybe you should find out."

"You just like to hear yourself say you're engaged."

Kit beamed. "With him? Yeah."

No wonder she and Jack were a match. They were both delightedly insufferable once they got comfortable.

"I can't tell him. If I do now, it's all over. The whole deal we made and what it was built on is the fact that he doesn't get to know who I am. A blank slate. No one has to deal with all the dark and scary bits under the bed."

"You don't have to deal with it."

"I really don't like you right now, Kit. I can be whoever I want to be."

"Yet you went to the ballet with him. You shared yourself and your life, even if not all of it. You look the same, even in those ratty clothes." Kit looked her up and down with another smile. "It looks like you chose to be yourself."

"If I start to tell him who I was—" She thought of his shadows. His mother. "He's had enough on his plate for a lifetime, Kit."

"So have you."

Avril clenched her teeth together. "I've been lying to him all this time."

Kit's eyes widened in mock horror. "Oh dear. Avril does have a conscience."

Reaching over, Avril whacked Kit with the back of her hand.

"If I told him—" Avril forced herself to take a deep breath. "If I managed to tell him everything—and I don't think I can. I don't think I can tell anyone about that. I don't want to."

"Start small."

"What? *Hello, my name is Avril Isobel Maison McClair Queen, and I'm a previously famous burlesque dancer and sex model who entertains to every kinky need?*"

Kit laughed. "Well, it does have a confidence to it."

"What's to say he doesn't drop the entire deal? His family is full of"—Avril sought for the word—"propriety and trophy wives who lost their virginities after their coming-out parties. They wear white. Even if he didn't …"

What if he still leaves?

She knew that Kit had heard the second question.

"What's so wrong with that then?"

"What?"

"Being happy."

Happy?

"Even if it is just for now," said Kit with a shrug.

She opened her mouth to say, *Maybe not.* Maybe for once in her life, it wouldn't be so bad at all.

Avril froze as she heard the fast scamper up the stairs. The door opened before Avril could even bring herself to scan for another exit.

"Seriously, that girl looks at me like I'm going to eat her or something."

Jack let the door slip closed as he stared at the two of them on the couch. He was as dark and handsome as ever. He dropped his camera bag gently and crossed the space between them, eyes locked on Kit's polite posture and the pained expression Avril portrayed.

Kit's smile faltered.

Jack noticed, slowing down halfway to kneel in front of the two of them. "Hey, Queen, you all right?"

That's not my name, Avril heard in her head, the same way she'd told Reed every time he slipped up before. This time, however, she let the name hang.

She stared at Jack until she gave a shake of her head. "I'm fine."

An expression of relief overcame his shadowed expression.

Avril glanced back over to Kit.

She watched the exchange with heightened interest.

"I should probably go."

"Oh." Kit nodded, adjusting herself. "Jack will drive you."

"It's fine."

"I'll drive you." Jack stood back up, reaching for his coat before seeing Avril's hanging. Pulling it off the hook, he extended it for her to slip on as the blanket fell back into its own plush mountain around Kit's feet. Jack gave a tentative smile to her. "I'll be back in a bit."

"Have fun."

Avril wasn't sure that was the opportune send-off, even as she accepted her jacket. Surprisingly, Jack didn't say another word as they made it onto the street from the side door, stumbling down creaky wood steps. With a twirl of his keys, he unlocked the formidable green Jeep he'd had for as long as Avril could remember.

Avril looked at the open passenger door, the polite arm to help her in.

"No questions," said Jack. "Promise."

Heat streamed out of the vents, the car still warm from Jack just getting home. Avril settled farther into the seat, looking down at her hands and back up toward the road whenever Jack made a turn. She waited for him to say something, listening to the hum of the engine and then the low music when Jack reached for the radio dial.

Her eyes flickered up to him at the sound of indie rock.

Jack cleared his throat. "You know I'm terrible with silence."

She did. As well as his lack of secret-keeping skills, he had a problem with keeping his mouth shut when he wanted to say something. She should've been giving him a round of applause.

Instead, she took a breath.

"Congratulations."

He glanced at her.

"You and Kit," Avril clarified, looking out the front window. "You really didn't fuck that one up, did you?"

"Ha." A minor laugh escaped him. "I tried not to."

She nodded, only imagining.

"Thanks."

They continued after that in the quiet, moody tones of the music until Jack slid the gear into park. Unbuckling, Avril opened the door.

Jack reached out, catching her hand.

She looked down at it before peering up at her friend.

"Find me when you're ready to talk, all right?"

Avril didn't answer. She watched Jack let go of her hand before she got out of the Jeep. Turning around, she stopped.

"Start small," Kit had told her.

"I will."

Jack twisted to look at her in the eyes. His were bright as they widened. "Good. I have a lot to say."

He always did.

He idled there in the street until she walked up the steps of the porch and opened the door, gratefully still unlocked.

Pausing, Avril looked around. A thick breeze tunneled through the covered porch, sweeping up the corner of her coat. When she'd gotten out of the Jeep, she almost hadn't realized that she expected Jack to drop her off back at the townhouse. She didn't remember giving him the address.

Kit must've told him where she was going before they left.

Avril moved into the house with a shake of her head, shutting the door behind her as the warm air circled her. Draping her coat over the table, she looked up, thinking if she should call out to Ian if he was still there. Turning, however, Avril stopped in her tracks.

There was Ian, standing by the fireplace.

And there was a tree.

CHAPTER THIRTY

"*A*ll work and no play, I think was the phrase you once said to me?" Ian quirked the corner of his mouth into a timid smile.

"I didn't think you took it to heart." Avril couldn't believe what she was seeing.

"I figured it would be a shame for you to lose your traditions altogether either way."

Avril stared at the nearly bare tree. Branches looked to have been torn out of the one side in bunches. "Is it real?"

"It is. From down the block in front of the scary bodega you don't like."

She resisted the urge to roll her eyes and smile all at once at the poor, ugly plant. "We're going to kill it."

"Oh, probably," Ian agreed, taking in the view. "Traditionally nonetheless."

"I can't believe you did this."

"Yeah, neither can I." Ian smirked, looking around at the slowly transforming space.

"What happened to the whole fresh and ideal year-round look

you were hoping to create for your potential buyers?" Avril teased.

Detangled holiday lights were strewn across the floor.

"To be honest," Ian began cautiously, "I wasn't sure if you were coming back."

"Why would you say that?"

He cocked his head to the side. "You're having a moment, aren't you?"

"What?" A moment? It made her sound like a Victorian woman being overcome by the vapors. "Of course not. I'm not someone who freaks out."

Ian was not convinced. He didn't look horrified otherwise still, which was a good start.

"I'm perfectly fine. Like I said, I had a friend to meet up with today."

"I thought it was an appointment."

Avril paused, but Ian looked, if anything, the opposite of mad. He looked like he might even have a secretive laugh in him as he bit his lip.

"Come on." Ian lifted the ornament in his hand. It was their ornament, the one they'd made the other week together in the glass stand. "Do the honors?"

Avril shook her head, though she walked up next to him. "Nope. Go ahead. I call the star."

"Of course you do."

"It's only fitting."

He chuckled as he found a sturdy enough branch to hang the small shadow-filled orb. It appeared more solid than it had the last time she stared into it.

Avril glanced toward a wide bowl sitting on the edge of the ottoman.

"What's with the popcorn?"

"I thought we could string it since we don't have any oranges, like you mentioned how you celebrated before," Ian explained.

"Only when I opened the popped bag, I realized you'd chosen ultra-butter or whatever the hell it is."

Avril grabbed a bunch and shoved it all into her mouth at once. Buttery heaven was what it was. She barely had to chew as it melted on her taste buds. She also realized how hungry she was.

She took another handful, popping each kernel into her mouth one at a time. Ian only watched with light interest, looping the lights around the stout tree.

Lifting her last piece, she raised her eyebrows at Ian. Seeing her, he rolled his eyes but lifted his chin nonetheless as the popcorn flew through the air.

He caught it in his mouth. He carefully chewed before swallowing.

"Show-off."

"Get over here and help re-create your childhood holiday dreams."

Staring at him, she shook her head but moved over to him to grab the excess of lights out of his hands, layering them over the back branches near the window. "This is definitely nothing like my childhood holidays."

"No?"

"So far, the food is a lot better."

Laughing, Ian shook his head with her. "I'd have to agree."

"I would have expected more from your holidays—on the Ashton side at least."

His eyes flared in a memory. "Have you ever had a fruit cake Jell-O mold instead of cookies? Sometimes, there wasn't even fruit in them."

"What was in them?"

"At worst, it was just a mold of meat."

Avril gagged.

"Exactly. My father's wives were not the most domestic."

"No wonder you're like this."

Ian laughed again, louder than the last.

Reaching into the box the lights appeared to come out of, Ian handed Avril a few glass ornaments, each in a coating of faded newspaper.

"The first time I ever made Christmas cookies was when I lived with Reed's family. His mother, Paula, had a whole list of different kinds she would bake and put on trays to take around the neighborhood and to her church. Whenever she went out with them, she only ended up coming back with more." She reached for her stomach, remembering how much it'd hurt from semisweet chocolate chips.

Ian smiled. "I think you need to talk to Reed."

Avril angled herself to carefully loop the piece of ribbon around the branch. "You don't even know him."

"I still think you need to talk to him."

She sighed. "Probably."

They continued to slowly decorate. Avril grabbed her underused phone, still sitting on the table, to play holiday tunes. She bopped back into the living room with their packet of cookies Ian had obviously thought he'd hidden well in the back of the cabinet. She peeled back the top and offered one to him.

"I promise, they are meat- and gelatin-free."

He looked at her, hiding his amusement as he took a bite of the shortbread. They really needed some milk.

Avril tapped her own biscuit with his. They both looked around the place. Hours ago, there had been basically nothing in this room. There was furniture, and that was all. There wasn't even a television over the fireplace. Now, a loose garland swooped over the edge, and the tree was sparsely glittered.

"Where did you get all this stuff anyway?" Avril asked.

"I found a lot in the basement when I cleaned it out. It was probably from when my mother and I stayed here."

Avril looked at it all again from the corner as she sat down in the wingback chair. "You don't have to answer if you don't want to."

Ian stiffened.

"Why did she leave?"

He sucked on his cheek, nodding, as if he was trying to find the right words.

"I don't know. I have thought about it a lot and have come up with plenty of reasons, but honestly, I don't know." Ian shrugged as he took a step closer to her. He gestured for her to stand.

Rolling her eyes, Avril stood. He moved past her and collapsed into the chair. Raising her eyes, she watched as he patted the space on his lap. With a deep breath, Avril took him up on it, squeezing next to him as she kicked her legs over the other arm. She breathed him in, and the entire space felt homey and warm.

"You said something about her wanting to be independent," Avril mentioned. "Stand on her own with you."

He shook his head, looking forward and then at Avril. "She did. She was clearly unhappy here, always feeling like the other woman, I'm sure. We both were. I remember him coming to visit sometimes, but I mostly remember it just being us two in his big house. It felt even bigger before, when I was young."

Avril could only imagine.

"Reminds me." Ian propped himself up. "Our other invitation I told you about is coming up this weekend."

"The other scary Whitlock?"

He nodded. "Another fun family tradition. My father always hosts something before the holidays for everyone he knows from the office and elsewhere."

"Where does he live?"

"One of those big townhouses by the river. My latest step-mother is apparently preparing the decorations this year."

"A shame if we missed out on those." Avril thought of all the other townhouses by her own little castle on the river. Most of them usually hired out to seasonal decorators to put up lights and garlands of at least a half dozen shades. "Fancy digs and all."

"My father wouldn't have it any other way."

Avril looked up around the house they sat in again. With the two of them sitting there, so close together, it did feel large, looming around them. "You don't say?"

Ian huffed a distracted sound. "If you aren't comfortable, we don't have to go."

"You don't want to go."

"I don't want to do many things at this point in my life, as you are well aware."

Eat pop-toasties. Stay in Ashton. Wake up at a reasonable hour that wasn't before eight a.m.

"The problem is, my father along with my half brother, who likely knows where I live currently. I wouldn't put it past him to show up, half drowned in top-shelf bourbon, just to cause a scene on the doorstep."

"A scene?" Now, that was something she'd love to see.

"You can only imagine. It wouldn't be the first time my brother has attempted to demean me, saying how I'm a disgrace to the family."

"You're kidding." Avril couldn't help but smile.

He lifted his gaze to her, less amused than her.

"When it was just the two of us, he took it upon himself to make sure I understood exactly what my mother did during her life. At first, I made a fool of myself, trying to make sure he didn't get the last word, but after a while"—Ian shrugged, disappointed —"I just had to let him go with it until he tired of whatever obscure entertainment I had to offer. He didn't know of the bad times I had with my mother after we ran off, taking care of ourselves. He didn't understand those weeks when things didn't go as planned or I couldn't help whatever was happening to my mother, from the men to the sickness. To me."

Avril said nothing as he spoke openly. She leaned her chin down onto her knee as she watched him.

"He doesn't know what it is like to have a childhood so full of joy in only such small moments that in order to move forward, you let it obscure your perception of all the horrible things."

He stared at Avril for a moment, as if she knew what he was talking about.

She did. "You look into the darkness, and whatever monsters stare back aren't all that frightening. You don't let them be."

Because who would they call to check for monsters under the bed? When their only other person could be just as afraid and uncertain.

Ian carefully nodded.

Avril attempted to lighten his mood. His joy from earlier had to be lingering somewhere in there yet. "You just need to look at the entertainment value. A reality television show would eat that shit right up. What's his name again?"

"My brother?"

"Yeah, your likely frat-boy brother who doesn't know how to handle his liquor, if I am catching this very kitsch drift right."

"Unfortunately"—Ian shook his head—"you are, and I try to stay as far away from him as possible. He's named after his father, Marcus."

"Marcus Whitlock. How stately."

Ian grunted in agreement. "When I once came home from school for the holidays my first year, he yanked me out of the shower and locked me in the backyard. It was snowing. The college students who were living in their parents' summer home beside us found me when their motion light kept going off from my shivering corpse."

"Oh God. That must've been—"

"Frosty. Indeed," Ian confirmed. "I ended up staying at school for the holidays and most breaks after that incident."

"What a jealous ass."

"Jealous?"

Avril looked up at Ian and found their eyes locked on one another. "Your brother. He is obviously jealous of you. You look like your father, for one thing. For the most part anyway."

Not counting Ian's beautiful yet professionally chopped hair —not tainted from what Avril could only assume was a cocaine phase from the '80s, turning Mr. Whitlock's blond locks more nicotine yellow than Ian's soft golden highlights.

"Wow, you really did do your research."

"Your brother is probably following in his father's footsteps, right? Yet for some reason, he just can't seem to capture your father's attention. Not like you seemed to."

"We were raised nearly the same."

"Nearly."

That was the key word.

"Where is Marcus's mother?" Avril asked as she thought of it.

Ian stretched his legs out in front of them onto the ottoman. His arm curled around Avril, pulling her into him. She took a deep breath as she laid her cheek against his chest, which gently vibrated as he spoke. "After the divorce? I don't know. Last I heard, she decided to move to the islands off Capri to be alone."

The woman had style.

Avril countered him with his own phrase. "Nearly the same."

"Hmm?" Ian's forehead creased in concentration.

Avril raised her eyebrows and looked around the gifted house outside the city, all for Ian and his mother Mr. Whitlock had tried to hide until Mrs. Whitlock found out most likely.

For years.

"Like I said, if you aren't comfortable, we don't have to go," Ian said.

If she didn't believe Ian, she would have thought he was getting on the verge of some sort of manly begging. She'd rather like to see that.

"I'll go."

"Are you sure?"

She nodded, as if he were kidding. "I already have my outfit picked out."

He still didn't look at ease.

Avril took a deep breath. "You know when I left today?"

Ian's attention pulled back, directly on her. Gentle and easy.

"I ended up seeing someone I hadn't in a long time," Avril said. "I hadn't seen her since I was with my mum. Suzanne. She was my godmother, of a sort. At least, my mom used to tell me that. Suzanne looked just as shocked when she saw me. She said that when she noticed me, she thought I was a ghost."

She forced herself to look up at him. She needed to see Ian's reaction as she continued on.

"She thought I was my mother."

Avril swallowed. She felt her forehead crease as she thought of the expression on Suzanne's face when she'd first seen her. "It turns out that she was supposed to be the person who took me if something happened to my mother. When something happened to her. All I can think about is, what would have happened if she had?"

Ian's fingers gently traced swirls up and down her forearm.

"If Suzanne had managed to get the letter my mother had left her before everything, I would've never been sent to live with my uncle and his family. I would've never then been tossed from home to home after my uncle got a little too drunk and little too angry one night at my aunt and beat her so terribly that my cousin, my brother—" That was what he was to her after all. What her aunt had made sure to introduce him as, the smiling and waving redhead only a bit older than she was. "We had to drag her into the back of the pickup to drive her to the hospital."

.   .   .

HER BROTHER WAS BARELY fifteen by then. Still, he didn't hesitate as he hauled Avril up into the back of the truck. Avril's aunt looked at her, eyes flickering until they remained half closed when she spoke.

"Pray, sweet girl. Pray to God. He will save us," she begged.

Avril shook her head at it all then, eleven and shivering as another rush of blood pulsed onto her hand-me-down jeans from the cut along her aunt's head. But then, it might've been one of the only times Avril ever looked up to the dark sky and prayed like a Christian.

There was no manifesting, no offerings. She only had herself covered in muck and blood.

She prayed to one god. To any. She prayed to the stars as her mum had always done late at night when she said she felt too much and didn't know what else to do but beg to be taken away.

"Please," Avril whispered, as if she herself were a god in that moment who could breathe life back into her aunt. Born out of blood and night. "Please, take me away."

"I SAW my brother again after my own accident with my back. I hadn't seen him in years, and when I did, it was like this well opened up in me, and I couldn't stop remembering that night. But for some reason, I can't find myself regretting being there or being angry. I would have never met Reed."

She shook her head at that one. Who would she have ever turned into without Reed? The two of them misfits in the land of ash and suburbia. They'd made themselves a home together. "I would've been here, in Ashton probably. Eventually."

Maybe she still would have met Reed at some point. Then again, maybe not.

"I wouldn't have ever…" Avril drifted off as she thought of the past year, closing her eyes for a short moment.

When she opened them again, Ian paused his soft touches. He pulled something out of his pants pocket. Immediately, the stark gold caught in the fairy lights.

Avril's eyes widened at the ring.

"I want you to have this."

"No, Ian." She shook her head.

"I made a rule, and you made me a promise with that rule," Ian said. Transitioning the ring from his palm to holding it between two fingers. A silent invitation. "Think of it as a reminder. To keep living."

You're not going to die, not unless you want to.

"Take it."

"Ian."

"You'll give it back to me when you're done using it," he said.

Holding her right hand, he slipped the small ring on her fourth finger. The finger was symbolic of passion, creativity and, most of all, promise. The ring was snug, but fit. The diamond, like her mother's brooches, winked as it caught the dim light from the fire.

She felt a flare inside of her stomach.

What was so wrong with happy for now?

Small steps.

"We still need the topper." Avril stood up, pushing off Ian to get out of the cushions. Reaching toward the bottom of the ripped box, she unwrapped the tiny, sparkling gold star from tissue paper. Lifting it up, she extended her arms to the top of the tree before looking at the wingback chair and then Ian.

He gave a deep chuckle, realizing what she was waiting for. Walking over, he wrapped his arms around her hips. "You realize, it would be easier if you let me do it."

"Ah, but where's the fun in that?"

CHAPTER THIRTY-ONE

*T*he air whipped against Avril's cheeks all the way to the metro. Crowds packed each car, families trying to get into the city for their last-minute shopping and meet and greets with a round-bellied Santa at the village center.

Avril watched the younger children. They seemed to jiggle in their seats from the excitement of the season. There was something in the air that jolted them into a different tone of elation.

Perhaps that was what also made the distance between Ian's house and Avril's castle smaller every time she made the journey. Of course, she hadn't been to her own house in a while. Longer than she thought it'd been.

When she arrived, she got off a stop early. She took her time as she walked across the bridge, holding her hat to her hair so it didn't blow away. Then, she was there.

She stood and looked at the looming presence of her townhouse, her castle, for a long moment, noting the multicolored light strands twisted around the pole.

Another addition since she had last been there.

Ascending the steps, she fished for her key in her bag, but before she could put it into the lock, the door swung open.

Reed stood there, one hand still on the brass knob.

He inhaled. "I wasn't sure if you were coming in."

Avril stepped past him and into the foyer. The warmth soaked into her skin as she stood in front of him. She sniffed, looking around the place, though it sounded empty. It was just the two of them.

"I know. I'm sorry, okay?" Reed slumped with immediate apology.

Avril took a step back. Her heel connected with the bottom step of the stairs before she managed to steady herself. She caught the end of the wood railing.

"I should have never contacted him. I needed to talk, and I never meant for us to—"

"Wait a second." Avril put up a finger to silence him.

It worked.

"Wait," she repeated. "You think that I'm angry with you because you and Dixon are together? Oh my gods."

"Aves."

"No, you're wrong, just—" She wasn't sure what to say. As she decided, she wandered over to the couch, flopping onto it as she stared at him.

Reed leaned against the rounded frame, seeming content to wait for her.

Dixon had been right when she came to the house before. Reed really thought he was in the wrong for needing something, someone.

"I love you."

"What?" Reed stiffened with shock.

"You know it," Avril snapped the words at him, as if they were a curse. Might as well have been. Better than *stay with me*. "I fucking love you, you weirdo. It hurts me to think that all this time, for some reason, you have been so focused on me and my career."

"You know that I loved every second of it."

"And then what happened—"

"You mean that fucking shithead I hated from the start?" Reed shook himself out of his flare of anger. "I should have been taking care of you. I should've watched out for you, even after you disappeared for so long after. I should've at least tried to look for you."

Where? In the middle of nowhere, where she'd ended up spending most of her time when she walked away from Reed the first time in the spring? When she'd walked away from everything.

Avril shook her head at him again, but slowly. "No, Reed, you shouldn't have."

"What are you talking about?"

"I'm a bitch. That's what I am saying."

He paused, considering this. "Well, yeah, but we both already knew that."

Avril dared to crack a smile.

So did he.

"I need you to know though. I mean, I have my studies and my research I've been focusing on, and I love what I do even though it's made me drift out of your weird and fabulous life recently, but you and me, Aves, that's always been it."

And it always would be.

Reed's eyes flickered side to side to combat what might've been tears.

Avril reached out to her best friend as he crossed the room. He took her hand in his as he sat down next to her on the blue couch, which he'd argued was too ostentatious in the rest of the wallpapered room. It'd felt right then.

Both them leaned until their heads lolled over the back cushion. Their ceiling was very similar to Ian's.

"Reed," Avril said, "you don't have to watch out for me. Not anymore, okay?"

"I'm not—"

"No, please," Avril cut him off.

"Wow." He seemed shocked. "A please."

Avril might've given a single laugh. "Stop. Just listen to me."

He stopped. Listened. He knew better by now.

"I'm sorry that when we first came to Ashton, you felt like I put that pressure on you to keep up with me all the time. To save me. But now, it's not like when we were kids in high school anymore. Though I am so fucking grateful. You are the absolute best thing that has ever happened to me, but you don't have to be that person for me anymore if you can't always be. Okay? You're my best friend."

"You're mine."

She knew that. "Wow. We must be really old and getting bored with each other if we are picking these ridiculous sorts of fights, huh? I want you to be happy, Reed. If you thought I was shocked to see a very comfortable Dixon in the house a few weeks ago, coming out of your bed, well, you'd be right."

Reed coughed a sound of laughter.

"But only for a second."

He laughed some more.

"I was much more pissed that you hadn't told me. You were living this whole different life from me because you thought I couldn't handle it."

"For a while there, Aves"—Reed rolled his head side to side —"I wasn't so sure you could."

Avril held in a long breath, trying to remember those times when she'd first come home from the incident. There was Reed's arms around her. Her back—the rest of the memories she shoved away. Then, there had been the parties of one. The drinking just so she could fall asleep for a few hours, where Reed would hold her hair back while she dry-heaved into their fancy guest toilet.

Stars, the thought made her cringe. It was only months ago.

It might as well have been a lifetime. But how could she explain that to Reed, who had seen it all?

"I'm doing better, you know."

Reed smiled. "I see that. When I saw you standing outside the house before you came up the porch, I had to do a double take. I swore, for the slightest second, I saw Queen out there."

She might've been peeking through. But then again, so was Avril. One and the same, just like all the names and personas she had taken on, and Ian had seen that enough to add another that was all his—and hers really. She felt the warmth stir at the thought of him murmuring his soft pet name into her ear.

My Rose.

She shivered, peeling herself back up to sitting so she could look at her friend better. He did the same. "Don't judge."

"Me?"

Turning with a raised eyebrow, she managed her best to not look bemused. "You. I have been staying with someone."

"Who?" Reed asked.

"Ian."

He nodded, interested, but Avril paused as he rested his cheek on his hand. She narrowed her eyes. "Jack called you already, didn't he?"

"Yeah."

"That fucker."

AVRIL MOVED through her room with ease, yanking open the closet, where hems swung against perfectly lined up shoes below.

Had someone cleaned her room?

She couldn't think long on it as she searched for the dress she was looking for. She and Reed had already wasted enough time talking about Dixon and how sad he was that Avril wasn't there to make some chocolate monstrosity before the holidays, which he would mainly be spending the days up to playing piano at private parties. She messaged Ian, saying that she'd meet him at his father's house on time.

Reed raised his eyebrows. "Back to using technology?"

Not answering, she threw the phone back on the bed beside him. "Red or black?"

"Red."

"You barely even looked at them."

"You're going into the lion's den. Red."

"I think you're thinking of bulls."

"It's all the same bullshit to Whitlock's people," Reed said. "Plus, you know, holiday."

Avril sighed and looked down at the red dress on the hanger. Simple with thin straps and a high slit. "Well, if we want to start talk."

"We are the best kind of gossip."

Very true, Avril thought as she finished getting dressed.

She went with the red, showcasing a daringly dipped neckline, where a single jewel swayed from a necklace so thin that it could have been a fishing line, naked to the eye, until you caught the other sparkling centerpiece attached to the deep V.

Adding her mother's ruby brooch, Avril cinched her long coat shut.

"How do I look?"

Reed only rolled his eyes at her, as if she'd asked the most unreasonable question there was.

When Dixon saw the two of them hugging goodbye before the entryway, Avril could've sworn something like relief crossed his face.

"Happy solstice, darling. Go fuck him," Reed encouraged.

She turned around with a single wave. "Already did!"

"Wow, is it just me, or do you feel like a father sending your child off into the world?"

"God, no, Dix. What the hell?" Reed shut the door by the time she made it past the window.

CHAPTER THIRTY-TWO

*S*he'd maybe walked by the house once without realizing it. It was one of the statelier townhouses by the river, farther away from the bridge than Avril's castle was. Here, the shutters were painted brown, and the doorknobs shone, just in case someone was more interested and looking to where they were putting their hand rather than where they walked into.

The Christmas lights were white. They trailed up the columns and railing.

Ian's eyes widened when he saw her. "I almost believed you were too nervous to show."

Avril looped her arm around his. "Just wanted to make sure I was properly adorned, is all."

"You look stunning."

Let's hope the rest of the place thinks so.

She gripped his wool-covered forearm a little tighter, and it was only then that Avril realized they'd stopped moving at the base of the front steps.

Ian stood, frozen, looking up at the house as if he'd just seen a ghost peeking out of the witch windows on the third floor.

"Something wrong?"

"I need a minute."

"All right."

Steady beside Ian, Avril held tight to him and his shirt he'd had to press every time she brought up the Christmas party the past few days. It might as well have been mainly starch, as he straightened and tucked it into his pleated pants.

Avril decided after all this time, she actually did rather like the dark academia look.

When she reached out to tug on one of the belt loops, Ian's glove grasped her own.

Avril stared down at it for a long moment before she had to remind herself to breathe. Giving him his moment, Avril lifted her chin to look at the house with him again. Letting out that breath, she watched it float away.

She couldn't imagine having lived in a house like her own now or Ian's father's, when she was young. A stone's throw from the height of downtown Ashton, Avril could only imagine the sort of trouble she would've gotten in.

"You seem tense."

"Me?" Ian tried to laugh. It didn't come out that way, sounding choked. "Not at all."

She smiled at him. "All right."

He sighed.

"Just focus on me. Like how I am about to turn into a human Popsicle. I can't imagine I'm as delicious as I am when thawed."

Looking her up and down, Ian let her shimmer with frost for another moment before nodding.

Walking with her stuck at his side, Ian opened the door and ushered her through before shutting the door behind him again, just as swiftly. The house smelled of warm mulled wine and pine. They had to be pumping the scent through the vents.

The house was so different compared to her own and not just because it was double the size. Dozens of people were scattered throughout without feeling like they were actually interacting.

Soft holiday music played. The modern stone fireplace wasn't just for decoration, but ran steadily with gas. The bookshelves surrounding it were painted a crisp clean white, along with the rest of the house. They were filled with less books and more clocks and knickknacks in the shape of snowflakes and gold memorabilia no one knew the origin to.

She let Ian unbutton her coat for her as she looked around.

He seemed to be unable to stop his hands from doing something even if she had a few better ideas for him, if only he asked. She felt a strange feeling slip over her, the longer she stood there, arms bare as Ian exposed her silk scarlet dress. The fabric practically begged for Ian to unwrap her.

But another sensation also pricked at her skin, dry and claustrophobic.

"You'll surely make a welcome sight." Ian's lip quirked to the side. He still shifted uneasily, looking around the place as if he wouldn't be surprised if something popped out of the hall closet.

"You sure you're okay?"

He swallowed.

"Is that a yes or a *I should hustle you out the back door or into another closet, so we scandalize the party and are never invited back?*"

"Yes," Ian said. He held a beat. "The first one."

"No fun."

"Behave yourself."

"I'll try, but…" Avril remembered Reed calling out the front door.

"Rose."

"I will say it again." She tilted her chin down to peer through her thick lashes. "No fun."

"Well, let's meet the hellhounds," Ian bemoaned into her ear.

"That's my brother's biker gang." Avril smiled.

"Ian! How wonderful it is to see you." A woman arrived ahead of them. She already looked to be finished with her first drink, waving an empty glass until a man with an empty tray easily extracted it from her grip.

Avril could only smile at the character of a woman who was dressed in feathers, unlike all the cashmere and red plaid that made Avril wonder if she'd stepped into an awkward family photo shoot.

"Idena," Ian said her name in greeting.

"Aren't you a sight for tired eyes? And by tired, I mean, bored," Idena proclaimed, putting a hand to her grown-out gray hair, swept back into a loose French twist.

Ian glanced down to Avril. "Idena used to work for my father."

"I was a secretary years ago."

Ian might've once said Avril had a mask of sorts, but his just as easily slipped into place with a flat, serious expression. His practiced smile was so different than the devilish glee he gave when getting the upper hand. "We've all gone our separate ways."

"Sounds like you were lovers," Avril added.

Ian twisted back down at her.

Idena only gave a boisterous laugh, coughing as she trailed off. "Oh, I love your friend, Ian."

"I'm sure she's thrilled." Ian continued to stare at her, though she wasn't quite sure what he was thinking with such an even look. She wanted it to crack open.

Let her see him.

"We can always use some color around here." Idena herself looked around the place, as if to prove the fact. "Of course, you two should come in. Don't sit around by the doorway unless you plan to make a mad dash."

"The offer has been made and is still on the table."

Idena laughed once more. "Oh, Ian dear, you have yourself a pistol with this one."

Ian only smiled again. His cheeks were going to hurt if he kept it up. But then he pulled his hand away from hers and wrapped it around Avril's waist to murmur in her ear, low enough so only she heard, "I didn't know she was loaded."

She smiled right back at him.

Ian exhaled a breath that must have been holding him up since the second they'd walked through the front door.

From around the corner, stuffed with a gathering of men in suits squishing the holiday decorations, another man in similar attire approached them. He buttoned the center over his full stomach. Immediately, Avril knew who it was from the shock in his eyes that quickly turned from unsureness to steady ease in his own house. She had heard of Mr. Whitlock spending thousands every year to different businesses around the holidays to write off on taxes, Rosin getting a few thousand one year when he likely had no idea who he was donating to.

Extending his arm, Mr. Whitlock shook his own son's hand. "Ian, I wasn't sure you'd come."

"I said I would."

"Of course." Mr. Whitlock nodded, as if he hadn't made such an absurd statement at all. "How are you? You've been working? I told you if you needed to get in contact with me, just to ring."

"I have been in town since the summer, working on the house."

"You've planned to stay? Like I said—"

"I've planned on selling at the end of the month."

Avril lifted her gaze up to Ian for a swift second.

Mr. Whitlock blinked. "I see."

Ian cleared his throat before looking back down to Avril next to him. She already began to look behind to the other rooms for an alternate escape route. A new stream of music trailed into the air from where it looked like some were dancing, table pressed up against the other wall.

"This is Ro—Avril."

Mr. Whitlock's eyes practically skimmed over her until Ian's hand brushed against her. The moment he looked at her, however, there was no doubt in Avril's mind. He knew exactly who she was.

Avril gave a bright smile, mouth stretching wide.

"I thought you were bringing that friend of yours. Clara?"

"Cynthia."

Mr. Whitlock's gaze flicked back to Avril. "Right."

"Change of plans," Ian said. His eyes did not leave his father's, as if they were in an intense staring contest.

Ian won.

"Can I have a moment?" Mr. Whitlock turned to Ian.

Ian licked his lips as he nodded. He turned back to Avril. "Can you behave yourself for a few minutes?"

"I think I'll manage." She smiled something dangerous just to scare him.

His eyes flared, as if he was unsure whether or not he actually wanted her to keep herself in check.

"He's smitten," Idena said.

"If you say so."

"You do look oddly familiar, dear."

Avril lifted a shoulder. "Just one of those faces."

Idena winked, though she still looked as if she was trying to place her. She'd get it eventually. Idena was one of the most generous when it came to all theatrical arts in Ashton after all.

"I believe I'm going to need a drink," Avril said, moving toward the other end of the house.

"Don't we all?" Idena already searched for her next group to infiltrate for a more interesting conversation. "We'll talk again."

Avril slowly wandered through the mansion of a home with too much open space, even with the people. Avril admired the clean surfaces and mused over the food table, topped with strange seed-covered crackers and shrimp sans sauce.

Picking up a crystal champagne glass, Avril tilted the bubbles toward her lips. She hadn't had bubbly since the first office party she and Ian had gone to and would never force herself to settle for such subpar celebratory cocktail again.

She took a longer sip before extending her hand to be topped off.

The man in the suit, hired by a company, obviously understood that she was a plus-one. Smiling, he let the foam almost crest past the rim.

"Thanks, darlin'." She lifted it into a cheers before turning back around toward the other side of the room, where she could better view the women giving each other the side-eye and laughing when one tried to make a joke.

Avril gave it a try, laughing from the back of her throat, just enough to choke herself with another sip of champagne. Looking beside her, she could imagine Reed there, easily making the night at the very least somewhat interesting. Reed could easily find a group to insert themselves into until they were the talk of the night.

She glanced down at her dress. She pressed her hand against her hip as she stood, looking over the rest of the crowd. She wanted to add the brooch underneath rather than only on her coat, but it showed through. Much to her dismay, she still hadn't had the chance to tease Ian how she wasn't wearing any underwear—truly this time.

The back of his neck would surely flare with a light blush. Her crudeness was the only thing she'd noticed that made it appear, though it would disappear just as quickly.

"Hello there."

A woman beside her settled in front of her. "Are you the girl I heard Marcus's son Ian had brought with him?"

Avril grinned, teeth still against the fine crystal flute. "I suppose I am."

"I thought so," she twittered. "Forgive me, I'm Marcus's wife."

No matter how hard she tried, which wasn't much, Avril's eyes widened at the woman before her. So pleasant and …

young. Ian hadn't told her much about his new stepmommy or whatever she was to him, but she hadn't expected, well, this woman.

Avril looked her up and down with simple appreciation. "Pleasure to meet you, Mrs. Whitlock."

"Oh." The woman put a hand to her chest. She reached the other hand up to tuck a golden-blonde curl behind her ear. "Bianca is fine, thank you."

"Avril."

"Avril." Her eyes squinted as she said her name, a slight sort of twitch of recognition.

Avril gently grinned, baring a single canine to see how far she could go before she scared the pretty petal off. "You throw a lovely party."

"Thanks. I've always loved Christmas. The lights. The presents."

Ian came up behind her.

Avril leaned into his chest.

"I was always more of a solstice gal myself."

Her serene expression at last faltered. "Nice to see you, Ian."

"Bianca." Ian squeezed Avril's shoulder. "Drinks?"

"Nothing sounds better right now. I'm empty. I'm sure we'll talk later, Bianca."

As they walked away, Bianca gave a tiny wave that didn't reach her fingertips.

"Rose."

"Oh gods, when you start with that name, it sounds rather serious," Avril purred.

When Ian said nothing, however, Avril twisted herself to look at him. They weren't going to the drink table. He looked straight ahead to the other side of the room. His father was swiftly coming toward them once more.

"Time for the escape plan?"

"Please, just be polite. We won't be staying long."

Avril stopped breathing. He was going to make her talk to that man. In front of him?

"Are you sure? I'm not wearing any underwear."

Ian's attention snapped to her, and the only blush she saw on him was the wantonness in his eyes.

Escape route, option two.

They were close to a reliably sturdy table by the looks of it.

Mr. Whitlock turned over his slightly pudgy hand before Avril could convince Ian to make use of the flat surface.

"Do you like to dance, *Avril?*"

CHAPTER THIRTY-THREE

*H*e held her lower back as they danced. Nearly crushing his hand as she reached behind herself, she slid it higher.

"You're quite the dancer, Mr. Whitlock."

"As are you," he muttered. "But if you think I don't know who you are, Miss...Queen, is it? You're mistaken."

Avril let out a light peal of laughter, as if he'd said the most interesting piece of gossip she'd heard all night. He did as well. The sound sent a heavy brick down into her stomach, putting pressure on each of her next words. But she had known from the moment she laid eyes on Ian's father what his game was. Little did he know, she'd played it before.

"I didn't take you as a fetish man, Mr. Whitlock. Or at least to pronounce it so openly." She raised her voice near the end. "Then again, I appreciate the fact that you never once frowned upon the common sex worker."

His kind disposition soured, the one side of his face wincing. He knew better than to look around to see if anyone was listening. "Keep your voice down or else my son will hear you."

"How many of your friends have visited someone like me?"

His eyes shifted from her for a hasty second.

"Also, please. He's as much your son as I am."

Whitlock had the audacity to look hurt. "He's still mine, whatever he told you. I gave him everything."

"And let me guess. It still wasn't enough? Is that why you take to threatening his dear friends at your annual holiday bash?"

"Is that all you are? Like you said, I unfortunately can't blame my son for his taste."

To that, Avril had no answer.

A stalemate on all fronts.

"What do you want?" asked Avril.

"What makes you think I want anything from you?"

"Everyone wants something."

Thus, the world went around.

"Even my son?"

Again, Avril didn't answer. All she knew Ian wanted was to get the hell out of Ashton, and to be honest, it was hard for Avril to dissuade him.

"I want what is best for him," Mr. Whitlock said. His voice was like stone.

"What makes you think I don't want the same?"

Avril's smile faltered as she looked up toward the ceiling. Dim lighting didn't give her much to find up there. "Mr. Whitlock, I will tell you what your son already did. He's leaving at the end of the month once he's finished working on the house you gave him and putting it up for sale."

"But that's not—"

She stopped him.

"He's told me he is leaving. He finished his final days of contract at the library." Avril swallowed. "Now listen closely when I say this. Ashton is my home."

And she'd be staying here, not going anywhere else.

"Perfect."

It was just how she wanted it. Ian. The deal and them

going their separate ways without him ever finding out who she was or why she was doing all of this, even if Avril hadn't thought she'd be leaving on two feet in the beginning. The shadows had kept fading and fading further from her view when she stopped thinking about them. Hours and then days had begun to go by when she felt as if she'd left them behind completely, only leaving an uneasy pit in the bottom of her stomach.

She felt the disquiet now, but it no longer seemed to overtake her.

Glancing over her shoulder, she searched the corners for Ian. "And now that the song has passed, I believe it would be appropriate for us to depart the floor. Don't you agree?"

Taking a step away from her, he guided her past another couple to the edge of the room.

"A pleasure."

"All mine," Mr. Whitlock assured her as his hand dropped back down to his side.

Still, Avril gritted her teeth. "I do prefer when men bow to me when they share such a wonderful moment with me, Mr. Whitlock."

He chuckled with a single nod. Without a bow or a kiss to the toe of her heel, Ian's father turned his back on her and walked toward the other end of the room. Standing there for another moment, tall with a light smile on her face, Avril watched as the eyes turned carefully toward her in curiosity.

She never minded the stares, even as she gave her own, looking around the crowded house for one in particular.

Ian was nowhere to be found. He wasn't near the dance floor or getting himself a drink to drown whatever had been irking him before he and Avril made it to the front door.

She would find him again, or he would find her.

Right now, she needed a moment.

As she moved toward the front of the house, the sound of

chattering dulled. Leaning against the stair banister, alone, Avril closed her eyes. And took a deep breath to steady herself.

Five, six, seven—

"I've seen you before."

Avril hummed with irritation before placing a careful smile to face the voice coming down the staircase. She glanced up as he rounded the bottom step. Ian's older brother smirked down at her.

He looked similar to Ian, strangely enough, like pieces of him were lingering. Tall in build, he filled out more in the way of a fit linebacker than Ian's bookworm. His smile though, that was all his father, up to the light crow's-feet starting to bridge from the corners of his eyes.

He seemed to like the way her eyes fell over him. "It was at a show in Chicago about three years ago. I was there on a med-pharm conference trip."

"You're a doctor."

"That's right. Pediatrics." Marcus practically patted himself on the back.

Avril couldn't help but be surprised at the turn of events, expecting young Marcus with his carefully gelled hair to be following in his father's bland outlook of life, keeping an eye on a friend's steadily growing hedge fund.

She narrowed her eyes as she thought back to when she had been in Chicago. The last time she'd traveled west had to have been about the time he was talking about. Three years ago. It had been a packed house, larger than anything Rosin could ever hold in its close and cozy quarters.

Still, she hadn't seen him before at all that she could remember.

"I thought I overheard Ian had brought someone unexpected tonight," said Marcus. "Can I ask you a question?"

Avril narrowed her eyes. His tone was enough to send her further over the edge.

"I can only imagine you are going to."

When he leaned down, his hot breath seeped into her ear. "Does my little bastard brother know you're a slut who flashes the world?"

"I see you don't fall far from your daddy's tree."

"Not like it would be surprising. I might be like my father, but if so, so is my brother. Don't you think? Rather jovial, taking in a whore to save, like his mother."

Ian's mother. She thought back to what she knew about her. How Ian smiled when he talked about her. Mother, prostitute, lover, woman who knew how to hold her own and live that way.

Avril swallowed. "A whore?"

He only waited as if he knew she had some sort of angry comeback to give to him.

He would be sadly mistaken.

Avril only smiled. "You realize that glorious little word is a term of endearment where I come from."

"Is that so?"

"It is," Avril said, forcing her voice to remain in cadence. Slow and steady. "When someone calls a woman or a man a whore, there's a significant power dynamic. A give and take of sorts."

"And how much would it cost for a night with the Queen?" Marcus droned.

Avril shoved him away but only to take a step back in. Her heel positioned itself between his legs as she went up on her toes.

"Depends. What do you want, darling? A usual rate for what I think you want—to be seduced, dominated perhaps after a long day?" Avril grinned as she turned her head, musing to him like a siren. "Nothing too fancy?"

He couldn't look away.

"Or maybe not. Do you want more than just a little tease? I once ran my nails down the back of a man until he bled. I watched while a handsome friend of mine with a wicked smile twice as sharp as mine whipped him until all he could do was cry and beg and open up his wallet for more. That was tame, if you like it rough. I offered to lick his wounds for a price. I hope you hide your bank account from prying eyes, darling.

"But, of course, the only games I play anymore are consensual. So"—Avril took another step forward—"how about you take a step back or lick my eight-hundred-dollar stilettos? Because with that kind of wit, the only someone who will want to sleep with you, you're going to have to pay for. Nothing wrong with that, of course."

Of all the things Ian had told her about Marcus, which was little, somehow, in her mind, she'd still imagined there was hope for a teenage asshole to have evolved. She had been one certainly.

"As long as you don't mind lowering yourself, like your brother, to another slut like me. Little do you know, your brother is more of a fucking man than I think you have ever been or will be. I might fuck a lot of men, Marcus. But you know what?"

Marcus still stared at her. His hand at the side of his leg was clenched.

"I still wouldn't fuck you."

Avril's eyes flickered from it back up to his eyes full of pent-up anger and something else. Fear.

"You'll regret this," Marcus sneered.

"Regret what?"

Before he could think of an answer, Marcus turned around and stormed away.

Avril finally let out another single fucking breath that she had come to be alone for.

Now, however, from standing on her aforementioned heels, Avril's back already started to ache from both the strain and stress. Moving around the banister, Avril needed to find a better spot to rest. Maybe then, Ian would be able to find her.

"Well, he doesn't look very happy. Should I be afraid?"

Looking up, Avril saw one of the last people she'd expected to. The house produced them one after another, like rabbits. Avril was thrown back to a month ago. The door opening in front of her, Avril forcing herself to stand tall, shoulders back in the hall, eye to eye with the one and only artist being showcased in downtown Ashton.

Cynthia.

She ran a hand through her sharp black bob, a beautifully androgynous Jordan Baker, ready to tip glasses with Mr. Gatsby himself. Perhaps they'd be wearing matching jumpsuits, her legs flaring out at the bottoms.

"Not sure yet," Avril began slowly. "I guess we'll see."

Cynthia nodded, glancing back at the retreating form already turning into another of many rooms. The music seemed to be louder than it had been moments ago when Avril was full of making threats.

She swallowed then, concealing her hands in one another so Cynthia didn't know how they wavered. "I'm Avril."

"Cynthia."

"Yes. I know—"

"Right. We didn't have the best introduction, did we?" Cynthia smiled. "I knew you though, before. I admire your work."

"Oh." Avril blinked, her words feeling like sand in her mouth, grainy and not quite in the right order as they slipped away. "Thank you."

"I was actually hoping to catch a show while I was in the city. I never got to see you perform on your home turf or whatever the city is to you."

"The city is everything to me."

Cynthia paused, noting Avril's sudden passion in the words. Ashton kept coming up, as if they weren't standing on the edge of it. Not Marcus. Not Cynthia. Only Avril, who was constantly feeling like she was the only one on the other side of the snow globe.

"Of course."

"I haven't been performing recently either," Avril softly informed her. "Not for a while now."

"So I heard," Cynthia said, a bit of sadness in her voice.

Avril couldn't tell if the disappointment was sincere. She also couldn't tell if it was for herself or Avril.

"Will you be returning to the stage soon?" Cynthia asked.

"I'm not sure."

No. She had told Kit a month ago, soot in her mouth as she'd said the word. *No, I'm not going back.*

Now, Avril said the words, confused. "I suppose we'll see."

"You'll have to let me know somehow when you plan on making your grand reentrance. Who knows where I'll be at the time? But I have a feeling if it's here in Ashton, I won't want to miss it. I've admired your presence and clothing onstage alone."

"A friend of mine is a prevalent lingerie designer. She creates the most sublime corsets."

Her eyes widened in admiration. "Of course. This city is so full of art and culture. I can't believe I haven't spent more time here since I visited with Ian once years ago."

For a moment, Avril had almost forgotten who Cynthia was. "It's a well-kept secret. I'll make sure you get a ticket if the unpredicted happens in the near future. I didn't realize you'd be here. Not that I know anyone here."

"Not your scene?"

"Not in the slightest."

"Ian invited me a long time ago, before the show opening," Cynthia said simply. "And I also know Bianca, strangely enough. Marcus's wife? A funny coincidence."

Avril waited for more. She didn't believe in coincidences.

"She was the first to buy one of my pieces when I was studying at the Sorbonne."

"Paris," Avril replied numbly.

Cynthia pursed her lips happily all the same. "I loved it there. Of course, not as much as Italy. The food, the wine."

"The men."

With a bark of a laugh, Cynthia did not answer. "It is a dream to have done well enough to travel. I've always wanted to see the world. All the colors of the rainbow and all that, I suppose."

"It used to be one of my favorite parts. Even in economy, the luxury of it."

"Mmhmm," Cynthia agreed. "My first trip abroad is how I met Ian, you know."

Avril nodded. "Florence."

She had the decency not to hide her minor shock. Then, pleasure skewed her lips. "That's right."

Avril turned around to look for any sign of Ian. She lifted her hand to tuck a curl behind her ear.

"Wow."

Eyes narrowed, Avril followed Cynthia's gaze. The golden ring. Ian's mother's ring on her right hand glimmered there.

Avril stared down at it for a moment longer. She'd almost forgotten it was there. The fine metal felt like a second skin. She hadn't taken it off since Ian had slipped it on the other night.

"I'm not going to lie; it was a shock when I walked in on the two of you at the show. For one thing, I never knew Ian to be so"—Cynthia looked for the word for only a second—"bold."

Avril wondered for a moment if she should say something, tell Cynthia that it wasn't Avril Ian had been taking the risk that night for. Instead, she thought about the Ian she knew. Upright with a stare that could knock anyone else over, including her at times.

He was a different type of bold.

"No?"

"I mean, of course, he's had his moments, but he is always so hesitant and looking for direction. He was never one to make a big decision unless he could play it all out in his own head. I think that's why he always latched on to other people, like Noah and me."

"You?"

"I've always had this theory about Ian. He's a bit of an enigma, you know. He always seems to meet the right people at the right time. He's like the opposite of a collector." Cynthia nodded as she thought it all through. "Somehow, he is constantly drawn by this need to be more whether that's because his upbringing he doesn't talk about, or what. He's drawn to extraordinary people. I always wondered if he pocketed them like loose change, just in case, one day, he'd eventually have enough to cash them all in."

Avril remained quiet as she stared at Cynthia.

Grinding her teeth, Avril gave a small laugh as she smiled.

"Wasn't it you though," Avril asked, "who cashed him in? I assume Ian's stepmother didn't just stumble upon your work by accident when, soon after, you managed to gain wider acclaim."

Hesitating, Cynthia faltered before regaining her expression toward Avril with a look of approval. "I suppose you're right."

"Everyone needs a little help and direction now and then," Avril replied, words falling out of her mouth. "To get to the top. Ian has been something of a … godsend to me recently. He's everything I didn't know I needed."

"People change then," Cynthia said to sum up.

"Some of the time."

"I'm glad. I see by the way you look at me that you know that there had been something of an on-again, off-again spark between Ian and I that never really caught. I hope you know not to worry about that. We weren't a good fit for more than a few reasons I've come to see. He's obviously taken with you."

Avril looked around, as if he would be there any minute. "You aren't the first to say so."

"I'm happy for the two of you."

"Thank you."

"Well, I hoped to catch you. Now, I have. I'm going to another get-together. Have a nice night." Cynthia gave an elegant wave of a hand before she clutched her handbag.

"Have a good night," Avril said, watching her turn. "Maybe I'll see one of *your* shows next time you're near town."

She gave a light smile. "That'd be nice. Tell Ian I stopped by. I only saw him for a moment earlier."

Avril clamped her teeth closed. "Of course."

CHAPTER THIRTY-FOUR

The moment Cynthia was out of sight, Avril turned hard on her heel. She ignored the shot of pain that snuck up from the base of her spine. Her mind as well roared with her next possible comeback, her next quip she needed to think up if someone else was going to approach her, as sweat beaded down the back of her neck.

She hadn't been around this many people in a bizarrely long time.

Through the side room, where a few couples sat in chairs with wine on the rests, Avril swiftly edged past them toward the sliding back door. When she snuck out, the cold air sucked whatever breath she needed out of her. She grasped for another as she stepped farther out into the yard of curved pavers. No one would see her by the side of the house in the dull light of the lanterns.

Reaching behind her back, Avril interlaced her fingers to stretch side to side. She braced herself on her knees, unable to fold herself over altogether. Not in this dress.

"I noticed you made an enemy."

Avril sighed with relief when she heard Ian's voice. He shut the door with a reassuring snap as he made his way toward her.

Her enemy list seemed to grow every day—not that Cynthia was an enemy by any means, though she'd rather not run into her in this sort of position, let alone again in the near future. What she really doubted was how she wasn't on Marcus's or his father's. A very long line they'd be in.

A very long time they would be waiting, only to find out she had already been brought down by force to her knees.

She forced herself to stand. "Unfortunately."

"I hope you said something terrible to him."

"So that I deserve whatever comes from it?"

"No, because he does." Looping his arms around Avril's waist, Ian pulled her against his shirt. Against him, warm and hard at her back. "It's cold out here."

"I'm aware."

Ian's fingers began to carefully knead her lower back. "This was the place where my brother locked me out, you know."

Avril hummed in pleasure at the gentle massage. It covered the appropriate amount of laughter she wanted to exude, remembering the story.

The heat from his laugh bled into the back of her neck. He had to tilt down to kiss her there. Ian continued to soothe as well. He smoothed her tight muscles in her upper back with the pads of his fingers.

Stars, she leaned more weight into his hands. They held her up without faltering. He felt good.

"Naughty."

"Naughty or knotty?" Avril asked with a smirk. "Because with what you are doing, it could be either."

Tilting his head down so that his mouth pressed against her curls, his voice was muffled, yet perfectly chilled from the cold air by the time it hit her ear. "I asked you to behave yourself tonight, you do understand."

"I did warn you."

"You did," Ian admitted as his hand skimmed the edge of her

dress's hem. His hands against her skin were warm. "I also see you at least don't lie. You aren't wearing any panties."

"Didn't want any lines."

"I'm strangely grateful for fashion's manufacturing errors right now."

"Seriously, darling Ian, what are you doing? You look like you indulged while we were apart." Looking up at him, she traced the softened lines where his jaw had been clenched since they'd arrived.

He smiled softly, his hands continuing to roam her previously chilled skin. His lips tasted sweet, like more than just a glass of wine from the kitchen. Maybe two, loosening his arms as they massaged and made their way over her accentuated shape.

"The situation has warranted raiding the small wine cellar in the basement." Forehead pressed against hers, Ian glanced down her frame, hitching her hem in one smooth motion over her hip, pressing his body against hers to guide her deeper into the darkness, where no one would see.

He had good taste.

She looked down at where his eyes stared at her.

All of her.

Obviously, he had good taste.

"Are you ready for an escape? Is this how we are getting out of here? You certainly have the route down," she goaded, tingling excitement building in her chest as she leaned her head back, opening her neck for his nose to brush. The motion sent shivers over her skin. No longer from the cold.

Ian's fingers stopped their gentle prodding.

Avril's heart leaped at the implication.

His palms slowly worked their way in long strokes down her body. Ian's eyes locked on hers, watching her reaction as he slid a hand between her legs, caressing her inner thighs. Avril immediately parted them farther for him. She pushed up into his hand, where she was met with a single finger, teasing the bundle of nerves there.

Ian listened to the breathless sound of rapture while her eyes fluttered. He lowered his mouth back against her throat while his other hand cupped her breast. When he ran his thumb over her sensitive nipple, Avril only strained toward him, and his dark laugh hummed directly to her core. She luxuriated in the sound, the feeling, no longer contemplating the pressure on her back, the pressure from all over in that house.

Only when her choked moans urged him on did Ian slide a finger inside her.

Avril gasped in two octaves.

Ian pulled back. His eyes flickered to her. "Not too loud now, my Rose. You don't want anyone to hear us, do you?"

Avril didn't care if the entire house—prude, not, or in between singing "Jingle Bell Rock" around the perfectly silver Christmas tree—heard her.

As she squirmed beneath him, he stilled, finger playing a hair-breadth outside of her. She inched closer, but to no avail.

"I want you."

"I don't understand."

"I want you."

"What was that? I think you are going to have to be more specific for an old man like me."

Avril could no longer help herself as she laid out her demands. She looked up at the darkened sky and barked a laugh at how he played with her. Teased her for all the times she had him. "I want your brilliant cock inside me, Ian. I want you to put your fingers inside me and lick me. I want you to fuck me, pretty please."

"What language," Ian chided, but his laughter rolled against her as he dipped closer to her. "But since you asked so nicely."

Instead, Ian slipped a second finger inside of her, capturing her lips as he gently pumped in a slow rhythm. She wondered what would happen if someone walked outside for a breath of air and saw them in the corner. Would they stand and watch? On edge while Ian coaxed wanton sounds from Avril's lips. She continued to undulate her hips against his hand, driving him deeper.

Each of her gasps rose higher on the wave of need and desire that hit the back of her throat. She was so close as Ian's fingers suddenly slid out of her.

Her parted lips shivered with shock in the cold.

Avril groaned, drooping toward him before finding her own balance against the brick. "You started this; you finish it."

"I did start this, but I've decided not to finish it just yet. Behave. There is something else I would love to do."

Delayed satisfaction was not her pleasure. She stared at Ian, grinning down. His pupils were wide as he put his fingers covered with the sheen of her in his mouth. He tasted her in one smooth movement.

He then leaned back in for one more kiss until Avril felt like she needed to hold on to his belt loops to stay upright. She pulled on them in a silent plea.

When he took a step back, however, she knew it was not going to be answered.

Ian extended the same hand that had pleasured her moments ago toward her. "Will you dance with me, Avril?"

Catching her breath, she looked around the backyard. Just the two of them stood in the cold. Avril closed her eyes and breathed the frost and scent of Ian lingering all over her in, feeling the weight lifted off her back that had been there before. A ribbon that had looped, so unlike the tautness of the shadows, around her heart loosened and drew her toward him, as if wrapping around his as she accepted his hand.

That strum of a drum, a beat, pulsed down the line.

"Lead the way," Avril said.

"You'll let me lead?"

"We'll see how you do."

Ian laughed into her now slightly mussed hair as he spun her once as they went back inside. He just as smoothly pulled her back into his arms on the makeshift dance floor she had been on earlier.

His hand gently clasped her palm, directing her other to his shoulder. "How am I doing?"

His eyes could've been sparkling with diamonds, not that it mattered. Avril couldn't break their stare. Her heart fluttered in her chest, and she noticed something strange she hadn't noticed before.

There was no fear there.

There was no question.

She was there in the moment. She was with him. It didn't matter whose house they were in. It didn't matter who was inside of it or what they'd be met with.

Avril wanted to dance.

And Ian held her as if she were the most delicate of things in the world. A relic. A rare unread book.

It was her city, and it always had been, ever since she'd declared it her home. She'd danced alone just fine in it before, but she wasn't sure she could go back to the way it had been as Ian let her sway in his stable arms.

Emotion swelled in her throat before pressing against the backs of her eyes. Good thing she had to look upward to meet his. They rolled right back down deep inside, where she needed them to stay.

"Beautiful."

He took her for another loop, not even pausing his stride when the music changed. "Rose?"

She turned her head, so he knew she was listening. A loose strand of hair, flattened from their previous antics, fell in front of her eyes.

He brushed it away with the backs of his fingers. "Will you always dance with me?"

As long as he held her up.

Her toes seemed to glide across the floor with him, as if there were no movement at all, just a breath of space, not even that, between them.

"Well, like I've told you …" Avril smiled lightly. Her air of confidence, her mask, much like his, dulled from the soothing wine of Provence, France, easing the creases. "I do love to dance."

"Then, that's how long we'll dance for."

"Forever?" Avril snickered.

Maybe he'd had a bit more to drink than she'd previously thought, but instead of joking, Avril melted even closer to him than was decent. Who cared if the rest of the party stared? She wondered if he felt the way her heart mimicked his too.

She relished the feeling of the buttons of his tailored sports coat with the elbow pads.

"Until you wish to stop."

Then, forever it would be.

Or at least until Avril lifted her head away from Ian's chest, unable to reach his shoulder, to the harsh noise radiating toward them from the other side of the room.

"Don't do this."

Marcus shoved the perfectly manicured hand of his step-mother away.

Wide eyed, Bianca immediately met Avril's stare with swift understanding.

Ian might've indulged a bit to take the edge off, but Marcus had put on a whole other persona the rest of the room was also keenly aware of. They shifted out of the way, leaving them in a straight warpath.

"Ian," Avril breathed.

Although he'd let go of her, Ian's hand still held to her hip. He stepped in front of her.

"Marcus, good to see you."

"Oh, cut the shit, Ian," Marcus snarled, flashing his overly white teeth.

Ian raised his eyebrows. He let the stagnant quietness of the room between them speak for itself. The rest of the house still clattered with dishes and voices, but even the music playing from the pod speakers slowed as the song changed.

"You come in here like you actually think anyone wants you here."

"I was invited."

"You show up here and act like you really care about Dad and Bianca when you weren't even at the wedding. You never showed up before. All of this was never yours. Yet, for some reason, when you step through the door, everyone just looks at you as if…" Seeming to find himself as he sputtered on, Marcus turned his attention to Avril.

Do it, Avril silently dared him. The other side of her wanted to reach forward and clamp her hand around his mouth for the words that it was about to expel, but instead, she just stood there, waiting.

Say it, Marcus.

"You think you are so smart, little brother? So above us all now that you showed up here, pretending you are a part of this family?"

"I never said I was above you."

"You don't have to. I hear it every fucking holiday. How smart Ian is. How many schools Ian went to. I'm a doctor, a surgeon. I'm the smart one who has actually made something of myself. So intelligent. Fuck, you don't even know who your girlfriend there is."

Ian said nothing, his jaw clenched along with his hand on one side.

Avril glanced down to the polished flooring.

They'd replaced the original hardwood.

"Avril Queen. Have you heard of her? Or are you going to pretend to be a little saint too? Your girlfriend you brought here, into this house, is a stripper. She sells herself for loose change. A whore."

Avril shut her eyes for a long moment. The stagnant pause was still there, no one moving.

Of course, Marcus seemed all the ready to break it with a grin. "Or do you know? Are you paying her right now?"

"Don't you dare say something like that to her," Ian snapped.

"What?" Marcus scoffed. "The truth? You don't even know half the shit about her that half the city already does or has read across *Page Six*."

Avril had never taken Marcus to be the gossip column type.

"That little slut ruined a friend of mine's life, you know. Basically ran him out of town with a single lie. She is a dirty, home-wrecking bitch. So, finally, gladly, I am happy to fill you in on how not smart you are, *little* brother, when you can't even see who is standing right in front of you."

That was where Avril had recognized Marcus before. It wasn't the way he held himself like his father or that pieces of him were reflected backward on Ian. She had met him, half drugged out of her mind after she stole *his* pills out of the medicine cabinet, thinking they would make her sick so she wouldn't have to go to the benefit. To Ashton's hospital, where he was supporting his buddies.

Avril swallowed, eyes stuck back on Ian.

He opened his mouth to bark a retort. Avril could see it and prepared to hear the beautiful melody of hate. She hoped it would be loud. She hoped he would blast him with words Marcus wouldn't dream of even knowing the meaning of from books he paid others to read for his literature classes in college.

Instead, Ian shoved and made his way toward the door in steady harmony.

It stayed silent as eyes followed each movement until everyone was sure he made it to the top.

Marcus let his face fall into his veined hands, only looking up when he slid them to his cheeks, the way Avril did after throwing up after a night of a party gone wrong. Only he appeared to do it with words.

Unfortunately, words were harder to hide.

She wasn't. Stepping closer, she threw any lesson she had taught herself away and shoved him back another step.

Anger loosened his jaw.

Bitterness surely took its place deep toward the back of Avril's tongue.

"You're a doctor, correct?"

This was who they had putting people back together?

"Yes," Marcus spat the word.

"Could've fooled me."

CHAPTER THIRTY-FIVE

*A*nxious relatives and wide-eyed friends Avril never had the opportunity or interest to be introduced to since they'd arrived started to whisper as they followed Avril's steps back to the front of the house.

"What the hell happened in there?" Now adorned with a tumbler of liquor, Mr. Whitlock peered toward the room where music began to play again.

The song was only a little louder than the thoughts that swirled through Avril's head.

It wasn't supposed to happen like that.

It wasn't supposed to happen at all.

He was going to leave. Ian was going to leave, and she would never have to tell him who she was or what she had done. She knew he was going to go eventually, but what happened to their happy for now?

She was supposed to have more time.

Stars, she wanted to go back and wrap her hands around Marcus's unproportionate neck. When she blinked, another odd feeling also stirred inside. Something like relief when she glared at Marcus, holding his gaze, just as she realized. It wasn't just him that set her on edge. It wasn't the understanding he had seen her naked along with hundreds of others, at a show in Chicago.

It was because Marcus had worn a similar suit once before, and Avril remembered through a shadow-filled haze seeing him in it. He'd had a similar look of distaste as his friend basically dragged her limp body around the party until ditching her by a table, where she couldn't even keep down the olives people had left in their martini glasses.

Avril was so sick that night when he made her go to that function.

"Excuse me." Whitlock's hand wrapped around Avril's wrist.

Avril yanked it away. Her hand flew upward, as if she was about to slap the man, though her palm was up. He didn't flinch, and all that came to mind was the fact of how Ian always talked with his hands. Had his mother?

"Excuse me," Avril scolded. "Maybe if you'd taught your son better manners, nothing would have happened."

Whitlock didn't have to ask which son, as it was quite obvious.

Avril rolled her eyes at the man. "And you were worried about me being the most unappealing thing in your house, Mr. Whitlock? Someone spoiled our little secret all on their own. Now, if you would truly excuse me, I would like to exit your house, which, if you didn't know, I have one similar to, two blocks over."

"I did."

She smiled, beholding the surroundings. The air felt too hot, the space still tingling with upset against her skin. "I walked by this place before and wondered what it looked like inside. I'm not impressed."

With a step aside, Avril yanked her coat off the hook Ian had hung it on, his no longer there.

Outside, it was as if she'd stepped back into the Ashton art gallery, going outside to the cool breeze to find no one in its wake.

Only this time, as she swiped her hair out of her face in the cold wind, the ring was on her finger.

"Ian?" Avril called out, but didn't raise her voice.

He couldn't be that far.

No one answered.

Pulling her coat farther over her shoulders, she overlapped the buttons. Heels snapped against each of the stairs down to the sidewalk. Great. How fantastic.

Avril had been left at a party before, but she really didn't think it was Ian's taste. Then again, clearly, she was no longer Ian's taste.

"Wait!" a voice trilled from behind.

Twisting around, she didn't make a move back to the house. Did everyone want to make her exit from the house of gentle horrors a process?

She waited as the blonde baby doll made her way down the block after her on her holiday jingle heels.

"I'm really sorry."

Avril sighed and looked upward, so she didn't roll her eyes at Bianca. "Don't be."

"Marcus, he hasn't been himself since his dad and I got married," she said with a shrug. "Understandable reasons, I guess."

That might have been part of it, along with Marcus's other heaps of toxic masculinity to work through.

"His father loves Ian, you know," Bianca said quickly. "I could never get it out of him, but I think … I think Ian reminds him of himself, in an odd way, and I think Marcus noticed that over the years."

"Why? Because he brought home a whore?"

"You aren't a whore, Avril." Bianca smiled at the suggestion, words sincere.

Closing her eyes, Avril nodded. Right.

"And aren't we all anyway, when there's something we really want enough?"

Avril assessed Bianca from the top of her head all the way down to her Miu Miu designer flats, much slower than she had before. She saw then what she hadn't seen inside when all there was in front of her was a happy young homemaker with labels at the back of her blouses and red-bottomed shoes by the dozen.

"You got that right."

Bianca pointed back to the house. "Do you need me to call you a car service?"

Avril glanced at the buildings, tall and looming in front of her. It was cold, but she tapped her foot to the beat of frost these days. "I'm good. Thank you."

The one side of her lips lifted into a smile.

"Can you tell me something?"

Avril could've laughed. She only shook her head again at her. "Let's hear it."

"Do you think you'll ever dance again?"

She hadn't expected that question, taking a step back. "Oh, um, I don't know."

"I won't ask what happened, obviously something," said Bianca. "You've always been a bit of an inspiration to me when I came to Ashton. Of course, even after seeing your shows at Rosin, I still expected you to be ... I don't know—"

"Taller?"

"That too." She giggled. "Intimidating, I think."

But Avril let her mask slip. From the moment Marcus had put her life out in front of everyone and Ian, Avril had let her mask slip, an open invitation to view her small desolation. "It was nice to meet you, Bianca."

"See you around?"

Avril looked back to the path she still had to walk, if that was what she was doing, all the way home.

Home.

She cringed. Again.

She shrugged and tossed her arms to either side. "I guess we'll see."

"If Marcus said anything in there to persuade Ian otherwise of what he feels about you, he'd be a fool."

Avril smiled down to her chest. "We both know that."

Bianca laughed, folding her arms around herself.

"We'll see if he does."

"Good luck."

"Happy holidays."

"Merry Yule?"

Avril closed her eyes and nodded. Good enough. "Give 'em hell, darling."

"I plan to."

SILENCE FLOWED from the dimly lit bathroom. She still held on to her coat tightly, as if she were still preparing to make a run for it all the way up the stairs. She made her way through the house, locking the door behind her. A different sort of sound strummed through the floorboards, the air.

The universe seemed to be waiting for something to happen.

She tilted her head to the side as she remembered the sound of water cascading over the edge of a bathtub she'd had to clean up with ocean-blue towels that scratched her sore palms once as she was done being shoved under—a hand on the back of her neck, the front of her throat squeezing, gasping.

Eyelashes fluttering against her still cold and flushed cheeks, Avril took another step toward the bathroom. The door slipped open at her fingertips.

Ian sat in the empty bathtub. Empty, but for the tousled man inside it. His hand dangled over the edge. Without looking up, he ran a hand through his hair. The tips stuck straight up in the front, where he'd so carefully groomed it before they left. Now, he tugged it away from his forehead.

"Do you …" Ian did not meet Avril's wandering eyes that started at the top of his head and went all the way down his pressed pants. His dress shoes were scuffed, yet tied in neat knots. "Don't you ever just want to die?"

Yes.

"Of course, you promised me to say no, didn't you?" Ian stared at her, eyes glossy.

Avril glanced down at her hand that Cynthia had noticed earlier. Ian's mother's ring gleamed there. The dainty little reminder.

"You want to die?"

Stepping into the bathroom, Avril watched as he paused.

He shook his head.

One knee at a time, Avril knelt beside the wide bathtub. She was shorter than the edge. Still, she managed to reach to where his shoes were perfectly tied and twisted the faucet. A thick cascade of water expanded over his hemmed pants, soaking veins of string.

"What are you doing?"

"Drowning you."

Ian stared at her. Instead of yelling at her about messing up his expensive pants or when she had taken a turn into crazy— long ago being the answer—Ian might as well have joined her. Laughter bubbled up from inside of his chest. He brought the mounds of his hands against his eyes before peeking through them at her.

"See? Breathless? A little nervous. Shaky hands. This is how it all starts." Avril attempted a smile of her own, though she was the one with the shaking hands.

He felt them when he reached out and touched them, gripping the sides of the bath.

"I think you are getting two very different events confused."

"I'm surprised you even want to touch me."

Shaking his head, Ian swallowed. "Let's not talk about that right now."

"You knew, didn't you?" She could see it in his eyes now. Where she'd sought surprise, there was only pain. She couldn't quite decide whether or not it was directed at her.

"Like I said, let's not talk about that now."

"Fine." For once, Avril would agree with him. "Later."

"I'm sorry that I put you through all that. I'm sorrier I left you there. I can't believe I did that. I just knew in that moment, if I had stayed and Marcus kept talking, I would've …" He gritted his teeth together to keep even the words in.

Avril shook her head again as she stood, not quite understanding all the different directions. "Later."

He didn't nod. He didn't even try to hold on to her as the water continued to pour.

He only watched her, as if he couldn't believe she stood before him.

That made two of them, as she'd debated on her way back to the house if she should come back at all. But there was that tug, that pull of shadow, she still couldn't bring herself to ignore until now, standing in front of him. She was unafraid—or at least pretended not to be.

One motion at a time, Avril leaned over the edge and slipped her hands beneath the warm, smooth surface of water until they were fully submerged.

Trailing her fingers over the thinning hair at his ankles, she slid his shoes away. Socks were next along with each and every button.

Now, truly, all that was left was a man in a bathtub.

All Avril was, was a stripper, like Marcus had said. So, she peeled away her little dress of fire. It slipped past her knees and onto the plush bathmat in front of him. No dance. No frills.

Just her.

And Avril never thought it was right for a beautiful man to be in the bathtub, all naked and alone.

Heels clattered as they slipped off the rug and onto the tiles, and Avril stood.

Ian's eyes were half closed and tired, but it didn't matter. His chest lifted, breaths heavy, as he trailed from her ankles to where her thighs pressed together with sudden nerves. She had never been so bare.

When she brushed her foot over the surface of the water, warmth encased her skin as Ian's even warmer hands slid up to help her down. She slid over his legs. Inch by inch, Avril couldn't help herself as she shut her eyes and felt the molten heat seep into her.

A beat surrounded the two of them when Ian had to reach forward, the water pooling around their waists, and twisted the knob off.

"You know," Avril said, her voice oddly soft, "I have a tub sort of like this at my home. Of course, mine is better."

His eyes softened. "Of course it is."

"But only for one reason really. I had it installed with a specific purpose in mind."

"And what would that purpose be?"

"That it be big enough for two."

Ian's fingers smoothed up her back as the water continued its gentle rumble. He cupped the sides of her face. "You've bewitched me."

"That's what they always say." Avril was surprisingly breathless.

She needed to control herself, though it was hard when Ian's nose brushed the nape of her neck. A shiver laced up her skin. Bumps were exposed on every spot she suddenly very much wanted to be touched. They traveled down each vertebra, hardened the tips of her breasts.

She shook her head.

"No more secrets."

Ian stared at her. Seriousness depleted with a softness she hadn't noticed before, right in the corner slants of his eyes.

"No more secrets."

CHAPTER THIRTY-SIX

*T*he shadows pulsed with their agreement, both teeming with nervous energy. Avril squeezed her legs around him tighter, as if to keep him from slithering away as the water submerged them both up to their waists. Her hands started there, sliding up to his shoulders until she had to look directly at him. Mouth set in all harsh, beautiful lines.

"I love it when you look at me like that," Ian said suddenly.

Avril turned to meet his expression. "Like what?"

"Like you see someone. More than just someone."

Placing her hands on his chest, Avril took a deep breath. He was more than someone.

No more secrets.

"I want to try and tell you something."

"Okay," Ian whispered and waited, his own hands beginning to trail behind her body, holding her.

Both of them were afraid what would happen if they let go, the cold air of the room able to lick their skin wherever they did not touch.

"You have to promise that you won't think I'm acting ridiculous or lying about why I wanted to find you after that night at the gallery, just because of what you know now of me."

"Masks off." Ian gave a gentle stroke of his thumb across her cheek.

She nodded, feeling her eyes water with fear and anticipation. "Masks off."

It was only her here.

With him.

"When I was little, there was a woman. My godmother, the one I told you about the other day. She told me about you."

"About me?"

Avril dipped her chin in a light, affirming nod. "She is something of a fortune-teller. A self-taught psychic really. I don't think anyone noticed how good she was already when she started. But before my mother died, I was over at her house, and she told me about you—or not you really. But she drew cards for me. It was a game we played, though no matter what, all the cards she pulled for me to try and answer a question or even flesh out a simple thought made no sense."

"Like my cards."

Avril sniffed. "Exactly. That day, though, on our second try, I decided to think of nothing. I was so tired to begin with, recovering from night terrors, that I thought of nothing but myself when she pulled my cards. Finally, they started to make a bit of sense."

Ian's eyes stared at her as he listened closely. "What did they say?"

"They were filled with hardship and magic, Suzanne said. High highs and the lowest of lows. There was one card, however, that stood out more than the others. She said the card brought great change and even destruction, based on where it was placed. It was a card that foretold a person or single action outside of my control. For the longest time, I let myself think I'd met the person who made that action, that changed my life and ruined it, but then—"

She shook her head.

"The card was the Knight of Swords."

"The card my mother drew that you said looked like me," Ian said with growing understanding. "The one with the clouds. The shadows."

"Yes. The shadows. A man of shadows." Avril took a deep breath, trying to prepare herself. All of it sounded ridiculous as it came out of her mouth, she knew that.

Still, Avril continued, "For the longest time, my godmother insisted that I was attuned, sensitive to the world around me, just like she was. She didn't even know before she pulled those cards what I was seeing every day, what I had been going through, living how we were. We were constantly up and running place to place when we couldn't manage the rent or when my mother had a boyfriend who wouldn't leave us alone. I saw the shadows."

"Like on the card."

"They were as clear as any bad dreams I had that Suzanne attempted to cure. All my life, I saw these dark splotches as casually as I saw dust on the table."

Ian said nothing, hopefully an invitation for her to continue.

So, she did. She couldn't stop now. Not now that she'd made it this far.

"It didn't take long for my mother to notice something was off with me. It didn't take me long to realize that no one else saw what I did. I have always been so afraid of losing control like her. There I was, even as a child, not quite right, even though I felt right somehow. It was only the other day, honestly, that I found out what the shadows were, according to my godmother."

Avril had sort of known all along what they were. Whether it be from the well-meaning therapist Reed had taken her to or Suzanne, the pieces had just begun to fit in her mind.

"The shadows are sort of a manifestation or *something*." Avril tried to explain it all, though it sounded crazy to hear, even to her own ears. "They're trauma and deep-rooted memories that hold too much emotion to be contained. I've seen stains on people or older objects. They even trail behind me as I walk, if I think too much about things I shouldn't be. Like a sign—a warning.

"They are always there until, sometimes, they're not." Avril swallowed. "I wanted to find you because of the shadows. It wasn't just to give you back your mother's ring. The shadows are all over you and are so similar to mine. I needed to know why or more than that, I was ready to simply succumb to them. After this past year where I haven't been *good*...I was ready to face this nightmarish shadow man who was going to ruin me once and for all. I wanted it to all be over. That way, I didn't have to keep on trying to find this person I am, but may never be again. I didn't have to keep seeing the pity on Reed's face when he looked at me every day.

"So, when I saw you, I followed. I ran after you. But then it was you and this charade we were playing, and it all got messed up in my head."

Ian stared at her as tears built in the corners of her eyes. "Why didn't you say anything?"

"I didn't want to. I didn't want you to know who I was at some point because it was cleaner the other way and because I didn't want ..." She searched for the right words. "I didn't want you to look at me the way your brother did tonight, even though I knew that was exactly what I deserved. For a while, I got to pretend on stage that I was someone, and, stars, I loved it. But I'm not someone. I'm no one and should be no one to anyone, and nothing is what I thought I deserved this past year."

And she still did, a little.

"Rose."

"All I do is mess things up and tear apart perfectly good lives, like Reed, who would've maybe been better off without me. He would've traveled the world on his own or had his own conquests as he wrote books on Roman emperors or whatever the hell he works on."

"Rose, stop," Ian said, pained. "Please."

She shook her head. She herself was shaking, her hands between them. "I know I sound crazy and that all of this makes no sense—"

Ian grasped her hands. "Where?"

Avril paused her stammering as she caught Ian's single word. "Where?"

"The shadows. On me. Right now. Where are they?" Ian asked carefully, his chest once again moving in steady, long breaths, as if encouraging her to mimic.

She looked down at how it rose and fell and did as she had been told, the shadows too thick not to. She took one breath and then another before he let go, and Avril's hands shook a little less, even as her nerves rose higher and higher from their home deep in her stomach.

All over Ian from the back of his neck, where he shivered at the possessive touch, swooping over his shoulders like snakes, the shades twisted and bent all the way around to the base of his back.

Just like hers did.

Coming to her knees, slowly, Avril tried to calm herself further, the tips of her fingers only shivered. Wet eyelashes stuck against her cheeks as Avril opened her eyes to stare into his. They were filled with gray shadows in their own right, and she wanted to look where they trailed over her the longest.

"Show me, Rose."

Starting at his temples, Avril smoothed her hands over where his shadows began. They didn't flinch or retreat when she touched them, only hovered, waiting as Avril continued her leisurely descent around his ears. She traced the way they swirled at his throat and knit together at his shoulder blades.

Water dribbled and dripped as she went, as if she were

painting on a dry canvas. Still, Avril continued until she touched every inch of where the shadows fought and eased against each other. Ian watched her, looking down at the damp design, similarly to how he'd looked at his own shadows the first time without realizing, covered in thick gray swaths of paint, the day she started to help him with the house.

Avril released an unsteady, long breath before meeting Ian's eyes again.

"This is what you see when you look at me? My darkness?"

She nodded before she could deny the simple truth. She didn't have many of them. "Not all the time. Sometimes, it's like I see right past it. As if there were never anything there at all. The shadows are like that."

"Fickle," Ian said, "They sneak up on you."

Like her dreams. Her memories that sent her running out of his arms and the house altogether some days when it was all too much.

Avril still did not ask Ian what they meant—his shadows. Though, for some reason, so close, she didn't find herself fearing any answer he might give.

"Some bare their stories easier than others."

"Like sins."

Scrunching her nose, Avril leaned her head against his. "How can you find humor right now? You're—I'm sitting naked on your lap in your house's new, otherwise pristine bathtub, basically saying I see dead people."

Still, she found herself chuckling by the end with him.

"Is that all?" Ian pressed his thumb into her bottom lip.

Her low rumble of laughter pitched higher. They laughed together, holding each other closely until Ian brought his lips to cover the tip of his thumb. Avril let her body press into him until she was sure there couldn't be even a drop of water holding them apart. He was so large compared to her, and their bodies didn't fit perfectly.

But that wasn't the point. They fit well enough.

They breathed heavily as they caught their breaths.

She had to say one more thing before their chests settled, before her head picked back up and began to race. Her lashes fluttered as she skimmed his face.

"Ian, about what happened at the party with what Marcus said—"

"Look at me." A strange sort of smile played on Ian's usually stern lips. "Did you really think I didn't already know?"

CHAPTER THIRTY-SEVEN

"Did you really think I didn't already know?" Ian asked. He gently wiped off each section of Avril's damp skin with a towel before lifting one of his extra-long T-shirts up into the air. He slipped it over her head. "All this time?"

Avril sat on the edge of his bed before moving back to the pillows. She held down the hem of the shirt to her thighs as she tried to understand what he was saying.

That was exactly what she'd thought. This whole time.

He flicked on the side lamp after grabbing loose pajama pants. Light bloomed over the angles of his face like a baroque portrait. The mattress dipped as he sat down next to her, in wait for her reaction. "I knew the moment you came to live at the house. Or at least, I started to piece it together."

"Sure you did."

"I saw the frilly wedding invitation you stuck on the fridge before you came to find me in the cemetery that night. I realized you didn't know, but the person who got me to accept the job at the library wasn't Noah."

"What do you mean?"

"Noah never even considered me as someone who would take a temporary position. He knew I had enough money to lean back on with the house that I wouldn't need to work for only a few months over the holidays. Also, to be fair, I was never much of a people person."

Forehead creased, Avril snuck out a chuckle. At this point, it was laugh or cry.

"Jack Carver got me the job. Of course, it helped that I knew Noah after he realized that I was serious, but Jack was the one who told me I would be a fool not to take the house and mooch off the art school that it's common knowledge my father isn't a patron of," Ian explained.

Jack. That fucker.

It still made no sense.

"How do you even know Jack?"

"How do *you* know Jack?" Ian jokingly asked.

He was having far too much fun with her sudden ignorance.

"I jumped into a random man's car—excuse me, Jeep—after a rather fantastic party that was busted one evening. And you?" Avril asked again.

"I met him a few years ago in New York. He was trying to sober up from what I assume was a one-night stand and hitch a ride somewhere, but he honestly had no idea where he was going. Noah, who was with me at the time in the city, offered our services to transport him to Midtown. He needed to get to a friend's show."

Her show. That was her show.

Avril couldn't come up with the words, knowing where this was going. Her lips parted as she stared at Ian. Ian had been at one of her shows with Jack, and she hadn't even noticed.

He had been there, and all the while, Avril had been so pissed that Reed wasn't the one who'd accompanied her on that trip and that Jack had left her at the club the night before without a word due to the fact that he'd lost another phone in the back of some random cab.

Still, he'd managed to get there just before she went on.

She remembered it all so clearly.

"Red-haired vixen. That is what he referred to you as when Noah asked who we were racing him to see. That kid was always too good for the city. Too trusting to let Jack jump in a cab with us, especially when we showed up to some sort of extravagant venue. But there we all were, and I saw that redheaded woman take the stage. She stood up there with such poise and fearlessness I knew had to be running through her veins.

"Jack and I somehow kept in touch, after, mainly because, for some reason, we kept running into each other. I'd knock into him in random cities," explained Ian.

"You're serious."

"Once, when I was studying off campus for my PhD. Another few, I was trying to visit Cynthia wherever she was traveling with her work. Somehow, I would walk into a hotel or restaurant, and Jack would also be there. Sometimes you would be there too, somewhere. I never saw you though. Not after that first night.

"Jack and I'd get dinner or share a drink while he talked about his magical life in Ashton. I had enough ties to understand. And by then, he knew who I was. Mostly anyway." Ian shook his head. "I can't believe I didn't notice who you were in the gallery right away. You looked so different then, so not like that woman I had seen onstage those years ago. I didn't recognize you at all—or didn't want to. Not at the gallery or even at the faculty party I took you to, thinking you were some random artist still hanging around the school."

Avril sighed, shaking her head.

"It didn't take long to figure out that wasn't the case. Then, there was the invitation, like I said, but I didn't want to even think about it still. We had a deal. I didn't want to break the rules."

One of her first rules. He couldn't go searching for more answers of who she was.

She couldn't believe this.

"Then?"

"Then, I ran into Jack at the theater when we saw *The Nutcracker*. You were using the restroom. I was so angry at him, telling me what I already knew, because by then, I also knew there was no turning back. I saw how you watched the show and listened to the music, and, God, Rose, all I could think of was that night in the cemetery. All I wanted to do was lick away your tears, just like you had for me, not caring if anyone else noticed before I took you away. I might as well have fallen in love right there."

Avril's heart stopped somewhere in her chest. It could have been floating around in there, but she no longer felt it.

"Jack, of course, wasn't in on our little deal."

"Stupid Kit." Avril knew better than to think her friend could've kept the entire secret from Jack, yet that tiny sliver of hope remained.

Ian laughed. "She wasn't, it seemed, either. He wanted to warn me."

"Warn you?" Avril began to sit up so that she could look at him, but Ian held her tight against his chest.

"Yes. He wanted to warn me about you. Apparently, you'd eat my heart out and watch as you showed me the wreckage or something like that. He went on and on about you and your terribly wild tendencies toward the perhaps demonic. He smiled, however, as he said it."

"That sadist." He was going to be in a world of pain of his own when she tracked him down.

"You could give Jack a hundred pussies, and he would let them all out of the bag." She'd once told that to Kit.

"I should take my own advice for once."

"What would that be, Rose?" Ian's breath was hot against her lips, finding himself very interested as she suffered.

"Never trust Jack for anything minutely important," Avril decided.

"I'll keep that in mind."

He'd have to from now on. He might have met the all-knowing Jack, who knew everyone, a fact that was becoming clearer and clearer, but he didn't know him like Avril did. Not yet.

"I guess we don't have to go over what Marcus said back there."

"I don't think we need to speak of him ever again," Ian said grimly.

She could live with that. "I think I made a friend with your stepmother."

"Why am I not surprised?"

"Maybe you do know me better than I thought."

"I did warn you."

He had.

"You also said something else a minute ago," Avril reminded him.

The words were still floating around them both, causing a silence in her head. She couldn't remember the last time it had been so quiet in there.

Ian hummed. "You mean that I fell in love with you."

That was the one.

Avril stared at him with wide eyes.

He chuckled, reaching out to hold her again in his arms. They were too far away from each other, the space of the bed suddenly too far. She had nowhere else to be or wanted to be right then but in his arms.

"I love you, Rose. Avril. Whoever you want to be on any given day as long as for me, it's always you, no mask you put on for the rest of the world. From the first time I saw you and still, I think you are the most vibrant and captivating woman I've ever met in my entire life, and I have no intention of letting anyone else get in the way of that."

Avril rolled her eyes, but her lips couldn't help themselves as she smiled.

"That's my new rule. Perhaps my final," murmured Ian. His fingers reached out as if to touch her curved lips. "I love you."

The words were as thick and as dark as the plum of a bitten memory forming in the back of Avril's vision. The emotion formed a different kind of shadow as a tear puffed under her lashes.

I love you.

Love? You?

Another voice seemed to chortle at the possibility.

She pressed her eyes closed.

"Rose, are you all right?"

Avril cleared her throat, looking around, as if she could somehow sense her mother in the room, still warning her. Her every nerve warned her, even as the shadows wavered and faded between them, *Beware.*

The thought made her huff a laugh. Stars.

Avril breathed into the delicate skin of his neck, bathing in his scent as she inched over toward him on the bed. "I think I want to say it back."

"You don't have to. Not yet."

But she wanted to. She wanted to scream the words for once in her life and actually mean it. She wanted to tell Ian how sweet and caring and absolutely infuriating he was for not telling her all of this sooner.

She wanted to tell him how for the first time in her life, when she was in his arms, she felt safe.

The words, however, got caught, one syllable at a time, in the back of her throat.

Just let me stay here, for just a moment, Avril seemed to plead with herself as she fell into this moment and no other. Into him.

For the first time ever, the shadows seemed to murmur back to her in harmony. *We can do that.*

"I just"—Avril peered up at him—"I'm confused."

"Why?" His eyebrow wrinkled, as if he were studying where in this conversation he wasn't clear enough.

"You're leaving. You told me—"

"My contract at the library is up since it was just a temporary position."

"I bet Noah is still thanking the gods for no more late nights, going over children's story-time themes." But it still didn't answer her question. Her assertions.

Ian surprised her with a smile, ignoring her. "Do you remember the other day, when I had to go out for a little while for a meeting?"

"With the realtor?" Something in Avril's stomach dropped as she remembered, thinking then about how he was likely leaving sooner.

The house, even with her diversions, had been completed before deadline.

The stager had even given their final approval on everything. They even conceded on the tree in the living room so long as it didn't drop any needles onto the furniture. They'd even given accolades to the bland-colored walls.

"I had an interview at The Ashton Institute of Art."

Avril's attention snapped away from her thoughts.

"A few interviews actually. It was rather intensive. I was offered a job. As of next semester, I am supposed to start as a new and much-needed English professor."

He was kidding.

Avril forgot to breathe for a moment. When she did, a choked stream of laughter came out of her. "You're joking. You took the job here? In Ashton?"

"I did."

"You did."

"I can't tell if you are horrified by this or not," Ian said.

"My, oh my." Avril put a hand to the side of her face. "Congratulations, Professor Whitlock."

Everything seemed to rush into her mind at the realization of what had just happened. Ian was staying in Ashton. He had taken a job in Ashton. She was in Ashton.

"Can I have the honor of being your first student? I think I have already broken half the curriculum," Avril mused. Emotion bubbled up behind her ribs, a feeling she couldn't quite name.

She could save the guessing game for another time.

A hand slipped over hers as Ian grinned, twisting her around to get a better look at the offender. She watched as his eyes closed when she rocked her hips into his. She felt him harden between her legs, only covered by his shirt that he'd dressed her in. The cotton hem slowly inched higher with the heady movement.

"I wouldn't doubt it." Without hesitating, Ian captured her lips with his once again.

Avril leaned into the kiss, hard and heavy, until they broke apart. Their movements remained deliberate yet soft as they touched each other this time. They took each second, leisurely feeling the curves of where the muscles curved and flexed, still damp from the bath.

Avril helped him push his bottoms back off his hips. She let her hands wander as they made their way back up to stroke her thumb over his cheek, flecked with stubble.

She rocked her hips into his, and with one smooth motion together, they were no longer playing.

He was inside her. She felt so full as he began to thrust with hard strokes. She gripped his shoulders to stay up with him, holding his eyes for as long as she could before her lips parted in a deep moan. He pressed his palm into her lower back, keeping her close as he growled just below her ear.

"Look at you," he murmured. "My extraordinary."

She sought his lips and groaned louder at the taste of him. Her mouth opened a little farther to take him in as he teased his tongue against hers. Teeth scraped against his bottom lip.

Ian hauled her up against him, reaching down to stroke the bundle of nerves at the apex of where they met. Avril couldn't tell how high she gasped, a pitch breaking one climax into the next. He continued to thrust into her, never letting go as his forehead creased.

Pulling out of her, he grunted as he twisted her onto her stomach.

Heart stuttering, Avril almost shook her head, said for him to stop as the shadows began to curl up the sides of the bed, unable to see. She expected hands to grip her hips from behind and for him to thrust deep into her, but instead, Ian's warm, heavy body lay over top of her, knees nudging her thighs apart.

The weight was almost unbearable, but her heart began to slow, feeling his heartbeat strum against her spine. He brushed her curls over her shoulder, their eyes meeting for a stark moment.

A sound hitched in the back of his throat.

"Ready?" he whispered. A look of unbridled yearning swept over his expression.

If she said no, if she made one single move to the contrary, Avril had no doubt that he would stop.

"Yes."

With a kiss on the back of her neck, gently and then all at once, Ian pushed back into her without hesitation.

Avril thought about him and only him as he used her body. She could feel him all around her every breath, grinding down into the comforter.

Just make it go away. Make me forget, she'd begged him that first night after she thought the nightmares would never stop. She never expected they could ever stop.

Take away the shadows. The darkness.

Ian did again and again, each of them lifting to meet the other as he kept moving, making love to Avril in a way no one had before—thoroughly, as if they had all the time in the world and not a clock about to stop on them both.

Ian grunted Avril's name, the name he had given her, as he slammed his hips against hers once more before stilling. After another moment, he carefully pulled out, drooping down so he lay next to her, watching her face for a sign of ill expression.

Silence dripped into Avril's ears, only interrupted by their panting breaths. Avril felt as if it were the middle of the day instead of night, full of light and ease.

She almost laughed as she smiled.

Ian grinned, liking the quiet howl.

"Since the other night," Avril managed to say, "when I was walking around the house, alone, after I woke up from a dream, I saw you sleeping right here. The shadows were thin, and I knew somehow."

And it'd scared her so much that she swore. She had run from the door like a coward and fallen asleep on the couch instead, just in case it was, too, a dream. But now, she was here, in the arms and body of a man who for so long had been on his own, thinking he wasn't good enough.

She was his extraordinary? No.

He was extraordinary in his own right.

Even if he didn't think so, she did.

Her heart crackled in anger at the thought of how she herself knew the feeling and hardships he had for far too long. But, he was staying. He was here, her man of shadows she'd waited for, drawn to, bringing forth a different sort of change, a light in the darkness that twisted all around them.

And it would always linger.

She might not have been able to say the words, not yet.

But Ian murmured them back into her skin all the same before turning out the light.

———

AVRIL GAVE a sharp inhale as she woke back up to the darkness of the room. She had fallen asleep, but she hadn't woken back up from a nightmare. Disbelief coated her senses as she blinked, but she didn't move to get out of the bed. She only shifted, pulling the sheet in closer to her.

Before she shut her eyes, she felt the body behind her shift as well. As he rolled over, Ian's legs were already tangled in hers, and she didn't move to get away from them. His arm curled over her front, pulling her closer to him.

He must've heard her wake up.

If there was any question, a soft kiss grazed her shoulder and then the side of her neck.

Avril inched herself into his warmth until there was no room left between them. He was stiff against her. With an arch of her back, he let out a low breath, his other hand slinking around her hip.

His fingers deftly found what he was looking for, making slow circles at the apex of her thighs, dipping in and out of her until she squirmed. Her legs opened farther, trying to create room for him as their heavy breaths hung in the air.

Rolling her farther onto him, he hitched her leg over his hip and sank into her.

Eyes closing, Avril gripped on to his thigh, soft under her palm.

They listened closely to each other's responses as heat poured from her core under the thick blankets. All Avril could feel was him as they shifted, grinding themselves into each other with small yet potent movements. They were slow and easy as pleasure coursed up through her stomach. It was like they were simply breathing, being, as they connected, moving until, finally, they simply relaxed into each other, hot and sated.

He stayed in her for a long time as her head lolled back to his shoulder.

Avril fell asleep once more.

CHAPTER THIRTY-EIGHT

*A*vril pushed her foot off the desk, twirling in the office chair once more, a blur of empty bookshelves and drifting sunlight through the French doors. Leaning her head back, she held her phone closer to her ear. She wasn't sure she'd ever used it before so casually, the screen cold and—

"To what do I owe the pleasure of this call?" Reed answered before it made it to the second ring.

Avril laughed as she told him about everything that had happened over the weekend. The family party, the outing via Marcus …

"What a complete asshole."

Avril agreed. She almost told him that it wasn't surprising, based on the fact that Avril remembered him from her time with—

She shook her head, hoping it could be blurred back from her memory again, tossing the shadow aside.

"So, basically, I'm calling to tell you that I've gone to hell, but before you get here to join me, I'll make sure we procure nice accommodations. Any requirements?"

"King-size beds and a booze fountain would be nice. We want to impress the big guy after all when he's invited over."

Good point.

Reed cleared his throat. "So, he knows then."

"Who knows?"

"Ian. He knows who you are now?" Reed clarified.

"Oh, right," Avril huffed. "Turns out, he's known for a while."

"You're kidding."

Again, she shook her head, thinking of all the worry and stress she could've saved, before she realized Reed couldn't see her. She was sure he had gotten the message nonetheless. "Looks like Jack might not force me to talk to him, but he sure as hell wants to be in for a pounding when I do."

"So does half the city. Someone must've seen you out the other night. Got a call from PR, who said you graced the gossip columns again for the first time in a while."

"Really?" Avril couldn't help the curve of her lips. "Whose? What'd they say?"

"Letters from Zelda."

"Stars, I love that girl."

Out of all the gossip columns and blogs that kept an eye on Ashton, she was the only one that Avril appreciated. The posts and weekly newsletters she sent held facts along with the steady, glamour-filled prose. The girl could write.

"She's become rather the under feeder when it comes to information sourcing as of late."

Avril's smile faltered. She repeated her last question, this time slower. "What did she write?"

"You were spotted on a few different occasions since your return to the city, is all. The holiday market. The theater … et cetera. It's mainly an inference piece, is all."

Mainly.

"What else?"

"Avril."

She waited on the line.

"All she said was that it looked like you had someone new on your arm. A tall and handsome professor of the institute. Professor?"

"It's a new development." Avril waved off the question. If that was all.

"She went on to say that perhaps he's the reason Queen has disappeared over the past year. She questions a comeback. It, um, it looks like she has managed to dig up some information."

"On what?"

"On *him*."

Reed knew better, just like her, than to say his name. He didn't get one. And he shouldn't have been allowed a single moment of airtime.

"A few friends of friends have talked to her about how things ended, it looks like, as well as their understanding of you, not in a particularly caring light. The post that also mentions seeing you with I assume our new friend, Ian, ends with, *Has our favorite feminist burlesque Queen turned into a sugar baby, only looking for her keep?*"

"Fabulous."

"Don't worry about it, Aves."

"I'm not," Avril said, her voice dead. She peeled away the gunk of how many people read it, looked further into it all for the dirt Reed had already promised was well closed. She swallowed it down. "I have more important things to worry about. I think Ian's taking me on a date."

"A date?" Reed asked, intrigued. "Have you ever been on one of those?"

Avril pursed her lips before she could answer. No. She didn't think she had. Not a real one anyway.

"Don't be rude. I think that is what is happening. He won't tell me where we are going, like a surprise. He thinks of everything, and I'm sure it will be great. I'm wearing my good black pants that make my ass look great." Even if she had to squeeze into them one leg at a time after getting out of the shower, still damp from Ian massaging suds into her hair and soap along every inch of her.

"I also can finally wear my red-soled heels long enough that my back doesn't ache, so I will almost be of a reasonable height next to him." Avril laughed. "You have a point."

"Of course I do. But you sound …" Reed drifted off, as if whatever thought had crossed his mind greatly perplexed him.

"What do I sound like?"

"Like you're in love with him."

Opening her mouth, Avril couldn't find the words to reply.

"It's not that I don't want to be happy for you, but—"

"But."

Reed sighed. "But need I mention again how you've freaked me out this past year? It's hard for me to believe you're just over it."

She thought of the article he'd just read her. She knew he was leaving quite a bit out.

"Well, I am."

Reed paused. "If you say so, I want to believe you."

"Then, believe me."

"I do."

"You sure?" Avril asked. "Because maybe I'm hearing you wrong, but someone sounds a little jealous behind all that well-meaning worry."

"I'm just trying to ask. I know you told me about him when you were over here, and I looked him up as best I could, but—did you think about it at all?"

Avril narrowed her eyes, brushing the shadows that speckled around her like flecks of dust. "About what?"

"How he'll fit into your life. I mean, I don't know him, Aves, but from what I gather, I'm not sure your professor's a *Friday night orgy, Saturday night party after DuCain* sort of guy. I'm glad he's a good lay, but does he play? Will he play with you?"

Again, Avril thought about how he'd gripped her skin and bitten all the spaces that made her gasp. She squirmed in the leather office chair as she continued to listen.

"Have you asked him what he thinks about your job? No pressure by any means. I don't know if you've been thinking about coming back anytime soon. It's up to you."

"No, I have," Avril admitted as she chewed on her lip.

The more comfortable she had gotten the past few days, the more she'd thought about the days after next. The new year was almost here, and Avril used to have a grand performance, blending Rosin and DuCain to bring the year in with a bang. More than one.

Kit and Jack had attempted to pull the sinful shindig off last year with decent results from what Avril had heard, and this year would still be a bust. No stage, no girls splashing glitter onto each other's tits in the dressing room before they danced.

A warm excitement at even the possibility filled a space that had been hollow for so long in Avril's chest. It wasn't just the memory.

"I've thought about it." Only she hadn't really been thinking about Ian standing by her side, as Reed had. At least not when she imagined the way the crowds at times leered while they cheered or as she kissed a player at DuCain onstage for showmanship value.

The shadows, however calm recently, started to bleed out of her fingerprints onto the desk. She yanked her hand back and turned away, but not before she blinked, and suddenly, a deep and scolding voice drifted over her shoulder with her.

"Disgusting. You realize what they all think of me, don't you? That I am the guy who bagged a whore. My God, you're proud of what you do? I don't understand why you think this isn't an embarrassment."

"I knew you said you liked him, but I didn't expect you of all people to just…"

Fall so quickly? Avril thought about the last time she had done that. Turned off her brain for a little while and felt.

"He knows that you've never been in a monogamous relationship for long before as well, correct?" Reed asked.

I don't want to share.

"He knows who I am," Avril snapped suddenly. It was finally out there in the open. He'd said he knew. She shoved any and all other insertions away. "Here I was, trying to give a pleasant phone call to my best friend, who uses the time to chastise me."

"I trust you."

"Mmhmm," Avril intoned, listening to more of his gentle reminders drift through the phone receiver. "I'm not going to screw this up, Reed."

"I hope not, darling. You're not giving me a lot of hope."

How honest, though not refreshing. Rolling her eyes, she stopped turning the chair.

Ian stood in the doorway to the living room.

Ready to go? he mouthed.

"Gotta go, darling."

"Are you ever going to bring him by?" asked Reed.

"Hey, like you said, it's not my fault he's a good lay," Avril purred into the phone before giving a short laugh. "You did tell me to fuck him."

"You sleep with everyone."

So then, why was Ian any different?

Ian glared at her from the other room. She gave him a horrified face that he dared to listen in on her very private call.

He rolled his eyes, but not before he exposed a small smile, touching the corners of his lips.

"I really do have to go unless you want me to be late for my mysterious date." Avril stood.

"Would you be pissed if Dixon and I went caroling without you?"

"I'm hanging up now."

"He has a much better vocal range."

She was certain that he did. Still, she hit the red button and dropped her phone back into her bag. Dixon probably also knew all the words, most of which Avril always made up. And hers were almost always better.

Walking out, Avril closed the doors behind her. Ian's eyes raked her over.

"Reed?"

"He had some very pressing matters to discuss."

"Such as?" Ian asked. "Looked like they were all good."

Avril's eyes widened as she nodded.

After they made their way to the front door, leaning down, Ian helped her into her coat one arm at a time before zipping up his own. "That didn't look very convincing."

"It looks like my escapades with you around town have been noticed," explained Avril, but she felt herself hesitating as she fiddled with the buttons Ian had just clipped shut. *It's nice*, she thought, perhaps for the first time, *to be taken care of*. "My favorite gossiper is now on my hit list."

"That bad?"

"Just the average conspiracy theory." As well as a slow, deep dive into her life that would likely only continue now that it was poked out. A beast alongside the shadows stirred inside of her. "I thought I would have more time until they noticed that I was back and I had to make this decision."

"About returning?"

Avril met his eyes as he listened to her. She studied the way he stood, no control. Not even hurry. It was only a question. "Yes. About returning."

"You can take your time, you know. No one else has to decide for you. The Queen is never late."

No, she wasn't.

"You still want to go out tonight?"

Avril shook out the side of her hair and walked out the door Ian held open. The streetlights twisted with red and gold, just starting to turn on one at a time down the block.

"I'd be more ready if you told me where we were going," Avril said. "Don't tell me we are actually going to another last-minute holiday party. For someone who doesn't know anyone around here, you are invited to a lot of things."

"Not a single more invitation unless you count Noah's D&D party."

"Like Dungeons and Dragons?"

Ian nodded. He looked the slightest bit impressed.

"Will there be dress-up? Cosplay? You know it's really just nerdy role-playing. Could turn mighty sexy," Avril added. "D&D orgy."

"With you there, I wouldn't put it past—"

"We should go."

"We're not going."

"Come on. I think I can handle it. Have fun on this Yule-tide Day. Live a little. I'll dress up as a sexy elf or something."

"As delightful as that sounds…" Ian trailed off.

"You could be a warrior fairy or whatever, you know. You're tall enough. Could have magical powers or what have you. A staff. Though you already have one of those."

He glared.

"See? You're halfway there. Or you could live out your vampire fantasy. I could get into that."

"I do not have—" He noticed the gleam in her eyes as he traced the careful bites he'd placed down her collarbone. "We're not going."

"Why not?" Avril argued.

"Are you listening to yourself?"

She was always listening to herself. She was as highly enter-taining as she was exhausted. "Name one thing better."

"Dinner. You and me."

The sidewalks were bustling, but Ian was already proving his point as they maneuvered through the city's crowded sidewalks, filled with a vibrant vibration of the season.

As she gripped his arm tighter, Ian led Avril another block until they were in front of a restaurant with large front windows. Their outside dining fireplace was lit, but Ian led her inside, where almost all the tables were full.

"This is it then. The final outing of our deal." Avril tilted her chin up at him as the heater above the doorway sent warm air over her head.

"Truly the end of an era."

She pressed her lips together. "Do you regret it?"

The question seemed to shock him. "Why would you ask that?"

She only shook her head.

"No," Ian said, staring right down at her. "Not for a second."

When he mentioned his name at the hostess stand, the curly-haired waitress smiled somehow, even when she jingled with every step from the bell attached to her name tag. The table was in the middle, near the electric fireplace.

Ian pulled out her chair, and Avril smiled as he sat across from her as she unbuttoned her coat to drape behind her.

"Rather cozy."

"Your server will be with you in a moment."

"Thank you." Ian pursed his lips over the cocktail list that she'd left at the edge of the table. "Wine or something called a Naughty Rudolph?"

"Sounds decadent."

"Is that a yes?"

"Wine," Avril said. "Please."

"Wow, manners and everything this evening. Should I be concerned?" Ian raised an eyebrow.

Avril shook her head, looking around the place again. It was nice.

Ian's eyes crinkled at her outward pleasure.

Maybe she was a date kind of girl, after all. Once in a while anyway.

A curl came loose from the side of her head she'd pinned up. She tucked the strand carefully behind her ear.

When their server appeared, Ian asked for a bottle of red.

"Are we celebrating outside the holiday this evening?" the server asked. As he shifted his weight onto his other foot, his name tag jingled.

"In a way."

Avril narrowed her eyes. The server already trailed off to another section, where another patron made a large sweeping motion, gesturing for the check. As she leaned across the table, the wine was already being poured into glass globes. "What are we celebrating?"

"One or two things."

"Am I to guess?"

"As of today, you can also tell me I'm nearly a decade older than you."

Avril's eyes widened in further shock before utter delight, cupping her hands over her mouth, careful not to smudge her deep red lips. "It's your birthday? I can't believe you."

He glanced up with a dark smile.

"I should've found out if they would do something," Avril started. "They'd probably sing or give us free cake."

"They won't. I already checked. This is a birthday-free restaurant." Ian leaned back in his chair, however, carefully giving death stares to any waiter who came back in that moment within a five-foot radius. It didn't take much more than that stare.

Only Avril would lean closer to it, voice low. "You're such a Capricorn. I can't believe I didn't see this sooner."

"Does it make you change your mind about me?" He lifted his full glass.

Avril did the same, tilting it against his as they locked eyes. She couldn't help the feeling of hers wavering.

"Makes me rethink my entire existence."

There glasses clinked softly. The dry flavor pleasantly stripped her tongue as she took a prolonged sip.

"Thirty-two. My, oh my, Professor."

He rolled his eyes at the inflection once more.

"Now, who's the indecent one? Falling in love with a twenty-four-year-old queen of the party girls." She rocked her head back and forth, as if such a statement didn't compute. Falling in love. Staying in Ashton.

Honestly, all of it didn't make much sense.

"What would your father say?"

She took another sip of wine and watched the drips fall back down the inside.

"Not sure. I think my mother would've loved you."

Avril stopped thinking.

"She would have looked at you and paused. She might've even given you a hard time, but I think she would've yelled at me already for the way I first treated you."

"I did steal your girlfriend," Avril said slowly.

"She was never my girlfriend," Ian said with a confused shake of his head.

"Is that so?"

"Very much."

Avril opened her mouth to say something else, but it was lost to the air. Instead, she laced her fingers together as a perch for her chin after they ate each course and Ian refilled her wide glass of wine. It went down smooth, filled with a light spice that remained toward the back of her tongue after each sip.

She leaned back languidly as she set the glass back down in front of her, watching Ian take his own gentle taste. "It's a big day for you, and I didn't even get you a present."

Ian looked at her—from her fingers all the way down to where she disappeared below the table. The tip of his loafer nudged her ankle. "I only have one thing I want for my birthday right now."

Avril smiled, eyes sparkling, before she noticed his sudden hesitation.

"I know you are on edge about being back out in the city and that person writing about something that obviously upset you, but I never asked before, how did you get started dancing?"

All thoughts suddenly escaped from her mind. "You want to know about the night I started dancing?"

He nodded.

"Well …" Avril tried not to smile nervously. A weight of all the other things he could've asked fell off her shoulders. In the dim light of the restaurant, she couldn't find a single shadow as she thought back. "All right. It was an accident really."

Ian snorted.

"What?"

"Come on."

"You don't believe me."

"Do you blame me?" he asked.

Avril rolled her eyes. "It was. Sort of."

He raised his eyebrows in victory.

"I would like to throw my napkin at you."

"It's my birthday."

Fair.

Taking a deep breath, she continued, "Remember how I told you I worked for a lingerie shop downtown?"

He nodded.

"My good friend—Jack's fiancée, you may know of—runs the place now and is doing a hell of a job. But along with selling to the general public, one of her big clients has always been the burlesque lounge downtown, Rosin."

"I might have done some research."

"I'm impressed." Avril dipped her chin. Trying to imagine the many pages he'd found with a single search button.

He didn't look at all afraid. She wondered why she still thought he would, pressed and perfect.

"We were there almost every weekend. As a part of the job, I helped the girls get dressed and replaced seams that had run away from them after their last performance. Stars, I sucked at sewing. Still, I was in love with everything about Rosin—from the way the inside looked to the most glamorous speakeasy to the people who attended the show. It reminded me of all the Technicolor movies I'd watched as a kid, only now, there I was. I'd tried to make Cherry, the owner of Rosin, let me onstage more than once."

"Now, this seems more honest."

Her eyes flared, warning him. Did he want to hear this story or not?

He opened his hands in invitation.

Thank you. "Now, where was I?"

"About to cause trouble for an owner over statutory stripping?" Ian suggested.

"Right. Of course, she said no and was getting more irritated with every time I asked. I showed up to their rehearsals and elsewhere until I started to get their routine down. Some of the older dancers saw me as a mascot, I'm sure. They all put up with me. I was the one making sure they didn't look like hot messes onstage after all. But one day, a new girl didn't show up. I had been admiring her costume. She had this gorgeous white pearl strung corset she'd had to practice getting in and out of for the past two weeks, and there was a reporter at the club. What was there to do?"

Ian chuckled. They both knew exactly what she had done.

"Like I said, some of the girls put up with me. Others wanted me gone before I helped them into their G-strings." Avril beamed down at herself. "Stars knows why. Anyway, the ones who disliked me the most were the ones who immediately started helping me into the delicate costume, encouraging me to go on. They thought I would make a fool out of myself. Cherry sure as hell wouldn't believe me if I blamed my opening night on them. When I went onstage though, I ruined that costume. It was so delicate that while I danced, I tugged and teased, as if I wasn't sure what was going to fall next and I didn't. Pearls cascaded across the stage along with me. I was the best goddamn dancer Rosin had ever seen. I was Queen."

Ian still watched her closely as her voice softened.

"Cherry put me on and in every dance she could that weekend once the reviews came out."

Shaking her head side to side, she looked around the restaurant with a returned vigor of being outside, in the world. In her city.

Just talking about Rosin made her want to go there. She imagined taking Ian there right then, hand in hand, to see her world. To see all of it. As she was about to stand and tell him that it was her turn to surprise him, Avril's eyes caught on a figure adjusting her bangs as they stood on the other side of the restaurant. They swept harshly over her forehead.

"So, why did you stop?"

"What?" Her eyes remained locked on the woman. She gave a fake smile to the server, bringing more attention to her frown lines and expensive dangle earrings hanging heavily from her lobes.

Ian's voice rang out somewhere around her, but it was as if she were somewhere else entirely, and he didn't quite break through.

"I don't feel well."

"Are you all right?" Ian asked. "Tell me what's wrong."

"We need to leave," Avril stuttered, knocking her knee into her chair as she stood abruptly. The wine left in her glass nearly sloshed over the rim. "I need to go."

"Okay, we'll go. Let me just go and pay. Stay with me?"

Avril couldn't focus on him. She could only watch the woman getting closer and closer to her. If she didn't move, she would see her. She and her husband, whose sharp tone stirred something deep in her spine, as if the fractures had never healed, would see Avril and then—

"I'll wait outside." She was already putting on her coat.

Looking around for what she was staring at, Ian couldn't seem to find it. "You'll wait for me?"

Avril swallowed at the terse tone of voice. When she looked at him, his eyes were full of worry. "I just need some air."

"I'll be right there."

She nodded again, swallowing as she swept around toward the front entrance. She felt eyes on her back. She hoped they were Ian's as she kept walking, but she only made it out the door by the time she knew that they were following her.

She couldn't even make it down the block when she finally forced herself to turn around and met a pair of dark eyes that so easily brought all the shadows back once more.

As if they'd never left.

CHAPTER THIRTY-NINE

"I see you've gotten over your whole sad and depressed act rather quickly."

The woman stood only a few steps in front of Avril. She barely knew the woman's name. Only her last. She never actually met the woman until afterward—when Reed had first tried to help her go back to the high-rise apartment she'd been living in with *him* for months prior to get her things.

She never got them.

She only remembered the way his mother had looked at her, as if she were dirt. Just as she looked at her now.

This time though, remembering to breathe, Avril tried to stand tall, rolling her shoulders back so as not to stutter. Not that she could find any words. She had nothing to say.

"Just plan on running away from the mess you made once again. Very confrontational."

Her husband remained behind. A dark look passed over his face as he watched.

"What? You suddenly have nothing to say?"

Avril swallowed, looking toward the door. Ian should be there any second. "If you are waiting for me to say something particular, you are going to have to be more specific."

"You are a disgusting child. You probably don't even know what you've done, do you? Do you know how people look at us now? You know what they think? And you think that you can just walk around here, like nothing is wrong. Does your little friend I saw you sitting with know what you are? Or is he still unaware of how you ruin people's lives?"

"Your son ruined me," Avril snarled. Already, she clenched her eyes to hold back the tears, instead letting her gaze fill over with anger instead.

That was better. That felt finally right.

Because she only crossed her arms and smirked. "My son said you were a good actress. I gave him the benefit of the doubt, but look where that got us."

She shook her head. Ian would find her or call her if he needed to now. She needed to walk away before … something. She clenched her teeth. The sound of her grinding them down to nubs was the only thing she heard before footsteps caught up and yanked her elbow.

Avril twisted around and shoved the woman back. She might have fallen had she not caught herself on the building. A pity.

The woman gasped. "How dare you!"

"Apparently," Avril screeched, stuck in her steps now as she leaned forward to scream, "both you and your son don't know how not to touch someone who doesn't want you to fucking touch them!"

Her lips quivered as she searched for words while her husband breached the few paces behind. He continued to slip on his Barbour leather gloves.

"You dirty little bitch."

She'd been called worse.

"Avril." Ian finally came out of the restaurant, walking steadily, though when she met his eyes, some sort of emotion must have been inside them that made him speed up to a halting jog.

Carefully coming to her side, he glanced toward the other two. They appeared to still be waiting to see what other filth could likely come out of Avril's mouth.

She could think of plenty. All of a sudden, she had a lot to say. All of it, however, was jammed in her throat like glass, cutting through tendons to be let out.

Instead, she looked down to the sidewalk and bit the inside of her cheek. She wanted to look at Ian, but she couldn't.

She couldn't do anything.

"Is there a problem here?" Ian questioned.

Avril didn't answer.

The fact of it only let the woman in front of her stand up straighter to look between Avril and Ian.

"I believe there is. You are?"

Ian said nothing, clenching his jaw as he assessed the situation. He seemed to understand the pain that was causing every muscle in Avril's body to become catatonic.

"I see. Did she not tell you that she was a little whore yet as well?" the woman bit. "Best to find out sooner rather than later, I assure you—Ian, was it?"

"Ian," Avril murmured.

She wanted to go. They needed to go.

"A stripper, to make it better. My son, of course, thought better of that. He wasn't one to judge, like most of us would. But there she was, sleeping with other men, when she's supposed to be with one. She's just as well a common prostitute."

Ian flinched.

Avril was never a prostitute. She never slept with others after her son, after he told her that he couldn't take it. Not like that.

"No wonder my son was in such a state of utter disrepair after what you did to him, flaunting yourself about. You know that he lost his job because of you? He had to leave his home. Yet you say he ruined you?" The woman released a sharp, humorless cackle. "You ruined his life. I haven't been able to say a word, but now is my time. You listen to me, you little slut." She only screeched at Avril louder, higher pitched than the car horns brawling around them, the carolers singing as they turned the corner to go to the park, nothing new in seeing two women nearing a brawl on the streets around the holidays.

Rather stressful time of year.

"Excuse me!"

Avril hadn't realized until then that Ian was shouting too.

"Back off. We are leaving, and I suggest you do the same."

"Obviously, she can't help herself from ruining other people's lives." She stared at Avril before turning toward Ian.

He was already trying to usher Avril away. Her footsteps were heavy and unwilling. Rage swelled inside of her that bent and shook yet was unable to take full form.

"Or she just can't stand being alone to keep her poison to herself. You should get her out of your life now before you become the talk of the town. Lose your friends. Your career!"

"Val—" The voice of her husband cut through, though he stood just as stiff as Avril as they bickered, his anger only seen in frozen rage.

Awful, vehement feeling twisting within it, Avril's stomach jumped before sinking lower and lower and lower from the break of adrenaline. The scene flared heavy and unshakable, even as Ian practically carried her around the corner.

This wasn't right. None of it was right.

When she finally looked up at Ian, he looked straight ahead, jaw locked, knowing exactly which corners to take where, which direction pointed home.

"It's going to be okay," he might've said.

Or maybe he didn't. Avril wasn't paying attention.

Either way, it wasn't going to be okay. How could she ever have thought it would be?

It wasn't going to be anything.

Clenching her own jaw shut so her teeth wouldn't chatter, Avril looked up to the stars.

There weren't any. The lights reflected off the buildings too brightly. There was no direction there, only shadows and the frosted heat that seeped into Avril's bones.

She shut her eyes altogether.

CHAPTER FORTY

Somehow, they made it back to the house. She barely realized before Ian was shuffling her coat off her shoulders. He guided her into the kitchen, pulling out a chair at the island she stood next to, but didn't take in her silence. He was talking to her, she was sure, but Avril didn't want to listen. She just kept playing the scene of what had happened outside of the restaurant, where for a moment, it had only been her and Ian in the entire world that mattered.

And then it wasn't.

It was just her. Always her.

She brought a hand to her head.

Ian set a glass of water in front of her. "Drink it. Please."

Face still set in concentration, Avril reached for the glass. One sip turned into two until half the water was gone. The bottom of the cup slid easily as she pushed it away. She still didn't take the seat offered in front of her. She needed to stand. To move.

"Are you going to tell me what just happened?"

Avril swallowed. She could right now; she could tell him everything. When she looked up and saw his eyes, though, she already began to see what would happen if she told him. The sadness and the pity and all she could feel was anger for herself. He didn't need to know. She never had to go to that side of town again, in case she ran into those awful people. She would figure out how to keep the press at bay with all the questions.

No one needed to know.

"I'd rather not. No."

Closing his eyes, he fought with himself, lifting his own hand that clenched in his short hair. "Avril."

Not Rose? She wasn't his pretty little thing anymore.

"Why don't you tell me?"

"I don't want to."

"I thought you said no more secrets?" Ian said. "No more lies."

Avril bared her teeth and grinned. Huffing, she wouldn't let him see her falter. She wouldn't let him see her break under the same eyes that watched her fall apart in front of him in ecstasy rather than pain. "I didn't lie!"

"Omitted then. It's all been the same to you these past weeks, hasn't it?"

"I never lied to you."

"You never told me the truth until a few days ago either."

She rolled her eyes.

"Take off the mask when you talk to me!"

Avril stared at him and then anywhere but him as her heart pounded. The shadows rose like a protective coating, cold and hard.

"How am I supposed to protect you if you don't tell me what is going on?"

"I don't need protection," Avril yelled. "I thought you got that. I thought..."

She needed a moment to collect herself, to gather her thoughts about how everything had gone to shit so suddenly in front of her and she couldn't stop it.

She couldn't stand to stop it, and maybe she shouldn't have ever thought she could.

She clenched her fists.

Ian stammered as shadows crawled up his neck, "You can't just conveniently leave out particular parts of yourself you think I won't like or don't fit with whatever persona everyone else sees. I thought that we were in this together, shadows and all."

Avril wanted to laugh at such a statement. Whose shadows were they talking about?

"I don't care if you never tell me what your favorite fucking color is, but whatever *this* is, I've been seeing it all this time since the moment I met you, your shadows, and they're eating you alive."

Avril flinched at his curse. He never swore.

"I want to see you."

But he did.

Too much.

"Like you haven't been lying to me," Avril snarled, her voice once again finding purchase, like poison dripping off the tip of her tongue. "Omitting the occasional thing you don't want to share."

"What are you talking about?"

"Your shadows, Ian."

"What about them?"

"Why do you have them?" Avril screamed. "Have I asked? No. I haven't, because it doesn't matter to me. It doesn't matter to me if you never want to share whatever the hell is weighing down your shoulders, digging craters into the back of your neck for who knows how long. Yet here you are, wanting me to bare my soul, my fucked-up life, including every bit and piece, like I haven't already given you enough!"

He shook his head. "This isn't about me."

Avril looked toward the hallway. Her exit. She continued instead to pace. She didn't want to leave.

"I need to know. What happened with that man you were with a year ago? Is what that woman said true? Did you decide to ruin him? Blackball his name or something across the city with the influence you had because he had cheated on you? Didn't like you?"

"Cheated on me?"

Ian shook his head, knowing it didn't quite fit. "Tell me what happened."

"I can't even believe that you would think—"

"That's just it, Avril. I don't know what to think. What am I supposed to think?"

Shadows felt as if they ripped into her skin. The world was pitch black, creeping in on her, a never-ending void she forced herself not to step into. It wasn't the night she had known and loved to rule all her life.

There are no stars.

Ian paused, eyebrows scrunching as his hand gestured around him boldly, as if trying to form something with them as he spoke. "You didn't answer the question."

He always talked with his hands. Avril had come to notice that not long after they had their conversations that lasted longer than a few moments, and she loved those hands. When he was excited, or nervous, or was trying to figure something out that was on the tip of his tongue, they splayed with annoyance and concentration.

Now, his hands flared with exasperation as they yelled back and forth again and again until their words no longer made sense.

There was hot rage that boiled inside of Avril, a beast that would not back down. Darkness bled into her vision, and she couldn't even be sure what was her and what was the man in front of her, trying to get her to see reason, trying to get her to scream louder.

She was Avril Isobel Maison McClair Queen, just like her mother had told her, and she needed no one.

"You are a hypocrite!"

"Why don't you trust me?"

"I have given enough."

"I know."

Avril shoved hands into her hair, catching on her ring. Ian's ring.

"Then, why do you keep pushing me on this? This is your fault!"

"My fault?" Ian put a hand to his chest with a dark laugh. "Fine, if that is what you want, I'll take the blame. Doesn't hurt me one bit."

"I can't be perfect for you. I can't be your extraordinary for you to pick pieces off of, if that's what you wanted. And I'm not your mother either, Ian. You can't save me," Avril insisted through gritted teeth. "Why can't you see that this is what was supposed to happen this whole time?"

She was to be ruined. Her life shattered in pieces.

This was what she deserved, finally out in the open for all to see. Life was a brutal tease.

She stepped forward, closer to his face. Let him see who she was. Let him see the little girl who had grown up on expired food stamps and the kindness of gross men who let her sleep on the couch, filled with bedbugs, while they and her mother shared the other room. Let him see the whore he fucked and thought he loved, who ruined people's lives. She was doing him a favor really.

Giving him a swift exit.

"That's not—why do you have to fuck everything up?" He closed his eyes in frustration, and a hand went to his head while the other swung outward before either of them realized what that step forward could do, what those beautiful, articulate hands could do.

They made an impact.

An imprint.

Though perhaps it wasn't words that had done it.

Less than words. Less than anything anyone wanted to linger over and savor like the religion Avril had found days ago when her lips were on Ian's skin and she so desperately wanted to say the words only their bodies fully understood.

The next thing Avril understood, she was on the floor.

A sharp gasp choked itself in the back of her throat as her back twisted. It jerked in a way it hadn't in some time, ached like she hadn't felt in longer.

The fresh tile was hard and cold under her palm. She had been doing so good. So good for so long. When she looked up, tears streamed down her face, blurring her vision. But she didn't cry.

Avril didn't cry.

Not since *he* had been above her, like *he* was now.

"Avril." He was breathless. He reached out. The shadows spun, prepared to take her captive. "I'm so sorry. I didn't mean—"

"NO. No! Stay away from me. Please, stay away." Putting up a hand, Avril shoved herself farther away with a painful cry.

Slowly, *he* flickered above her with each of her blinks. The shadows instead began to settle back in. It was Ian there, horrified, as he stared down at her. His hand shook midair. It never came down. Not once.

Still, Avril couldn't find it in herself to breathe, turning away, no matter the hurt. "P-please, don't touch me."

"Okay. Okay," he said carefully.

He said…carefully?

The screws in his head began to turn as his eyes flickered left and right over his newly decorated kitchen. He'd lifted her onto that counter before. His mouth had trailed between her legs over there. They'd made pancakes and burned the pan with chocolate chips.

Avril folded in on herself. She couldn't stop shaking, gasping for air as she looked away. Anywhere but at him, so she would never have to remember the face again.

Him.

Ian.

Her mind traded back and forth one face for another. One emotion for another slid back and forth in her chest until she couldn't make sense of them.

"Okay." Ian twisted on his heel. "I'll be right back, all right? Stay here. I'll be right back."

Stay here. *Stay here.* The words replayed in her head while the creak of the stairs rebounded off the suddenly empty walls. Avril bit back a whimper as she forced herself to stand on uneasy legs.

"Stay here," Ian had said.

He had said.

But they weren't playing by his rules anymore. The memory was over.

The deal was shattered.

Avril knew better. Her eyes drifted to the ceiling as she braced her back with a hand.

She didn't want to think of *him* or Ian or anything, but she did anyway, all the way out the door.

CHAPTER FORTY-ONE

*S*he didn't remember telling the driver where to go. She must have because within what felt like minutes, but had to at least have been half an hour as the streets began to clear from the cold, Avril stood in front of the Riverside house. She and Reed joked that it was her own personal castle.

She really saw it that way as she looked up at the looming pillars and different-sized windows. Here was her castle, overlooking Ashton City. The Ash River was her moat to keep out invaders.

Now, she was one herself as she turned the brass knob. It didn't budge.

Letting her head fall against the solid oak door, Avril shut her eyes. Her body felt numb. As if that was all she was, a body to be used how she saw fit. Her head leaned against the door while her fist pounded against solid wood.

Bang. Bang. Bang.

After a dozen, Avril felt herself droop against the surface before the door opened.

Reed peered at her, rich brown eyes wide and confused. "Avril, what's going on?"

She shoved past Reed.

She ignored the other man sitting on her sofa with alarm. As Reed tried to grab on to her, Avril screamed until her throat burned, and Reed let her make her way up to her room alone.

She didn't want to talk. She didn't need his help. She didn't need anyone.

She was fine.

All she needed was to get inside. To be home, and now she was. Flinging the door behind her, Avril tore out bobby pins one at a time from her hair and tore the pin clasped to the front of her shirt, watching as the fabric pulled before it teared.

She threw the stupid thing across the room.

The sharp metallic sound it made as it hit the wall before tumbling back down to the floor stopped her heart already racing in her chest, and the whole of it resounded in her ears over and over again as well as Ian's voice did when it broke.

Ian.

That was Ian, with eyes wide in horror.

She wiped at her own as she stood on shaking legs toward the pin. It still lay there as she reached for it. Perfectly intact.

"Ruby. For passion and power," her mother had told her.

Well, fuck that.

Fuck her.

She let it drop back down to the floor, more intent now on the hand that even dared to pick it up, still sparkling with the thin golden band—her reminder not to die. Her reminder to keep moving forward. She had nowhere else to go.

Avril stumbled, trying to get from one end of the room to the other, prying the dainty piece of jewelry she never asked for off her swollen finger. It wouldn't begin to dislodge over her knuckle, stuck.

Strange sounds extracted themselves from her chest as she continued to yank before giving up altogether, feeling the shadows intermixing with her tears. Her eyes were swollen as she clenched them shut.

Avril lay down and finally felt the burning, heat-filled pain that radiated up from her back that she'd ignored the entire way home. Her hands shook, one with a reminder that didn't want to go away when they pulled up blankets to cover her limp knees.

All of her shook, even as she warmed. A frost entered her veins as she gasped, and her teeth chattered.

She could still hear the voice radiating in her head.

She could feel the way each word stung in whatever likely combination she wanted to put them together in the darkened void she would likely be in until she was dead, ring or no.

Shadows didn't stop their fight. They traveled up the walls until the hazy soot transformed into wallpaper and charcoal became its own creation. The darkest of shadows swirled above her on the ceiling.

You're mine. The shadows seemed to whisper.

You're mine.

Are you mine?

Avril clenched her fists in sheets and shut her eyes.

Her name was Avril Isobel Maison McClair Queen.

And she was no one else's.

Only it didn't feel that way, even as she clenched her eyes shut and prayed once more to whatever gods of the darkest nights that would listen to make it so.

———

AVRIL DIDN'T KNOW for how long she lay there. She didn't remember the last time she'd changed the sheets either, let alone slept in them. Cotton was soft against her skin as she let the edge of her quilt cradle her chin.

Every once in a while, Avril slowly peeled off layers until Reed came in to help her change into a camisole and sweats.

Days it felt like, though, it couldn't have been that.

It might've been only hours. A different sort of lifetime.

The elastic of the waistband of her pants fit her again, compared to when she had shown up a month ago to the house after so long away. They'd hung before, but again, she was healthy and full.

Reed used the fit to securely hold the hot pad against her spine. She flinched when he placed it the first time.

She flinched whenever someone touched her.

"Truth for me this morning. Please, Avril? Start with I," Reed requested. Whenever he used to ask why she was so angry, he would always say that. *Start with I.*

It was easier to place blame on anyone but herself if she didn't start that way.

"I'm fine."

Avril blinked a few times, adjusting her eyes after being closed for so long. Somehow, she'd managed to fall asleep, and it had taken her heavy and deep before she could think.

But now, something about the look made Reed turn his head. She expected to see the Reed she thought they had just gotten over again, full of pity and selflessness. Instead, all she saw was Reed, reaching forward with the lightest of smiles to brush a clump of hair away from her forehead.

"Try again," he requested.

Avril sighed. Shaking her head, she looked up to the ceiling before she decided what to say. It all sounded so wrong in her head. Even the truth. For the longest time, the truth and the shadows had the habit of mixing in with the rest of her mind, no matter where it was kept, in sealed compartments, better to be left for a rainy day.

A never day.

"I don't know what to do."

Her forehead creased in concentration. There was no way to

sift through it all. "I really fucked it all up this time, Reed. This was all for nothing."

Reed pulled himself further into the bed beside her. They must've made quite the sight, the two of them. They always did, but this time, Avril looked down. Her, half dressed in sweats, and him, prepared, as if he were going out to the opera.

"Can you tell me what happened, darling?"

With a sniff, Avril still wanted to shake her head, but the words fell out of her from the start. She told Reed about the stupid deal he'd already known about. How Ian was the most infuriating man with a stick up his ass she had ever met. How she'd confided in Ian before he even knew who she was—or so she'd thought. That he loved her.

She was so willing to throw it all away.

"You were right—and don't even look at me like you knew. I hate myself because I loved him so much. It's so stupid."

"Loved?" Reed asked, careful to make sure to pronounce the past tense.

Love.

The present made her heart ache a little worse.

Still, Avril shook her head. This was right. She wasn't meant to have someone like Ian.

Liar. Whore.

She was all those things and more, and Ian—

"I even said it to him. Almost anyway."

"When, the other night?"

"After the party, when we …" Avril cradled her aching face in her hands.

Reed shrugged. "Well, no one can take that for anything concrete."

"I can't believe I thought this could've ended any differently." She'd so desperately wanted it to end differently, but it didn't matter. This wasn't one of Ian's romance novels she read late at night, crying at the end, no matter what the final words were. She couldn't even remember most of them.

She only remembered that they always mattered.

"How Ian looked at me though after that woman attacked me, it was as if I were keeping something huge from him."

Reed adjusted himself again, reaching to turn up the heat of her heating pad. "Stop moving before the thing falls behind the frame."

"He doesn't know me. Not all of me, and he said he was fine with that. He said I didn't have to talk about it or anything. Not until I was ready. And I wasn't even if all I could think about was what you said about that stupid article the gossiper posted."

"Did you look at it?" Reed asked with a cringe.

"It's bad, huh?" She wondered how long it had been up before that woman attacked her on the street. How long would that take for someone to read about?

Reed said nothing.

It was likely for the best. For now. "Until I'm ready, he doesn't deserve to know every piece of me."

"No, he doesn't."

"I said such fucked-up things, Reed."

"I don't think after all of what you two managed to fit into a month, he would be surprised, Aves."

A breath of a laugh puffed through her lips. "There was this moment in the kitchen. Gods, I was loud."

Reed only smiled lightly.

She shook her head. "I was standing there, and then, the next moment, I was on the ground."

That smile flipped on a dime. Suddenly, Reed moved to get a better look at her face. Since she had started talking, her friend had appeared to relax considerably, not taking the severity of this situation seriously enough until right now.

"He hit you?"

"No. Stop. It was an accident, in a way. He didn't even touch me. High heels and high stress whenever someone's expressive hands move, well, it's not a great combination." Avril patted the tense arm of her pacifist friend.

She leaned her head up onto his shoulder, and his hair tickled her cheek, so he had to relax again.

The realization of everything that had happened had come to her a while ago, hours after she lay down and Reed put her hot pad into place for the first time, careful not to disturb her. The dark corners of her room called, so she stared into the shadows. There, they spoke to her in hushed tones until she put together in her mind and saw what had really happened, piece by piece.

She had fallen, she'd flinched, she had been scared, not of Ian exactly, but who he might've been.

Like he was afraid of whatever was left inside that she was keeping from him. Her deep, dark nightmares that woke them both up.

The two of them nestled further into Avril's cocoon of blankets and sorrow.

"What are you going to do?" asked Reed.

"I don't want to do anything." So, for right now, she was going to lie here.

"But..."

Avril turned back up to him. *But.* She could hear the words he was going to say next, and it came with the fluidity of someone reading from a children's book, an English professor reading an English gothic novel, knowing exactly where the twist was coming on the next page.

Either way, Avril startled every time it was read, whenever the time came to realize. That was it. This was where everything changed.

"We are no longer the kids in the closet."

"Or a girl with monsters under her bed," Avril finished. Using his hand in hers, she brought her sheet up closer to her chest. She was suddenly very tired again. "I made a home under that bed."

"I know you did."

In the darkness. The longest nights.

The *shadows.*

"I think the boy in the closet and the girl under the bed have both been scared. I'm sorry."

"Don't."

"I will be anyway." Avril rolled her eyes. "You know I don't say it often. Take it."

"Save it for a rainy day," Reed whispered. "I'm going to have to call the doctor about your back to get something for it."

"Don't."

"You need to heal—in more ways than one."

"Don't."

And Reed wouldn't anyway. He only nodded, as if putting a pin in this conversation. He would eventually come back to it again when she woke up from a nightmare and the sudden pain in her back that she hadn't felt like this in some time would be all too much for her. She wouldn't be able to say no forever if it went on. If she went on.

Not like this.

"I'm going to be fine, Reed," Avril said. A tear betrayed her, however, running from her eye and into her hair.

"I know."

"I will be."

He brushed her hair back again into a more manageable space, and Avril closed her eyes so she wouldn't have to watch his face as she shifted.

"You just need some time."

"I took time."

"No one said you couldn't have more."

"I'm just tired." Avril shook her head. "I haven't slept in so long."

Reed nodded. He knew. "Rest then."

"You can stay if you want, if you aren't going to bake cookies or bang your boyfriend. I approve of both though."

"I'll stay for a little while."

THE NEXT TIME Avril woke up, it was to tea and water. At another, a cup of coffee sat, still hot. She drank only a sip or two. It was filled with enough sugar that her heart pumped hard in her chest. When she put her hand there, over her ribs, her skin was warm against the cold metal of the ring still stuck on her right hand, but she could feel it.

Still beating on.

Sometimes, when she woke up, and the daylight was too bright to ignore, the car horns too loud, she wondered if Ian had tried to find her. Called out her name when he came back downstairs, wondering where she'd wandered off to.

Or maybe he didn't, still pissed and glad to be rid of her, as he should've been by now.

She was better off alone.

How many times did she need to remind herself of that? It was all going to be fine in a little while. Avril would be Avril, alone in her tower, deciding what to do next with her life, which still did not seem to be slipping away as vastly as she'd thought it would, and he—Ian—would either stay or go, and that would be entirely up to him.

The thought only sent her body to tingle with detachment.

She shut her eyes, though the sensation only went away when she peered them open again.

Someone sat in her chair across from her. She usually sat just like that to lace up her boots or adjust her heels. She'd practiced the pose her favorite burlesque shoot had depicted on that chair.

Head back, crown perched on top, and grinning like the devil Avril prayed one day she would come to be.

Only now, here he was. Waiting for her. A demon to match her own.

A man of shadows.

CHAPTER FORTY-TWO

*H*e sat on the edge of the soft rose-hued fabric with his elbows on his knees.

At Avril's single intake of breath at the sight of him, he lifted his eyes to meet hers from across the room. They were red-rimmed and hard.

Parting her lips, Avril meant to say something, anything along with the question of how the hell he'd found her. But of course, he had. But why?

All of it died somewhere between her brain and lips as she still tried to remember how to form any of those words at all.

Instead, her breath, her voice, her everything wavered at the scene of him there, in front of her. It was as if she had woken from a dream instead of a nightmare.

"Hi."

"You scared the hell out of me."

That made two of them. Trying to sit up, Avril winced.

Ian crossed the room but paused halfway, as if remembering her screaming at him, telling him to stay away. So, he stood, neither waiting for permission nor asking for it.

"I came back downstairs and didn't know where you had

gone, and, God, Avril." Her name held less bite than it had the last time he said it. "God, you scared me."

Ian grimaced at the words, and Avril only stared at him, rocking back and forth on his feet, as if trying to find purchase on solid ground.

"You found me," Avril whispered, eyes still adjusting to the forever darkness swirling around them both.

"I found you."

She looked around the space, even though he was only looking at her. His eyes lay on her, heavy and stilled, as if he now was having trouble finding the right words to say too. She was sure, for some people, it would be *sorry*.

"Not what you expected?" she asked, glancing at the wallpaper.

He shook his head. "Avril, you've always been exactly what I expected."

"And what's that?" Scandalous? Different from the so-called other girls? A good lay who could make him laugh after he came?

She had promised most of that.

"Frustrating," Ian said.

Avril met his strained eyes.

He extended a hand to the side, as if the whole rest of what she was lay in the palm of his hand. "Infuriating and crude and maddening when I can't seem to get you out of my head from the first night I ever saw you."

"You did say I bewitched you."

Teeth flashed in a grimace as he nodded, correcting her. "When I saw you for the first time, Avril."

"What do you mean?"

"On that stage in New York where Jack had to run to meet you at—I watched you take the stage and I had no idea who you were. Yet, for some reason, I felt as if someone had sucked something right out of my chest that night. You danced, and I couldn't breathe. Noah whacked me on the back to make sure I wasn't going to pass out in the crowd. You were this fiery, beautiful woman who stood up there and grinned. I'd never seen anyone more exquisite in my entire life. You flung splashes of black lace ribbons to each side under the light. So proud. So perfect."

"I'm not perfect."

"Oh, I know," Ian said seriously. "When I saw you that first time, I had no idea what the hell I was going to do with my life. Until recently, I still had no clue. But when I saw you, for those few minutes, it didn't matter. You held nothing back. You left everything you ever wanted to say or be right there in front of everyone and told them to take it or leave it. When I saw you for the first time in my life—"

"Let me guess. Time stopped?" Avril cut in. "Sounds like one of those books you love."

"So what if it does?"

Avril took a deep breath, turning her stare back down to her hands. They caught each other as they fisted the bedsheet between her legs. She thought of the first time she had seen Ian—no, felt Ian in that closet. She felt as if all the fear she had been running away from, all the people, had slipped away. The only person she'd cared about then and there was the man slipping his hand over her hip. The man who made that tiny flame deep in her stomach spark when it had long since been snuffed out.

"What I saw in you that night was someone who had such fire and strength in her eyes. I didn't know your name, yet for some reason, I felt this pull. I loitered around after, trying to convince Noah to go as he talked and met other people, with this *need* to meet you. I had no idea what I was going to say, but I felt this yank, as if someone wanted to pull me right to you."

She shook her head. "I never met anyone that night."

"By the time I got backstage, you and Jack were gone. In that moment, when I realized I hadn't gotten that chance, that second to get to you in time, all the weight on my chest returned that I'd lost for those few hours since Jack had run into me. The heaviness was there, still there. I knew I had just wasted this big moment and I wouldn't get it back." Ian took a deep breath. "I went into a closet at a gallery opening for a girl I thought was meant for me after praying to whoever would listen in the darkness for one thing to work out for me, thinking of that night in the club when I'd felt that pull. I needed my life to have purpose because I was done waiting, no matter what it was that I had to do to make it happen."

And then Avril had arrived.

"When I came back downstairs the other night, having not the slightest plan of what to do next, I found you gone. It was that night in the club in the middle of New York City all over again when I had known I missed my chance of something that would change my life."

Avril lifted her eyes back up in slow increments, afraid of what she'd find. Something lodged in her chest. She wanted to scream everything she felt and everything she didn't. She wanted to shriek that he wasn't alone. That she felt, as if for the past few years, when she was on every magazine cover and stage around the world, like she still hadn't quite found what she was looking for in this grand world she hoped truly revolved around her.

"You were right too," Ian said, taking another step closer when she didn't object. "I haven't been honest with you. There are things I don't want to talk about."

"You don't have to."

"But I should. Just like you should, when you're ready."

Would she ever be? He didn't seem to understand. It didn't matter how she felt, how he felt. All of this was wrong. This wasn't how it was all supposed to end.

She didn't know how it was supposed to end, but this couldn't be right. Not for her.

"Ian," Avril choked. "I'm sorry."

"Don't."

"I should have never brought you into this, my life. Not like this. You were ... an escape." They both had to have known it until somewhere along the line, it'd morphed. She should have known better. "We made a mistake."

"No."

She was never any good at sticking to plans. Following rules.

"You were never a mistake," Ian insisted. "This could not have been a mistake after everything. This was the opposite of a mistake."

"I just keep fucking up. You're right. That woman the other night was right. Even Cynthia at that party was right, the way she looked at me." As if Avril were someone else entirely that no one recognized anymore. "I fuck up everything."

"No. No, that isn't—I didn't mean that. Not one bit. At least, not in any way but a fun way," Ian said, tears in his eyes, but there was something of a joke in his voice.

Avril sniffled, unable to hold back her own small, pained chuckle. It felt like acid in her throat. "Are you trying to make a joke?"

"Is it working?"

"I don't know."

"I know the truth isn't pretty, Avril," Ian said softly. "Mine isn't either."

"Oh, please," Avril nearly snarled.

Ian remained silent.

If he was waiting for her still to take the leap first, he'd have to wait. Forever maybe.

"I don't want to—"

"Then, don't. You don't have to say a word you don't want to me. Not right now. I'm here in front of you, for you. All of you. Like I said, you were right back there. I haven't told you everything. I haven't been completely truthful about my life, or what I have always really wanted, or my mom. They are"—he shivered at the word—"shadows."

Avril's eyes locked on him, tracing the thick black snakes slicing through his skin.

"Just listen." Ian reached out a hand and paused before taking hers into his own. Supple and warm. "My shadows, the ones you talk about, the ones you see all over me, I don't want to talk about them. I have a feeling I know all too well where they came from, and like a garden, I watered my darkest bits daily for a long time. I still do."

Avril waited for him to say more as he gathered himself.

"I'm sorry I made you feel like you had to come out with it all to me before, but now, I'm going to tell you about me. And I just want you to listen. Can you do that?"

After a moment, Avril shifted to make room on the bed.

He swallowed. "I don't even know where to start."

"The beginning is always a good place."

CHAPTER FORTY-THREE

"My mother was all I knew. Even when we were in Ashton, it felt like I was in another world, away from everyone else. It was just me and her. Occasionally, I would see my father, of course. He'd stop in a lot sometimes, and then other times, not so much," Ian began, sitting down on the far edge of Avril's bed.

Listening closely, Avril flipped back the one blanket, watching as it caught on his knee. He gripped it like she gripped her end. The two of them tethered by each corner, like the dark, tattered ribbon that had seemed to yank them both together in the first place for some reason, confused and unaware of the damage two wrong ends tied together could cause.

"One day, my mother was a mess. Something had happened. I never worked the courage to ask her what, but we left before morning. She filled a bag of my things before getting her own. I remember watching Ashton and the lights of all the buildings fade behind us the farther we got. I question it all the time—if she regretted leaving, if it was rash, but I don't have answers. I don't know if she didn't feel safe or as loved as how she once had by my father." Ian shrugged a single shoulder.

"All I know is that at some point, my mother returned to what she had been taught to do for most of her life. She sold any piece of herself in order to get by. She didn't have the same options or didn't know or want them. Still, I found her crying late in the evenings more often than not, especially in the coldest parts of the winter, when things got tight and she was laid off again from whatever seasonal position she'd found in whatever town we made our way through."

Avril knew of those months, the ones where her mother had come off a sort of high of the holidays, so full of light and sugar and people who had it in their hearts to notice all those around them rather than a select few, reaching out their hands, crying for help on the sides of the street.

"Her favorite time was the holidays," Ian went on. Lost in thought, he made himself more comfortable. "There was always work at a department store, putting up sales and restocking shelves. They never cared who she was, where she had come from, or how much education she had. They needed help, and if there was one thing about my mother, it was that she was soft. She was nearly always willing to give it."

He flashed a strange smile with the front of his teeth.

"She always treated herself and me to little things when she had her discount. 'Just a little something,' she'd say. She tied it up, no matter what it was, with a bow from the wrapping department."

"That's sweet," Avril managed.

"She once brought home a chess set. It had been on clearance. The pieces were tiny, but we spent hours playing."

"No wonder you always beat me."

"You need to remember what each of the pieces do."

"They should do whatever I want them to."

Ian pressed another smile, as if he couldn't believe this was where his conversation had led him, glad that it had.

A dip of his chin moved him forward, backward. "We had

good years at the start. Even if they didn't always feel that way. We were independent people, she would remind me. I always remembered that. We took care of ourselves. When you told me about your mother, about Isobel..." Ian said Avril's mother's name like a bell, calling out for her.

It struck a chord somewhere in Avril as she remained silent, forcing herself to focus on him and not the stark gray shades surrounding her own memories sneaking in between.

"It reminded me of that. Of course, like I said, my mother was very good at giving help, just not receiving it. She refused the doctors since it would leave me alone in the house and probably would only bring a prescription she couldn't afford.

"We took care of each other the best we could. We tried to keep each other safe, whatever that meant to us at the time.

"My father had been trying to find her, trying to find me, since we'd left the city. He was worried something would happen to me, all alone with her. He didn't believe I was getting a proper education or living up to his name, which, I suppose, he was right. None of that mattered at the time. We were much more concerned with making sure the house and ourselves were cleaned and mostly fed. My mother still was struggling on the latter, already losing an appetite years before she left Ashton." Ian scrunched his mouth to the side. He sighed. "Don't you hate when people eventually have a point?"

"What happened?" Avril barely heard herself ask the question.

"It wasn't uncommon for my mother to take clients at home when the need called for it. It was never odd to me either. She explained it as one would go into the office. She also said it was safer. I was about nine, I think, almost ten. Each night, she would leave me in the kitchen with the pocket door nearly closed. I watched cartoons. It was the only time we really had the television on, which had been left behind by the last tenant. Otherwise, my mother would set me up with a book in the corner.

"One day though, a client came by. He brought a friend to

wait for him. Noticing me in the kitchen, he came in. He sat for a while. It wasn't the first time someone had done that, even changing the channel without asking. This time, he didn't change the channel."

Avril could taste the metallic copper of ash in her mouth. The shadows that shuddered as Ian continued to speak. She shut her eyes before opening them again, knowing Ian needed her to listen and to look at him while he spoke, no matter how much she wanted him to stop.

Her hands reached out before she could stop them.

Ian held them in his lap. She couldn't tell if he noticed the gesture fully, but his thumb smoothed over the backs of her palms.

"I found his kindness in how he tipped my mother so strange. He'd come in, and my mother would attend to her client, and he would sit and ask me all sorts of questions about myself. How old I was. How I liked the town. What I wanted to be most when I got older. I'm not sure what I said to any of those questions, and once, while he was asking me them, he started to get closer to me. Embrace me, like a father." Ian swallowed. "I can't blame her, of course. I could never blame her."

Avril shook her head.

"Sitting next to me in the kitchen, he reached over, and his fingers gripped into my skin, right behind the neck. Forcing me over the table. He asked me if I was proud of what my mother did. Why couldn't I be more of a man to help her? He started to threaten me about how he would go to the police. He'd tell them what my mother did or kill her if I said anything about what happened. I froze under him, the pain as he held me shot all the way down to the base of my spine as he held me there, yanking at me."

"Ian," Avril breathed.

He turned to look at her. "But nothing happened. Nothing got to happen, not before my mother came in all of a sudden and I heard the dollar-store frying pan left out on the stove hit that man right on the side of his head. My mother didn't stop either. She beat him as he screamed. We never had to move to a new town so quickly. We barely packed before we left.

"I can't blame my mother," Ian repeated as before. "My mother and I couldn't look at each other for a long time. She was ashamed, and so was I. It was easier not saying a single word. Eventually though, like she wanted it to, like I wanted it to, the entire situation faded. It was just a nightmare not to be spoken of. Still, I could never forget that man or what he'd said about how I wasn't doing enough to help her. That something, anything, could happen to her, all because of me. I stopped going to school because of it, too afraid that something would happen while I was gone. I wouldn't be there to stop it or to take care of her."

There was a moment of silence as Ian debated on how to continue. His eyes narrowing as the scenes played out in front of him

"I didn't want you to know this piece of me. My past."

"I want to know you."

"Well…" *Now, you do*, Ian seemed to say, knowing she heard it all the same. "She never took clients at home after that. Maybe going out only exerted her condition and killed her sooner. I don't know. No one besides me and her ever came inside of our home again, not until the day she died in her bed. She begged me through tears to run and bring a priest."

"So, you did?"

"I'd never run so fast," Ian vowed. "The priest looked rather taken aback, of course. She was never made for that kind of life. She hadn't chosen it, or at least, she felt like she'd had to for some reason."

They would never fully know.

Avril fell silent as he came to the end of the story, letting it settle in the air like a thick, overbearing blanket, more likely to suffocate than warm. He waited for her to speak, his eyes begging for something that wasn't clear, likely a pronouncement of some sort. A passing judgment in her loosening hands.

"And the worst part is that when she died, I was grateful. So grateful."

"Ian."

"It's the truth. I watched her fade. She was done suffering, yes, but all I remember thinking was how terribly grateful I was to have even a single ounce of the pressure lifted off me.

"When she died, my father sent his secretary, Idena, to pick me up at the airport. I had no idea what was going to happen to me, but mostly, I was indebted to whatever god had made that decision to take her right then. I was so tired, in all the ways," Ian managed to get out.

"I was unwilling to suffer another second for her, who had done everything she could for me."

"To survive."

Ian twisted his chin away from her.

Not before she could catch it. "Ian, look at me."

His silver eyes shone like the most beautiful of precious metals. "You did what you had to do. You felt what you needed to feel and made it through because you are a survivor. You endured the darkest bits—what should be anyway. So what if you were thankful your mother had died? So what if you cried out of joy instead of pain?"

The shadows swirled around him as if that was exactly what had happened.

"You took the darkness that had made a home around you and used every foothold you could to still head toward the bright parts, Ian. You are extraordinary more than anything because of that."

Avril glanced down at her ring as she gripped his hand.

"You kept moving forward, even when you felt guilt that you shouldn't have and were told not to."

"I was selfish. I still am."

"So what?"

Ian stared at her.

"So what if you are? So what if I am? We can afford to be selfish, to be whatever the fuck we want. So, fine. I'm selfish. I'm a liar. I'm the whore of Ashton to more people than I could probably count. I'm someone who ruined someone's life and doesn't want to look back. I'm full of hatred and rage, and I've let that be my own personal fuel for as long as I can remember because I like to watch things burn. But that's not just me, is it?"

Wasn't it?

"Just like feeling terrible all because you wanted to breathe and see a magical life like the ones of the stories that brought you solace isn't just you."

When she swallowed, the shadows seemed to waver at the acceptance of her own words, stirring deep in her stomach, as if more of them had bred there in her lower back, a different sort of reminder than the tiny diamond of starlight on her finger.

"I didn't know at first how awful *he* was," Avril whispered. "He was kind and caring and made more than just me laugh when I met him at a random bar with Jack."

Ian tried to cut in, but she shook her head.

She needed to continue. If she stopped now, she knew she would never say the words at all.

"I'm pretty sure he only approached me first because one of his friends had dared him to. They all knew who I was, whether or not he did. It was easy enough to see from where I was perched on the edge of the bar, my feet in Jack's lap as he flirted with the girl next to him. I remember I saw him though, right as I brought the final sip of my drink back down from my lips. My body seemed to go still as he walked toward me. I thought it was some sort of sign, but maybe it was just me. An animal realizing that it was suddenly prey. I smiled nonetheless. I tried to play my game as he played his, so shy and trim in his wrinkled suit. All of those boys wore them after coming from work." Avril shut her eyes, focusing on the buttons and rolled sleeves rather than the faces in them.

The shadows were all too happy to oblige, reminding her of any pieces she'd missed.

"I still wonder how much cash they all lost that night. I would've paid them all double now, if they'd just minded their own fucking business."

Ian's hand still held Avril's, but as she talked, he shifted, folding them together as they lay. Legs tangled in the blankets with hers. His hands slowly moved down so as not to startle Avril as he extracted the heating pad from her back. He gently stroked the cool space.

The story began to come out as he soothed away the burden and hesitation.

"Everyone liked him. All the other girls said how lucky I was to have a man who bought me flowers and looked like he cared so much about my life. But they didn't know. No one did. I didn't even know for a long time, not until it felt like it was all too late.

"We moved in together when it all really started. He needed to know where I was going and who I was with all the time. He told me that I needed to stop going out so late at night when other men were out. He worried for me so much and got so angry when I didn't listen to him. Of course, I never really listened to anyone. He didn't understand my past, I thought, though I didn't tell him much of it. He didn't know I could handle myself. But that wasn't it. Not really."

"He abused you."

Closing her eyes, Avril shook her head before she realized that wasn't right. "He never hit me. Not for a long time did he ever actually raise a hand to me at all. He so easily situated himself into my life, insisted that he wanted to take care of me. To be honest, some days, after so long, it sounded so nice."

Avril swallowed, feeling the pressure building and not just from the darkness settling in.

"Take a second."

She didn't want one. There was a lump in her throat she needed to go away.

"At first, I thought he was so interested in the culture of my work, which I loved, especially DuCain. He wanted to be dominant in the way Jack was, knowing that I'd played on stage with him before—I assume from one of his friends. But he was no Dom." Avril's face contorted. "He wanted to dominate. No real Dom would ever do the things he did. I know that, but for some reason, I let it go. He called me all sorts of ugly things. He used anything I'd ever trusted him with against me, saying it was all the more reason I was a slut, an embarrassment. He meant it too."

Ian's jaw clenched.

"I don't know why I didn't leave. There were just these moments—these quiet, beautiful moments—some days, whether it be after a fight or just in the middle of the afternoon, where we'd be sitting there across from each other, and everything felt all right.

"I'd been with men before. Men and women and everyone, but never singularly. I never let myself put that kind of energy into something. Risk that kind of feeling. But I did with him.

"I had from the moment he said hello to the seconds where he manipulated me so plainly. I didn't want to see it. I stayed and tried to see a different future with someone who smiled at me for no reason when he saw me, even when that meant leaving my job, my family, my entire world. And why did I—the scum off the street, who fancied herself a well-off sex worker—deserve anything different? Anyone who loved me better?"

Ian listened. His arms stilled around her.

"He hollowed me out, and I let him. I *let* him fill me with his screams, and I only sometimes screamed back. I screamed back that final night before I left. He was in a rare mood, angry that I had been going out to Rosin. I was only with Jack and then Kit while he was away on business, but seeing them and the city..." Avril rolled her eyes.

"You were able to be alive."

For the slightest of seconds, the nights breezed by.

"He began to see everything I did as a sort of threat. My heels were too loud. My opinions were too loud. I was too loud, and in the very back of my mind, I started to like that. I liked it so much that after months, I sharpened all my edges when he came back and I let him have his way until there was nothing left for him to scream at me. I knew it all, and I had already given so much. But then I took a step forward when I dared to counter him, and he hit me."

There was really no other way to put it.

"He shoved me. It's all semantics at this point. I had seen it coming, but I didn't move. My back twisted as I fell into the wall and cracked my head on the floor."

She met Ian's gaze, intently focused on her.

"The other night, when you were in front of me, it was as if I couldn't differentiate the two moments, the two shadows brushing up against one another, fighting for which one mattered most. You were him, and I was the me I had thought I'd moved on from. All during our time that night, I thought I'd somehow managed it. I'd managed to fit the pieces of myself back together, even if they weren't perfect. For the longest time, I wasn't sure I would ever be able to, but then there you were, decorating a tree and pulling me on your lap, like I mattered."

"You matter," Ian said.

"I broke and healed, and I was supposed to be better. But I wasn't," Avril went on as if she hadn't heard him, her voice cold and clouded. She scrunched her face, trying to focus, but those stupid dreaded tears slipped from the corners anyway.

"I'd never seen myself as my aunt from when I was first sent away, being rushed to the hospital, until then. He was crying more than I was, not able to look at me. He was so sorry, he said. So sorry that I'd made him so furious. He'd make it up to me. But I was alone. He left out the door not long after. He left me there, shaking on the floor. I was all alone and had no one but myself to pick up the phone and make a call to save myself. If not then"— Avril sighed, letting the entire reaction wash over her—"never."

She wasn't sure what would've happened if she hadn't called Reed then. He'd seemed to be waiting by the phone for a long time.

He also might've been the angriest when he came to get her, bringing along Jack, who was able to help her rise from the floor. Reed swore when he saw what *he* had done and continued a steady round of expletives Avril couldn't help but laugh at as she cried in the back seat of Jack's Jeep. She just kept laughing so loud, all the way to the house when she denied going to the emergency room. They would've only put an ice pack where she was sore.

And she'd hurt all over.

Avril was terrified at what she would see when she looked finally at Ian next to her. There could be anything in that flat stare, so steady. He must've always had to hold himself so solid and strong.

But now, his face held nothing but devastation.

"I couldn't go back after that," Avril said, breathing through her open mouth. "I couldn't go back."

To anything.

To anyone.

To herself. She wasn't sure anymore if she ever would.

Somehow, Ian understood it all as he opened his arms, and she let herself fall into them.

CHAPTER FORTY-FOUR

"*W*hy didn't you say anything?" Ian asked.

"I didn't want to." It seemed the simplest excuse as she continued to cling to him. "Just for a moment, when I was with you, I wasn't anyone. I wasn't anything. I really liked how you had no idea who I was and didn't care. For a little while, I could pretend I was no one."

She'd wanted to be no one.

"Most of the time, I could pretend that what had happened didn't, and I was okay. But then…"

"You didn't want to pretend anymore."

Avril hadn't even realized that he was gently stroking her back again until she finally pulled back to see his face. When she looked at him this time, neither of them flinched because, now, finally, they knew what had happened next.

The world had just kept on burning.

And she'd let it.

It was too much. She was always too much.

"Look at me."

She curved away.

Ian gently turned her face back, fingers below her ear. "Look at me, Rose. You are not too much. Ever. You were always *mine*, even when I didn't realize or thought I didn't deserve it. I am going to love you, and no matter what, it is going to be worth it. You are worth it all to me."

"You don't mean that."

"I do," Ian said. "What can I do to make you see that I mean it all? Every word?"

She didn't know. She only stared at him.

"You came looking for me?"

Ian narrowed his eyes at her. A breath escaped him. "I did."

He had. Maybe that was all she needed to hear because at the words, something stilled inside of her chest.

"No wonder," Avril said morosely. "We're both pretty fucked up, huh?"

"I thought of it more along the lines of broken."

"Shattered." Avril could only agree. "Then stitched back together, mostly anyway, like Frankenstein."

"I'm much handsomer than any Frankenstein."

She'd have to agree as she reached out, and Ian, already intrinsically knowing, leaned down to her.

"I'm only just your average monster."

Ian chuckled. His breath was hot on her skin. His scent was so familiar that Avril felt emotion swell upward. Paper and pine, he was right here in front of her.

He guided her hand up to the side of his face, gritty with thicker stubble than she remembered.

"Just let me kiss you," Ian bade. "I just want to kiss you. Hold you."

Avril had never been the girl who someone just wanted to steal a kiss from. She was the girl who had once sucked off three guys on the baseball team at the same time just because she could and she wanted to and they knew it. She was never the girl who wanted to just kiss.

She wanted to devour.

Yet Ian—her Ian—was warm and easy and full of sharp edges like her own. He bent and smoothed them over for her, and she melted into his mouth. A kiss. It broke the hardship and fear, reminding them who they were.

She could kiss him forever, his lips soft and easy against hers.

To kiss him like this, to be with him like this, she fought against all the pain and fear of what all of this meant. She had never felt this way for anyone before, never desired someone like she desired the single person in front of her.

"I love you."

For the longest moment, neither of them seemed to realize who had said the words. They pulsed as they came from Avril's lips, full of joy and emotion that crept up on her, bleeding into her eyes.

Ian gazed down at her from where he was just barely holding himself steady on a leash she so wanted to snap.

"I love you." Avril laughed the words as tears poured down her cheeks. "Every piece."

When he brushed them away with his thumbs, the leash pulled. Ian bent back down onto her in a rush. Her head fell back as he kissed her neck, teeth nipping at the tendon that made her shiver. He bit down hard enough that she gasped.

She loved him. She loved Ian.

The fear was still there and holding, just slowly fuzzing around the edges. For another day. Another time that was not this one because right now, all that mattered was that Ian had found her. He had come looking for her. He wanted her, and she wanted him back so much that his heartbeat under her hand turned into music, a steady beat as they moved.

Already stretched across the sheets of her bed, Avril pulled his shirt overhead, so she could get closer to that beautiful sound.

Ian chuckled. "Not too much there, my little fury."

"I thought you believed I was a witch."

"Guess I'll have to stay close to find out." Ian set his head back into that perfect spot where their lips just nearly touched. Breath tossed back breath. "God, Rose, you scared me."

"I know."

"Is that so?"

She swallowed all the heavy feeling inside of her throat as she nodded. They were there now, in her bed, in her turret of the house she'd bought just for herself—and Reed, of course. She had never let anyone else in before. Not like this.

"I scared me too."

Ian leaned his head against hers as they slumped farther down into the bed, a nest of strewn blankets. "I might've thought I wanted something of my own, away from the world, something I thought would only then be extraordinary. I am very good at being alone, even when I don't actually want to be. But, Rose, you helped me find joy."

"Joy." Avril spoke the word like it was foreign.

"Here. In a house. In Ash. Turns out, what I was missing and looking for was you."

"Ash? Don't you sound like a city dweller?"

Blinking his eyes slowly, Ian continued to peruse Avril's body with his hands, as if making sure she was still there and he wasn't a part of a very strange dream. "Please, be mine."

Avril closed her eyes, feeling his heartbeat against her skin. His.

"I suppose we can strike up some sort of deal," Avril ruminated. She looked upward, away from him, as if already seeing a contract being drawn up before her eyes.

He laughed. "Tomorrow."

"Tomorrow."

She was pretty sure the sun had already risen and set between them. Another beautiful night for her shadows, now twisting calmly over his skin. She brushed a finger over them as he shut his eyes partway, peering at her between lashes.

"Are you tired?" Avril whispered into his ear. Unlike Reed's long locks, she didn't need to brush anything aside as she cradled herself on his shoulder.

"Exhausted."

"So am I."

Ian stroked a piece of hair away from her forehead. "I might not always be able to be gentle with your heart, but don't you think that there is a single part of you, Avril Isobel…"

"Maison."

"Maison McClair Queen." Ian chuckled before adding another name. What was one more? "My Rose. There is not one part of you that I couldn't love. I mean it. I love you."

"I'm yours."

CHAPTER FORTY-FIVE

*F*or the next few days, the two of them convalesced in bed, watching movies and drinking coffee Ian had brought up for the two of them, though he never put enough sugar in her mug. Maybe there was a reason as they spent most of their time sleeping, only waking to the pleasant movements of Avril finding her body pressed up against someone else's.

Every time she opened her eyes, she was surprised to find that remnants of the shadows were still there, twisting and turning like stuck knots, never disappearing from Ian's skin or hers. Perhaps they never would.

Reed seemed to keep his own distance as her back healed. She only heard the sounds of him and Dixon having an argument downstairs.

Avril leaned farther into Ian. At this point, she might as well have burrowed. "How does it feel to be in the mysterious castle of Ashton's underworld?"

Ian huffed a light laugh. "Very privileged, I must say. The decor, of course, is definitely not stager approved."

Hopefully, her appalled expression showed how much she cared.

"You did manage to make this place feel like a home."

"I needed it to be. An imaginary home for misfits," Avril whispered, thinking of all the people over the past years who had managed to call the townhouse home for at least a little while until they found their footing, nowhere else to go but to the bottom, where all the fun was.

There was also royalty.

They found it all when they least expected it, just like she and Reed had.

"You know, I think this is the point where I tell you that if you do stay—"

"I'm staying."

He might need to tell her that a few more times.

"If you do stay," Avril went on, "your life might change forever."

Nestling himself so his chin rested on top of Avril's head, Ian didn't seem the least perturbed by this. "I didn't really like my life before I was debauched at an art show recently anyway."

"Must've been a hands-on show."

"You have no idea."

Avril smiled at the memory. It didn't hold the bite it once had. The shadows did not snap like a snake at any mere movement she made in the wrong direction. Still, she cleared her throat. "I'm not going back, I've decided. Not right away."

Ian nodded.

"I figure I should actually do what I've been told for a little while."

"Are you sure you didn't hit your head on the way down the other day?"

Avril sighed but didn't move out of his touch as he gently searched for lumps. "Unfortunately."

She just wasn't ready to take a step back out into the light. The cameras. The people all asking her what had happened.

What was next?

"Tomorrow."

"What?" Ian asked, pulling them back down.

"Tomorrow, my darling. My love."

He hummed with pleasure at the name.

It sounded right on her lips, even if she could only whisper it. "Tomorrow, I want to show you everything. I want to show you Ashton. My Ashton."

"It would be an honor," Ian murmured into the space between her earlobe and throat.

Avril made a similar hum of pleasure. A smile coming out before she had a moment to think about it.

He only lifted his gaze when he heard the sound. His eyes of molten gray and silver swirled. "When else will I ever get to say I've been shown around the kingdom by the Queen herself?"

"You don't know?"

"Tell me."

She smiled as she put a finger on his lips, pushing him carefully on his back. "You'll be the king."

KNEELING BEFORE HER, Ian swiftly laced up her knee-high boots with surprising ease as they prepared for the evening, which had started with a bath in her tub made for two. Her heels were the final item of her outfit. The rest of her was just as structured to keep her standing and comfortable—from her tight pants to the simple corset near the back of her closet. It was one of the first corsets she'd ever bought when she worked for Emilie at the lingerie shop.

The piece spoke to her, saying something between debutante and femme fatale. The silk satin was both glamorous as well as practical.

She ran her fingers over the stiff boning.

Adjusting each piece until it lay right, as if she were going out into the battle zone, Avril prepared herself for anyone to strike. Who knew who she'd see? Except, of course, the one person she needed to stop specifically for, already warning Ian of what the evening had in store.

Avril ran through Ian's light hair with nimble fingers. She really did love him on his knees.

"You sure you've never done this before?"

Ian stood up again, tall above her. He gave her a kiss as he headed to the other side of the room.

Ian had already made himself at home in her space, and she couldn't find herself angry about it as she stood for one last look in the mirror. When she popped her lips, the bold red was stark against her skin and revealed freckles she let scatter any which way they pleased against her cheeks. She rolled her shoulders back. She stood tall.

She forced herself to open the door and walk downstairs toward the low volume of music playing over the speakers. Dixon was likely still there. He was the only one she could imagine who would set up a playlist of what she could describe as classical a cappella.

The clang of pans pulled her down the hallway toward the kitchen. Dixon dripped batter down into a frying pan, listening as it sizzled. He handed Reed a plate of finished pancakes, and Reed barely looked Avril's way before sliding the plate toward her. They were fluffy and golden brown.

"Eat," Reed commanded, as if it wasn't Dixon behind him who was doing the actual cooking.

She raised her eyebrows at both of them. She pushed the stack back away to Reed. He still didn't look up from the journal he was reading. "I'm going out. Hey, Dix."

He smiled. Flour was smeared at the edge of his jawline. Since Reed said nothing about it to him, neither did she.

"Have fun. It's good to see you, Avril."

"When I'm not yelling at you, right?"

Dixon glanced down at his tray with another smile. "That always helps."

Slowly sliding herself around the island until she was closer to Reed, she rested her cheek against her hand, waiting for him to look at her. When she pretended to read over his shoulder, he could only last so long.

Reed glanced up at her. "What?"

"Did you call him?" Avril asked.

Pressing his lips together as if debating, he nodded.

Avril wrapped her arms around her friend and held him close. She kissed him hard on the cheek before holding him even tighter.

Dixon roared with a cheerful laugh, as if he'd been hoping for this strange outcome for a long time. He hissed after another moment though, turning back to his cooking. An overdone pancake smoked up into the range hood.

"Thank you, Reed."

Reed mildly pushed her back, finally looking over what she was wearing. "You look yourself."

He thought she'd looked like Queen the other day, standing outside and looking at the townhouse, wondering if she was willing to enter and risk his wrath, to risk her own, but this was a whole new dream come to fruition.

"Reed."

"Don't even."

She just stared at him, feeling the guilt continuing to climb into her stomach as she held on to his hand. It wasn't a stretch to understand how much it must've killed him to open her phone and search for Ian's name after being the one she called for so many years.

"You know I don't make a habit of groveling."

Reed rolled his eyes at her even suggesting it.

"But thank you, Reed. For everything. I know I owe you."

"Is that all?"

"You are the absolute most wonderful person on the face of the earth that the stars guided me to. My soul mate. My friend. My knight in oddly patterned armor."

Reed laughed, the stark sound finally escaping him once and for all. It sounded like chimes. A truce. "Stop. I'll call in all my many favors you owe me eventually."

"I'll plan on it."

"You look like you are going somewhere?"

"I thought it was time to show Ian my Ashton." From where Avril had bloomed from the gutter.

Reed seemed to understand, a new humor-filled look crossing his face of what that entailed. He must've also had to fight himself to ask if she was sure. If she was ready.

Avril cocked her head and glanced down at herself in answer. She was as ready as she was going to be. One day or now.

"Ahem," Dixon piped in over his shoulder.

"Excuse me." Reed held her hand, tapping the fist they'd made against his knee propped on the other chair. "Are Dixon and I allowed to join you on your evening out on the town?"

"Next time," Avril promised. "I have a few extra stops to make tonight."

Reed held his tight smile as he looked over his shoulder. He didn't let go, hand limp as Avril walked away to the hall. Ian stood there, looking even taller in the passage. Her friend looked between the two of them before shaking his head.

"Don't," Avril warned, eyes flaring.

He shook his head. "I'm not saying a word this time."

BEFORE SHE COULD CHANGE her mind, Avril sauntered inside the looming building and down the aisle. Ian held back in the atrium. The space used to be the ticket counter of the old converted theater, now the formidable DuCain.

Everything was a shadow in DuCain. Maybe that was why Avril always liked it so much, even more than Rosin some days when the dark red velvet walls weren't enough to entice. There were places to hide at DuCain, as well as places to put yourself as the center of attention on stage, bedecked in a sparkling black gloss, as if a piece of the night sky captured.

A man dropped his overcrowded gym bag, not filled with only sweats, on the edge of the stage before pulling himself up to sit.

Jack's legs dangled over the side as he watched Avril stroll toward him. He assessed her up and down. Blinked once.

"So, I take it you didn't break our poor librarian's heart?" He spoke first, a power move of sorts. His voice echoed through the empty theater, booming toward her.

"I never took you as someone who had friends in academic places, Jack."

"Well"—Jack shrugged, letting her cross the aisle to stand in front of him—"he kept popping up like a little troll I couldn't get rid of on my shoulder whenever I was usually about to do something I shouldn't. Much like someone else I know, though he didn't cheer me on. I like to keep a few surprises up my sleeves."

She wasn't surprised.

"Plus, I remembered an old friend who had once told me she didn't meet just anyone for no reason." He tried to sound light, but his voice was unable to handle it by the end, dropping. With a hop, he descended off the stage, as if he couldn't bear to be staring down at her any longer. He shoved his hands into his dark jean pockets. "You're talking to me now?"

Avril raised her eyebrows. Looked like it.

"Avril."

"Jack, don't."

He was getting closer with each step, and her heart raced. Not because he was close. Too close. It was because it was him, and Avril needed all the space she could get in order to find the right words to say first.

He came up with plenty.

"Why didn't you come to me?" Jack asked.

Avril knew he wasn't talking about recently. He meant a year ago, broken and slowly decaying and feeling as if no one had noticed, as if it was all just her insides rotting like she'd imagined they would eventually anyway.

"I couldn't look at you."

"Why not?" Jack asked. "Because you hadn't listened when I told you not to go home with him when we were at the bar that night? It wouldn't be the first time."

No, it wouldn't have been the first time.

"I was just so ..." She shook her head, blinking so as not to smudge her eyeliner. It had been ages since she'd put any on, and she wasn't going to screw it up now.

"Avril?" Jack stared at her. "Look at me."

She did.

"Fuck you."

Avril's teeth jarred together as she snapped her mouth shut. "Jack."

"Seriously, fuck you."

Avril leaned forward, her lip curling back over one side of her mouth. How could he?

"FUCK YOU."

The words again were puckered on the edges of Jack's plush lips. They seemed to quiver at her sudden outburst; instead, out surged a loud, boisterous laugh. His crow erupted through the space for the second time. This time, the owner, Nik, who must've been behind the bar the entire time, did look up with raised eyebrows at the exchange. They wisely knew to say nothing.

Instead, they gave a wave with a polished glass.

Jack wiped a tear from the corner of his eye before it spilled over from his absurdity. "Man, I missed you, A. You were my friend. My good-ass friend. One of my first around here."

"Such lies."

"What?"

"You had at least half the patrons in this place already after you."

"But none like you, Queen. None like you."

Avril paused at the name, finally said by someone else who wasn't her and wasn't Reed. She let the rest of the stale air in her lungs release. "Well, you got that right."

Jack stilled, stared at her without another curve of a smile in sight on that cross face. "I don't know though now. I still don't hear an apology anywhere in there."

"I'm sorry," Avril said, coming out more of an exasperated question. "What, you want me to get down on my knees?"

Jack raised his eyebrows. He didn't say anything to the contrary.

Inhaling, Avril looked either way in the empty space. For the second time today, she felt naked, only this time, not in a good way. Apologizing was one of the worst things ever invented. Slowly, Avril dropped one knee at a time before him. Her balance was a little wobbly, as was her grace in her tight corset, but she was on the floor. The correct position for beggars.

Throwing her hands out to either side, she waited. Was this good enough for him?

He waved his hand. He was listening.

"Please, my most formidable friend. Jack-of-all-trades, Jack the panty ripper, do you forgive me?"

Puckering his lips, as if he had to really think about it, Jack nudged his boot out in front of her.

Oh, hell no. She slapped his calf. Avril was not going to kiss his feet. That was one thing too far. She propelled herself back up from the grimy ground and kicked her sadistic friend in the shin. "Come on now. Seriously?"

Jack grinned once more, another loud laugh erupting through

the space. "Queen, I forgave you the moment you walked through the door. I just wanted to see how much you meant it."

"You ass."

He shrugged.

The two of them shook their heads as they leaned back against the stage again. They'd made more than just a few memories in this place. She'd helped him make a name for himself, one of the first people at DuCain she properly loved.

"Did you mean it?"

Jack glanced his cool eyes to her. "Mean what? My undying love for you? Of course. Kit doesn't mind sharing."

"No." Avril smiled, though, thinking of the two of them together again. What a strange pair. What a strange world. "When you told Kit when she first met me a year ago that I was someone who collected lost things."

"She told you that?"

Avril dipped her chin, not betraying her feelings about it all. It seemed right, the more she thought about it. People came into her life, seeking solace, a haven. Even if that meant they would take it from the devil herself.

"If you didn't collect us, Queen, who the hell knows where we'd be? That moment you jumped in my car with Reed by accident or on purpose"—Jack sighed, a weight in each word—"I'm grateful for it every day."

She looked at him again, her dark and brooding warrior, so willing to fight alongside her. *Grateful.* So was she.

"Are you coming back then, Queen?"

Avril considered the place. The familiarity pulsed through her. The stirring of madness deep in her stomach nearly screamed with the desire for performative sin.

Still, she shook her head. "Not yet."

After a moment, Jack bobbed his head.

"I'll be around, but turns out, I need to figure some shit out."

"That'll take a while," Jack muttered.

She hit him in the arm. "All the better to plan my return coronation. These suckers around here so love a surprise to make things interesting. I also still need to find you a wedding gift."

One thing at a time.

"Are you at least planning on staying for the night before getting on my amazing wedding present? It'd better be good. I'm thinking a trip to Bali. Or maybe you could find it in your schedule to take a trip and pluck one of your favorite stars out of the sky for me. I want to make sure it keeps my wish going for the rest of my life."

Avril rolled her eyes, thinking about when he must've made that kind of wish. She wondered what it was. For love? Or for the strange breed of life he'd been given?

"Seriously though, Kitten should be here any minute."

"I'm surprised she still lets you play with others."

"Only if she gets to watch or is at least in the building, the jealous thing." Jack shrugged, just as amused or as likely turned on the horny devil probably was by his future wife. "Rules are rules."

She couldn't imagine the look on Kit's face when she got here, the hiding and games over. Avril turned to look toward the front door anyway. Her own very tall and handsome escort was waiting.

He was far too punctual when she said she'd only need a few minutes.

"We have plans actually."

"Oh?" Jack glanced up, giving Ian a wave. "Plan on making the rounds?"

"Something like that."

"Then, I won't keep you." Standing, Jack gave her a graceful bow. Leaning in, he kissed her on the cheek.

With a swat from her, he smirked.

But not before he whispered in her ear, "I really did miss you, Queen."

She shrugged a single shoulder.

"I might've missed you."

———

JACK'S EYES followed her all the way back up the aisle toward Ian.

He cocked his head to the side, shifting between the two. "Have a good talk?"

"The beginning of one." Avril eyed Ian as he wrapped his arm around her. "I'm not stupid. Jack's not going to let me off the hook that easy."

"What do you mean?"

"I mean, I am really going to have to get him one hell of a wedding gift," Avril said. A small price to pay.

"Are we not staying then?" Ian asked, eyes somehow steady on her when there was so much to take in around DuCain.

Avril smiled. "Another night."

He extended an arm to her. "Set to go then?"

"Me?" Avril looked up at the building, suddenly pausing.

Jack had already headed toward the back entrance, walking around the stage to greet Kit. Another time.

When she gripped on to Ian, her ring flashed against his thick coat. They had all the time in the world.

She nudged his new oxfords, instead of loafers, to get moving. "I am when you are. Are you sure that you're prepared?"

"I've primed my delicate disposition, as warned."

Yes, he'd do nicely.

They walked in the cold, under the lamplights, steadily shining their path for them. They weren't too far away from where they needed to be. A few blocks from her one home, and they ran into the other.

Much less statuesque, Rosin's converted brownstone glimmered from the moment you looked to the windows, cloaked in sheer curtains. A perfect hideout for guests arriving at the front door, whispering to one another, as if truly entering an art deco fantasy.

At the rise of voices already inside, bodies moving behind the curtains, a crescendo of sound trilled a similar beat inside Avril's chest before they made it to the front stairs.

She stopped Ian in his tracks.

He looked down at her, waiting carefully for her explanation. In his eyes, one word, and they would leave. All that and more looked back at her.

"Come on." Avril tugged on his sleeve, turning them around from the small crowd of mostly ladies in front of them, one with a sash around her chest. "I have a better idea."

Following without question, Ian looked around as Avril pulled him around the corner of the building, nudging aside the loose fence and trash cans until she saw the red light bleeding through the cracks in the back door.

Personnel only.

They'd both read that sign before.

Turning back to watch his expression turn from confused to intrigued, Avril reached up for him, yanking him down by his collar to meet her. His lips were warm as she kissed him. Breaking apart from him, Avril hummed with sudden happiness. In a few moments, Ian would know another piece of her. Another shadow.

A great light.

"Ready?"

"Don't we need to check in through the front?"

"Please." Avril grinned.

She pushed open the back hatch door, exposing the neon lights, puffed velvet wallpaper, and sounds of cheers over the deep roll of music, life. Holding his hand with both of hers, she dragged him and his amused smirk inside.

"Like you said, darling, you're with the Queen now."

EPILOGUE

"*T*here are to be no frilly words at this ceremony. No. Absolutely not. I don't care that you think it would be fun right now, Jack." Kit spoke into the phone, most certainly not having fun by any indication of her voice, transitioning into a higher, squeakier pitch.

Though they had agreed on not seeing the bride before the ceremony, it appeared that once Kit had caught wind of the nontraditional marriage vows discussed over a final bachelor beer, she'd thought one was better to panic now rather than later.

"You want me to pass out in front of your family, don't you? No, I do not want you to gracefully catch me, Jack. If I get to the vows that have been the same for the past hundred years and suddenly go blank from your brother showering us with strange words from a movie that don't end in *I do*, I think I will pass out, and then who will be there to marry you, hmm? And don't say Avril. She's officially mine."

Kit passed over the window and looked out from the farmhouse to where the chairs were set up between a row of vines.

Avril smiled as she watched Kit roll her perfectly lined eyes at every single detail, however thankful that Jack had taken over. It was a lot, Kit had admitted to her, much like she'd feared it would be.

"No, I don't mean that. I just … please? Pretty please? You can tell all your extra vows to me later."

Kit's cheeks flushed pink.

"Exactly then. I love you. Yes, I'm sure."

"You didn't ask if he was sure?" Avril smiled as she moved in on Kit.

She tossed the phone before turning to Avril. She stood in her delicate lingerie of silk and French lace she'd made for herself. Garter on, hair in place.

Her dress was smooth and simple as she held the sleeves up to slip her hands through. More carefully arranged lace trailed down to the creases of her arms. It was Jack's mother's dress. She'd insisted Kit wear it since she didn't have her own there today. It was just Kit, marrying into Jack and the rest of his large, vivacious family Avril had been glad to finally meet.

Kit would look lovely in anything, but the dress seemed to have been perfectly made for her. Only a few alterations had been needed that she had done herself along with what was underneath.

Jack was a lucky man.

"Honestly, I'm afraid of the answer."

Avril looped her hand around her friend's waist. "He's sure."

"He's sure," she repeated.

Meltdowns were a staple for Kit, but this one was on an entirely new level.

Avril reached up to flick a wayward strand of fringe out of her eyes as she finished taking a deep breath. "He is absolutely one thousand percent sure in love with you. Which, knowing Jack, is very strange, as you now know, so count yourself as the most fabulous, sexy, yet also adorable woman alive."

Kit laughed, blushing at the compliments. "Wow, I think I need a drink."

Avril reached for the tiny cups that had been left at the door from Jack's brothers. "Vodka, whiskey, or whatever this stuff is?"

"I'm not sure I can take that kind of risk." She reached for the vodka but only drank about half before handing it back.

Avril downed the rest. "Now, are you ready?"

Pressing her perfectly pink lips together, as smooth as any fresh bloom, Kit cleared her throat. "Lace me up before buttoning, will you?"

"Of course." Avril moved toward the back of her dress. On her fingers flared a delicate wisp of a shadow, reminding Avril of when she had thrown a corset at Kit the first time they met— officially anyway. She'd said similar words. Though she might've barked them, more of a command than pleasant request. "I believe it is my turn."

Nimble fingers tugged and pulled until Kit took long and even breaths. Rubbing her lips together in the mirror, she looked at herself, touching the braids that looped over her head one last time.

Avril smiled, taking a step back to look at her up and down. She heard the door creak open behind her. "I think it might be showtime."

Before she could back up and turn to see the other person in the room, Kit flung her hands around Avril. "Thank you."

"Don't."

"Thank you so much for everything, Avril."

She hadn't done anything. She just … shook her head, pulling back with a sniff. "If you mess up your makeup again."

Kit shook her head, smiling at the large man behind the two of them in the doorway. He watched with soft eyes.

"You think you can take over from here, Brian?" Avril asked, still holding her friend's hand. She pulled Kit to walk with her, slowly gliding her fingertips into Jack's father's.

"You look stunning. You know, Jack's mom and I had a lot of

fun on our wedding day in the fall. Now, we have a spring one. All sounds fitting, doesn't it?"

Avril made her way back down the hallway of the farmhouse, far outside the city Jack had escaped to. On the staircase, photos of him and his three other brothers were scattered in frames along the wall. She could easily tell which was him though. The Carver men all had the same striking eyes, but Jack's smile, which had stretched ear to ear until he was at least thirteen, no longer covered in dirt as he climbed trees and rolled his eyes at his brothers as they were forced to stand together, said it all.

The plucking of guitars near the back of the house continued to tune as Avril made her way out into the grass field, trees strung with fairy lights and streamers.

Jack was already up front, waiting with his brother, volunteered officiant. Otherwise, Jack kept to his word. There was no extra. Only him and Kit, no bridesmaids or groomsmen. Just the two of them, where his parents and their parents before them had declared each other theirs for the rest of their lives.

Kit would come as she was.

And that would be enough.

Jack grinned when he saw Avril.

Avril grinned back, giving a small thumbs-up as she slid into her row on the end. Looking behind her, Reed and Dixon lounged in their suits, contrasting country wicker chairs near the back. Ian shifted over, but still pulled her into his side as she sat.

"How is she?" Ian asked, bending to murmur near her shoulder.

Over the past few months, he and Kit had become close out of everyone Avril often spent time with. Both of them were quiet enough, and Avril was sure they only laughed about how much peace they were getting when no one else was around.

"As well as expected."

Giving her a quick peck, Ian hushed Avril before she could scold him or say another word. The acoustic sound of music began to play, and the crowd of Jack's family and family friends rose.

Clinging to Jack's father's arm, Kit walked down the grass aisle. Shadows flickered to mark the forever memory of their footsteps all the way up to the front, where Jack rocked on his heels, smiling wide.

Jack beamed as she walked toward him, giving her a wink that made Kit's strained expression relax into a pleasant laugh by the time their hands met at the end.

Jack's brother said a few words as the sky turned from sunlight to a rosy purple above them. He didn't crack a joke anyone had to answer with anything but a laugh. He kept to the vows, traditional yet full, as he asked Jack and Kit to repeat after him as they placed their respective rings on each other's fingers.

Choked up, Jack cleared his throat, but it did nothing to hide the tears building on the edges of his eyes.

Kit gently patted his hand as he soldiered on.

"I do."

Of course he did, eyes still watering.

That was surely what he would say to explain the waterworks. The sap.

Married, Jack finally did not stop himself as he swooped Kit over into a dip against him as they kissed. He pulled her back up in front of him. Her cheeks were flushed, and he couldn't help himself, it looked like, as he kissed her again. Once more for the crowd before heading back down the aisle.

From the moment they hit the end, the fairy lights grew brighter. Children ran around the yard and fields beyond without care, and the rest of the wedding quickly turned into a party, music playing as they shoved the chairs out of the way for the makeshift dance floor set between portable outdoor heaters.

Everyone laughed and yelled over top of each other as they spoke and ate food left out until the tarp was attached between the tree and house. At one point, as Jack and Kit took their first dance as a newlywed couple, a cup was shoved into Avril's hand.

Looking down at the deep red liquid, she took a sip, blinking in both horror and interest at the sweet yet deadly mixture.

"Be careful with that," Ian said, coming up alongside her from wherever he'd wandered off to. "I heard it's a neighbor's sangria. Apparently, it's truly the meaning of getting the party going."

With a small chuckle, Avril took another long gulp before setting the cup on a nearby table. It went down easy, warming her insides as she grasped both Ian's hands.

She gave them a light tug. "Dance with me."

"Always," he said, moving with her to where others began to gather as well, together and apart.

Kit's dress near the center swooshed against her mid-calf as she looked at Jack and then up to the stars, also gracing them all with their presence tonight.

They all danced beneath them from one song to the next. The beat was an unnecessary guide as Ian held Avril close and swayed. She could only expect so much, though Avril was sure if she got enough of that sangria in him, anything was possible.

"I'm not sure I like that look."

She grinned. "You realize we still have another party to go to tomorrow before our lovely newlywed friends jet off to some undisclosed location."

"There's another reception?"

Avril nodded. "You ready to see me and my entire family once and for all? I suggest you prepare your fragile disposition again."

"It's no longer fragile."

"Tell that to how you flinched at Rosin the other day," Avril reminded.

Ian displayed his reaction again at watching one of the girls attempt to twirl their new fire pasties. She'd had to agree that it didn't look the most comfortable. Highly entertaining, on the other hand …

He smiled into her neck. "Where is it?"

"DuCain."

"And then?"

"And then what?" Avril laughed as he nestled himself farther into her perfectly clipped curls that were already slowly unraveling themselves over the tips of her ears.

He still had to slouch significantly.

"What will we do with each other after?"

They'd love each other.

And have a hell of a lot of fun while they did it.

For some reason, the words seemed to settle nicely now where only sticky emotions had before in Avril's chest. Maybe it wasn't only the content of the sangria that felt warm as she wrapped herself back around him. Warmer.

She tilted her chin up until he looked her in the eyes as they moved to the right, continuing their languid dance without caring who was around them. How strange they might have looked together. The vixen and the professor.

What a scandal Jack and his friends had brought to the small farming town indeed.

"Well, first, we will indulge in very good-luck sex that must happen after a wedding," Avril told him. "We don't want to ruin things for our very happy bride and groom after all."

Ian chuckled. There was no argument.

"Then, we take over the world, of course."

"Or burn it to the ground," Ian suggested, giving her a small twirl before pulling her back into his lapels.

"One or the other."

He smirked, leaning down closer so only she could hear. "Only as long as I still get to see you dance."

Avril smirked right back, feeling the weight of a crown gilded in glitter and thick shadows poised on the top of her head.

She could live with that. After the past few months, she had been debating when the right time was to grace the stage. There was no *if ever* in her repertoire now. Only *when*.

Ian cheering for her as she gave private performances was no longer quite enough.

Her hands slid upward. She traced his shadows that swirled and turned over his skin, flaring when they looked at her in something like delight. A height of emotion surged. It was not good and maybe not bad at all, but enough that when he looked at her, Ian would remember Avril and their blissful exploits forever, like any harsh imprint. She'd make sure of it.

"But if we are staying in that house of yours for any period of time..." Avril started.

She peeled herself up onto her toes, so her words reverberated close against his lips.

"Yes?" he ventured.

"We're going to need to repaint."

Ian grinned, swiping a finger down her cheek, where they both remembered where their last painting adventure had ended. Right there, in front of each other. Shadows visible.

Breathing heavy. Smiling.

This was how it'd all happened.

"Deal."

ACKNOWLEDGMENTS

Avril has been with me from the beginning. Or at the very least, near it. I started writing her story about seven years ago. I wrote between, during, and after classes. I wrote at least two dozen different versions of her story, never fully completed, but always featuring a bold burlesque dancer re-finding herself while escaping past traumas. But this past manuscript was different.

It had been years as of November 2020 since I'd last written about Avril. Her snarky voice was never far from my mind, yet still, I wasn't sure if I was going to be able to tell her story. Of course, then, when nothing seemed to be going right, I said quite plainly, *screw it*. I listened to days' worth of *The Queen's Gambit* soundtrack and let the story flow however it wanted to. Suddenly, I was writing. I was the writer I had known I wanted to be once more, and instead of a story about leaving behind trauma to start anew, this story evolved into finding the grace to dance and move forward with it and as the person our main character always was. Avril waited for me to catch up to her and her story, and I am so glad she did.

I hope you readers are glad, too, because without you, these books wouldn't be possible. Every time I see a photo of my book somewhere or someone commenting about how they are reading it, my heart aches in a joyful sort of way in hopes of how, one day, I will be able to write and think about stories every day of my life.

The stories of Ashton would never have been possible or published without my wonderful friend, Taylor Whelan. You've truly been a gift sent to me even if it is mostly for me to freak out to about a scene not flowing correctly, or an amazing book you recommended, distracting me from writing altogether.

A big shout must go out as well, to my dear friend, Alyse Fryer. There couldn't have been anyone else who would've hid with me between library reference shelves to talk about my fictional worlds and fictional characters as I began to find myself as a writer. You listened to me go on and on about these characters for hours at a time—especially Avril. At times, I remember thinking that you knew my made-up worlds better than I did. Or at least, you really nailed the whole, "smile and nod" expression, which I deeply appreciate to this day. I hope I finally gave Avril the story worth her bold charisma and sass that drew us both in from the start.

My parents also cannot go without being mentioned. Since I published my first novel, you've been my biggest cheerleaders and supported me as I grew and flourished wherever my own story took me.

In Ashton, there are still more stories to be told.

ABOUT THE AUTHOR

Kendra Mase is the author of *The Strings That Hold Us Together*. She holds a BA in English publishing and editing and is a graduate of The Columbia Publishing Course in New York City.

ALSO BY KENDRA MASE

The Strings That Hold Us Together
Everything You Never Had: An Ashton Holiday Novella
Words That Burn Like Ash